By Nora Roberts
Trilogies and Quartets

The Born In Trilogy:
Born in Fire
Born in Ice
Born in Shame

The Bride Quartet:
Vision in White
Bed of Roses
Savour the Moment
Happy Ever After

The Key Trilogy:
Key of Light
Key of Knowledge
Key of Valour

The Irish Trilogy:
Jewels of the Sun
Tears of the Moon
Heart of the Sea

Three Sisters Island Trilogy:
Dance upon the Air
Heaven and Earth
Face the Fire

The Inn Boonsboro Trilogy:
The Next Always
The Last Boyfriend
The Perfect Hope

The Sign of Seven Trilogy:
Blood Brothers
The Hollow
The Pagan Stone

Chesapeake Bay Quartet:
Sea Swept
Rising Tides
Inner Harbour
Chesapeake Blue

In the Garden Trilogy:
Blue Dahlia
Black Rose
Red Lily

The Circle Trilogy:
Morrigan's Cross
Dance of the Gods
Valley of Silence

The Dream Trilogy:
Daring to Dream
Holding the Dream
Finding the Dream

Nora Roberts also writes the In Death series using the pseudonym J.D. Robb

NORA ROBERTS

ROBERTS

SHADOW SPELL

piatkus

PIATKUS

First published in Great Britain in 2014 by Piatkus

A CIP catalogue record for this book
is available from the British Library.

HB ISBN 978-0-7499-5863-3
C Format 978-0-7499-5862-6

Printed and bound by CPI Group (UK) Ltd, Croydon, CR0 4YY

Papers used by Piatkus are from well-managed forests
and other responsible sources.

MIX
Paper from
responsible sources
FSC® C104740

Piatkus
An imprint of
Little, Brown Book Group
100 Victoria Embankment
London EC4Y 0DY

An Hachette UK Company
www.hachette.co.uk

www.piatkus.co.uk

For my own circle,
family and friends

Coming events cast their
shadows before.

——THOMAS CAMPBELL

The ornament of a house is
the friends who frequent it.

——RALPH WALDO EMERSON

1

Autumn 1268

Mists spiraled up from the water like breath as Eamon rowed the little boat. The sun shed pale, cool light as it woke from the night's rest and set morning birds to their chorus. He heard the cock crow, so arrogant and important, and the bleating of sheep as they cropped their way across the green fields.

Familiar sounds all, sounds that had greeted him every morning for the last five years.

But this wasn't home. No matter how welcoming, how familiar, it would never be home.

And home he wished for. Home brought him wishes aching down to his bones like an old man's in damp weather, longings bleeding through his heart like a lover scorned.

And under the wishing, aching, longing, bleeding, lived a simmering rage that could bubble up and scorch his throat like thirst.

Some nights he dreamed of home, of their cabin in the great woods where he knew every tree, every turn of the track. And some nights the dreams were real as life, so he could smell the peat fire, the sweet rushes of his bed with the lavender his mother wove through for good rest and good dreams.

He could hear her voice, her singing soft from below the loft where she mixed her potions and brews.

The Dark Witch, they'd called her—with respect—for she'd been powerful and strong. And kind and good. So some nights when he dreamed of home, when he heard his mother singing from below the loft, he woke with tears on his cheeks.

Hastily brushed away. He was a man now, fully ten years, head of his family as his father had been before him.

Tears were for the women.

And he had his sisters to look after, didn't he? he reminded himself as he set the oars, let the boat lightly drift while he dropped his line. Brannaugh might be the eldest, but he was the man of the family. He'd sworn an oath to protect her and Teagan, and so he would. Their grandfather's sword had come to him. He would use it when the time came.

That time would come.

For there were other dreams, dreams that brought fear rather than grieving. Dreams of Cabhan, the black sorcerer. Those dreams formed icy balls of fear in his belly that froze even the simmering rage. A fear that made the boy inside him want to cry out for his mother.

But he couldn't allow himself to be afraid. His mother was gone, sacrificing herself to save him and his sisters only hours after Cabhan had slaughtered their father.

He could barely see his father in his mind's eye, too often needed the help of the fire to find that image—the tall and proud Daithi, the *cennfine* with his bright hair and ready laugh. But he had only to close his eyes to see his mother, pale as the death to come, standing in front of the cabin in the woods on that misted morning while he rode away with his sisters, grief in his heart, fresh, hot power in his blood.

He was a boy no longer, from that morning, but one of the three, a dark witch, bound by blood and oath to destroy what even his mother could not.

Part of him wanted only to begin, to end this time in Galway on their cousin's farm where the cock crowed of a morning, and the sheep bleated in the fields. The man and witch inside him yearned for the time to pass, for the strength to wield his grandfather's sword without his arm trembling from the weight. For the time he could fully embrace his powers, practice the magicks that were his by birth and right. The time he would spill Cabhan's blood black and burning on the earth.

Still, in the dreams he was only a boy, untried and weak, pursued by the wolf Cabhan became, the wolf with the red stone of his black power gleaming at his throat. And it was his own blood, and the blood of his sisters, that spilled warm and red onto the ground.

On mornings after the worst dreams he went to the river, rowed out to fish, to be alone, though most days he craved the company of the cottage, the voices, the scents of cooking.

But after the blood dreams he needed to be away—and no one scolded him for not helping with the milking or the mucking or the feeding, not on those mornings.

So he sat in the boat, a slim boy of ten with a mop of brown hair still tousled from sleep, and the wild blue eyes of his father, the bright and stirring power of his mother.

He could listen to the day wake around him, wait patiently for the fish to take his bait and eat the oatcake he'd taken from his cousin's kitchen.

And he could find himself again.

The river, the quiet, the gentle rock of the boat reminded him of the last truly happy day he'd had with his mother and sisters.

She'd looked well, he remembered, after how pale and strained she had looked over the long, icy winter. They were, all of them, counting the days until Bealtaine, and his father's return. They'd sit around the fire then, so Eamon had thought, eating cakes and tea sweetened with honey while they listened to his father's tales of the raids and the hunting.

They would feast, so he had thought, and his mother would be well again.

So he'd believed, that day on the river when they'd fished and laughed, and all thought of how soon their father would be home.

But he'd never come, for Cabhan had used his dark magicks to slay Daithi the brave. And Sorcha, the Dark Witch—even though she'd burned him to ash, he'd killed her. Killed her and somehow still existed.

Eamon knew it from the dreams, from the prickle down his spine. Saw the truth of it in the eyes of his sisters.

But he had that day, that bright spring day on the river to remember. Even as a fish tugged on his line, his mind traveled back, and he saw himself at five years bringing a shining fish from the dark river.

Felt that same sense of pride now.

"Ailish will be pleased."

His mother smiled at him as he slid the fish into the pail of water to hold it fresh.

His great need brought her to him, gave him comfort. He baited his hook again as the sun warmed and began to thin the fingers of mists.

"We'll need more than one."

She'd said that, he remembered, that long ago day.

"Then you'll catch more than one."

"I'd sooner catch more than one in my own river."

"One day you will. One day, *mo chroi*, you'll return home. One day those who come from you will fish in our river, walk our wood. I promise this to you."

Tears wanted to come, blurred his vision of her, so she wavered in front of his eyes. He willed them away, for he would see her clear. The dark hair she let fall free to her waist, the dark eyes where love lived. And the power that shone from her. Even now, a vision only, he sensed her power.

"Why could you not destroy him, Ma? Why could you not live?"

"It was not meant. My love, my boy, my heart, if I could have spared you and your sisters, I would have given more than my life."

"You did give more. You gave us your power, almost all of it. If you'd kept it—"

"It was my time, and your birthright. I am content with that, I promise you as well." In those thinning mists she glowed, silver-edged. "I am ever in you, Eamon the Loyal. I am in your blood, your heart, your mind. You are not alone."

"I miss you."

He felt her lips on his cheek, the warmth of her, the scent of her enfolding him. And for that moment, just that moment, he could be a child again.

"I want to be brave and strong. I will be, I swear it. I will protect Brannaugh and Teagan."

"You will protect each other. You are the three. Together more powerful than I ever was."

"Will I kill him?" For that was his deepest, darkest wish. "Will I finish him?"

"I cannot say, only that he can never take what you are. What you are, what you hold, can only be given, as I gave to you. He carries my curse, and the mark of it. All who come from him will bear it as all who come from you will carry the light. My blood, Eamon." She turned her palm up, showed a thin line of blood. "And yours."

He felt the quick pain, saw the wound across his palm. And joined it with his mother's.

"The blood of the three, out of Sorcha, will lay him low, if it takes a thousand years. Trust what you are. It is enough."

She kissed him again, smiled again. "You have more than one."

The tug on his line brought him out of the vision.

So he had more than one.

He would be brave, he thought as he pulled the fish, flapping, out of the river. He would be strong. And one day, strong enough.

He studied his hand—no mark on it now, but he understood. He carried her blood, and her gift. These, one day, he would pass to his sons, his daughters. If it wasn't for him to destroy Cabhan, it would be done by his blood.

But he hoped, by all the gods, it was for him.

For now, he'd fish. It was good to be a man, he thought, to hunt and fish, to provide. To pay back his cousins for the shelter and the care.

He'd learned patience since being a man—and caught four fish before he rowed the boat back to shore. He secured the boat, strung the fish on a line.

He stood a moment, looking out at the water, the shine of it now under the fullness of the sun. He thought of his mother, the sound of her voice, the scent of her hair. Her words would stay with him.

He would walk back through the little woods. Not great like home, but a fine wood all the same, he told himself.

And he would bring Ailish the fish, take some tea by the fire. Then he would help with the last of the harvest.

He heard the high, sharp cry as he started back to the cottage and the little farm. Smiling to himself, he reached into his satchel, drew out his leather glove. He only had to pull it on, lift his arm, and Roibeard swooped out of the clouds, wings spread to land.

"Good morning to you." Eamon looked into those golden eyes, felt the tug of connection with his hawk, his guide, his friend. He touched the charmed amulet around his neck, one his mother had conjured with blood magicks for protection. It carried the image of the hawk.

"It's a fine day, isn't it? Bright and cool. The harvest is nearly done, and we'll have our celebration soon," he continued as he walked with the hawk on his arm. "The equinox, as you know, when night conquers day as Gronw Pebr conquered Lleu Llaw Gyffes. We'll celebrate the birth of Mabon, son of Mordon the guardian of the earth. Sure there'll be honey cakes for certain. I'll see you have a bit."

The hawk rubbed its head against Eamon's cheek, affectionate as a kitten.

"I had the dream again, of Cabhan. Of home, of Ma after she gave us almost all there was of her power and sent us away to be safe. I see it, Roibeard. How she poisoned him with a kiss, how she flamed, using all she had to destroy him. He took her life, and still . . . I saw the stirring in the ashes she made of him. The stirring of them, something evil, and the glow of red from his power."

Eamon paused a moment, drew up his power, opened to it. He felt the beating heart of a rabbit rushing into the brush, the hunger of a fledgling waiting for its mother and its breakfast.

He felt his sisters, the sheep, the horses.

And no threat.

"He hasn't found us. I would feel it. You would see it, and would tell me. But he looks, and he hunts, and he waits, as I feel that as well."

Those bold blue eyes darkened; the boy's tender mouth firmed into a man's. "I won't hide forever. One day, on the blood of Daithi and Sorcha, I'll do the hunting."

Eamon lifted a hand, took a fistful of air, swirled it, tossed it—gently—toward a tree. Branches shook, and roosting birds took flight.

"I'll only get stronger, won't I?" he murmured, and walked to the cottage to please Ailish with four fish.

BRANNAUGH WENT ABOUT HER DUTIES AS SHE DID EVERY day. As every day for five years she'd done all that was asked of her. She cooked, she cleaned, tended the young ones as Ailish always seemed to have a baby at the breast or in the belly. She helped plant the fields and tend the crops. She helped in harvest.

Good honest work, of course, and satisfying in its way. No one could be more kind than her cousin Ailish and her husband. Good, solid people both, people of the earth, who'd offered more than shelter to three orphaned children.

They'd offered family, and there was no more precious gift.

Hadn't her mother known it? She would never have sent her three children to Ailish otherwise. Even in the darkest hour, Sorcha would never have given her beloved children to anyone but the kind, and the loving.

But at twelve, Brannaugh was no longer a child. And what rose in her, spread in her, woke in her—more since she'd started her courses the year before—demanded.

Holding so much in, turning her eyes from that ever-brightening light proved harder and more sorrowful every day. But she owed Ailish respect, and her cousin held a fear of magicks and power—even her own.

Brannaugh had done what her mother asked of her on that terrible morning. She'd taken her brother and sister south, away from their home in Mayo. She'd kept off the road; she'd shuttered her grief in her heart where only she could hear it keening.

And in that heart lived the need to avenge as well, the need to embrace the power inside her, and learn more, learn and hone enough to defeat Cabhan, once and done.

But Ailish wanted only her man, her children, her farm. And why not? She was entitled to her home and her life and her land, the quiet of it all. Hadn't she risked it by taking in Sorcha's blood? Taking in what Cabhan lusted for—hunted for?

She deserved gratitude, loyalty, and respect.

But what lived in Brannaugh clawed for freedom. Choices needed to be made.

She'd seen her brother walk back from the river with his fish, his hawk. She felt him test his power out of the sight of the cottage—as he often did. As Teagan, their sister, often did. Ailish, chattering about the jams they'd make that day, felt nothing. Her cousin blocked most of what she had—a puzzlement to Brannaugh—and used only the bit she allowed herself to sweeten jams or coax bigger eggs from the hens.

Brannaugh told herself it was worth the sacrifice, the wait to find more, learn more, be more. Her brother and sister were safe here— as their mother wished. Teagan, whose grief had been beyond reaching for days, weeks, laughed and played. She did her chores cheerfully, tended the animals, rode like a warrior on her big gray Alastar.

Perhaps some nights she wept in her sleep, but Brannaugh had only to gather her in to soothe her.

Except when came the dreams of Cabhan. They came to Teagan, to Eamon, to herself. More often now, clearer now, so clear Brannaugh had begun to hear his voice echo after she woke.

Choices must be made. This waiting, this sanctuary, might need to come to an end, one way or another.

In the evening she scrubbed potatoes, tender from the harvest. She stirred the stew bubbling low on the fire, and tapped her foot as her cousin's man made music on his little harp.

The cottage, warm and snug, a happy place filled with good scents, cheerful voices, Ailish's laugh as she lifted her youngest onto her hip for a dance.

Family, she thought again. Well fed, well tended in a cottage warm and snug, with herbs drying in the kitchen, babes with rosy cheeks.

It should have contented her—how she wished it would.

She caught Eamon's eye, the same bold blue as their father's, felt his power prod against her. He saw too much, did Eamon, she thought. Far too much if she didn't remember to shutter him out.

She gave him a bit of a poke back—a little warning to mind his own. In the way of sisters, she smiled at his wince.

After the evening meal there were pots to be cleaned, children to tuck into bed. Mabh, the eldest at seven, complained, as always, she wasn't sleepy. Seamus snuggled right in, ready with his dreaming smile. The twins she'd helped bring into the world herself chattered to each other like magpies, young Brighid slipped her comforting thumb in her mouth, and the baby slept before his mother laid him down.

Brannaugh wondered if Ailish knew both she and the babe with his sweet angel face would not be without magick. The birth, so painful, so *wrong*, would have ended them both in blood without Brannaugh's power, the healing, the seeing, the doing.

Though they never spoke of it, she thought Ailish knew.

Ailish straightened, a hand on her back, another on the next babe in her womb. "And a good night and happy dreams to all. Brannaugh, would you have some tea with me? I could do with some of your soothing tea, as this one's kicking up a storm tonight."

"Sure and I'll fix you some." And add the charm as she always did for health and an easy birthing. "He's well and healthy that one, and will be, I suspect, as big a handful on his own as the twins."

"It's a boy for certain," Ailish said as they climbed down from the sleeping loft. "I can feel it. I've not been wrong yet."

"Nor are you this time. You could do with more rest, cousin."

"A woman with six children and one in the pot doesn't see much rest. I'm well enough." Her gaze fixed on Brannaugh's for confirmation.

"You are to be sure, but could do with more rest all the same."

"You're a great help and comfort to me, Brannaugh."

"I hope I am."

Something here, Brannaugh thought as she busied herself with the tea. She sensed her cousin's nerves, and they stirred her own.

"Now that the harvest is in, you might settle in with your sewing. It's needed work, and restful for you. I can see to the cooking. Teagan and Mabh will help there, and I'll tell you true, Mabh's already a fine cook."

"Aye, sure and she is that. I'm so proud of her."

"With the girls seeing to the cooking, Eamon and I can help our cousin hunt. I know you'd rather I didn't take up the bow, but isn't it wise for each to do what we do well?"

Ailish's gaze veered away a moment.

Aye, Brannaugh thought, she knows and, more, feels the weight of asking us not to be what we are.

"I loved your mother."

"Oh, and she you."

"We saw little of each other the last years. Still she sent messages to me, in her way. The night Mabh was born, the little blanket my girl still holds as she sleeps was there, just there on the cradle Bardan made for her."

"When she spoke of you, it was with love."

"She sent you to me. You, Eamon, Teagan. She came to me, in a dream, asked me to give you a home."

"You never told me," Brannaugh murmured, and carried the tea to her cousin, sat with her by the peat fire.

"Two days before you came, she asked it of me."

With her hands clasped in her lap over skirts as gray as her eyes, Brannaugh stared into the fire. "It took eight for us to travel here. Her spirit came to you. I wish I could see her again, but I only see her in dreams."

"She's with you. I see her in you. In Eamon, in Teagan, but most in you. Her strength and beauty. Her fierce love of family. You're of age now, Brannaugh. Of age where you must begin to think of making a family."

"I have a family."

"Of your own, as your own mother did. A home, darling, a man to work the land for you, babes of your own."

She sipped her tea as Brannaugh remained silent. "Fial is a fine man, a good man. He was good to his wife while she lived, I can promise you. He needs a wife, a mother for his children. He has a fine house, far bigger than ours. He would offer for you, and he would open his house to Eamon and Teagan."

"How could I wed Fial? He is . . ." *Old* was her first thought, but she realized he would be no older than her Bardan.

"He would give you a good life, give a good life to your brother, your sister." Ailish picked up her sewing, busying her hands. "I would never speak of it to you if I believed he would not treat you with kindness, always. He is handsome, Brannaugh, and has a fine way about him. Will you walk out with him?"

"I . . . Cousin, I don't think of Fial in that way."

"Perhaps if you walk out with him you will." Ailish smiled as she said it, as if she knew a secret. "A woman needs a man to provide, to protect, to give her children. A kind man with a good house, a pleasing face—"

"Did you wed with Bardan because he was kind?"

"I would not have wedded him hadn't he been. Only consider it. We'll tell him we wait until after the equinox to speak to you of it. Consider. Will you do that?"

"I will."

Brannaugh got to her feet. "Does he know what I am?"

Ailish's tired eyes lowered. "You are the oldest daughter of my cousin."

"Does he know what I am, Ailish?"

It stirred in her now, what she held in, held back. Pride stirred it. And the light that played over her face came not only from the flickers of the fire.

"I am the oldest daughter of the Dark Witch of Mayo. And before she sacrificed her life, she sacrificed her power, passing it to me, to Eamon, Teagan. We are the three. Dark witches we."

"You are a child——"

"A child when you speak of magicks, of power. But a woman when you speak of wedding Fial."

The truth of that had a flush warming Ailish's cheeks. "Brannaugh, my love, have you not been content here these last years?"

"Aye, content. And so grateful."

"Blood gives to blood with no need for grateful."

"Aye. Blood gives to blood."

Setting her sewing aside again, Ailish reached for Brannaugh's hands. "You would be safe, the daughter of my cousin. And you would be content. You would, I believe it, be loved. Could you want more?"

"I am more," she said quietly, and went up to the sleeping loft.

BUT SLEEP ELUDED. SHE LAY QUIET BESIDE TEAGAN, WAITING for the murmurs between Ailish and Bardan to fade away. They would speak of this match, this good, sensible match. They would convince themselves her reluctance was only a young girl's nerves.

Just as they had convinced themselves she, Eamon, and Teagan were children, like any others.

She rose quietly, slipped on her soft boots, her shawl. It was air she needed. Air, the night, the moon.

She climbed silently down from the loft, eased the door open.

Kathel, her hound, who slept by the fire, uncurled and, without question or hesitation, went out before her.

Now she could breathe, with the cool night air on her cheeks, with the quiet like a soothing hand on the chaos inside her. Here, for as long as she could hold it, was freedom.

She and the faithful dog slipped like shadows into the trees. She heard the bubbling of the river, the sigh of wind through the trees, smelled the earth, and the tinge from the peat smoke rising from the cottage chimney.

She could cast the circle, try to conjure her mother's spirit. She needed her mother tonight. In five years, she'd not wept, not allowed herself a single tear. Now, she wanted to sit on the ground, her head on her mother's breast, and weep.

She laid a hand on the amulet she wore—the image of the hound her mother had conjured with love, with magick, with blood.

Did she stay true to her blood, to what lived in her? Did she embrace her own needs, wants, passions? Or did she set that aside like a toy outgrown, and do what would ensure the safety and future of her brother and sister?

"Mother," she murmured, "what should I do? What would you have me do? You gave your life for us. Can I do less?"

She felt the reaching out, the joining of power like a twining of fingers. Whirling around, she stared at the shadows. Heart racing, she thought: *Ma*.

But it was Eamon who stepped into the moonlight, with Teagan's hand in his.

The keen edge of her disappointment sliced like a blade through her voice. "You are to be abed. What are you thinking wandering the woods at night?"

"You do the same," Eamon snapped back.

"I am the oldest."

"I am head of the family."

"The puny staff between your legs doesn't make you head of the family."

Teagan giggled, then rushed forward, threw her arms around her sister. "Don't be angry. You needed us to come. You were in my dream. You wept."

"I am not weeping."

"In here." Teagan touched a hand to Brannaugh's heart. Her deep, dark eyes—so like their mother's—searched her sister's face. "Why are you sad?"

"I am not sad. I only came out to think. To be alone and think."

"You think too loud," Eamon muttered, still smarting over the "puny" comment.

"And you should have more manners than to listen to others' thoughts."

"How can I help it when you *shout* them?"

"Stop. We will not quarrel." Teagan might have been the smallest of them, but she didn't lack in will. "We will not quarrel," she repeated. "Brannaugh is sad, Eamon is like a man standing on hot coals, and I . . . I feel like I do when I've had too much pudding."

"Are you ill?" Brannaugh's anger whisked away. She peered into Teagan's eyes.

"Not that way. Something is . . . not balanced. I feel it. I think you do, and you do. So we will not quarrel. We are family." Still holding Brannaugh's hand, Teagan reached for Eamon's. "Tell us, sister, why you're sad."

"I . . . I want to cast a circle. I want to feel the light in me. I want to cast a circle and sit in its light with you. Both of you."

"We rarely ever do," Teagan said. "Because Ailish would we didn't."

"And she has taken us in. We owe her respect in her home. But we are not in her home now, and she need not know. I need the light. I need to speak with you within our circle, where no one can hear."

"I will cast it. I practice," Teagan told her. "When Alastar and I ride away, I practice."

On a sigh, Brannaugh ran a hand down her sister's bright hair. "It's good you do. Cast the circle, *deirfiúr bheag*."

2

―――― ⚜ ――――

B RANNAUGH WATCHED TEAGAN WORK, HOW HER SISTER
pulled light, pulled fire out of herself, gave the goddess her
thanks as she forged the ring. A ring wide enough, Brannaugh thought,
with amusement and with gratitude, to include Kathel.

"You did well. I should have taught you more, but I . . ."

"Respected Ailish."

"And worry as well," Eamon put in, "that if we use our power too
much, too strong, he'll know. He'll come."

"Aye." Brannaugh sat on the ground, looped an arm around Kathel.
"She wanted us safe. She gave up everything for us. Her power, her
life. She believed she would destroy him, and we would be safe. She
couldn't know whatever black power he bargained with could bring
him out of the ashes."

"Weaker."

She looked at Eamon, nodded. "Yes, weaker. Then. He . . . eats power, I think. He'll find others, take from them, grow stronger. She wanted us safe." Brannaugh drew a breath. "Fial wishes to wed me."

Eamon's mouth fell open. "Fial? But he's old."

"No older than Bardan."

"Old!"

Brannaugh laughed, felt some of the tightness in her chest ease. "Men want young wives, it seems. So they can bear them many children, and still want to bed with them and cook for them."

"You will not wed Fial," Teagan said decisively.

"He is kind, and not uncomely. He has a house and farm larger than Ailish and Bardan. He would welcome you both."

"You will not wed Fial," Teagan repeated. "You do not love him."

"I don't look for love nor do I need it."

"You should, but even if you close your eyes, it will find you. Do you forget the love between our mother and father?"

"I don't. I don't think to find such a thing for myself. Perhaps one day you will. So pretty you are, and bright."

"Oh, I will." Teagan nodded wisely. "As you will, as Eamon will. And we will pass what we are, what we have, to those who come from us. Our mother wanted this. She wanted us to live."

"We would live, and well, if I wed Fial. I am the oldest," Brannaugh reminded them. "It is for me to decide."

"She charged me to protect you." Eamon folded his arms across his chest. "I forbid it."

"We will not quarrel." Teagan snatched their hands, gripped hard. Flame shimmered through their joined fingers. "And I will not be tended to. I am not a babe, Brannaugh, but the same age as you when we left our home. You will not marry to give me a home. You will not deny what you are, ignore your power. You are not Ailish, but Brannaugh, daughter of Sorcha and Daithi. You are a dark witch, and ever will be."

"One day we will destroy him," Eamon vowed. "One day we will avenge our father, our mother, and we will destroy even the ash we burn him into. Our mother has told me we will, or those who come from us will, if it takes a thousand years."

"She told you?"

"This morning. She came to me while I was on the river, in the mists and the quiet. I find her there when I need her."

"She comes to me only in dreams." Tears Brannaugh wouldn't shed clogged her throat.

"You hold what you are so tight." To soothe, Teagan stroked her sister's hair. "So not to upset Ailish, so to protect us. Perhaps you only allow her to come in dreams."

"She comes to you?" Brannaugh murmured. "Not only in dreams?"

"Sometimes when I ride Alastar, when we go deep into the woods, and I hold myself quiet, so quiet, she comes. She sings to me as she used to when I was little. And it was our mother who told me we will have love, we will have children. And we will, by our blood, defeat Cabhan."

"Am I to marry Fial then, bear him the child, the blood, who will finish it?"

"No!" Tiny flames flickered at Teagan's fingertips before she remembered control. "There is no love. The love comes, then the child. This is the way."

"It is not the only way."

"It is our way." Eamon took Brannaugh's hand again. "It will be our way. We will be what we are meant, do what we must do. If we don't try, what they sacrificed for us is for nothing. They would have died for nothing. Do you want it so?"

"No. No. I want to kill him. I want his blood, his death." Struggling, Brannaugh pressed her face to Kathel's neck, soothed herself with his warmth. "I think part of me would die if I turned away from what I am. But I know all of me would if a choice I make brings harm to either of you."

"We choose, all of us," Eamon said. "One by three. We needed this time. Our mother sent us here so we could have this time. We are not children now. I think we were no longer children when we rode from home that morning, knowing we would never see her again."

"We had power." Brannaugh breathed deep, straightened. Though he was younger, and a boy for all that, her brother spoke true. "She gave us more. I asked you both to let it lie still."

"You were right to ask it—even if we woke it now and then," Eamon added with a smile. "We needed the time here, but this time is coming to a close. I feel it."

"As I do," Brannaugh murmured. "So I wondered if it meant Fial. But no, you're right, both of you. I am not for the farm. Not for kitchen magicks and parlor games. We will look, here within the circle. We will look, and see. And know."

"Together?" Teagan's face glowed with joy as she asked, and Brannaugh knew she'd held back herself, her sister and brother too long.

"Together." Brannaugh cupped her hands, brought the power up, out. And dropping her hands down like water falling, she made the fire.

And the making of it, that first skill learned, the purity of the magick coursed through her. It felt as if she'd taken her first full breath in five years.

"You have more now," Teagan stated.

"Aye. It's waited. I've waited. We've waited. We wait no more. Through the flame and the smoke, we'll seek him out, see where he lurks. You see deeper," she told Eamon, "but have a care. If he knows we look at him, he will look at us."

"I know what I'm about. We can go through the fire, fly through the air, over water and earth, to where he is." He laid a hand on the small sword at his side. "We can kill him."

"It will take more than your sword. For all her power, our mother couldn't destroy him. It will take more, and we will find more. In time. For now, we look only."

"We can fly. Alastar and I. We . . ." Teagan trailed off at Brannaugh's sharp look. "It just . . . happened one day."

"We are what we are." Brannaugh shook her head. "I should never have forgotten it. Now we look. Through fire, through smoke, with shielded sight as we invoke. To seek, to find, his eyes we blind, he who shed our blood. Now our power rises in a flood. We are the three. As we will, so mote it be."

They gripped hands, joined their light.

Flames shifted; smoke cleared.

There, drinking wine from a silver cup, was Cabhan. His dark hair fell to his shoulders, gleamed in the light of the tallows.

Brannaugh saw stone walls, rich tapestries covering them, a bed with curtains of deep blue velvet.

At his ease, she thought. He had found comfort, riches—it didn't surprise her. He would use his powers for gain, for pleasure, for death. For whatever suited his purpose.

A woman came into the chamber. She wore rich robes, had hair dark as midnight. Spellbound, Brannaugh thought, by the blind look in her eyes.

And yet . . . some power there, some, Brannaugh realized. Struggling to break the bonds that locked it tight.

Cabhan didn't speak, merely flicked a hand toward the bed. The woman walked to it, disrobed, stood for a moment, her skin white as moonshine glowing in the light.

Behind those blind eyes, Brannaugh saw the war waged, the bitter, bitter fight to break free. To strike out.

For a moment, Eamon's focus wavered. He'd never seen a grown woman fully naked, nor one with such large breasts. Like his sisters he sensed that trapped power—like a white bird in a black box. But all that bare skin, those soft, generous breasts, the fascinating triangle of hair between her legs.

Would it feel like the hair on her head? He desperately wanted to touch, just there, and know.

Cabhan's head came up, a wolf scenting the air. He rose so quickly, the silver cup upended, spilling wine red as blood.

Brannaugh twisted Eamon's fingers painfully. Though he yelped, flushed as red as the fire, he brought his focus back.

Still, for a moment, a terrible moment, Cabhan's eyes seemed to look straight into his.

Then he walked to the woman. He gripped her breasts, squeezed, twisted. Pain ran over her face, but she didn't cry out.

Couldn't cry out.

He pinched her nipples, twisted them until tears ran down her cheeks, until bruises marred the white skin. He struck her, knocking her back on the bed. Blood trickled from the corner of her mouth, but she only stared.

With a flick of his wrist, he was naked, and his cock fully erect. It seemed to glow, but not with light. With dark. Eamon sensed it was like ice—cold and sharp and horrible. And this he rammed into the woman like a pike while the tears ran down her cheeks and the blood trickled from her mouth.

Something inside Eamon burst up with outrage—a vicious, innate fury at seeing a woman treated thus. He nearly pushed through that fire, that smoke, but Brannaugh gripped his hand, twisting bone against bone.

And while he raped her—for it was nothing else—Eamon felt Cabhan's thoughts. Thoughts of Sorcha, and the terrible lust for her that he'd never quenched. Thoughts of . . . Brannaugh. Of Brannaugh, and how he would do this to her, and more. And worse. How he would give her pain before he took her power. How he would take her power before he took her life.

Brannaugh quenched the fire quickly, ended the vision on a snap. And as quickly grabbed Eamon by both arms. "I said we were not ready. Do you not think I felt you gather to go?"

"He hurt her. He took her power, her body, against her will."

"He nearly found you—he sensed something pushing in."

"I would kill him for his thoughts alone. He will never touch you as he did her."

"He wanted to hurt her." Teagan's voice was a child's now. "But he thought of our mother, not of her. Then he thought of you."

"His thoughts can't hurt me." But they'd shaken her, deep inside herself. "He will never do to me, or to you, what he did to that poor woman."

"Could we have helped her?"

"Ah, Teagan, I don't know."

"We did not try." Eamon's words lashed out. "You held me here."

"For your life, for ours, for our purpose. Do you think I don't feel what you feel?" Even the secret fear drowned in an icy wave of rage. "That it stabbed a thousand times to do nothing? He has power. Not what he had, but different. Not more, but less, and still different. I don't know how to fight him. Yet. We don't know, Eamon, and we must know."

"He's coming. Not tonight, not tomorrow, but he'll come. He knows you . . ." Eamon flushed again, looked away.

"He knows I can bear children," Brannaugh finished. "He thinks to get a son from me. He never will. But he's coming. I felt it as well."

"Then we must go." Teagan tipped her head to Kathel's flank. "We must never bring him here."

"We must go," Brannaugh agreed. "We must be what we are."

"Where will we go?"

"South." Brannaugh looked at Eamon for confirmation.

"Aye, south, as he is still north. He remains in Mayo."

"We will find a place, and there we will learn more, find more. And one day we will go home."

She rose, took both their hands again, let the power spark from one to one. "I swear by our blood we will go home again."

"I swear by our blood," Eamon said, "we or what comes from us will destroy even the thought of him."

"I swear by our blood," Teagan said, "we are the three, and will ever be."

"Now we close the circle, but never again close off what we are, what we have, what we were given." Brannaugh released their hands. "We leave on the morrow."

EYES WEEPY, AILISH WATCHED BRANNAUGH PACK HER SHAWL. "I beg you to stay. Think of Teagan. She's but a child."

"The age I was when we came to you."

"As you were a child," she said.

"I was more. We are more, and must be what we are."

"I frightened you by speaking of Fial. You cannot think we would force a marriage upon you."

"No. Oh no." Brannaugh turned then, took her cousin's hands. "You never would. It is not for Fial we leave you, cousin."

Turning, Brannaugh packed the last of her things.

"Your mother would not want this for you."

"My mother would want us to be home, happy and safe with her and our father. But that was not to be. My mother gave her life for us, gave her power to us. And now her purpose to us. We must live our lives, embrace our power, complete our purpose."

"Where will you go?"

"To Clare, I think. For now. We will come back. And we will go home. I feel it as true as life. He will not come here."

Turning back, she looked into her cousin's eyes, her own like smoke. "He will not come here or harm you or any of yours. This I swear to you on my mother's blood."

"How can you know?"

"I am one of three. I am a dark witch of Mayo, first daughter of Sorcha. He shall not come here nor harm you or yours. You are protected for all of your life. This I have done. I would not leave you unprotected."

"Brannaugh . . ."

"You worry." Brannaugh laid her hands over her cousin's hands, which rested on the mound of her belly. "Have I not told you your son is well and healthy? The birthing will go easy, and quickly as well. This I can promise as well, and I do. But . . ."

"What is it? You must tell me."

"As you love me so still you fear what I have. But you must bide me now, in this. Your son, this one to come, must be the last. He will be healthy, and the birthing will go well. But the next will not. If there is a next, you will not survive."

"I . . . You cannot know. I cannot deny my husband the marriage bed. Or myself."

"You cannot deny your children their mother. It is a terrible grieving, Ailish."

"God will decide."

"God will have given you seven children, but the price for another will be your life, and the babe's as well. As I love you, heed me."

She took a bottle from her pocket. "I have made this for you. Only you. You will put it away. Once every month on the first day of your courses, you will drink—one sip only. You will not conceive, even after you take the last sip, for it will be done. You will live. Your children will have their mother. You will live to rock their children."

Ailish laid her hands over the mound of her belly. "I will be barren."

"You will sing to your children, and their children. You will share your bed with your man in pleasure. You will rejoice in the precious lives you brought into the world. The choice is yours, Ailish."

She closed her eyes a moment. When she opened them, they turned dark, dark. "You will call him Lughaidh. He will be fair of face and hair, blue of eye. A strong boy with a ready smile, and the voice of an angel. One day he will travel and ramble and use his voice to make his living. He will fall in love with a farmer's daughter, and will come back to you with her to work the land. And you will hear his voice across the fields, for he will ever be joyful."

She let the vision go. "I have seen what can be. You must choose."

"This is the name I chose for him," Ailish murmured. "I never told you, nor anyone." Now she took the bottle. "I will heed you."

Pressing her lips together, Ailish reached into her pocket, took out a small pouch. This she pushed into Brannaugh's hand. "Take this."

"I won't take your coin."

"You *will*." The tears fell now, spilling down her cheeks like rain. "Do you think I don't know you saved me and Conall in the birthing? And even now you think of me and mine? You have given me joy. You have brought Sorcha to me when I missed her, for I saw her in you day by day. You will take the coin, and swear to me you will be safe, you will come back. All of you, for you are mine as I am yours."

Understanding, Brannaugh slipped the purse into the pocket of her skirts, then kissed Ailish on each cheek. "I swear it."

Outside Eamon did his best to make his cousins laugh. They asked him not to go, of course, asked why he must, tried to bargain with him. So he wound stories of the grand adventures he would have, smiting dragons and catching magick frogs. He saw Teagan walking with a weeping Mabh, saw her give Mabh a rag doll she'd made herself.

He wished Brannaugh would hurry, for the leave-taking was a misery. Alastar stood ready. Eamon—he was head of the family, after all, had decided his sisters would ride, and he would walk.

He would brook no argument.

Bardan came out of the little stable leading Slaine—Old Slaine now, as the broodmare was past her prime, but a sweet-natured thing for all that.

"Her breeding days are done," Bardan said in his careful way. "But she's a good girl, and she'll serve you well."

"Oh, but I can't be taking her from you. You need—"

"A man needs a horse." Bardan set his calloused hand on Eamon's shoulder. "You've done a man's work for the farm, so you'll take her. I'd give you Moon for Brannaugh if I could spare him, but you'll take Old Slaine here."

"It's more than grateful I am to you, for Slaine and all the rest. I promise you I'll treat her like a queen."

For a moment, Eamon let himself be just a boy, and threw his arms around his cousin, the man who'd been a father to him for half his life. "We'll come back one day."

"Be sure you do."

When it was done, all the farewells, the safe journeys, the tears, he swung up on the mare, his grandfather's sword and sheath secured against his saddle. Brannaugh mounted behind Teagan, leaned down once to kiss Ailish a last time.

They rode away from the farm, their home for five years, from their family—and south toward the unknown.

He looked back, waved as they waved, found himself more torn in the leaving than he'd expected. Then overhead Roibeard called, circled before spearing the way south.

This was meant, Eamon decided. This was the time.

He slowed his pace a bit, cocked his head at Teagan. "So, how does our Slaine feel about all this then?"

Teagan looked down at the mare, cocked her head in turn. "Oh, it's a grand adventure to her, to be sure, and she never thought to have another. She's proud and she's grateful. She'll be loyal to the end of her days, and do her very best for you."

"And I'll do my best for her. We'll ride through midday before we stop to rest the horses, and eat the first of the oatcakes Ailish packed for us."

"Is that what we'll be doing?" Brannaugh said.

He tossed up his chin. "You're the eldest, but I have the staff, however puny you might think it is—which it isn't at all. Roibeard shows the way, and we follow."

Brannaugh looked up, watched the flight of the hawk. Then down at Kathel who pranced along beside Alastar as if he could walk all day and through the night.

"Your guide, mine, and Teagan's. Aye, we follow. Ailish gave me some coin, but we won't be spending it unless we must. We'll be making our own."

"And just how are we doing that?"

"By being what we are." She lifted her hand, palm up, brought a small ball of flame into it. Then vanished it. "Our mother served her gift, tended us, her cabin. We can surely serve our gift, tend ourselves, and find a place to do both."

"Clare's a wild place I hear," Teagan offered.

"And what better place than the wild for such as us?" The pure joy of freedom ripened with every step. "We have our mother's book, and we'll study, we'll learn. We'll make potions and do healings. A healer is always welcome, she told me."

"When he comes, it will take more than healing and potions."

"So it will," Brannaugh said to her brother. "So we learn. We were safe five years at the farm. If our guides lead us to Clare, as it seems they will, we may have the next five there. Time enough to learn, to plan. When we go home again, we'll be stronger than he can know."

They rode through midday and into the rain. Soft and steady it fell from a sky of bruises and broodings. They rested the horses, watered them, shared oatcakes, with some for Kathel.

Through the rain came the wind as they continued their journey, past a little farm and cabin with smoke puffing out of the chimney, sending out the scent of burning peat. Inside they might be welcome, be given tea and a place by the fire. Inside the warm and dry.

But Kathel continued to prance, Roibeard to circle, and Alastar never slowed.

And even the gloomy light began to die as the day tipped toward night.

"Slaine grows weary," Teagan murmured. "She won't ask to stop, but she tires. Her bones ache. Can't we rest her a bit, find a dry place and—"

"There!" Eamon pointed ahead. Near the muddy track stood what might have been an old place of worship. Sacked now, burned down to the scorched stone by men who couldn't stop destroying what those they vanquished had built.

Roibeard circled over it, calling, calling, and Kathel bounded ahead.

"We'll stop there for the night. Make a fire, rest the animals and ourselves."

Brannaugh nodded at her brother. "The walls stand—or most of them. It should keep the wind out, and we can do the rest. It's nearly end of day. We owe Mordan and Mabon who came from her our thanks."

One wall had fallen in, they discovered, but the others stood. Even some steps, which Eamon immediately tested, circled up to what had been a second level. Whatever timber had been used had burned to ashes and blown to the winds. But it was shelter of a sort and, Brannaugh felt, the right place.

This would be the place of their first night, the equinox, when the light and the dark balanced.

"I'll tend the horses." Teagan took the reins of both. "The horses are mine, after all. I'll see to them, if you make us a place, a dry spot I'm hoping, and a good fire."

"That I'll do. We'll give our thanks, then have some tea and some of the dried venison before we—"

She broke off as Roibeard swooped down, perched on a narrow stone ledge.

And dropped a fat hare on the ground at Eamon's feet.

"Well now, that's a feast in the making. I'll clean it, Teagan tends the horses, and Brannaugh the fire."

A dry spot, she thought, and shoving back the hood of her cloak imagined one. Drew up and out what she was, thought of warm and dry—and flashed out heat so bright and hot it nearly burned them all before she drew it down again.

"I'm sorry for that. I haven't done any of this before."

"It's a cork out of a bottle," Eamon decided. "And it poured out too fast."

"Aye." She slowed it, carefully, carefully. She didn't mind the wet for herself, but Teagan was right. The old mare's bones ached, even she could feel it.

She eased back the wet, slowly, just a bit, just a bit more. It trembled through her, the joy of it. Loosed now, free. Then the fire. Magickal tonight. Other nights, as their mother had taught them, a body gathered wood, put the work into it. But tonight, it would be her fire.

She brought it, banked it.

"A bit of the oatcake, and some wine," she told her brother, her sister. "An offering of thanks to the gods for the balance of the day and night, for the cycle of rebirth. And for this place of rest.

"Into the fire," she told them. "The cake, then the wine. These small things we share with thee, we give our thanks we servants three."

"At this time where day meets night, we embrace both dark and light," Eamon continued, not sure where the words had come from.

"We will learn to stand and fight, to use our gifts for the right and the white," Teagan added.

"In this place and hour, we open to our given power. From now till ever it will be free. As we will, so mote it be."

The fire shot up, a tower, red, orange, gold, with a heart of burning blue. A thousand voices whispered in it, and the ground shook. Then the world seemed to sigh.

The fire was a fire, banked in a tidy circle on the stony ground.

"This is what we are," Brannaugh said, still glowing from the shock of energy. "This is what we have. The nights grow longer now. The dark conquers light. But he will not conquer us."

She smiled, her heart full as it hadn't been since the morning they'd left home. "We need to make a spit for the hare. We'll have that feast tonight, our first. And we'll rest in the warm and dry until we journey on."

EAMON CURLED BY THE FIRE, HIS BELLY FULL, HIS BODY warm and dry. And journeyed on.

He felt himself lift up, lift out, and fly. North. Home.

Like Roibeard, he soared over the hills, the rivers, the fields where cattle lowed, where sheep cropped.

Green and green toward home with the sun sliding quiet through the clouds.

His heart, so light. Going home.

But not home. Not really home, he realized when he found himself on the ground again. The woods, so familiar—but not. Something different. Even the air different, and yet the same.

It all made him dizzy and weak.

He began to walk, whistling for his hawk. His guide. The light changed, dimmed. Was night coming so fast?

But not the night, he saw. It was the fog.

And with it, the wolf that was Cabhan.

He heard the growl of it, reached for his grandfather's sword. But it wasn't at his side. He was a boy, ankle deep in mists, unarmed, as the wolf with the red gem glowing around his neck walked out of the fog. And became a man.

"Welcome back, young Eamon. I've waited for you."

"You killed my father, my mother. I've come to avenge them."

Cabhan laughed, a rolling, merry sound that sent ice running up Eamon's spine.

"It's spirit you have, so that's fine and well. Come avenge then, the dead father, the dead witch who whelped you. I will have what you are, and then I'll make your sisters mine."

"You will never touch what's mine." Eamon circled, tried to think. The fog rose and rose, clouding all, the woods, the path, his mind. He gripped air, fisted it, hurled it. It carved a shaky and narrow path. Cabhan laughed again.

"Closer. Come closer. Feel what I am."

He did feel it, the pain of it, the power of it. And the fear. He tried fire, but it fell smoldering, turned to dirty ash. When Cabhan's hands reached out for him, he lifted his fists to fight.

Roibeard swooped like an arrow, claws and beak tearing at those outstretched hands. The blood ran black as the man howled, as the man began to re-form into the wolf.

And another man came through the fog. Tall, his brown hair damp from the mists, his eyes deep and green and full of power and fury.

"Run," he told Eamon.

"I will not run from such as he. I cannot."

The wolf pawed the ground, showed its teeth in a terrible smile.

"Take my hand."

The man grabbed Eamon's hand. Light exploded like suns, power flew like a thousand beating wings. Blind and deaf, Eamon cried out. There was only power, covering him, filling him, bursting from him. Then with one shattering roar, the fog was gone, the wolf gone, and only the man gripping his hand remained.

The man dropped to his knees, breath harsh, face white, eyes full of magicks. "Who are you?" he demanded.

"I am Eamon son of Daithi, son of Sorcha. I am of the three. I am the Dark Witch of Mayo."

"As am I. Eamon." On a shaky laugh, the man touched Eamon's hair, his face. "I am from you. You're out of your time, lad, and in mine. I'm Connor, of the clan O'Dwyer. I am out of Sorcha, out of you. One of three."

"How do I know this to be true?"

"I am your blood, you are mine. You know." Connor pulled the amulet from under his shirt, touched the one, the same one, Eamon wore.

And the man lifted an arm. Roibeard landed on the leather glove he wore.

Not Roibeard, Eamon realized, and yet . . .

"My hawk. Not yours, but named for him. Ask him what you will. He is yours as much as mine."

"This is . . . not my place."

"It is, yes, not your time but your place. It ever will be."

Tears stung Eamon's eyes, and his belly quivered with longing worse than hunger. "Did we come home?"

"You did."

"Will we defeat him, avenge our parents?"

"We will. We will never stop until it's done. My word to you."

"I wish to . . . I'm going back. I feel it. Brannaugh, she's calling me back. You saved me from Cabhan."

"Saving you saved me, I'm thinking."

"Connor of the O'Dwyers. I will not forget."

And he flew, over the hills again, until it was soft, soft morning and he sat by Brannaugh's fire with both his sisters shaking him.

"Leave off, now! My head is circling over the rest of me."

"He's so pale," Teagan said. "Here, here, I'll fix you tea."

"Tea would be welcome. I went on a journey. I don't know how, but I went home, but 'twasn't home. I need to sort through it. But I know something I didn't. Something we didn't."

He guzzled some water Brannaugh pushed on him, then shoved the skin away again. "He can't leave there. Cabhan. He can't leave, or not far. The farther from home, from where he traded for his new powers, the less they are. He risks death to leave there. He can't follow us."

"How do you know this?" Brannaugh demanded.

"I . . . saw it in his mind. I don't know how. I saw it there, that weakness. I met a man, he's ours. I . . ." Eamon drew a long breath, closed his eyes a moment.

"Let me have some tea, will you then? A little tea, then I have a tale to tell you. We'll bide here awhile yet, and I'll tell you all. Then, aye, aye, south for us, to learn, to grow, to plan. For he can't touch us. He won't ever touch you."

Whatever boy he'd been, he was a man now. And power still simmered inside him.

3

Autumn 2013

WHEN CONNOR WOKE EARLIER THAN HE LIKED, HE hadn't expected to meet an ancestor, or the greatest enemy of his blood. He certainly hadn't anticipated starting his day with an explosion of magicks that had all but knocked him off his feet.

But, in the main, he liked the unexpected.

With the dawn barely broken, there'd been no hope his sister might be busy in the kitchen. And his skin meant too much to him to risk waking her and suggesting she might like to cook up breakfast.

More, there hadn't been a hunger, and he always woke ready to break the night's fast. Instead there'd been an odd energy, and a deep need to get out, get about.

So he'd whistled up his hawk and, with Roibeard for his companion, had taken himself into the mists and trees.

And quiet.

He wasn't a man who required a great deal of quiet. He preferred, most of the time, the noise and conversations and heat of company.

But this soft morning, the call of his hawk, the scrabble of rabbit in the brush, and the sigh of the morning breeze had been enough for him.

He thought he might walk over to Ashford Castle, let Roibeard soar in the open, over the greens there—and that would give any early-rising guests at the hotel a thrill.

Thrills often drummed up business, and he had one to run with the falconry school.

He'd aimed for that exactly, until he'd felt it—the stir of power, within and without. His own rising without his asking it, the dark stain of what was Cabhan, smudging the sweetness of the dewy pines.

And something more, something more.

He should have called his circle—his sister, his cousin, his friends, but something pushed him on, down the path, through the trees, near the wall of vines and uprooted tree where beyond lay the ruins of the cabin that had been Sorcha's. Beyond where he and his circle had battled Cabhan on the night of the summer solstice.

There the fog spread, the power thrummed, dark against white. He saw the boy, thought first and only to protect. He would not, could not, allow harm to an innocent.

But the boy, while innocent enough, had more. The something more.

Now, the fog gone and Cabhan with it, the boy gone back to his own time, his own place, Connor stayed as he was—on his knees on the damp ground, fighting to get his breath fully back into his lungs.

His ears still rang from what had sounded like worlds exploding. His eyes still burned from a light brighter than a dozen suns.

And the power merged with joined hands sang through him.

He got slowly to his feet, a tall, lean man with a thick mop of curling brown hair, his face pale yet, and his eyes deep and green as the moss with what still stirred inside him.

Best to get home, he thought. To get back. For what had come through the solstice, and hidden away till the equinox lurked still.

A bit wobbly in the legs yet, he realized, unsure if he should be amused or embarrassed. His hawk swooped by, landed with a flutter of wings on a branch. Sat, watched, waited.

"We'll go," he said. "I think we've done what we were meant to do this morning. And now, Jesus, I'm starving."

The power, he thought as he began to walk. The sheer force of it had hulled him out. Turning toward home, he sensed his sister's hound seconds before Kathel ran toward him.

"You felt it as well, did you now?" He gave Kathel's great black head a stroke, continued on. "I'd be surprised if all of Mayo didn't feel a jolt from it. My skin's still buzzing like my bones are covered with bees."

Steadier yet with hound and hawk, he walked out of the shadows of the woods into the pearly morning. Roibeard circled overhead as he walked the road with Kathel to the cottage. A second hawk cried, and Connor spotted his friend Fin's Merlin.

Then the thunder of hoofbeats broke through the quiet, so he paused, waited—felt a fresh stirring as he saw his cousin Iona, his friend Boyle astride the big gray Alastar. And Fin as well, racing with them on his gleaming black Baru.

"We'll need more eggs," he called out, smiling now. "And another rasher or two of bacon."

"What happened?" Iona, her short cap of hair tousled from sleep, leaned down to touch his cheek. "I knew you were safe, or we'd have come even faster."

"You all but flew as it is—and not a saddle between the three of you. I'll tell you inside. I could eat three pigs and top it off with a cow."

"Cabhan." Fin, his hair dark as his mount's, his eyes the dark green of Connor's when the power had taken him, turned to stare into the trees.

"Him and more. But Iona has the right of it. I'm fine and well, just starving half to death while we stand here on the road. You felt it," he added when he began to walk again.

"Felt it?" Boyle stared down at Connor. "It woke me from a sound sleep, and I don't have what the three of you do. I've no magick in me, and still whatever it was shot through me like an arrow." He nodded toward the cottage. "And it seems the same for Meara."

Connor looked over, saw Meara Quinn, lifelong friend, his sister's best mate, striding along toward them—tall and lush as a goddess in her flannel sleep pants and old jacket, he thought, and her long brown hair a tangle.

She made a picture, he mused, but then she ever did.

"She stayed the night," he told the others. "Took Iona's room as you stayed over at Boyle's, cousin. Good morning to you, Meara."

"Good morning be damned. What the bloody hell happened?"

"I'm after telling you all." He slipped an arm around her waist. "But I need food."

"Branna said you would, and she's already seeing to it. She's shaken, and pretending not to be. It was like a bleeding earthquake—but inside me. That's the devil of a way to wake."

"I'll see to the horses." Boyle slid off Alastar. "Go on in, stuff something in your belly."

"Thanks for that." Smiling again, Connor lifted his arms so Iona could drop into them from Alastar's back. Then she wrapped around him.

"Scared me," she murmured.

"You're not alone in that." He kissed the top of her head, his pretty cousin from America, the last of the three, and keeping her hand in his, went into the cottage.

The scent of bacon, of coffee, of warm bread hit his belly like a fist. In that moment he wanted to eat more than he wanted to live— and needed to eat if he wanted to live.

Kathel led the way back to the kitchen, and there Branna worked at the stove. She'd tied her dark hair back, still wore the flowered flannel pants and baggy shirt she'd slept in. That alone showed her love, he mused, as she'd have taken the time to change, to fuss with herself a little knowing there'd be company—and Finbar Burke most especially.

Saying nothing, she turned from the stove, handed him a plate holding a fried egg on toast.

"Bless you, darling."

"It'll fill the worst of the hole. There's more coming. You're cold," she said quietly.

"I hadn't noticed, but I am, yes. A bit cold."

Before she could flick a hand toward the kitchen hearth, Fin did so, and the little fire flashed.

"You're quivering some. Sit, for God's sake, and eat like a human." Voice brisk, Meara all but shoved him into a chair at the table.

"I'm not a one to brush away some fussing, and truth be told, I'd kill for coffee."

"I'll get it." Iona hurried over to the pot.

"Ah, what man can complain with three beautiful women pampering him. Thanks, *mo chroi*," he added when Iona gave him the coffee.

"You'll not be pampered long, I can promise. Sit down, the lot of you," Branna ordered. "I've nearly got this fried up. When his belly's full enough to settle him, he'll damn well explain why he didn't call for me."

"It was fast and done. I would've called for you, for all of you. It wasn't me in harm's way, I'm thinking. He didn't come for me this morning."

"And who then, when the rest of us were asleep in our beds?" When Branna would have lifted an enormous platter of food to bring to the table, Fin simply took it from her.

"Sit then, and listen. Sit," he repeated before she could snap at him. "You're as shaken as he is."

The minute the tray hit the table, Connor began to scoop eggs, sausage, bacon, toasted bread, potatoes onto his plate and into a small mountain.

"I woke early, and with an edge on," he began, and took them all through it between enthusiastic bites.

"Eamon?" Branna demanded. "The son of Sorcha? Here and now? You're sure of it?"

"As sure as I know my sister. I only thought him a boy at first, and in Cabhan's path, but when I took his hand . . . I've never felt the like, never. Not even with you, Branna, or you and Iona together. Even on the solstice when the power was a scream, it wasn't so big, so bright, so full. I couldn't hold it, couldn't control it. It just blew through me like a comet. Through the boy as well, but he held on to me, on to it. He's a rare one."

"What about Cabhan?" Iona demanded.

"It ripped through him," Fin said. "I felt it." Absently, he lifted a hand to his shoulder, where the mark of his blood, of Cabhan's blood scarred his flesh. His heart. "It stunned him, left him, I promise you, as shaken as you were."

"So he slithered away?" Boyle dug into eggs. "Like the snake he is."

"That he did," Connor confirmed. "He was gone, and with him the fog, and there was only myself and the boy. Then only myself. But . . . He was me, and I was he—parts of one. That I knew when we joined hands. More than blood. Not the same, but . . . more than blood. For a moment, I could see into him—like a mirror."

"What did you see?" Meara asked.

"Love and grief and courage. The fear, but the heart to face it, for his sisters, for his parents. For us, come to that. Just a lad, no more than ten, I'd venture. But in that moment, shining with a power he hasn't yet learned to ride smooth."

"Is it like me going to visit Nan?" Iona wondered, thinking of her grandmother in America. "A kind of astral projection? But it's not exactly, is it? It's like that, but with the time shift, much more than that. The time shift that can happen by Sorcha's cabin. You weren't by Sorcha's cabin, were you, Connor?"

"No, still outside the clearing. Near though." Connor considered. "Maybe near enough. All this is new. But I know for certain it wasn't what Cabhan expected."

"It may be he brought the boy, brought Eamon," Meara suggested. "Pulled him from his own time into ours, trying to separate him from his sisters, to take on a boy rather than a man like the sodding coward he is. The way you said it happened, Connor, if you hadn't come along, he might have killed the boy, or certainly harmed him."

"True enough. Eamon was game, by God, he was game—wouldn't run when I told him to run, but still confused, afraid, not yet able to draw up enough to fight on his own."

"So you woke and went out," Branna said, "you who never step a foot out of a morning without something in your belly, and called up your hawk. Barely dawn?" She shook her head. "Something called you there. The connection between you and Eamon, or Sorcha herself. A mother still protecting her child."

"I dreamed of Teagan," Iona reminded them. "Of her riding Alastar to the cabin, to her mother's grave, and facing Cabhan there— drawing his blood. She's mine, the way Eamon is Connor's."

Branna nodded as Iona looked at her. "Brannaugh to Branna, yes. I dream of her often. But nothing like this. It's useful, it must be useful. We'll find a way to use what happened here, what we know. He hid away since the solstice."

"We hurt him," Boyle said, scanning the others with tawny eyes. "That night he bled and burned as we did. More, I'm thinking."

"He took the rest of the summer to heal, to gather. And this morning tried for the boy, to take that power, and—"

"To end you," Fin interrupted Branna. "Kill the boy, Connor never exists? Or it's very possible that's the case. Change what was, change what is."

"Well now, he failed brilliantly." Connor polished off his bacon, sighed. "And I feel not only human again, but fit and fine. It's a pity we can't take the bastard on again now."

"You need more than a full fry in your belly to take him on." Rising, Meara gathered dishes. "All of us do. We hurt him on the solstice, and that's a satisfying thing, but we didn't finish him. What did we miss? Isn't that the thing we need? What did we not do that we need to do?"

"Ah, the practical mind."

"Someone needs to think practical," Meara tossed back at him.

"She's right. I've poured over Sorcha's book." Branna shook her head. "What we did, what we had, how we planned it, it should've worked."

"He changed the ground," Boyle reminded her. "Took the fighting ground back in time."

"And still, I can't find what we might add to it." Branna tossed a glance toward Fin, just a beat. He only gave her the most subtle shake of head. "So we'll keep looking."

"No, you sit." Iona took more dishes before Connor could do so. "Considering your dawn adventure, you get a pass at kitchen duty. Maybe I wasn't strong or skilled enough last summer."

"Do you need reminding of a whirlwind called?" Boyle asked her.

"That was more instinct than skill, but I'm learning." She glanced back at Branna.

"You are, yes, and very well indeed. You're no weak link if that's what you're thinking, nor have you ever been. He knows more than us, and that's a problem. He's lived, in his way, hundreds of years."

"That makes him older," Meara put in, "not smarter."

"We have books and legends and what was passed down generation to generation. But he lived it all, so—smarter or not—he knows more. And what he has is deep and dark. His power has no rules as ours does. He harms who he wants, no matter to it. That we can never do and be what we are."

"His power source—the stone he wears around his neck, wolf or man. Destroy it, destroy him. I know it," Fin stated, clenched a fist on the table. "I know it as truth, but don't know how it can be done. Yet."

"We'll find the way. We must," Connor said, "so we will."

Fin rose when Connor reached over the table to lay his hand on Branna's, and joined the others across the room with the clatter of dishes, the whoosh of water in the sink.

"Worrying for me won't help, and isn't needed. I don't have to look," he added, "to see."

"And if he'd harmed you and the boy, where would we be?"

"Well, he didn't, did he? And between us we gave him a solid boot in the balls. I'm here, Branna, as ever. We're meant for this, so I'm here."

"You're a thorn in my side half the time." Her hand turned under his until their fingers curled together and gripped. "But I'm used to you. You'll have a care, Connor."

"I will, of course. And the same for you."

"The same for us all."

IT AMUSED HIM, AND TOUCHED HIM WHEN MEARA FELL INTO step beside him as he left the house for the falconry school.

"Are you leaving your lorry then?"

"I am. I want to walk off that breakfast."

"You're guarding my body." He slung an arm around her shoulders, pulled her in so their hips bumped.

She'd dressed for work at the stables, rough pants and jacket, sturdy boots, and with all that hair braided back to hang through the loop of her battered cap.

And still she made a picture, he thought, the dark-eyed Meara with the gypsy in her blood.

"Your body can guard itself." She glanced up, watched the hawks circle in the heavy sky. "And you've got them keeping an eye out."

"I'm glad for your company all the same. And this gives you time to tell me what's troubling you."

"I think a mad sorcerer bent on our destruction's enough to go around."

"Something else brought you to Branna last night and had you staying through it. Is it a man giving you grief? Do you want me to lay him low for you?"

He flexed one arm, made a fist, shook it fiercely to make her laugh.

Then she sniffed. "As if I couldn't lay any I wanted low—or otherwise—myself."

He laughed in turn, sheer delight, and gave her hip another bump. "I've no doubt on that one. What is it then, darling? I can hear the buzzing in your head like a hive of angry wasps."

"You could stop listening." But she relented enough to lean against him a moment, so he caught the scent of his own soap on her skin. An oddly pleasant sort of thing.

"It's just my mother driving me half mad, which is a normal enough day in the life. Donal's got himself a girl."

"So I've heard," he said, thinking of her younger brother. "Sharon, isn't it, moved to Cong this past spring? A nice girl, from what I've seen. A pretty face, an easy smile. Don't you like her then?"

"I like her fine and well, and more to the point Donal's mad for her. It's lovely, really, to see him so taken, and happy with it, and her very much the same."

"Well then?"

"He's after moving out of the house, and in with his Sharon."

Connor considered that as they walked through the pretty morning toward work they both loved. "He's, what, twenty and four?"

"And five. And, yes, past time he moved out of his mother's house. But now my mother and my sister Maureen have their heads together and have come to the horrible conclusion I should move back in with Ma."

"Well now, that won't do, not for a minute."

"It won't." Now her sigh held relief, as he understood the simple and bare truth. "But they're laying it on like courses of brick. The guilt, the pressure, the bloody *logic* as they see it. Oh, Maureen's after saying our mother can't be left on her own, and me being the only one unhampered, so to speak, it stands I should be the one to right the ship. And Ma's right behind her with she'll have the room for me, and it would save me the rent, and how lonely she'll be without a chick or child around."

She shoved both hands in her pockets. "Bugger it."

"Do you want my opinion or only my condolences?"

She slanted a look at him, bold brown eyes both suspicious and speculative. "I'll take the opinion, though I may hurl it back in your face."

"Then here it is for you. Stay where you are, darling. You were never happy, not really, until you moved out to begin with."

"That's what I want, and what I know I should do for myself and my sanity, but—"

"If your mother's fretting about being lonely, and Maureen's fretting about your mother—who's her mother as well I'll add—being on her own, why wouldn't it be a fine idea for your mother to move in with Maureen and her family? Wouldn't it be a great help to Maureen to have her mother with her, with the children and all that?"

"Why didn't I think of that?" Meara pulled away long enough to punch Connor's shoulder, do a little dance. "Why didn't I think of that my own self?"

"You hadn't got through the courses of guilt." In an old habit, he gave her long, thick braid a tug. "Maureen's no right to push you to give up your flat, change your life just because your brother's changing his."

"I know it, but I know as well, Ma's next to helpless. She has been since my father left us. She did her best with a terrible situation, but she'll dither her way through the days, worry herself through the nights living all on her own."

"You've two brothers, two sisters," he reminded her. "There's five of you to help tend your mother."

"The smart ones got well away, didn't they? It's only me and Donal right here. But I can plant the seed in Ma's mind of moving in with Maureen. If nothing else, it should scare Maureen silent for a bit."

"There you have it." He turned, as she did, toward the stables.

Meara stopped. "Where are you going?"

"I'll walk you to work."

"I don't need my body guarded, thanks. Go on." She planted a finger in his chest, gave it a little push. "You've work of your own."

There was no harm in the day—he felt none at all. And after the early-morning clash, Connor felt Cabhan would be curled up in some dark cave, gathering.

"We've five hawk walks already booked today, and may have others before it's done. Maybe I'll see you on the paths."

"Maybe."

"If you text me when you're done for the day, I'll meet you here, walk back with you to the cottage."

"We'll see how it all goes. Mind yourself, Connor."

"I will. I do."

Because her eyebrows had drawn together, he kissed the space between them, then strolled off. Looking, to Meara's mind, like a man without a single care in the world rather than one with the weight of it on his shoulders.

An optimist to the bone, she thought, envying him a little.

But she pulled her phone out of her pocket as she took the path to the stables and her workday.

"Morning, Ma." And smiling to herself, prepared to give her annoying sister a shot right up the arse.

4

CONNOR SLIPPED THROUGH THE EMPLOYEES' GATE FOR the falconry school. As always, he felt a little flutter—a bit like beating wings—in his heart, along his skin. It had always been the hawk for him. That connection, like his power, came down through the blood.

He'd have preferred having some time to walk around the enclosures and aviary, greet the hawks, the big owl they called Brutus, just to see—and hear—how they all fared.

But the way he'd started his day meant he was a few minutes behind already. He saw one of his staff, Brian—skinny as a flagpole and barely eighteen—checking the feed and water.

So he only glanced around to be sure all was well as he crossed over to the offices, past the fenced-in area where his assistant, Kyra, kept her pretty spaniel most days.

"And how's it going for you today, Romeo?"

In answer, the dog wagged his whole body, clamped a gnawed blue ball in his mouth, and brought it hopefully to the fence.

"It'll have to be later for that."

He stepped into the office, found Kyra, her hair a short wedge of sapphire blue, busy at the keyboard.

"You're late."

Though she just hit five foot two, Kyra had a voice like a foghorn.

"Happy I'm the boss then, isn't it?"

"Fin's the boss."

"Happy I had breakfast with him so he knows what's what." He knocked his fist lightly on the top of her head as he moved by to a desk covered with forms, clipboards, papers, brochures, a spare glove, a tether, a bowl of tumbled stones, and other debris.

"We've had another booking come in already this morning. A double. Father and son—and the boy's just sixteen. I've put you on that, as you do better with the teenagers than Brian or Pauline. They're for ten this morning. Yanks."

She paused, sent Connor a disapproving look from her round, wildly freckled face. "Sixteen, and why isn't he in school, I want to know."

"You're such a taskmaster, Kyra. It's an education, isn't it, to travel to another country, to learn of hawks?"

"That won't teach you to add two and two. Sean's not coming in till noon, if you're forgetting. He's taking his wife in for her check with the doctor."

He looked up at that because he had forgotten. "All's well there, right, with her and the baby?"

"Well and fine, she just wants him there as they may find if it's a girl or boy today. That puts Brian on the nine with the lady from Donegal, you at the ten, and Pauline's at half-ten with a pair of honeymooners from Dublin."

She clicked and clacked at the keyboard as she laid out the

morning's schedule. Though she tended toward the bossy and brisk, Kyra was a wizard at doing a dozen things at once.

And—the fly in Connor's ointment—expected everyone else to do the same.

"I've set you on at two for another," she added. "Yanks again, a couple over from Boston. They've just come in from a stay at Dromoland in Clare, and they're having three days at Ashford before moving on. Three weeks holiday for their twenty-fifth anniversary."

"Ten and two then."

"They've been married long as I've been alive. That's something to think on."

Listening with half an ear, he sat to poke through the paperwork he couldn't palm off on her. "Your parents have been married longer yet, considering you're the youngest."

"Parents are different," she said—decisively—though he couldn't see how.

"Oh, and Brian's claiming there was an earthquake this morning, near to shook him out of bed."

Connor glanced up, face calm. "An earthquake, is it?"

She smirked, still clattering on the keyboard with nails painted with pink glitter. "Swears the whole house shook around him." She rolled her eyes, hit Print, swiveled around for a clipboard. "And he's decided it's some conspiracy, as there's not a word of it on the telly. A few mentions, so he claims, on the Internet. He's gone from earthquake to nuclear testing by some foreign power in a fingersnap. He'll be all over you about it, as he's been me."

"And your bed didn't shake?"

She flashed a grin. "Not from an earthquake."

He laughed, went back to the paperwork. "And how is Liam?"

"Very well indeed. I'm thinking I might marry him."

"Is that the way of it?"

"It might be, as you have to start on racking up those anniversaries sometime. I'll let him know when I've made up my mind."

When the phone jangled, he left her to answer, went back to clearing off a section of his desk.

So some felt it, some didn't, he thought. Some were more open than others. And some closed tight as any drum.

He'd known Kyra most of his life, he mused, and she knew what he was—had to know. But she never spoke of it. She was, despite her blue hair and the little hoop in her left eyebrow, a drum.

He worked steady enough until Brian came in and, as predicted, was full of earthquakes that were likely nuclear testing by some secret government agency, or perhaps a sign of the apocalypse.

He left Brian and Kyra batting it all around, went out to choose the hawk for the first walk.

As no one was watching, he did it the quick and simple way. He simply opened the aviary, looked into the eyes of his choice, held up his gloved arm.

The hawk swooped through, landed, coming in as obedient as a well-trained hound.

"There you are, Thor. Ready to work, are you? You do well for Brian this morning, and I'll take you out later, if I can, for a real hunt. How's that for you?"

After tethering the hawk, he walked back to the offices, transferred him to the waiting perch, tethered him there.

Patient, Thor closed his wings, sat watchful.

"We may get some wet," he told Brian, "but not a drench, I'm thinking."

"Global warming's causing strange weather around the world. It may have been an earthquake."

"An earthquake 'tisn't weather," Kyra stated.

"It's all connected," Brian said darkly.

"I think you won't see more than a shower this morning. If there's an earthquake or volcanic eruption, be sure you get Thor back home again." Connor gave Brian a slap on the shoulder. "There's your clients now, at the gate. Go on, let them in, give them the show around. I'll take Roibeard and William for the ten," he told Kyra when Brian hurried to answer the gate. "That leaves Moose for Pauline's."

"I'll set it up."

"We'll have Rex for Sean. He respects Sean, and doesn't yet have the same respect for Brian. Best not send him out with Bri yet, on their own. I'll take Merlin for the two, as he hasn't been on a walk in a few days."

"Fin's hawk isn't here."

"He's around," Connor said simply. "And Pauline can take Thor out again this afternoon. Brian or Sean, whoever you have for the last so far, can take Rex."

"What of Nester?"

"He's not feeling it today. He's got the day off."

She only lifted her beringed eyebrow at Connor's assessment of the hawk. "If you say."

"And I do."

Her round face lost its smirk in concern. "Does he need to be looked at?"

"No, he's not sick, just out of sorts. I'll take him out later, let him fly off the mood."

He was right about the shower, but it came and went as they often did. A short patter of rain, a thin beam of sun through a pocket of clouds.

By the time his double arrived, the shower had moved on, leaving the air damp and just misty enough. Truth be told, he thought as he took the father and son around, it added to the atmosphere for the Yanks.

"How do you know which one is which?" The boy—name of Taylor—gangling with big ears and knobby knuckles, put on an air of mild boredom.

"They look alike, the Harris's hawk, but they each have their own personality, their own way. You see, there's Moose, he's a big one, so he has the name. And Rex, beside him? Has a kind of regal air."

"Why don't they just fly away when you take them out?"

"Why would they be doing that? They've a good life here, a posh life come to that. And good, respectable work as well. Some were born here, and this is home for them."

"You train them here?" the father asked.

"We do, yes, from the time they're hatchlings. They're born to fly and hunt, aren't they? With proper training—reward, kindness, affection, they can be trained to do what they're born to do and return to the glove."

"Why the Harris's hawk for the walks?"

"They're social, they are. And more, their maneuverability makes them a fine choice for a walk in these parts. The Peregrines—you see here?" He walked them over to a large gray bird with black and yellow markings. "They're magnificent to be sure, and there's no faster animal on the planet when they're in the stoop. That would be flying up to a great height, then diving for its prey."

"I thought a cheetah was the fastest," Taylor said.

"Apollo here?" At the name, at Connor's subtle link, the falcon spread its great wings—had the boy impressed enough to gasp a little before he shrugged. "He can beat the cat, reaching speeds to three hundred twenty kilometers an hour. That's two hundred miles an hour in American," Connor added with a grin.

"But for all its speed and beauty, the Peregrine needs open space, and the Harris's can dance through the trees. You see these here?"

He walked them along. "I watched these hatch myself only last spring, and we've trained them here at the school until they were ready for free flights. One of their brothers is William, and he'll be with you today, Mr. Leary."

"So young? That's what, only five or six months old."

"Born to fly," Connor repeated. He sensed he'd lose the boy unless he moved things along. "If you'll come inside now, we've your hawks waiting."

"It's an experience, Taylor." The father, an easy six-four, laid a hand on his son's shoulder.

"Whatever. It'll probably rain again."

"Oh, I think it'll hold off till near to sunset. So, Mr. Leary, have you family around Mayo then?"

"Tom. Ancestors, I'm told, but no family I know of."

"Just you and your boy then?"

"No, my wife and daughter went into Cong to shop." He gave a grinning roll of his eyes. "Could be trouble."

"My sister has a shop in Cong. The Dark Witch. Maybe they'll stop in."

"If it's there and it sells something, they'll stop in. We were thinking of trying a horseback ride tomorrow."

"Oh, you couldn't do better. It's a fine ride around. You just tell them Connor said to give you a good time with it."

Stepping inside, he turned to the holding perches. "And here we have Roibeard and William. Roibeard's my own, and he's for you today, Taylor. I've had him since he was a hatchling. Tom, would you sign the forms that Kyra has ready for you, and I'll make Taylor acquainted with Roibeard."

"What kind of name is that?" Taylor demanded.

Thinks he doesn't want to be here, Connor mused. Thinks he'd rather be at home with his mates and his video games.

"Why it's his name, and an old one. He comes from hawks that hunted these very wood for hundreds of years. Here's your glove. Without it, as smart and skilled as he is, his talons would pierce your skin. You're to hold your arm up like this, see?" Connor demonstrated, holding his left arm up at a right angle. "And keep it still as we walk. You've only to lift it to signal him to fly. I'll tether him at first, until we get out and about."

He felt the boy quiver—nerves, excitement he tried to hide—as Connor signaled Roibeard to step onto the gloved arm. "The Harris's is agile and quick, as I said, and a fierce hunter, though since we'll be taking these chicken parts along"—he patted his baiting pouch—"they'll both leave off any thought of going for birds or rabbit.

"And here for you, Tom, is young William. He's a handsome one, and well behaved. He loves little more than a chance to wing through the woods, and have some chicken as a reward for the work."

"He's beautiful. They're beautiful." Tom laughed a little. "I'm nervous."

"Let's have ourselves an adventure. How's your stay at the castle?" Connor began as he led them out.

"Amazing. Annie and I thought this was our once in a lifetime, but we're already talking about coming back."

"Sure you can't come once to Ireland."

He walked them easy, making some small talk, but keeping his mind, his heart with the hawks. Content enough, ready enough.

He took them away from the school, down a path, to the hard paved road where there was an opening, with tall trees fringing it.

There he released the jesses.

"If you lift your arms. Just gentle now, sliding them up, they'll fly."

And the beauty of it, that lift in the air, that spread of wings, nearly silent. Nearly. A soft gasp from the boy, still trying to cling to his boredom as both hawks perched on a branch, folded their wings, and stared down like golden gods.

"Will you trust me with your camera, Tom?"

"Oh, sure. I wanted to get some pictures of Taylor with the hawk. With . . . Roibeard?"

"And I will. You turn, back to them, look over your left shoulder there, Taylor." Though Roibeard would answer without, Connor laid a bit of chicken on the glove.

"Gross."

"Not to the bird."

Connor angled himself. "Just lift your arm, as you did the first time. Hold it steady."

"Whatever," Taylor mumbled, but obeyed.

And the hawk, fierce grace in flight, swooped down, wings spread, eyes brilliant, and landed on the boy's arm.

Gobbled the chicken. Stood, stared into Taylor's eyes.

Knowing the moment well, Connor captured the stunned wonder, the sheer joy on the boy's face.

"Wow! Wow! Dad, Dad, did you see that?"

"Yeah. He won't . . ." Tom looked at Connor. "That beak."

"Not to worry, I promise you. Just hold there a minute, Taylor."

He took another shot, one he imagined would sit on some mantel or desk back in America, of the boy and the hawk staring into each other's eyes. "Now you, Tom."

He repeated the process, snapped the picture, listened to his clients talk to each other in amazed tones.

"You've seen nothing yet," Connor promised. "Let's move into the woods a bit. You'll all have a dance."

It never got old for him, never became ordinary. The flight of the hawk, the soar and swoop through the trees always, always enchanted him. Today, the absolute thrill of the boy and his father added more.

The damp air, fat as a soaked sponge, the flickers of light filtering through the trees, the swirl of the oncoming autumn made it all a fine day, in Connor's opinion, to tromp around the wood following the hawks.

"Can I come back?" Taylor walked back to the gates of the school with Roibeard on his arm. "I mean, just to see them. They're really cool, especially Roibeard."

"You can, sure. They'd be pleased with a bit of company."

"We'll do it again before we leave," his father promised.

"I'd rather do this than the horseback riding."

"Oh, you'll enjoy that as well, I wager." Connor led them inside at an unhurried pace. "It's pleasant to walk the woods on the back of a good horse—a different perspective of things. And they've fine guides at the stables."

"Do you ride?" Tom asked him.

"I do, yes. Though not as often as I might like. The best, of course, is hawking on horseback."

"Oh man! Can I do that?"

"That's not in the brochure, Taylor."

"It's true," Connor said as he gently transferred Roibeard to a perch. "It's not on the regular menu, so to speak. I'm just going to settle things up with your da if you want to go out, have another look at the hawks."

"Yeah, okay." He studied Roibeard another moment with eyes filled with love. "Thanks. Thanks, Connor. That was awesome."

"You're more than welcome." He transferred William as Taylor ran out. "I didn't want to say in front of the boy, but I might be able to arrange for him to have what we'd call a hawk ride. I'd need to check if Meara can lead your family—she's a hawker as well as one of the guides at the stables. And if you'd be interested."

"I haven't seen Taylor this excited about anything but computer games and music for months. If you can make it happen, that would be great."

"I'll see what I can do, if you give me a minute or two."

He leaned a hip on the desk when Tom stepped out, took out his phone. "Ah, Meara, my darling, I've a special request."

A FINE THING IT WAS TO GIVE SOMEONE THE LINGERING glow of memories. Connor did his best to do the same with his final client of the day—but nothing would quite reach the heights of Taylor and his da from America.

Between his bookings, he took the Peregrines—Apollo included—out beyond the woods, into the open for exercise and hunting. There he could watch the stoop with a kind of wonder that never left him. There he could feel the thrill of that diving speed inside himself.

As he was a social creature like the Harris's, he enjoyed doing the hawk walks, but those solo times—only himself and the birds and the air—made up his favorite part of any day.

Apollo took a crow in midstoop—a perfect strike. They could be fed, Connor thought as he sat on a low stone wall with a bag of crisps and an apple. They could be trained and tended. But they were of the wild, and the wild they needed for their spirit.

So he sat, content to wait, to watch, while the birds soared, dived, hunted, and prized the peace of a damp afternoon.

No fog or shadows here, he thought. Not yet. Not ever as he and his circle would find the way to preserve the light.

And where are you now, Cabhan. Not here, not now, he thought as he scanned the hills, rolling back and away lush and green. Nothing here now but the promise of rain that would come and go and come again.

He watched Apollo soar again, for the joy of it now, felt his own heart lift. And knew for that moment alone he would face the dark and beat it back.

Rising, he called the birds back to him, one by one.

Once all the work was done, he made a final round with the birds and checked on all that needed checking on, then shoved his own glove in his back pocket and locked the gate.

Then he wandered, at an easy stroll, toward the stables.

He sensed Roibeard first, pulled out the glove and put it on. Even as he lifted his arm, he sensed Meara.

The hawk circled once, for the pleasure of it, then swooped down to land on Connor's gloved arm.

"Did you have an adventure then? Sure you gave the boy a day he'll not be forgetting." He waited where he was until Meara rounded the bend.

Long, sure strides—a man had to admire a woman with long legs that moved with such steady confidence. He sent her a grin.

"And there she is. How'd the boy do?"

"He's mad in love with Roibeard, and expressed great affection for Spud, who gave him a good, steady ride. I had to stop once and give the sister a go at it or there'd have been a brutal sibling battle. She enjoyed it quite a lot, but not like the boy. And we won't be charging them for the few minutes of her go."

"We won't, no." He took her hand, swung it as they walked, kissed her knuckles lightly before letting it go. "Thanks."

"You'll thank me for more, as the mister gave me a hundred extra."

"A hundred? Extra?"

"That he did, as he judged me the honest sort and asked if I'd give half to you. Naturally, I told him it wasn't necessary, but he insisted. And naturally, I didn't want to be rude and refuse again."

"Naturally," Connor said with a grin, then wiggled his fingers at her.

She pulled euros from her pocket, counted them out.

"Well now, what should we do with this unexpected windfall? What do you say to a pint?"

"I say on occasion you have a fine idea. Should we round up the rest of us?" she wondered.

"We could. You text Branna, and I'll text Boyle. We'll see if we have any takers. It'd do Branna good to get out for an evening."

"I know it. Why don't you text her?"

"It's easier to say no to a brother than a friend." He met Roibeard's eyes, walked in silence a moment. And the hawk lifted off, rose up, winged away.

As Connor did, she watched the hawk for the pleasure of it. "Where's he going then?"

"Home. I want him close, so he'll fly home and stay tonight."

"I envy that," Meara said as she took out her phone. "The way you talk to the hawks, Iona to the horses, Branna to the hounds—and Fin to all three when he wants to. If I had any magic, I think that would be what I'd want."

"You have it. I've seen you with the horses, the hawks, the hounds."

"That's training, and an affinity. But it's not what you have." She sent the text, tucked the phone away. "But I'd just want it with the animals. I'd go mad if I could read people, hear their thoughts and feelings as you can. I'd forever be fighting to listen, then likely be pissed at what I'd heard."

"It's best to resist the eavesdropping."

She gave him an elbow poke and a knowing look out of dark chocolate eyes. "I know good and well you've had a listen when you're wondering if a girl might be willing if you bought her a pint and walked her home."

"That may have been the case before I reached my maturity."

She laughed her wonderful laugh. "You've not hooked fingers around your maturity as yet."

"I'm within centimeters now. Ah, and here's Boyle answering already. Iona's at the cottage practicing with Branna. He'll drag Fin with him shortly—and see if Iona will do the same with Branna."

"I like when it's all of us together. It's family."

He heard the wistfulness, swung an arm over her shoulders. "It's family," he agreed, "right and true."

"Do you miss your parents since they've settled down in Kerry?"

"I do sometimes, yes, but they're so bleeding happy there on the lake, running their B and B, and with Ma's sisters all chirping about. And they're mad about the FaceTime. Who'd've thought it? So we see them, and know what's what."

He gave her shoulder a rub as they walked the winding road to Cong. "And truth be told, I'm glad enough they're tucked away south for now."

"And here I'd be more than glad to have my mother tucked away most anywhere, and not for unselfish reasons such as your own."

"You'll get through it. It's but another phase."

"Another phase that's lasted near fifteen years. But you're right." She wiggled her shoulders as if shaking off a small weight. "You're right. I put a bug in her ear today about how she might enjoy a long visit with my sister and the grandchildren. And that's shoving the same bug straight up Maureen's arse, which she well deserves. If that doesn't stick, I'm planning to bounce her from brother to sister to brother in hopes she lands somewhere that contents her."

"I'm not giving up my flat."

"You'd go stark raving if you moved back in with your ma, and what good would that do either of you? Donal's done well by her, no question of it, but so have you. You give her your time, your ear, help with her marketing. You pay her rent."

He only lifted his eyebrows when she jerked away, narrowed her eyes.

"Be sane, Meara. Fin's her landlord, how would I not know? I'm saying you're a good daughter, and have nothing to feel selfish over."

"Wishing her elsewhere seems selfish, but I can't stop wishing it. And Fin doesn't charge half what that little cottage is worth."

"It's family," he said, and she sighed.

"How many times can you be right on one walk to the pub?" She shoved her hands in the pockets of her work jacket. "And that's enough bitching and carping from me for the same amount of time. I'm spoiling my own good day at work, and the extra fifty in my pocket."

They passed the old abbey where tourists still wandered, snapping photos. "People always tell you things. Why is that?"

"Maybe I like hearing things."

She shook her head. "No, it's because you listen, whether you want to hear it or not. I too often just tune it all out."

He stuck his hand in her pocket to give hers a squeeze. "Together we probably come average on the graph of human nature."

No, she thought. No, indeed. Connor O'Dwyer would never be average on any graph.

Then she let the worries and wondering go, walked with him into the warmth and clatter of the pub.

It was Connor who was greeted first by those who knew them— which was most. A cheery call, a flirtatious smile, a quick salute. He was the sort always welcome, and always at home where his feet were planted.

Good, easy qualities, she supposed, and something else she envied.

"You get us a table," he told her, "and I'll stand the first round."

She skirted through, found one big enough for six. Settling in, she took out her phone—Connor would be a bit of time due to conversing, she knew.

She texted Branna first.

Stop fussing with your hair. We're already here.

Then she checked her schedule for the next day. A lesson in the ring in the morning, three guideds—not to mention the daily mucking, feeding, grooming, and nagging of Boyle to make certain he'd seen to the paperwork. Then there was the marketing she'd neglected—for herself and her mother. Laundry she'd put off.

She could do a bit of the wash tonight if she didn't loiter overlong in the pub.

She checked her calendar, saw her reminder for her older brother's birthday, and added finding a gift to her schedule.

And Iona was due for another lesson in swordplay. She was coming along well, Meara thought, but now that Cabhan had put in an appearance, they'd be wise to get back to regular practice.

"Put that away now and stop working." Connor set their pints on the table. "Workday's done."

"I was checking on tomorrow's workday."

"That's your burden, Meara darling, always looking forward to the next task."

"And you, always looking to the next recreation."

He lifted his glass, smiled. "Life's a recreation if you live it right." He nodded as he spotted Boyle and Iona. "Family's coming."

Meara glanced around. And put away her phone.

5

A GOOD DAY'S WORK, A PINT, AND FRIENDS TO DRINK IT with. In Connor's estimation, there was little more to wish for. Unless it was a hot meal and a willing woman.

Though he knew the pretty blonde—name of Alice—tossing him the occasional glance would be willing enough, he contented himself with the pint and the friends.

"I'm thinking," he said, "now that Fin's joined us, you might consider combining the hawk and horse as Meara and I did today for the Yanks as a regular option."

Boyle frowned over it. "We'd need an experienced falconer as the guide, and that limits us to Meara."

"I could do it," Iona protested.

"You've only hawked a few times," Boyle pointed out. "And never on your own."

"I loved it. And you said I was a natural," she reminded Connor.

"You have a fine way with it, but you'd want to have a few goes on horseback. Even on a bike, as we do when we're giving the hawks some exercise in the winter."

"I'll practice."

"You need to be practicing more with a blade in your hand," Meara told her.

"You always kick my ass."

"I do." Meara smiled into her pint. "I do indeed."

"Our girl here's a quick study," Fin commented. "And it's an interesting idea."

"If we toyed with it . . ." Boyle sipped at his pint and considered. "The customers who booked the package would need some riding experience. The last thing we'd want is a rank novice going into a panic when a hawk lands on their arm and spooking the horse."

"Agreed there."

"The horses won't spook if I tell them not to." Iona angled her head, smiled. "Here's Branna."

She'd fussed with her hair, of course, and wore a red scarf over a jacket of strong, deep blue. The flat boots meant she'd walked from her cottage.

She ran a hand over Meara's shoulder, then dropped into the chair beside her. "What's the occasion?"

"Meara and I split a fine tip from an American today."

"Good. So you'll buy your sister a pint, won't you? I could do with a Harp."

"It's my round." Meara rose.

"She's been brooding about her mother," Connor said when she was out of earshot. "She could use a festive sort of evening. We'll have a meal, all right, and keep her mood up. I could do with some fish and chips."

"Whose stomach are you thinking of?" Branna asked.

"My stomach, her mood." He raised his glass. "And good company."

IT WAS GOOD COMPANY. SHE'D INTENDED TO HAVE ONE PINT, linger a bit, then go home, start the wash, throw together whatever was left in the larder for a quick dinner. Now she'd started on a second pint, and a chicken pie.

She'd leave her truck where it was at Branna's, walk home from the pub. Toss some wash in, make a market list—for herself and for her mother. Early to bed, and if she made the rise early enough, she could toss more wash in and be done with it.

Marketing on her lunch break. Go by her mother's after work—God help her—do her duty. Plant a few more seeds about going off to Maureen's.

Connor poked her in the ribs. "You're thinking too much. Try being in the moment. It'll amaze you."

"A chicken pie in the pub is amazing?"

"It's good, isn't it?"

She took another bite. "It's good. And what are you going to do about Alice?"

"Hmm?"

"Alice Keenan, who's signaling her churning lust across the pub like one of those flag people." She waved her arms to demonstrate.

"A pretty face, for certain. But not for me."

Meara put on a look of amazement, sent it around the table. "Are you hearing that? Connor O'Dwyer saying a pretty face isn't for him."

"Wants a ring on her finger, does she then?" Fin asked, amused.

"That she does, and as that's more than I can give, she's not for me to play with. But it is a pretty face."

He leaned toward Meara. "Now, if you were to snuggle up here, give me a kiss, she'd think, ah, well, he's taken, and stop pining for me."

"She'll have to pine, as other foolish women do." She scooped up more chicken. "My mouth's occupied at the moment."

"You put it on mine once."

"Really?" Iona pushed her plate aside, leaned in. "Tell all."

"I was but twelve."

"Just shy of thirteen."

"Just shy of thirteen is twelve." She feigned stabbing him with her fork. "And I was curious."

"It was nice."

"How could I tell?" Meara countered. "It was my first kiss."

"Aw." Iona drew in a sighing breath. "You never forget your first."

"It wasn't his."

Connor laughed, gave Meara's braid a tug. "It wasn't, no, but I haven't forgotten it, have I?"

"I was eleven. Precocious," Iona claimed. "His name was Jessie Lattimer. It was sweet. I decided we'd get married one day, live on a farm, and I'd ride horses all day."

"And what happened to this Jessie Lattimer?" Boyle wanted to know.

"He kissed someone else, broke my heart. Then his family moved to Tucson, or Toledo. Something with a *T*. Now I'm going to marry an Irishman." She angled over, kissed Boyle. "And ride horses all day."

Her eyes sparkled when Boyle linked his fingers with hers.

"Who was your first, Branna?"

The minute the words were out, the sparkle changed to regret. She knew. Of course she knew even before Branna flicked a glance at Fin.

"I was twelve as well. I couldn't let my best friend get ahead of me, could I? And like Connor for Meara, Fin was handy."

"That he was," Connor agreed cheerfully, "for he made sure he was where you were every possible waking minute."

"Not every, because it wasn't his first kiss."

"I practiced a bit." Fin tipped back in his chair with his pint. "As I wanted your first to be memorable. In the shadows of the woods," he murmured, "on a soft summer day. With the air smelling of the rain and the river. And of you."

She didn't look at him now, nor he at her. "Then the lightning struck, a bolt from the sky straight into the ground." She remembered. Oh, she remembered. "The air shook with it, and the thunder that followed. We should have known."

"We were children."

"Not for long."

"I've made you sad," Iona said quietly. "I'm sorry."

"Not sad." Branna shook her head. "A bit nostalgic, for innocence that melts faster than a snowflake in a sunbeam. We can't be innocent now, can we, with what's come. And what will come again. So . . . let's have some whiskey in our tea and take the moment—as my brother's fond of saying. We'll have some music, what do you say to that, Meara? A song or two tonight, for only the gods know what tomorrow brings."

"I'll fetch the pub fiddle." Connor rose, brushed a hand over his sister's hair as he left the table. And, saying nothing, gave her the comfort she needed.

Meara stayed longer than she'd intended, well past a reasonable time to think of doing wash or making market lists. Though she tried to brush him off, Connor insisted on walking her home.

"It's silly, you know. It's not a five-minute walk."

"Then it's not taking much of my time. It was good of you to stay because Branna needed it."

"She'd do the same for me. And it lifted my mood as well, though it didn't get the wash done."

They walked the quiet street, climbing the slope. The pubs would still be lively, but the shops were long snugged closed, and not a single car drove past.

The wind had come up, stirring the air. She caught the scent of heliotrope from a window box, and saw needle pricks of stars through the wisps of clouds.

"Did you ever think of going somewhere else?" she wondered. "Living somewhere else? If you didn't have to do what needs doing here?"

"I haven't, no. It's here for me. It's what I want and where. Have you?"

"No. I have friends who went off to Dublin, or Galway City, Cork City, even America. I'd think I could do that as well. Send money to my mother and go off somewhere, an adventure. But I never wanted it as much as I wanted to stay."

"Fighting a centuries-old sorcerer powered by evil would be an adventure for most."

"But it's no Grafton Street, is it now?" She laughed with him, turned the corner toward her flat. "Some part of me never thought it would happen. The sort of thing that happened in that clearing on the solstice. Then it did, all so fierce and fast and terrible, and there was no thinking at all."

"You were magnificent."

She laughed again, shook her head. "I can't quite remember what I did. Light and fire and wind. Your hair flying. All the light. Around you, in you. I'd never seen you like that. With your magick like the sun, all but blinding."

"It was all of us. We wouldn't have beaten him back without all of us."

"I know that. I felt that." For a moment, she just looked out at the night, at the village that had been hers all of her life. "And still he lives."

"He won't win." He walked her up the open stairs to her door.

"You can't know, Connor."

"I have to believe it. If we let the dark win, what are we? What's the purpose of it all if we let the dark win? So we won't."

She stood for a moment beside a basket from which purple and red petunias spilled. "I wish you'd let Fin drive you home."

"I have to walk off the fish and chips—and the pints."

"You have a care, Connor. We can't win without you. And besides all that, I'm used to you."

"Then I'll have a care." He reached up, seemed to hesitate, then gave her braid a familiar tug. "You have one as well. Good night to you, Meara."

"Good night."

He waited until she went in, until the door closed and locked.

He'd nearly kissed her, he realized, and wasn't entirely sure the kiss would've been . . . brotherly. Should've skipped the whiskey in his tea, he decided, if it so clouded his judgment.

She was his friend, as good a friend as he had. He'd do nothing to risk tipping the balance of that.

But now he felt edgy and unsatisfied. Perhaps he should've given Alice a whirl after all.

With so much happening, so much at stake, he couldn't be easy leaving Branna alone at night—even if Iona stayed at the cottage. And he couldn't quite feel easy bringing a woman home with him, especially given the circumstances.

All in all, he thought as he left the village behind and took that winding road on foot, it was inconvenient. And just one more reason to send Cabhan screaming into hell.

He liked women. Liked conversing with them, flirting with them. He liked a dance, a walk, a laugh. And, Jesus, he liked bedding them.

The soft and the heat, the scents and the sighs.

But such pleasures were on an inconvenient pause.

For how much longer, he wondered, as Cabhan had struck out again.

Even as he thought it Connor stopped. Stood still and quiet—body and mind—on the dark road he knew as well as the lines on his own hand. And he listened, with all of himself.

He's there, he's there. Not far, not far enough—not close enough to find, but not far enough for true safety.

He touched the amulet under his sweater, felt its shape, felt its warmth. Then he spread his arms wide, opened more.

The air whispered around him, a quiet song that danced through his hair, kissed along his skin as power rose. As his vision spread.

He could see trees, brush, hear the whisper of air through them, the beating hearts of the night creatures stirring, the faster pulses of the prey hunted. He caught the scent, the sound of water.

And a kind of smear over it—a shadow clinging to shadows. Buried in them so he couldn't separate the shapes or substance.

The river. Beyond the river, aye. Though crossing it causes pain. Water, crossing water unsettles you. I can feel you, just feel you like cold mud oozing. One day I'll find your lair. One day.

The jolt burned, just a little. Hardly more than a quick zap of static electricity. Connor drew himself in again, pulled the magick back. And smiled.

"You're weak yet. Oh, we hurt you, the boy and me. We'll do worse, you bastard, I swear on my blood, we'll do worse before we're done."

Not quite as edgy now, not quite as dissatisfied, he whistled his way home.

THE RAIN CAME AND LINGERED FOR A LONG, SOAKING VISIT. Guests of Ashford Castle—the bulk of their clientele—still wanted their hawk walks.

Connor didn't mind the rain, and marveled, as he always did, at the gear travelers piled on. It amused him to see them tromp along in colorful wellies, various slick raincoats, bundling scarves and hats and gloves, all for a bit of cool September rain.

But amused or not, he watched the mists that swirled or crawled—and found nothing in them but moisture. For now.

On a damp evening when work was done, he sat on the cottage stoop with some good strong tea and watched Meara train Iona. Their swords clashed, sharp rings though Branna had charmed them to go limp as noodles should they meet flesh.

His cousin was coming along well, he judged, though he doubted she'd ever match the style and ferocity of Meara Quinn.

The woman might have been born with a sword in her hand the way she handled one. The way she looked with one—tall and curved like a goddess, all that thick brown hair braided down her back.

Her boots, as broken-in as his own, planted on the soggy ground, then danced over it as she drove Iona back, giving her student no quarter. And those dark eyes—a prize like the gold-dust skin of her gypsy heritage—sparkled fierce as she blocked an attack.

Sure he could watch her swing a sword all day. Though he did wince in sympathy as she drove his little cousin back, back, in an unrelenting attack.

Branna came out holding a thick mug of tea of her own, sat beside him.

"She's improving."

"Hmm? Oh, Iona, yes. I was thinking the same."

Placidly, Branna sipped her tea. "Were you now?"

"I was. Stronger than she was when she came to us, and she wasn't a weakling then. Stronger though, and surer of herself. Surer, too, of her gift. Some of it's us, some of it's Boyle and what love does for body and soul, but most of it was always inside her, just waiting to blossom."

He patted Branna's knee. "We're lucky, we two."

"I've thought so a time or two."

"Lucky in who we came from. We always knew we were loved and valued. And what we have, what we are, was indeed a gift and not something to be buried or hidden away. The two of them striking swords in the rain? Not so lucky as we. Iona had and has her granny, and that's a treasure. But beyond that, for them their family's . . . well, fucked, as Meara's fond of saying."

"We're their family."

"I know it, as they do. But it's a wound that can't fully heal, isn't it, not to have the full love of those who made you. The indifference of Iona's parents, the full mess of Meara's."

"Which is worse, do you think? That indifference, which is beyond my understanding, or the full mess? The way Meara's da ran off, taking what money was left after he bollocksed all they had? Leaving a wife and five children alone, or just never giving a damn all along?"

"I think either would leave you flattened. And just look at them. So strong and full of courage."

Iona stumbled back, slipped. Her ass hit the soggy grass. Meara leaned down, offered a hand, but Iona shook her head, set her teeth. And rolled over, sprang up. Moved in, sword swinging.

Now Connor grinned, slapped his sister's leg.

"Though she be but little, she is fierce!"

"Because it's true, I'll forgive you for quoting the English bard when I've a pot of Guinness stew on the simmer."

His mind went directly to food. "Guinness stew, is it?"

"It is, and a fine round of sourdough bread with the poppy seeds you're fond of."

His eyes lit, then narrowed. "And what will I be doing to deserve it?"

"On your next free day I need you to work with me."

"I will of course."

"The magicks we made for the solstice . . . I was so certain it would work. But I missed something, just as Sorcha missed something when she sacrificed herself and poisoned Cabhan all that time ago. Every one of us since has missed something. We need to find what's missed."

"And we will. But you can't leave us out of it, Branna. You didn't miss, the whole of us did. Fin—"

"I know I have to work with him. I have, and I will."

"Does it help to know he suffers as you do?"

"A little." She leaned her head on his shoulder a moment. "Small of me."

"Human of you. A witch is as human as any, as Da always told us."

"So he did."

For a few moment they sat quiet, side by side, as swords rang.

"Cabhan's healing, isn't he?" She said it quietly, just to him. "Gathering himself for the next. I feel . . . something in the air."

"I feel it, too." Connor watched, as she did, the deep green shadows of the woods. "As his blood, Fin would feel more. Is there stew enough for the whole of us?"

She sighed in a way that told him she'd already thought of it herself. "I suppose there is. Ask them," she said as she rose, "and I'll make sure of it."

He took her hand, kissed it. "As human as any, and braver than most. That's my sister."

"The thought of Guinness stew's made you sentimental." But she gave his hand a squeeze before she went inside.

It wasn't the stew, though Christ knew it didn't hurt a thing. But he worried about her more than she knew.

Then Iona feinted left, spun, struck from the right, and it was Meara who stumbled, slipped, and landed on the wet grass.

Iona immediately let out a whoop, began to jump in circles, sword raised high.

"Well done, cousin!" he called out over Meara's strong, throaty laugh.

Iona made a flourishing bow, then on a squeak, straightened fast as the flat of Meara's sword slapped her ass.

"Well done indeed," Meara told her. "But I could've sliced open your belly while you were dancing about in victory. Finish me off next time."

"Got it, but just one more." She whooped again, jumped again. "That should do it. I'll put the swords away, and go brag to Branna."

"That's fair enough."

Iona took the swords, waved them both high, did another bow for Connor, then dashed inside.

"You trained her well," Connor commented as he rose to walk over and offer Meara what was left of his tea.

"Cheers to me."

"Did you let her knock you down?"

"I didn't, no, though I'd considered doing just that to give her a boost. Didn't prove necessary. She's always been quick, but she's learning to be sneaky as well."

She rubbed her ass. "And now I'm wet where I wasn't."

"I can fix that." He moved in a little closer, reached around her. His hands trailed lightly over the butt of her wet trousers.

Warmth seeped over, through, and his hands lingered. Something in her eyes, he thought, something in those dark, exotic eyes. He caught himself on the point of drawing her in when she stepped back.

"Thanks." She polished off his tea. "And for that as well, though I could use a glass of that wine Branna's so fond of."

"Then come in and have one. I'm calling on the others to come. There's Guinness stew and a fresh round of bread."

"I should go on." She shifted back, glanced toward her lorry. "I'm all but living here these days."

"She needs her circle, Meara. It would be a favor to me if you'd stay."

Now she looked over her shoulder, as if sensing something sneaking up behind her. "Is he coming already?"

"I can't say, not absolutely. I'll be hoping Fin can say more. So come inside and have some wine and stew, and we'll be together."

They came, as Connor knew they always would. So the kitchen filled with voices, the warmth of friends with Kathel stretched in front of the little hearth, and good, rich stew simmering on the stove.

As he'd get his Guinness in the stew, Connor opted for wine himself. Drinking it, he watched his besotted friend grin as Iona, once again, replayed her moment of victory.

Who would have thought Boyle McGraff would fall so hard, so fully? A man who said little, and in general paid more mind to his horses than the ladies. As loyal and true a friend as they came, and a brawler under the self-taught control.

And here was Boyle of the scarred knuckles and fast temper starry-eyed over the little witch who talked to horses.

"You're looking sly and satisfied," Meara commented.

"I'm enjoying seeing Boyle resemble an overgrown puppy when he looks at Iona."

"They fit well, and they'll make a good life together. Most don't."

"Ah now, not most." It pinched his heart to hear her say it, know she felt it. "The world needs lovers who fit, or how would we go on? To be only one of one for a life? That's a lonely life."

"Being one of one means being able to go as you please, and not facing being one of two, then ending up the one of one when it all goes to hell."

"You're a cynical one, Meara."

"And fine with it." She shot him a look under arched brows. "You're a romantic one, Connor."

"And fine with it."

She laughed, quick and easy, as she set the napkins she held on the table. "Branna says it's serve yourself from the pot on the stove, so you'd best get in line."

"That I will."

He fetched wine for the table first to give himself a moment to open a bit, to test the air for any sense or sign before they sat and ate, and talked of magicks. Light and dark.

The stew was a bit of magick itself, but then Branna had a way.

"God, this is good!" Iona spooned up more. "I have to learn how to cook like this."

"You're doing well with the side dishes," Branna told her. "And Boyle's a steady cook. He can handle that, and you'll do the sword fighting."

"Maybe so. After all, I did knock Meara on her ass."

"Will she never tire of saying it?" Meara wondered. "I see now I'll have to knock her on her own a dozen times to dim her victory light."

"Even that won't." Iona smiled, then sat back. "You didn't do it on purpose, did you?"

"I didn't, no, and I'm wishing I had so we could all pity you."

"We'll have a toast then." Fin lifted his glass. "To you, *deifiúr bheag*, a warrior to be reckoned with. And to you, *dubheasa*," he said to Meara, "who made her one."

"That was smoothly done," Branna murmured, and drank.

"Sometimes the truth is smooth. Sometimes it's not."

"Smooth or not, the truth's what's needed."

"Then I'll give you what I have, though it's but little. You hurt him," he said to Connor. "You and the boy, Eamon. But he heals. And you, the three, you feel that, as I do."

"He gathers," Connor said.

"He does. Gathers the dark and the black around him, and into him. I can't say how, or we might find a way to stop it, and him."

"The red stone. The source."

Fin nodded at Iona. "Yes, but how did it come to him? How was it imbued, how can it be taken and destroyed? What price did he pay for it? Only he knows the answers, and I can't get through to find them, or him."

"Across the river. How far I can't say," Connor added, "but he's not on our side of it, for now."

"He'll stay there until he's full again. If we could take him on before he gains back what you and the boy took, we would finish him. I know it. But I've looked, and can't find his lair."

"Alone?" Fury fired Branna's voice. "You went off looking for him on your own?"

"That slaps at the rest of us, Fin." Boyle's voice might have been quiet, but the anger simmered under it. "It's not right."

"I followed my blood, as none of you can."

"We're a circle." It wasn't anger in Iona's voice, in her face, but a disappointment that carried a sharper sting. "We're a family."

For a moment Fin's gratitude, regret, longing rose so strong Connor couldn't block it all. He caught only the edge, and that was enough to make him speak.

"We're both, and nothing changes it. Alone isn't the way, and yet I thought of it myself. As have you," he said to Boyle. "As have all of us at one time or another. Fin bears the mark, and did nothing to put it there. Which of us can say, with truth, if we were in his place, we wouldn't have done the same?"

"I'd have done the same. Connor has the right of it," Meara added. "We'd all have done the same."

"Okay." But Iona reached over to Fin. "Now don't do it again."

"I'd take you and your sword with me as protection, but there's no purpose to it. He's found a way to cover himself from me, and I've yet to find the way under it."

"We'll work longer and harder." Branna picked up her wine again.

"All of us needed time as well after the solstice, but we've not been hiding in the dark licking our wounds. We'll work more, together and alone, and find whatever we've missed."

"We should meet like this more than we have been." With a glance around the table, Boyle spooned up more stew. "It doesn't have to be here, though Branna's far better at cooking than me. But we could meet at Fin's as well."

"I don't mind the cooking," Branna said quickly. "I enjoy it. And I'm here or over in the workshop most days, so it's easy enough."

"Easier if it was planned, and we could all give you a hand," Iona decided, then glanced around as Boyle had. "So. When shall we six meet again?"

"Now it's paraphrasing the English bard." Branna rolled her eyes. "Every week. At least every week for now. More often if we feel we should. Connor'll be working with me on his free days, as you should, Iona."

"I will. Free days, evenings, whatever we need."

There was a pause that went on just a beat too long for comfort.

"And you, Fin." Branna broke the bread she'd barely touched in half, took a bite. "When you can."

"I'll keep my schedule loose as I can."

"And all of that, all of us, will be enough," Connor determined, and went back to his stew.

6

H E DREAMED OF THE BOY, AND SAT WITH HIM IN THE flickering light of a campfire ringed with rough gray stones. The moon hung full, a white ball swimming in a sea of stars. He smelled the smoke and the earth—and the horse. Not the Alastar that had been or was now, but a sturdy mare that stood slack-hipped as she dozed.

On a branch above the horse, the hawk guarded.

And he heard the night, all the whisperings of it in the wind.

The boy sat with his knees drawn in, and his chin upon them.

"I was sleeping," he said.

"And I. Is this your time or mine?"

"I don't know. But this is my home. Is it yours?"

Connor looked toward the ruins of the cabin, over to the stone marking Sorcha's grave. "It's ours, as it was hers. What do you see there?"

Eamon looked toward the ruins. "Our cabin, as we left it the morning my mother sent us away."

"As you left it?"

"Aye. I want to go in, but the door won't open for me. I know my mother's not there, and we took all she told us to take. And still I want to go in as if she'd be there, by the fire waiting for me."

Eamon picked up a long stick, poked at the fire as boys often do. "What do you see?"

It would hurt the boy's heart to tell him he saw a ruin overgrown. And a gravestone. "I see you're in your time, and I in mine. And yet . . ." He reached out, touched Eamon's shoulder. "You feel my hand."

"I do. So we're dreaming, but not."

"Power rules this place. Your mother's and, I fear, Cabhan's as well. We hurt him, you and I, so he brings no power here tonight. How long ago for you since we met?"

"Three weeks and five days more. For you?"

"Less. So the time doesn't follow. Are you well, Eamon? You and your sisters?"

"We went to Clare, and we made a little cabin in the woods." His eyes gleamed as he looked toward his home again. "We used magick. Our hands and backs as well, but we thought if we used magick we'd be safer. And dryer also," he added with a ghost of a smile. "Brannaugh's done some healing as we traveled, and now that we're there. We have a hen for eggs, and that's a fine thing, and we can hunt—all but Teagan, who can't use the arrow on the living. It hurts her heart to try, but she tends the horses and the hen. We've traded a little— labor and healing and potions for potatoes and turnips, grain and such. We'll plant our own when we can. I know how to plant and tend and harvest."

"Come to me if you can, when you have need. It might be I can get you food, or blankets, whatever you need."

Some comfort, Connor thought, for a sad young boy so far from home.

"Thank you for that, but we're well enough, and have coin Ailish and Bardan gave us. But . . ."

"What? You've only to ask."

"Could I have something of yours? Some small thing to take with me? I'll trade you." Eamon offered a stone, a cobble of pure white cupped like an egg in his palm. "It's just a stone I found, but it's a pretty one."

"It is. I don't know what I have." Then he did, and reached up to take the thin leather strap with its spear of crystal from around his neck.

"It's blue tiger eye—but also called hawk's eye or falcon's eye. My father gave it to me."

"I can't take it."

"You can. He's yours as I am. He'll be pleased you have it." To settle it, he put it around Eamon's neck. "It's a fine trade."

Eamon fingered the stone, studied it in the firelight. "I'll show my sisters. They were full of wonder and questions when I told of meeting you, and how we drove Cabhan away. And a bit jealous they were as well. They want to meet you."

"And I them. The day may come. Do you feel him?"

"Not since that day. He can't reach us now, Brannaugh said. He can't go beyond his own borders, so he can't reach us in Clare. We'll go back when we're grown, when we're stronger. We'll go home again."

"I know you will, but you'll be safe where you are until the time comes."

"Do you feel him?"

"I do, but not tonight. Not here. You should rest," he said when Eamon's eyes drooped.

"Will you stay?"

"I will, as long as I can."

Eamon curled up, wrapped his short cloak around him. "It's music. Do you hear it? Do you hear the music?"

"I do, yes." Branna's music. A song full of heart tears.

"It's beautiful," Eamon murmured as he began to drift. "Sad and beautiful. Who plays it?"

"Love plays it."

He let the boy sleep and watched the fire until he woke in his own bed with the sun slipping into the window.

When he opened his fisted hand, a smooth white stone lay in his palm.

He showed it to Branna when she came down to the kitchen for her morning coffee. The sleep daze vanished from her eyes.

"It came back with you."

"We were both there, solid as we are standing here, but both in our own time. I gave him the hawk's-eye stone Da gave me—do you remember it?"

"Of course. You used to wear it when you were a boy. It hangs on the frame of your bedroom mirror."

"No longer. I wasn't wearing it, or anything else, when I got into bed last night. But in the dream, I was dressed and it was around my neck. Now it's around Eamon's."

"Each in your own time." She went to the door to open it for Kathel, returned from his morning run. "Yet you sat together, spoke together. What he gave you came through the dream with you. We have to learn how to use this."

She opened the fridge, and he saw as she pulled out butter, eggs, bacon, that the story, the puzzle of it, and her need to pick over the pieces would net him breakfast.

"We heard you playing."

"What?"

"In the clearing. We heard you. Him so sleepy he could barely hold his eyes open. And the music came, your music, came to us. He fell asleep listening to you. Did you play last night?"

"I did, yes. I woke restless, and played for a bit."

"We heard you. It carried all the way there from your room."

He caught the flicker over her face as she set bacon to sizzle in the pan. "You weren't in your room then. Where?"

"I needed some air. I just needed the night for a bit. I only went to the field behind the cottage. I felt I couldn't breathe without the air and the music."

"I wish you'd find a way to mend things with Fin."

"Connor, don't. Please."

"I love you both. That's all I'll say for now." He wandered the kitchen rubbing the little stone. "The field's too far from the clearing for the music to carry, by ordinary means."

He circled the kitchen as she sliced soda bread, as she broke eggs into the pan.

"We're tied together. We three, those three. He heard your music. Twice now I've spoken to him. Iona saw Teagan."

"And I've seen or heard none of them."

Connor paused to pick up his coffee. "Eamon mentioned his sisters were jealous as well."

"I'm not jealous. Well, a little, I admit. But it's more frustrated, and maybe a bit insulted as well."

"He took your music into dreams, and smiled as he slept when he'd been sad."

"I'll take that as something then." She plated the bacon, the eggs she'd fried. Passed it to him.

"Aren't you having some?"

"Just some coffee and toasted bread."

"Well, thanks for the trouble."

"You can pay it back with another favor." She plucked toast out of the toaster, dropped one piece on his plate, and another on a smaller one. "Carry the stone he gave you."

"This?" He'd already put it in his pocket, and now drew it out.

"Carry it with you, Connor, as you wear the amulet. There's power in it."

She took her toast and coffee to the table, waiting for him to sit with her. "I don't know, can't be sure if it's suspicion, intuition, or a true knowing, but there's power in it. Good magicks because of where it came from, when it came from, who it came from."

"All right. I'll hope the hawk's eye does the same for Eamon, and his sisters."

IT WASN'T ALL HAWK WALKS WITH EAGER TOURISTS OR giving tours to school groups. An essential part of the school involved care and training. Clean mews, clean water for baths, weight checks and a varied diet, sturdy lean-tos for weathering the birds so they might feel the air, smell it. Connor prided himself on the health, behavior, and reliability of his birds—those he helped raise from hatchlings, those who came to him as rescues.

He didn't mind cleaning the poo, or the time it took to carefully dry a wet bird's wings, the hours of training.

The hardest part of his job was, and always would be, selling a bird he'd trained to another falconer.

As arranged, he met the customer in a field about ten kilometers from the school. The farmer he knew well allowed him to bring the young hawks he trained to hunt to that open space.

He called the pretty female Sally, and tethered her to his glove to walk her about and talk to her.

"Now Fin's met this lady who wants you to be hers, and he's even seen your new home should the two of you get along. She's coming

all the way from Clare. And there, I'm told, she has a fine house and
a fine mews. She's done her training as well as you have yours. You'll
be her first."

Sally watched him with her gold eyes, and preened on his fist.

He watched the spiffy BMW navigate the road, pull to a stop
behind his truck.

"Here she is now. I expect you to be polite, make a good im-
pression."

He put on his own game face, though his eyebrows rose a bit when
the willowy blonde with a film star's face stepped out of the car.

"Is it Ms. Stanley then?"

"Megan Stanley. Connor O'Dwyer?"

The second surprise was the Yank in her voice. Fin hadn't mentioned that either.

"We're pleased to meet you."

Sally, as advised, behaved well, merely standing quiet and watching.

"I didn't realize you were an American."

"Guilty." She smiled as she walked toward Connor, and earned a
point or two by studying the hawk first. "Though I've lived in Ireland
for nearly five years now—and intend to stay. She's beautiful."

"She is that."

"Fin told me you raised and trained her yourself."

"She was born in the school in the spring. She's a bright one, I'll
tell you that. She manned in no time at all. Hopped right on the glove
and gave me a look that said, 'Well then, what now?' I have her file
with me—health, weight, feeding, training. Did you hawk in America?"

"No. My husband and I moved to Clare—just outside of Ennis—
and a neighbor has two Harris's Hawks. I'm a photographer, and
started taking photos of them, became more and more interested. So
he trained me, then helped me design the mews, the weathering area,
get supplies. By his rules I wasn't to so much as think about getting a
bird until I'd spent at least a year preparing."

"That's best for all."

"It's taken more than two, as there was a gap when my husband moved back to the States and we divorced."

"That's . . . difficult for certain."

"Not as much as it might've been. I found my place in Clare, and another passion in falconry. I did considerable research before I contacted Finbar Burke. You and your partner have a terrific reputation with your school."

"He's my boss, but—"

"That's not how he put it. When it comes to hawks or birds of prey, you want the eye, ear, hand, and heart of Connor O'Dwyer." She smiled again, and the film-star face illuminated. "I'm pretty sure that's a direct quote. I'd love to see her fly."

"We're here for that. I call her Sally, but if the match between you seems right, you'll call her what suits you."

"No bells, no transmitter?"

"She doesn't need them here, as she knows these fields," Connor said as he released the jesses. "But you'll want them back in Clare."

He barely shifted his arm, and Sally lifted, spread her wings. Soared.

He saw the reaction he wanted, had hoped for in Megan's eyes. The awe that was a kind of love.

"You have a glove with you, I see. You should put it on, call her back yourself."

"I didn't bring a baiting pouch."

"She doesn't need baiting. If she's decided to give you a go, she'll come."

"Now I'm nervous." Her laugh showed it as she took her glove from her jacket pocket, drew it on. "How long have you been doing this?"

"Always." He watched the flight of the bird, sent his thoughts. *If you want this, go to her.*

Sally circled, dove. And landed pretty as a charm on Megan's glove.

"Oh, you beauty. Fin was right. I won't go home without her."

And, Connor thought, she would never come to him again. "Do you want to see her hunt?"

"Yes, of course."

"Just let her know she can. Do you not talk to the birds, Ms. Stanley?"

"Megan, and yes, I do." Now her smile turned speculative as she studied Connor. "It's not something I admit to most. All right, Sally—she'll stay Sally—hunt."

The hawk rose, circled high. Connor began to walk the field with Megan, following the flight.

"So what brought you to Ireland, and to Clare?" he asked her.

"An attempt to save a marriage, which it didn't. But I think it saved me, and I'm happy with that. So it's just me and Bruno—and now Sally."

"Bruno?"

"My dog. Sweet little mutt who showed up at my door a couple years ago. Mangy, limping, half starved. We adopted each other. He's used to hawks. He doesn't bother my neighbor's.

"A dog's an asset on a hunt. Not that she needs one." As he spoke, Sally dove—a bullet from a gun. As talons flashed, Megan let out a little hiss.

"Gets me every time. It's what they do, need to do. God or the world or whatever you believe in made them to hunt and feed. But I always feel a little sorry about it. It took some time for me to stop being squeamish about feeding them during molting, but I got over that. Have you always lived in Mayo?"

"Always, yes."

They exchanged some small talk—weather, hawking, a pub in Ennis he knew well—while Sally feasted on the small rabbit she'd taken down.

"I'm half in love with her already." Megan lifted her arm, and the hawk responded, flying over to land. "Some of that's just excitement and anticipation, but I think we'll make that match you spoke of. Will you let me have her?"

"You made arrangements with Fin," Connor began.

"Yeah, I did, but he said it would be up to you."

"She's yours already, Megan." He looked from the hawk to the woman. "Else she wouldn't have come to you after her feed. You'll want to take her home."

"Yes, yes. I brought everything, with my fingers crossed for luck. I nearly brought Bruno but thought they should get acquainted before a car trip."

She looked at Sally, laughed. "I have a hawk."

"And she has you."

"And she has me. And I think she'll always have you, so would you mind if I took a picture of you with her?"

"Ah, sure if you're wanting."

"My camera's in my car." She transferred Sally to Connor, dashed back to her car. And returned with a very substantial Nikon.

"That's quite the camera."

"And I'm good with it. Go to my website and see for yourself. I'm going to take a couple, okay?" she continued as she checked setting and light. "Just relax—I don't want a studied pose. We'll have the young Irish god with Sally, queen of the falcons."

And when Connor laughed, she took three shots, fast.

"Perfect. Just one more with you looking at her."

Obliging, he looked at Sally. *You'll be happy with her,* he told the hawk. *She's been waiting for you.*

"Great. Thanks." She slung the camera around her neck. "I'll email you the best of them if you want."

"Sure I'd like that very much." He dug out one of the business cards he'd remembered to stick in his back pocket.

"And here's one of mine. My website's on it. And I wrote my

personal email on the back when I got my camera. In case you have any questions or follow-ups about . . . Sally."

"That's grand." He slipped it into his pocket.

Shortly, after helping Megan settle Sally in her container for the trip, Connor climbed back in his lorry.

"That's grand? That's all you have to say about it?" He cast his eyes to heaven as he drove. "What's come over you, O'Dwyer? The woman was gorgeous, single, clever, and a keen hawker. And she gave you an open door a kilometer wide. But did you walk through it? You didn't, no. 'That's grand' is all you said, and let that open door sit there."

Was it simply distraction, the burden of what he knew would have to be done, and the not knowing when it could or would be done? But it had always been there, hadn't it, in the back of all? And had never interfered with his romantic maneuverings.

Had it all changed so much after the solstice? He knew he'd never known fear as sharp as when he'd seen Boyle's hands burning, seen Iona on the ground bruised and bloody. When he'd known the lives of all of them depended on all of them.

Ah well, he thought, perhaps it was best to stay unentangled from those romantic maneuvers for a bit longer. No reason at all he couldn't walk through that open door at a later date.

But for now, he needed to swing by the big stables, let Fin know the deal was done. Then his sister expected him, as this was, at least in theory, his free day.

He stopped at the stables where Fin made his home in the fancy stone house with a hot tub big as a pond on the back terrace and a room on the second floor where he kept magickal weapons, books, and everything else a witch might need—especially one determined to destroy a dark sorcerer of his own blood.

Beside it stood the garage with the apartment over it where Boyle lived—and where Iona would. And the barn for the horses—some for breeding, some for use at the working stables not far off.

Some of the horses cropped in the paddock beyond the one set for jumping practice and lessons.

He spotted Meara, which surprised him, leading one out.

He hopped down from the lorry to greet Bugs, the cheerful mutt who made the barn his home, then hailed her.

"I'd hoped to see Fin, but didn't expect to see you."

"I'm fetching Rufus. Caesar was on the slate for guides today, but Iona says he's got a bit of a strain—left foreleg."

"Nothing serious, I hope."

"She says not." She looped Rufus's reins around the fence. "But we agreed to give him a bit of rest and keep an eye. Fin's round and about somewhere. I thought this was your free day."

"It is, but I had to meet a customer over at Mulligan's farm. She bought Sally—one from the brood we had last spring."

"And you're a bit sulky over it."

"I'm not sulky."

"A bit," Meara said, and bent to give Bugs a scratch. "It's hard to raise a living thing, connect and bond with it, then give it to another. But you can't keep them all."

"I know it"—though he wished otherwise—"and it's a good match. Sally took to her right off, I could see it."

"She?"

"A Yank, moved here a few years ago, and intends to stay—even after her husband, now her former husband, moved back."

Meara's lips curved; her eyebrows lifted. "A looker, is she?"

"She is. Why?"

"No why, just I could hear it in your voice. Living hereabouts?"

"No, down in Clare. Still squeamish over the hunt, but a good hand and heart with the hawk. I thought I'd let Fin know we made the deal, then I'm off to home to work with Branna, as I promised."

"I'm off as well." She unlooped the reins. "Since you'll talk to

Branna before I do, tell her Iona's after a trip to Galway City to look for a wedding dress, and soon."

"That's months off yet."

"Only six, and a bride wants to find her dress before she digs into the rest of it."

"Will they live there, do you think?"

Meara paused in the act of mounting, glanced toward Boyle's rooms over the garage. "Where else? I don't see them trying to squeeze the pair of them into Iona's room at the cottage for the long term."

He realized he'd miss her—or more them as it was now. Talk over breakfast, conversation before bed whenever the two of them stayed at the cottage.

"Boyle's place is bigger than a single room, but sure it's not big when you add children."

"You're jumping some steps ahead," Meara observed.

"Not for the likes of Boyle and Iona." Idly, he stroked the horse as he studied what Fin had built for himself—and for others as well. "They'll want a house of their own, won't they, not a couple of rooms over a garage."

"I hadn't thought of it. They'll figure it." She swung onto Rufus. "For now she's thinking bridal dresses and bouquets, as she should be. There's Fin now, with Aine."

She studied the beautiful white filly Fin led out of the barn. "Soon to be a bride herself when we breed her with Alastar."

"No white dress and bouquet for her."

"But she'll get the stud, and for some of us that's fine and enough."

She rode off on Connor's laugh. And he watched her nudge Rufus into a lope as smooth as butter before walking over to meet Fin.

His friend crouched down to give Bugs a rub, smiling as the dog wagged everywhere and made growls in his throat.

Talking to the dog, Connor knew, as he himself did with hawks,

Iona with horses, Branna with hounds. Whatever ran in Fin's blood meant he could talk to all.

"Has he complaints then?" Connor wondered.

"He's only hoping I didn't forget this." Fin reached in the pocket of his leather coat for a little dog biscuit. Bugs sat, stared up with soulful eyes.

"You're a fine boy and there's your reward."

Bugs took it delicately before trotting off in triumph.

"Takes little to please him," Connor commented.

"Well, he loves his life and would choose no other. A man would be lucky to feel the same."

"Are you lucky, Fin?"

"Some days. But it takes more than a hard biscuit and a bed in a barn to content me. But then, I have more," he added and stroked Aine's throat.

"Sure she's the most beautiful filly I've seen in my life."

"And knows it well. But then modesty in a beautiful female's usually of the false sort. I'm after riding her over, letting her and Alastar gander at each other. So how did you find Megan?"

"Another beauty for certain. They took to each other, her and Sally. She gave me the payment on the spot."

"I thought they would." He nodded, didn't glance at the check Connor handed him, just shoved it in his pocket. "She'll be back for another in a month or two."

Now Connor smiled. "I thought the same."

"And you? Will you be traveling to Clare to visit them?"

"It crossed my mind. I think no, and can only think I think no because there's too much else crossing my mind." Connor shoved fingers through his breeze-tossed hair. "I wake each morning thinking of it, and him. I never used to."

"We hurt him, but he hurt us as well. We nearly didn't get through to Iona in time. None of us will be forgetting that. For all we had together, it wasn't enough. He won't forget that."

"We'll have more next round. I'm going to work with Branna." Lightly, he laid a hand on Fin's arm. "You should come with me."

"Not today. She won't want me round today when she's thinking it'll just be the two of you together."

"Branna won't let her feelings get in the way of what must be done."

"That's God's truth," Fin agreed, and swung himself into the saddle. He let Aine dance a bit. "We have to live, Connor. Despite it, because of it, around it, through it. We have to live as best we can."

"You think he'll beat us?"

"I don't. No, he won't beat you."

Deliberately, Connor slid a hand onto Aine's bridle, looked into Fin's stormy green eyes. "Us. It's us, Fin, and will always be us."

Fin nodded. "He won't win. But before the battle, and bitter and bloody it's bound to be, we have to live. I might choose another life if I could, but I'll make the most of the one I have. I'll come to the cottage soon."

He let Aine have her head, thundered away.

With his mood mixed and unsteady, Connor drove straight to the cottage. The light filtered through the windows of Branna's workshop, bounced over the colored bottles she displayed that held her creams and lotions, serums and potions. Her collection of mortars and pestles, her tools, the candles and plants she set about were all arranged just so.

And Kathel sprawled in front of her work counter like a guard while she sat at it, her nose in the thick book he knew to have been Sorcha's.

The fire in the hearth simmered, as did something in a pot on her work stove.

Another beauty, he thought—it seemed he was surrounded by them—with her dark hair pulled back from her face, her sweater rolled up at the sleeves. Her eyes, gray as the smoke puffing from the chimney, lifted to his.

"There you are. I thought you'd be here long before this. Half the day's gone."

"I had things to see to, as I told you clear enough."

Her brows lifted. "What's bitten your arse?"

"At the moment, you are."

No, his mood wasn't mixed, he realized. It had tipped over to foul. He stalked to the jar on the counter beside the stove. There were always biscuits, and he was slightly mollified to find the soft, chewy ones she rolled in cinnamon and sugar.

"I'm here when I could get here. I had the hawk sale to deal with."

"Was it a favorite of yours— Never mind, they all are. You have to be realistic, Connor."

"I'm bloody realistic. I sold the hawk, and the buyer was beautiful, available, and interested. I'm bloody realistic enough to know I had to come back here for you and this, else I'd be having myself a good shag."

"If a shag's so bleeding important, go get it done." Eyes narrowed, she fired right back at him. "I'd rather work alone than with you pacing about horny and bitter."

"It's that it *wasn't* so bleeding important, hasn't been so bleeding important since before the solstice that worries me." He stuffed one cookie in his mouth, wagged the other in the air.

"I'm making you some tea."

"I don't want any fucking tea. Yes, I do." He dropped down onto one of the stools at her work counter, rubbed Kathel when the dog laid his great head against Connor's leg. "It's not the shag or the woman or the hawk. It's all of it. All of this. All of it, and I let it bite me in the arse."

"Some days I want to climb up on the roof and scream. Scream at everyone and everything."

Calmer, Connor bit into the second biscuit. "But you don't."

"Not so far, but it could come to it. We'll have some tea, then we'll work."

He nodded. "Thanks."

She trailed her fingers over his back as she walked around him to the stove. "We'll have good days and bad until it's done, but until it's done we have to live as best we can."

He stared at the back of her head as she put on the kettle, and decided not to tell her Fin had said the very same.

7

H E THOUGHT TO GO TO THE PUB. HE WAS TIRED OF
magicks, of spells, of mixing potions. He wanted some light,
some music, some conversation that didn't center on the white or the
black, or the end of all he knew.

The end of all he loved.

And maybe, just maybe, if Alice happened to be about, he'd see
if she was still willing.

A man needed a distraction, didn't he, when his world hung in the
balance of things? And some fun, some warmth. The lovely, lovely
sound of a woman moaning under him.

Most of all, a man needed an escape when the three most important women in his life decided to have a wedding-planning hen
party—not a term he'd use in their hearing if he valued his skin—in
his home.

But he'd no more than walked outside when he realized he didn't want the pub or the crowd or Alice. So he pulled out his phone, texted Fin on his way to his lorry.

House full of women and wedding talk. If you're there, I'm coming over.

He'd no more than started the engine when Fin texted back.

Come ahead, you poor bastard.

On a half laugh he pulled away from the cottage.

It would do him good, Connor decided, after most of a day huddled with his sister over spell books and blood magicks to be in a man's house, in male company. Sure they could drag Boyle down as well, have a few beers, maybe play a bit of snooker in what he thought of as Fin's fun room.

Just the antidote to a long and not quite satisfying day.

He took the back road, winding through the thick green woods on an evening gone soft and dusky. He saw a fox slink into the green, a red blur with its kill still twitching in its jaws.

Nature was as full of cruelty as of beauty, he knew all too well.

But for the fox to survive, the field mouse didn't. And that was the way of things. For them to survive, Cabhan couldn't. So he who'd never walked into a fight if he could talk his way out of one, had never deliberately harmed anyone, would kill without hesitation or guilt. Would kill, he admitted, with a terrible kind of pleasure.

But tonight he wouldn't think of Cabhan or killing or surviving. Tonight all he wanted was his mates, a beer, and maybe a bit of snooker.

Less than a half kilometer from Fin's, the lorry sputtered, bucked, then died altogether.

"Well, fuck me."

He had petrol, as he'd filled the tank only the day before. And he'd given the lorry a good going-over—engine to exhaust—barely a month before.

She should be running smooth as silk.

Muttering, he pulled a torch from the glove box and climbed out to lift the bonnet.

He knew a thing or two about engines—as he knew a thing or two about plumbing, about carpentry and building, and electrical work. If the hawks hadn't taken him heart and mind, he might have started his own business as a man of all work.

Still, the skills came in handy in times such as these.

He played the light over the engine, checked the battery connection, the carburetor, flicked a hand to have the key turn in the ignition, studied the engine as it attempted to turn over with an annoying and puzzling grind.

He couldn't see a single thing amiss.

Of course, he could have solved it all with another flick of his hand and been on his way to mates, beer, and possibly snooker.

But it was a matter of pride.

So he checked the connections on the fuel pump, rechecked the connection on the battery, and didn't notice the fog swimming in along the ground.

"Well it's a bloody mystery."

He started to spread his hands over the engine, do a kind of scan—a compromise before giving up completely.

And felt the dirty smudge on the air.

He turned slowly, saw that he waded ankle deep in the fog that went icy with his movement. Shadows drew in, dark curtains that blocked the trees, the road, the world. Even the sky vanished behind them.

He came as a man, the red stone around his neck glowing against the thick and sudden dark.

"Alone, young Connor."

"As you are."

Spreading his hands, Cabhan only smiled. "I've a curiosity. You have no need for a machine such as that to travel from one place to another. You have only to . . ."

Cabhan swung his arms out, lifted them. And moved two feet closer without visibly moving at all.

"Such as we respect our gift, our craft, too much to use it for petty reasons. I've legs for walking or, if needs be, a lorry or a horse."

"Yet here you are, alone on the road."

"I've friends and family close by." Though when he tested, he found he couldn't quite reach them—couldn't push through the thick wall of fog. "What have you, Cabhan?"

"Power." He spoke the word with a kind of greedy reverence. "Power beyond your ken."

"And a hovel beyond the river to hide in, alone, in the dark. I'll take a warm fire, the light of it, and a pint with those friends and family."

"You're the least of them." Pity dripped like sullen rain. "You know it, as they do. Good for a laugh and the labor. But the least of the three. Your father knew enough to pass his amulet to your sister—to a girl over his only son."

"Do you think that makes me less?"

"I know it. What do you wear? Given you by an aunt, as consolation. Even your cousin from away has more than you. You have less, are less, a kind of jester, even a servant to the others you call family, you call friends. Your great *friend* Finbar chooses one with no power over you as partner, while you labor for wages at his whim. You're nothing, and have less."

He eased closer as he spoke, and the red stone throbbed like a pulse.

"I'm more than you know," Connor replied.

"What are you, boy?"

"I'm Connor, of the O'Dwyers. I'm of the three. I'm a dark witch of Mayo." Connor looked deep into the black eyes, saw the intent.

"I have fire." He threw his right hand out, held a swirling ball of fire. "And I have air." Stabbed a finger up, twirled it, and created a small, whirling cyclone. "Earth," he said as the ground trembled. "Water."

Rain spilled down, hot enough to sizzle on the ground.

"And hawk."

Roibeard dived with a piercing call, and landed soft as a feather on Connor's shoulder.

"Parlor tricks and pets." Cabhan raised his arms high, fingers spread wide. The red gem went bright as blood.

Lightning slapped the ground inches from Connor's boots, and with it came the acrid stink of sulfur.

"I could kill you with a thought." Cabhan's voice boomed over the roar of thunder.

I don't think so, Connor decided, and only cocked his head, smiled.

"Parlor tricks and pets? I bring fire, water, earth, and air. Test my powers if you dare. The hawk is mine for all time. He and me as part of the three will fulfill our destiny. Light is my sword, right is my shield, as long ago my path was revealed. I accept it willingly."

He struck out then, with the sword formed from the ball of fire, cleaved the air between them. He felt the burn—a bolt, a blade sear across the biceps of his left arm.

Ignoring it, he advanced, swung again, hair flying in the cyclone of air, sword blazing against the dark.

And when he sliced it down, Cabhan was gone.

The shadows lifted, the fog crawled away.

"As I will," Connor murmured, "so mote it be."

He let out a breath, drew in another, tasted the night—sweet and damp and green. He heard an owl hoot on a long, inquisitive note and the rustle of something hurrying through the brush.

"Well now." For a moment, Roibeard leaned in, and their cheeks met, held. "That was interesting. What do you wager my lorry starts up easy as you please? I'm off to Fin's, so you can go ahead with me there and have a visit with his Merlin, or go back home. It's your choice, *mo dearthair*."

With you. Connor heard the answer in his heart as much as his head. *Always with you.*

Roibeard rose into the air and winged ahead.

Still throbbing with the echoes of power—dark and light—Connor got back in the lorry. It started easy, purred, and drove smoothly the rest of the way to Fin's.

He walked straight in. A fire crackled in the hearth, and that was welcome, but no one sprawled on the sofa with a beer at the ready.

As at home there as he was in his own cottage, he started toward the back, and heard voices.

"If you want hot meals"—Boyle—"marry someone who'll make them."

"Why would I do that when I have you so handy?"

"And I was happy enough in my own place making do with a sand-wich and crisps."

"And I've a fine hunk of pork in the fridge."

"Why are you buying a fine hunk of pork when you don't know what in bloody hell to do with it?"

"Why wouldn't I, again, when I have you so handy?"

Though his head ached a bit, like a tooth going bad, the exchange made Connor chuckle as he continued back.

Strange, he felt he'd already had that beer. Quite a lot of beer, as he seemed to be floating right along, but on a floor tilted just a bit sideways.

He stepped into the kitchen where the lights burned so bright they made him blink, made his head pound instead of ache. "I could do with a hunk of pork."

"There, you see?" Grinning, Fin turned—and the grin fell away again. "What happened?"

"I had a little confrontation. Jesus, it's hot as Africa in here."

He struggled out of his jacket, weaving a little, then stared at his left arm. "Look at that, will you. My arm's smoking."

When he pitched forward, his friends leaped to catch him.

"What the fuck is this?" Boyle demanded. "He's burning up."

"It's hot in here," Connor insisted.

"It's not. It's Cabhan," Fin bit off the word. "I can smell him."

"Let me get his shirt off."

"The girls are always saying that to me."

Impatient, Fin merely jerked a hand over Connor, and had him bare-chested.

Connor stared at his arm, at the huge black burn, the peeling and bubbling skin. He felt oddly detached from it all, as if he looked at some little wonder behind glass.

"Would you look at that?" he said, and passed out.

Fin pressed his hands to the burn. Despite the pain that scorched through him, he held them there. Held the burning back.

"Tell me what to do," Boyle demanded.

"Get him water. I can stop it from spreading, but . . . We need Branna."

"I'll go get her."

"It'll take too long. Get him water."

Closing his eyes, Fin opened, reached out.

Connor's hurt. Come. Come quickly.

"Water's not going to help." Still Boyle knelt down. "Either of you. It's burning your hands. I know what that's like."

"And you know it can be fixed." Sweat popped out on Fin's face, ran in a thin river down his back. "I can't know how far this might take him if I don't hold it."

"Ice? He's on fire, Fin. We can put him in a tub of ice."

"Natural means won't help. In my workshop. Get— No need," he said with relief as Branna and Iona, with a wild-eyed Meara between them, popped into the kitchen.

Branna dropped down to Connor.

"What happened?"

"I don't know. Cabhan for certain, but that's all I know. He's feverish, a bit delirious. The burn under my hands is black, deep, it's trying to spread. I'm holding it."

"Let me see it. Let me do it."

"I'm holding it, Branna. I could do more, but not, I think, all. You can." He set his teeth against the pain. "I won't let him go, not even for you."

"All right. All right. But I need to see it, feel it, know it." She closed her eyes, drew up all she had, laid her hands over Fin's.

Her eyes opened again, filled with tears, for the pain under her hands was unspeakable.

"Look at me," she murmured to Fin. "He can't, so you look for him. Be for him. Feel for him. Heal for him. Look at me." Her eyes turned the gray of lake water, calm, so calm.

"Iona, put your hands over mine, give me what you can."

"Everything I have."

"It's cool, do you feel the cool?" Branna said to Fin.

"I do."

"Cool and clear, this healing power. It washes away the fire, floods out the black."

When Connor began to shiver, and to moan, Meara dropped down, pillowed his head in her lap. "Shh now." Gently, gently, she stroked his hair, his face. "Shh now. We're here with you."

Sweat poured down Connor's face—and ran down Fin's.

Branna's breathing grew shallow as she took in some of the heat, some of the pain.

"I'm holding it," Fin said between his teeth.

"Not alone now. Healing hurts—it's the price of it. Look at me, and let it go with me. Out of him we both love, slowly, coolly, out of him, into you, onto me. Out of him, into you, onto me. Out of him, into you, onto me."

She all but hypnotized him. That face, those eyes, that voice. And the gradual lifting of the pain, the cooling of the burn.

"Out of him," she continued, rocking, rocking. "Into you, onto me. And away. Away."

"Look at me." Now he told her as he felt her hands begin to tremble over his. "We're nearly there. Boyle, in my workroom, a brown apothecary bottle with a green stopper, top shelf behind my workbench."

Gently, he eased his hands back so they could see the wound. The burn, raw and red now, was no larger than a woman's fist.

"He's cooler," Meara said, stroking, stroking. "Clammy now, but cooler, and breathing steady."

"There's no black under it, no poison under it." Iona looked from Branna to Fin and back for confirmation.

"No, it's but a nasty burn now. I'll finish it." Branna put her hands over it, sighed. "Just a burn now, healing well."

"This?" Boyle rushed in with the bottle.

"That's it." Fin took it, opening it for Branna to sniff.

"Yes, yes, that's good. That's perfect." She turned up her hands for Fin to pour the balm into them.

"Here now, *mo chroi*." She turned her hands over, gently, gently rubbed the balm on the burn—now pink, now shrinking.

As she rubbed, as she crooned, Connor's eyes fluttered open. He found himself staring up into Meara's pale face and teary eyes.

"What? Why am I on the floor? I hadn't gotten drunk yet." He reached up, brushed a tear from Meara's cheek. "Don't cry, darling." He struggled to sit up, teetered a bit. "Well, here we all are, sitting on Fin's kitchen floor. If we're going to spin the bottle, I'd like to be the one to empty it first."

"Water." Boyle pushed it on him.

He drank like a camel, pushed it back. "I could do with stronger. My arm," he remembered. "It was my arm. Looks fine now."

And seeing Branna's face, he opened his arms to her. "You tended me."

"After you scared five lives out of me." She held on tight, tight until she could trust herself. "What happened?"

"I'll tell you, but— Thanks." He took the glass Boyle offered, drank. Winced. "Jesus, it's brandy. Can't a man get a whiskey?"

"It's brandy for fainting," Boyle insisted.

"I didn't faint." Both mortified and insulted, Connor pushed the glass back at Boyle. "I fell unconscious from my wounds, and that's entirely different. I'd rather a whiskey."

"I'll get it." Meara scrambled up as Iona leaned over, pressed a kiss to Connor's cheek.

"Your color's coming back. You were so pale, and so hot. Please don't ever do that again."

"I can promise to do my best never to repeat the experience."

"What was the experience?" Branna demanded.

"I'll tell you, all of it, but I swear on my life I'm starving. I don't want to be accused of fainting again if I pass out from hunger. I'm light-headed with it, God's truth."

"I've a hunk of pork. Raw," Fin began.

"You haven't put any dinner on?" Branna pushed to her feet.

"I was thinking Boyle would cook it up, then Connor came in. We've been a bit busy with this and that since."

"You can't cook up pork in a fingersnap."

Fin tried a smile. "You could."

"Oh, save your shagging pork, and get me a platter."

"That sort of thing's in the—" Fin gestured toward the large dining area off the kitchen with its massive buffets and china cabinets and servers.

She marched in, yanked open a couple of drawers. And found a large Belleek platter. After moving a nice arrangement of hothouse lilies, she set the platter in the center of the table.

"It's a frivolous use of power, but I can't have my brother starving to death. And since I had already roasted a chicken with potatoes and carrots tonight. So."

She shot the fingers of both hands at the platter. And the air went redolent with the scents of roasted chicken and sage.

"Thank all the gods and goddesses." With that, Connor dived straight in, ripped off a drumstick.

"Connor O'Dwyer!"

"Starving," he said with his mouth full as Branna fisted her hands on her hips. "I'm serious about it. What's everyone else eating?"

"Someone set the table, for God's sake. I need to wash up." She turned to Fin. "Have you a powder room?"

"I'll show you."

She'd never been in his home, he thought. Not once would she agree to cross the threshold. It had taken her brother's need to have her step foot in it.

He showed her the powder room tucked tidily under the stairs.

"Let me see your hands." She held herself very straight while the voices and good, easy laughter flowed from the kitchen.

He held them out, their backs up. With a sigh of impatience, she gripped them and turned them over.

Blistered palms, welts along his fingers.

"The balm will take care of it."

"Stop."

She laid her hands—her palms to his palms, her fingers to his fingers.

"I'm going to thank you. I know you don't want or need thanks. I know he's your brother as much as mine. The brother of your heart, your spirit. But he's my blood, so I need to thank you."

Tears trembled in her eyes again, a glimmer over the smoke. Then she willed them back and gone. "It was very bad, very bad indeed. I can't be sure how much worse it might have been if you hadn't done for him what you did."

"I love him."

"I know it." She studied his hands, healed now, then gave them both a moment. She lifted his hands, pressed them to her lips. "I know it," she said again, and slipped inside the powder room.

As deep and true as his love ran for Connor, it was a shadow beside what he felt for her. Accepting it, Fin walked back to the kitchen, watched his circle prepare for their first meal together in his home.

"WHY DIDN'T YOU CALL US?" BRANNA ASKED WHEN THEY'D settled in with the food and Connor's tale.

"I did—or tried. There was something different in the shadows, in the fog. It was . . . like being closed into a box, tight, so there was nothing else, not even sky. I don't know how Roibeard heard me or got through unless he was already inside the box, so to speak. The stone Cabhan wore beat like a heart, and the beats of it came faster when I called the elements."

"In tune with him?" Fin wondered. "Showing excitement, temper, fear?"

"I don't think fear, as he thinks so little of me."

"Bollocks." Meara stabbed a carrot. "He was mind-fucking you so you'd think little of yourself."

"She's right on that," Boyle agreed. "Trying to get under your skin, he was. Weaken your defenses. It's a common enough tactic in a brawl."

"I saw you brawl once." Iona thought back, smiled. "You didn't say much."

"Because I was punching the stupid. But if you're thinking your opponent's got skills, maybe even better than yours, mind-fucking, as our Meara put it, it's a good tactic."

"What the bastard thinks of me either way isn't something I worry myself about." Content enough now, Connor shoveled in potatoes. "The lightning strike gave me a jolt, I confess."

"He didn't strike you because you have the amulet, and that's protection," Branna considered. "And because he wants what you have more than your death. He tried to undermine your confidence, and put bad feelings between you and me, between you and Fin."

"He failed on all counts. And here's the thing. When I struck at him, the stone glowed brighter, but then—I felt something burn—nothing like it came to be, but a quick burning. And the gem, it dimmed after that. Dimmed considerable just as I struck out again, just before he vanished, and the shadows with him."

"What he did to you took considerable from him." Branna ran her hand down Connor's arm. "To close you in, then cause you harm, to, well, show off for you as well. It cost him."

"If I'd been able to call you, if we'd all been there."

"I don't know," Branna mused.

"We do know he wasn't willing to risk it. He's not ready to take us all on again, or hasn't the balls for it." Fin looked around the table. "And there's a victory."

"He wasn't weak, I'll tell you that. I could feel it pumping out of him. The dark, and the hunger of it. I didn't see him strike, and would swear he never touched me. Yet, I felt that burn."

"Neither your jacket or shirt were scorched. But your shirt?" Boyle gestured with his fork. "Smoke came through it from the burn on your arm. Yet you're wearing it now, and there's no mark on it."

"That's grand, as I'm fond of this shirt."

"He stayed as a man," Meara added. "Because he didn't choose to use his power for the change? He needed all he had to hurt Connor. If Fin hadn't kept it from spreading until Branna got here, it would've been far worse—is that right?"

"Much worse," Branna confirmed.

"And worse, much worse, would have taken more from you—from the three. He's studied you all your lives, one way or another, so surely he knew Branna would come, and she'd put all she had into healing Connor—that Iona would add what she could. But that much worse might've put Connor down for a day or two, depleted the three of you. He wanted that, risked that. But he didn't count on Fin," Meara explained.

"I was nearly here," Connor pointed out. "He had to suss it out here's where I'd come."

Impatient, Branna shook her head. "He's watched you, studied you, but he doesn't understand Fin at all. Not at all. He can't see beyond the blood shared between them. That I would be called and come, yes, but that Fin would take the pain, the risk, the burning to stop the spread? He doesn't know you at all," she said to Fin. "He never will. In the end, that might be his undoing."

"He doesn't understand family, and because he doesn't understand, he doesn't respect. He won't win this," Connor said, and helped himself to more potatoes.

AFTER THE MEAL AND THE CLEARING UP, CONNOR DROVE Branna home, Meara with them.

"Will you be staying?" he asked Meara.

"No—unless you want me," she said to Branna. "I know we'd planned a night of it."

"Go sleep in your own bed. We'll have our night of it, and wedding plans another time. Connor will drive you home."

"I walked from the stables." Meara leaned forward to look at Connor around Branna. "You could just drop me there."

"I'll drive you home. It's late, and it's an uneasy night at best."

"I won't argue with that."

So he dropped Branna off, and waited for her to go inside, though he doubted Cabhan could manage so much as a poke with a sharp stick that night.

"She'll want just you," Meara said quietly.

"You're never out of place with us."

"No, but she'll want just you tonight. I've never seen her so frightened. We're all standing in the kitchen, with her just pulling the chicken from the oven, and laughing over something I can't even recall. Then she went white as death. It was Fin calling her, though I don't know what he said."

Gathering herself, Meara paused a moment. "But she said only, 'Connor's hurt. At Fin's.' And she grabbed my arm. Iona grabbed the other. And I was flying. A blink, an hour, I couldn't say. All these years I've known you and Branna, and I never knew the like of that. Next I know we're in Fin's kitchen, and you're on the ground, paler even than Branna.

"I thought you were dead."

"It takes more than a bit of black magick to do me."

"Stop the lorry."

"What? Ah, are you sick. I'm sorry." He swung to the side of the road, stopped. "I shouldn't be joking when—"

His words, his thoughts, the whole of his mind dropped into a void when she launched herself at him, chained her arms around him, and took his mouth like a madwoman.

Like a hot, mad, desperate woman.

Before he could act, react, think, she pulled back again.

"What— What was all that? And where's it been?"

"I thought you were dead," she repeated, and latched that hot, mad, desperate mouth to his again.

This time he acted, grabbing on to her, trying to shift her around so he could find a better hold, gain a better angle. All the while her taste pumped into him like a drug, one never sampled, one he wanted more of. All of.

"Meara. Let me—"

She jerked back again. "No. No. We're not doing this. We can't do this."

"We already did."

"Just that—" She waved her hands in the air. "That's all of it."

"Actually, there's considerable more, if you'd just—"

"No." She threw her arm out, slapped a hand to his chest to stop him. "Drive. Drive, drive, drive."

"I'm driving." He pulled back onto the road, realized he was as unsteady as he'd been after Cabhan's attack. "We should have a talk about it."

"We won't be talking about it, as there's nothing to talk about. I thought you were dead, and it's got me shaken up more than I understood because I don't want you dead."

Because he could feel the chaos inside her roiling around, he tried for ease and calm to counter it. "Sure I'm glad you don't, and glad I'm not. But—"

"There's not a 'but' about it. And nothing more to it."

She leaped out of the lorry almost before he pulled in front of her flat.

"Go home to Branna," she ordered. "She needs you."

If she hadn't said the last, he'd have marched right up to her flat, pushed his way in if necessary. Then they'd have seen what they'd have seen.

But because she was right, he waited until she'd shut herself inside. Then he drove home, more puzzled than he'd ever been about a woman.

And more stirred by one than he could remember.

8

MEARA TOLD HERSELF TO FORGET ABOUT IT. TO PUT IT aside as a moment of insanity caused by extreme stress. It wasn't every day, was it, your two good friends grabbed hold of you and took you flying so you winked out of one place, winked into another?

Where you looked at a man you'd cared for the whole of your life, and thought him dead?

Some women would have run screaming, she thought as she put her back into mucking stalls. Some would have fallen into hysterics.

All she'd done was kiss the man who wasn't dead at all.

"I've kissed him before, haven't I?" she muttered and pitched soiled hay into the barrow. "You can't know someone almost from birth, run in the same pack all along, be best mates with his sister, and not. It's nothing. It's not a thing at all."

Oh God.

She squeezed her eyes shut, leaned on her pitchfork.

Sure she'd kissed him before, and he her.

But not like that. Not like that, no. Not all hot and heavy with tongues and teeth and her heart racing.

What must he think? What did she think?

More, what the bloody, bleeding hell was she to do when next she saw him?

"Okay." Iona stepped into the stall behind her, leaned on her own pitchfork. "I've given you thirty-two minutes, by my mark. That's my limit. What's going on?"

"Going on?" Flustered, Meara tugged the brim of her cap down lower, and tossed another scoop into the barrow. "I'm pitching horse shit, as you are."

"Meara, you barely looked at me, much less spoke when we got here this morning. And you're in here muttering under your breath. If I did something to piss you off—"

"No! Of course you didn't."

"I didn't think so, but something's got you muttering and hunching off with your eyes averted."

"Maybe I've got my monthlies."

"Maybe?"

"I couldn't think fast enough if I'd been bitchy recently when I did have them. My mother—"

Iona jabbed a finger to stop her. "You didn't think fast enough there either. When it's your mother, you spew. You're not spewing, you're hiding."

"I am not." Insulted, Meara angled away. "I'm merely taking some time with my thoughts."

"Is it about last night?"

Meara straightened up like a flag pole. "What about last night?"

"Connor. Black magickal burn."

"Oh. Well, yes, of course. Of course, it's that."

Eyes narrowed in speculation, Iona circled her finger in the air. "And?"

"And? That should be enough for anyone. It would send most people into hospital with collapsed nerves."

"You're not most people." Now Iona moved in closer, crowding the space. "What happened after you left Fin's?"

"Why would anything happen?"

"There!" Iona pointed. "You looked at the ground. Something happened, and you're evading."

Why, oh why, was she such a miserable liar when it mattered? "I'm looking at the horse shit I'm not shoveling."

"I thought we were friends."

"Oh, oh, that's below the belt." It was Meara's turn to point an accusatory finger. "That sorrowful look, the little catch in your voice."

"It is," Iona admitted with a quick smile. "But it's still true."

Losing the battle, Meara leaned on her pitchfork again. "I don't know what to say about it, or do about it."

"That's why you tell a friend. You're close to Branna—and I don't mean that below the belt. If you can talk to her, I'll cover for you while you go over."

"You would," Meara said with a sigh. "I'll need to talk to her, that's clear enough. I'm not sure how. It might be better to talk to a cousin rather than a sister right off. Sort of like stepping-stones. It's just that . . ."

She stepped to the opening of the stall, looked up, looked down to be sure Boyle, Mick, or any of the stable hands weren't loitering nearby.

"It was scary, last night. And I was turned upside down right off at being whisked magickally from one kitchen to the next in a couple blinks of the eye."

"You'd never flown before? Oh God, Meara, you had to be upside down. I guess I assumed Branna would have taken you now and then. For, well, fun."

"It's not that she won't use power for a bit of fun now and then. But she's pretty bloody responsible with it."

"You don't have to tell me."

"Then we're there, where we weren't, and Connor . . . In that first moment, I thought he was dead."

"Oh, Meara." Instinctively, Iona reached out to hug her. "I knew he wasn't—that connection among the three—and I nearly lost it."

"I thought I'd—we'd—lost *him*, and my head was already spinning, my guts twisted sideways. Then Branna and Fin working on him, and you as well. And I could do nothing."

"That's not true." Iona pulled back, gave Meara a little shake. "It took us all. It took our circle, our family."

"I felt useless all the same, but that's not important. It was such a relief when he came back, and so much himself. And I thought I'd calmed and settled. But when he drove me home, it started rolling around inside me again, and before I knew it, before I could think straight, I told him to pull over."

"Were you sick? I'm so sorry."

"No, no, and he thought the same. But I went a bit mad, really. I just jumped him, right there in his lorry."

Shock had Iona's mouth falling open as she took a jerky step back. "You— You hit him?"

"No! Don't be an idjit! I kissed him. And not at all like a brother or a friend, or someone you're welcoming back from death."

"Oh." Iona drew the syllable out.

"Oh," Meara echoed, doing a restless circle around the stall. "Then, as if that wasn't enough, I pulled back. You'd think I'd've got my head back in place, but no, I did it all over again. And being a man, after all, he had no objections, and would've moved on from there if I hadn't found my sanity again."

"I shouldn't be surprised. I'm not really surprised. I thought there was something . . . but when I first got here this winter, I thought there was something between you and Boyle."

"Oh Jesus." Completely done, Meara covered her face with her hands.

"I know there wasn't, ever, anything but family, friends. So I decided the something I thought I felt between you and Connor was the same."

"It is! Of course it is. This was a result of trauma."

"A coma's a result of trauma. Making out in a truck—lorry—is a result of something else entirely."

"It wasn't making out, just a couple kisses."

"Tongues?"

"Oh bloody hell." She yanked off her cap, tossed it down, stomped on it.

"Does that help?" Iona wondered.

"No." Disgusted, Meara grabbed the cap, beat it against her thigh. "How can I tell Branna I've been snogging her brother in his lorry on the side of the road like a horny teenager?"

"The same way you told me. What about—"

"Do the two of you intend to stand around all morning, or will you be hauling that manure out?" Boyle stepped to the opening, scowled at them.

"We're nearly done," Iona told him. "And we have something we have to discuss."

"Discuss later, haul manure now."

"Go away."

"I'm the boss here."

She merely stared at him until he shoved his hands in his pockets and stalked away.

"Don't worry, I won't say anything to him."

"Oh, it doesn't matter." Mortified all over again, Meara shoveled more manure. "Connor will for certain. Men are worse than women about such matters."

"What did you say to Connor? After."

"I told him that was the end of it, and I wasn't going to talk about it."

"Right." Iona managed to hold back the laugh, but not the toothy smile. "That'll work."

"We can't have a mad, momentary impulse twisting things up. We've more important things to concern us, as a whole."

Iona said nothing for a moment, then stepped over, gave Meara another hug. "I understand. I'll go with you when you talk to Branna if you want."

"Thanks for that, but it's best I do it on my own."

"Go this morning, get it off your mind. I'll cover for you."

"It would be good to get it out and gone, wouldn't it?" And maybe her stomach would stop rolling around, she considered as she pressed a hand to it. "I'll finish up here, then run over. Once it's said, I can put it aside and concentrate on what needs doing without it nagging at me."

"I'll smooth it with Boyle."

"Tell him I've my monthlies or some other female thing. It always shuts him up."

"I'm aware," Iona said with a laugh, and went back to her own stall.

DO IT QUICK, MEARA ORDERED HERSELF AS SHE STRODE through the woods. Get it over. Branna would hardly be mad about it—more likely she'd laugh, and think it a fine joke.

That would be grand, and then she could think of it as a fine joke herself.

Imagine Meara Quinn lusting for Connor O'Dwyer. And she could admit there were little pockets of lust burning in uncomfortable places.

But a talk with Branna would quash all that, and things would be back as things should be.

Maybe she'd had a little twinge over him now and then through the years. What woman wouldn't feel a twinge or two for the likes of Connor O'Dwyer?

The man made a picture, didn't he? All long and lean and that curling mop of hair, that pretty face, that knowing grin. Add in his caring ways, for he had that as much as the pretty.

A temper to be sure, but less than hers by far. By a few thousand kilometers, truth be told. And a far happier, steadier outlook on life than most, including herself.

For all he'd faced the whole of his life, he kept that happy outlook, those caring ways. You mixed the power in, for it was an awesome thing to behold even for one who'd known and seen it all her life, and the full package of him packed a solid punch.

And he knew it well, used it well—on more than a fair share of females to her way of thinking.

Not that she held that against him. Why not pluck the flowers along the way?

For her, for sense and logic, she'd stick with being his friend rather than part of a bouquet.

She sighed, hunched her shoulders as the air chilled. She'd have to speak to him of it—foolish to tell herself otherwise. But after she'd told Branna and they'd had a good laugh over it.

She'd be able to talk to Connor, make it all a fine joke, after she told Branna.

She dug into her pocket for her gloves as the wind kicked up. And to think they'd called for a bright morning, she thought as clouds smothered the sun.

And she heard her name on the wind.

Pausing, she looked over in that direction, saw she stood at the big downed tree by the thick vines. By the place where beyond lay the ruins of Sorcha's cabin, and the land that could slip in and out of time on Cabhan's whim.

He'd never before called to her, bothered with her. Why would he? She had no power, was no threat. But he called now, and the voice that oozed seduction pulled at something inside her.

She knew the dangers, knew all the warnings and risks, yet found herself standing at the curtain of vines without realizing she'd walked to them. Found herself reaching.

She'd just have a look, just a quick look is all.

Her hand touched the vines, and a dreamy warmth came with the touch. Smiling, she started to part them while fog oozed through their tangles.

The hawk cried as it dove. It sliced a path along those vines so she stumbled back. Shuddered and shuddered with the fog swimming nearly to her knees.

Roibeard perched on the downed tree, looked at her with eyes bright and fierce.

"I was going in, have a look. Can you hear him as well? It's my name he's calling. I only want to see."

When she reached out again, Roibeard spread his wings in warning. Behind her Branna's hound let out a soft woof.

"Come with me if you like. Why don't you come with me?"

Kathel caught the hem of her jacket in his teeth, pulled her back.

"Stop that now! What's wrong with you? What's . . . What's wrong with *me*?" she murmured, swaying now, knees watery, head light.

"Bugger it." She laid an unsteady hand on Kathel's great head. "Good dog, smart and good. Let's get away from here." She looked back at Roibeard, and at the shadows dimming again as the sun struggled through the mists. "Let's all get away from here."

She kept her hand on the dog, walking fast while the hawk swooped and glided overhead. Never in her life was she so glad to see the woods behind her, and the home of the Dark Witch so close at hand.

She wasn't ashamed to run, or to fling herself, just ahead of the hound, breathless into Branna's workshop.

In the act of pouring something that smelled of sugar biscuits from vat to bottle, Branna looked up. Immediately set the pot aside.

"What is it? You're shaking. Here, here, come by the fire."

"He called me," Meara managed as Branna rushed around the work counter. "He called my name."

"Cabhan." Wrapping an arm around Meara, Branna pulled her to the fire, eased her down into a chair. "At the stables?"

"No, no, the woods. I was coming here. At the place—outside Sorcha's place. Branna, he called me, and I was going. I wanted to go in, go to him. I wanted it."

"It's all right. You're here." She brushed her hands over Meara's cold cheeks, warmed them.

"I wanted it."

"He's sly. He makes you want. But you're here."

"I might not be but for Roibeard who came out of nowhere to stop me, then Kathel who came as well, and clamped right onto my jacket to pull me back."

"They love you, as I do." Branna bent down to lay her cheek to Kathel's head, to wrap around him for a moment. "I'm going to get you some tea. Don't argue. You need it, as do I."

She got Kathel a biscuit first, then stepped outside briefly.

To thank the hawk, Meara thought. To let him know all was well, and he had her gratitude. Branna always acknowledged loyalty.

To give her own thanks, and for comfort, Meara slid off the chair to hug Kathel. "Strong and brave and true," she whispered. "There's no better dog in the world than our Kathel."

"Not a one. Sit down, catch your breath." Branna busied herself with tea when she came back inside.

"Why would he call me? What would he want with me?"

"You're one of us."

"I've no magick."

"Not being a witch doesn't mean you don't have magick. You have a heart and a spirit. You're as strong and brave and true as Kathel."

"I've never felt anything like it. It was as if everything else went away, and there was only his voice, and my own terrible need to answer it."

"I'll be making you a charm, and you'll carry it with you always."

Warm now, Meara shrugged out of her jacket. "You've made me charms."

"I'll make you another, stronger, more specific, we'll say." She brought over the tea. "Now tell me all, as carefully as you can."

When she had, Meara sat back. "It was only a minute or two I realize now. It all seemed so slow, so dreamlike. Why didn't he just strike me down?"

"A waste of a comely maid."

"I haven't been a maid in some time." She shuddered again. "And oh, what a terrible thought it is. Worse, I might have been willing."

"Spellbound isn't willing. I can only believe he'd have used you if you'd gone through—taken you to another time, used you, and done what he could to turn you."

"He couldn't do that with any spell. Not with any."

"He couldn't, no, not that. But as you said about Fin, he doesn't understand family and love." Branna gripped Meara's hand, brought it to her cheek. "He'd have hurt you, Meara, and that would have hurt us all. You'll carry the charm I make you."

"Of course I will."

"We'll need to tell the others. Boyle will need to have more of a care as well. But he has Iona and Fin. You should stay here, with Connor and me."

"I can't."

"I know you value your own space—who'd understand more—but until we've settled on what we do next, it's best if—"

"I kissed him."

"What? What?" Stunned, Branna jerked back. "You kissed Cabhan? But you said you didn't go through. What—"

"Connor. I kissed Connor. Last night. I all but molested him on the side of the road. I lost my mind for a minute, that's all it was. The flying along, the seeing him lying on Fin's kitchen floor, all the pain in his face when the healing started. I thought, he's dead, then he wasn't, then he's shaking and burning up, and then he's ripping off a drumstick and chomping into it before he's so much as put his shirt on again. It all just boiled my brain until I was all but crawling over him and kissing him."

"Well," Branna said after Meara sucked in a breath.

"But I stopped—you have to know—well, after the second time I stopped."

Though Branna's mouth quirked at the corner, her tone stayed utterly even. "The second time?"

"I— It— He— It was a mad reaction to the evening."

"And did he have a mad reaction as well—to the evening?"

"I'd have to say, thinking on it, the first one took him by surprise, and who could wonder. And the second . . . he's a man, after all."

"He is that, indeed."

"But it went no further. I'll make that clear to you. I had him drop me home and drive on. It went no further."

"Why?"

"Why?" Blank, Meara just stared. "He dropped me home as I said."

"Why didn't he go with you?"

"With me? He needed to go home, to you."

"Ah, bollocks to that, Meara." Annoyance flicked out. "I won't be used as an excuse."

"I don't mean that, not at all. I . . . . I thought you'd be irritated or amused, or puzzled at least. But you're not."

"I'm none of those, no, or surprised in the least. I've wondered why it's taken the pair of you so bloody long to get to it."

"Get to what?"

"Get together."

"Together?" Pure shock had Meara surging to her feet. "Me, Connor. No, that can't be."

"And why can't it?"

"Because we're friends."

Meara sipped her tea, looked into the fire. "When I think of a lover who would touch more than my body, I think of a friend. To have only the heat without the warmth? It would do, and does, but only just."

"And what happens to the friend when the lover ends?"

"I don't know. I see our parents, Connor's and mine, happy still. Not blissful every second of every day, for who could stand that? But happy, and in tune most of the time."

"And I see mine."

"I know." Branna reached up, took Meara's hand to draw her down to sit again. "Those who made us give us each a different place to stand on it, don't they? I want, when I let myself want, that happy, that in tune. And you won't let yourself want at all because you see the ruin, the misery, and the selfishness under it all."

"He means too much to me to risk the ruin. And we've too much to fight for—as yesterday and today have proved—to tangle up our circle with sex."

"I believe Iona and Boyle have sex at every opportunity."

Now Meara laughed. "They're mad in love, and suited for it, so it's different."

"It's up to you, of course, and to Connor." And Connor, Branna thought, would very likely have a different thing or two to say about the matter. "But know I've no objection at all, if that was a worry to you. Why would I? I love you both. I'll say as well that sex is a power-ful magick of its own."

"So I should sleep with Connor to aid the cause?"

"You should do what makes you happy."

"It's all a bit confusing right now to be sure what does, what doesn't. But what I have to do is get back to work before Boyle gives me the boot."

"I'll make the charm first, and Kathel and Roibeard will go back with you. Walk clear of Sorcha's place, Meara."

"Believe me, I'll do that."

"Tell Iona and Boyle what happened. Boyle will see Fin's told, and I'll speak with Connor. Cabhan's growing bold again, so we best all be on our toes."

BRANNA DIDN'T HAVE TO TELL CONNOR, AS FIN WENT BY the school that afternoon, took Connor aside.

"Is she all right? Are you sure of it?"

"I saw her myself not an hour ago. She's fine and fit as ever."

"I've been busy," Connor said. "I barely noticed Roibeard wasn't about, then when I did, I knew he was at the stables. He likes it there, with the horses. With Meara. So I thought nothing of it, and he never sent me any alarm."

"As he and Kathel were all she needed. Branna made her a charm. It's a strong one—I had Meara show me. And the woman's strong as well. Still, it's time we were all a bit more careful."

Connor paced, boots crunching on gravel. "He'd have raped her. Strong or not, she couldn't have stopped him. I've seen what he's done to women over his time."

"He didn't touch her, Connor, and won't. We'll all see to that."

"I've worried for Branna on this. He wants power, and she is full of power. Named for Sorcha's firstborn, and the first of the three in the now to be passed the amulet. And . . ."

"The woman I love, who loves me even if she won't have me. You're not alone in your worry."

"And Meara is a sister to Branna. That might be making her more appealing to him," Connor considered.

"To strike at Branna through Meara." Fin nodded. "It would be his way."

"It would. And after last night . . ."

"After what he did to you? What has that to do with Meara?"

"Nothing at all. Well, indirectly." A man shouldn't lie or evade with his mates. In any case there was more on the line than discretion. "We had a moment, Meara and I, after leaving Branna at the cottage. A moment or two in the lorry, on the side of the road."

Fin's eyebrow winged up. "You moved in on Meara?"

"The other way." Distracted, Connor twirled a finger. "She moved in on me. And moved in with great enthusiasm. Then stopped cold, said that's the end of that, and take me home. I love women, Fin. I love them top to toe, minds, hearts, bodies. Breasts. What is there about a woman's breasts?"

"How long do we have to discuss it?"

Connor laughed. "True enough. We could take hours on breasts alone. I love women, Fin, but for the life of me there's so much of them impossible to understand."

"And that discussion would take days and never be resolved." Obviously intrigued, Fin studied Connor's face. "Tell me this, did you want that to be the end of it?"

"After I got over wondering where all this had been hiding, from both of us, all our lives, no, I didn't. Don't."

"Then, *mo dearthair*." Fin slapped Connor's shoulder. "It's up to you to follow through."

"I'm thinking on it. And now wondering if that moment or two on the side of the road might be why Cabhan took an interest in her today. Because I did, in that way? It's not far thinking."

"It's not, no. He hurt you last night. It may be he tried to hurt you again, through Meara, today. So have a care, both of you."

"I will, and I'll see she does. Ah, there's the three o'clocks. A mister and missus from Wales. Want to go along? I'll fetch you a pack and glove."

Fin started to decline, then realized it had been too long since he'd done a hawk walk with Connor. "I wouldn't mind that, but I'll get my own gear."

Connor glanced up, spotted Merlin in the sky. "Will you take him? Trust one of them with him?"

"He'd enjoy it as well."

"It'll be a bit like old times then."

When Fin went off for the gear, Connor took a quick glance at the time. As soon as he was able, he'd search out Meara. They had considerable to talk about, like it or not.

9

As if her day hadn't been fraught enough, Meara added on a frantic and weepy call from her mother that sent her searching out Boyle.

He sat in his office scowling as he was prone to scowl over paperwork.

"Boyle."

"Why is it the numbers never tally the first time you do them? Why is that?"

"I couldn't say. Boyle, I'm sorry to ask but I need to go. My mother's had a fire at the house."

"A fire?" He shoved up from his desk as if he'd rush off to put it out himself.

"A kitchen fire, I think. It was hard getting anything out of her, as she was near hysterical. But I did get she's not hurt, and didn't burn the place down around her. Still, I don't know how bad it all is, so—"

"Go. Go on." He rounded the desk, taking her arm, drawing her out of the office. "Let me know what's what as soon as you can."

"I will. Thanks. I'll do extra tomorrow to make up for it."

"Just go, for Christ's sake."

"I'm going."

She jumped in her lorry.

It would be nothing, she told herself. Unless it was something. With Colleen Quinn, you never knew which.

And her mother had been all but incoherent, wailing one minute, babbling the next. All about the kitchen, smoke, burning.

Maybe she was hurt.

The image of Connor, the black bubbling burn on his arm flashed through her mind.

Burning.

Cabhan. Fear spurted through her at the thought he might have played some part. Had he gone after her mother because in the end she'd resisted his call?

Meara punched the accelerator, rocketed around curves, raced her way with her heart at a gallop to the little dollhouse nestled with a handful of others just along the hem of Cong's skirts.

The house stood—no damage she could see to the white walls, the gray roof, the tidy dooryard garden. Tidy, true enough, as the small bit of garden in front and back was her mother's only real interest.

She shoved through the short gate—one she'd painted herself the previous spring, and ran up the walk, digging for her keys, since her mother insisted on locking the doors day and night in fear of burglars, rapists, or alien probes.

But Colleen rushed out, hands clasped together at her breast as if in prayer.

"Oh, Meara, thank God you've come! What will I do? What will I do?"

She threw herself into Meara's arms, a weeping, trembling bundle of despair.

"You're not hurt? For certain? Let me see you're not hurt."

"I burned my fingers." Like a child she held up her hand to show the hurt.

And nothing, Meara saw with relief, a bit of salve wouldn't deal with.

"All right then, all right." To soothe, Meara brushed a light kiss over the little burn. "That's the most important thing."

"It's terrible!" Colleen insisted. "The kitchen's a ruin. What will I do? Oh, Meara, what will I do?"

"Let's have a look, then we'll see, won't we?"

It was easy to turn Colleen around and pull her inside. Meara had gotten her height from her long-absent father. Colleen made a pretty little package—a petite, slim, and always perfectly groomed one, a fact of life that often made Meara feel like a hulking bear leading a poodle with a perfect pedigree.

No damage in the front room, another relief, though Meara could smell smoke, and see the thin haze of it.

Smoke, she thought—more relief—not fog.

Three strides took her into the compact, eat-in kitchen where the smoke hung in a thin haze.

Not a ruin, but sure a mess. And not one, she determined immediately, caused by an evil sorcerer, but a careless and inept woman.

Keeping an arm around her weeping mother, she took stock.

The roasting pan with the burned joint, now spilled onto the floor beside a scorched and soaking dish cloth told the tale.

"You burned the joint," Meara said carefully.

"I thought to roast some lamb, as Donal and his girl were to come to dinner later. I can't approve him moving in with Sharon before marriage, but I'm his mother all the same."

"Roasting a joint," Meara murmured.

"Donal's fond of a good joint as you know. I'd just gone out the back for a bit. I've had slugs in the garden there, and went to change the beer."

Fluttering in distress, Colleen waved her hands at the kitchen door as if Meara might have forgotten where the garden lay. "They've been after the impatiens, so I had to see about it."

"All right." Meara stepped over, began to open the windows, as Colleen had failed to do.

"I wasn't out that long, but I thought since I was, I'd cut some flowers for a nice arrangement on the table. You need fresh flowers for company at dinner."

"Mmm," Meara said, and picked up the flowers scattered over the wet floor.

"I came in, and the kitchen was full of smoke." Still fluttering, Colleen looked tearfully around the room. "I ran to the oven, and the lamb was burning, so I took the cloth there to pull it out."

"I see." Meara turned off the oven, found a fresh cloth, picked up the roasting pan, the charcoaled joint.

"And somehow the cloth lit, and was burning. I had to drop every-thing and take the pan there, where I had water for the potatoes."

Meara picked up the potatoes while her mother wrung her hands, dumped the lot in the sink to deal with later.

"It's a ruin, Meara, a ruin! What will I do? What will I do?"

The familiar mix of annoyance, resignation, frustration wound through her. Accepting that as her lot, Meara dried her hands by swiping them on her work pants.

"The first thing is to open the windows in the front room while I mop this up."

"The smoke will soil the paint, won't it, Meara, and you see the floor there, it's scorched from the burning cloth. I don't dare tell the landlord or he'll set me out."

"He'll do nothing of the kind, Ma. If the paint's soiled, we'll fix it. If the floor's damaged, we'll fix that as well. Open the windows, then put some of Branna's salve on your fingers."

But Colleen only stood, hands clasped, pretty blue eyes damp. "Donal and his girl are coming at seven."

"One thing at a time, Ma," Meara said as she mopped.

"I couldn't ring him up to tell him of the disaster here. Not while he's at work."

But you could ring me, Meara thought, as you've never understood a woman can work, does work, wants or needs to work, the same as a man.

"The windows," was all she said.

Not a mean bone in her body, Meara reminded herself as she cleaned the floor—not scorched at all, but only smudged with ash from the cloth. Not even selfish in the usual way, but simply helpless and dependent.

And was that her fault, really, when she'd been tended and sheltered the whole of her life? By her parents, then by her husband, and now by her children.

She'd never been taught to cope, had she? Or, Meara thought with a hard stare at the roasting pan, how to cook a fecking joint.

After wringing out the mop, she took a moment to text Boyle. No point in keeping him worried.

Not a fire but a burnt joint of lamb and a right mess. No harm.

Meara carted out the ruined meat to dump in the bin, scrubbed off the potatoes and set them to dry—as they were still raw because her mother had forgotten, all to the good, to turn the heat on under them.

She set the roasting pan in the sink to soak, put the kettle on for tea, all while Colleen despaired of being evicted.

"Sit down, Ma."

"I can't sit, I'm that upset."

"Sit. You'll have some tea."

"But Donal. What will I do? I've ruined the kitchen, and they're coming for dinner. And the landlord, this will put him in a state for certain."

Meara did multiplication tables in her head—the sevens, which buggered her every time. It kept her from shouting when she turned to her mother. "First, look around now. The kitchen's not ruined, is it?"

"But I . . ." As if seeing it for the first time, Colleen fluttered around. "Oh, it cleaned up well, didn't it?"

"It did, yes."

"I can still smell the smoke."

"You'll keep the windows open a bit longer, and you won't. At the worst, we'll scrub down the walls." Meara made the tea, added a couple of chocolate biscuits to one of her mother's fancy plates—and because it was her mother, added a white linen napkin.

"Sit down, have your tea. Let's have a look at your fingers."

"They're much better." Smiling now, Colleen held them up. "Branna's such a way with things, hasn't she, making up her lotions and creams and candles and so on. I love shopping in the Dark Witch. I always find some pretty little thing or other. It's a lovely little shop she has."

"It is."

"And she comes by now and then, brings me samples to try out for her."

"I know." So Colleen could have her pretty little things, Meara knew as well, without spending too much.

"She's a lovely girl, is Branna, and always looks so smart."

"She does," Meara agreed, and knew Colleen wished her daughter would dress smart instead of cladding herself for the stables.

We'll have to keep on being disappointed in each other, won't we, Ma? she thought, but said nothing more.

"The kitchen did clean up well, Meara, and thanks for that. But I haven't a thing now, or the time really, to make a nice dinner for Donal and his girl. What will Sharon think of me?"

"She'll think you had a bit of a to-do in the kitchen, so you called round to Ryan's Hotel and made a booking for the three of you."

"Oh, but—"

"I'll arrange it, and they'll run a tab for me. You'll have a nice dinner, and you'll come back here for tea and a bit of dessert—which I'll go pick up at Monk's Cafe in a few minutes. You'll serve it on your good china, and feel fine about it. You'll all have a nice evening."

Colleen's cheeks pinked with pleasure. "That sounds lovely, just lovely."

"Now, Ma, do you remember the proper way to deal with a kitchen fire?"

"You throw water on a fire. I did."

"It's best to smother it. There's the extinguisher in the closet with the mop. Remember? Fin provided it, and Donal put the brackets in so it's always right there, on the wall of the little closet."

"Oh, but I never thought of it, being that upset. And how would I remember how to use it?"

There was that, Meara thought. "Failing that, you can dump baking soda on it, or better all around, set a pot lid on it, cut off the air. Best of all, you don't leave the kitchen when you've got cooking going. You can set a timer on the oven so you're not wed to the room when you're baking or roasting."

"I meant to."

"I'm sure you did."

"I'm sorry for the trouble, Meara, truly."

"I know, and it's all fixed now, isn't it?" She laid a hand lightly over

Colleen's. "Ma, wouldn't you be happier living closer to your grand-children?"

Meara spent some time nourishing the seed she'd planted, then went to the cafe, bought a pretty cream cake, some scones and pastries. She dropped by the restaurant, made arrangements with the manager—a friend since her school days, circled back to her mother's.

Since she had a headache in any case, she went straight home from there and rang up her sister.

"Maureen, it's time you had a turn with Ma."

After a full hour of arguing, negotiating, shouting, laughing, com-miserating, she dug out headache pills, chugged them down with water at the bathroom sink.

And gave herself a long stare in the mirror. Little sleep left its mark in shadowed eyes. Fatigue on every possible level added strain around them, and a crease between her eyebrows she rubbed in annoyance.

Another day like this, she decided, she'd need all of Branna's creams and lotions—and a glamour as well—or she'd look a hag.

She needed to set it all aside for one bloody night, she told herself. Connor, Cabhan, her mother, the whole of her family. One quiet night, she decided, in her pajamas—with a thick layer of one of Bran-na's creams on her face. Add a beer, some crisps or whatever junky food she had about, and the telly.

She'd wish for no more than that.

Opting for the beer to begin—it wouldn't be the first time she'd taken a cold beer into a hot shower to wash away the day—she started toward the kitchen, and someone pounded on the door.

"Go away," she muttered, "whoever you are, and never come back."

Whoever it was knocked again, and she'd have ignored it again, but he followed up with:

"Open up, Meara. I know very well you're in there."

Connor. She cast her eyes to the ceiling, but went to the door.

She opened it. "I'm settling in for some quiet, so go somewhere else."

"What's this about a fire at your mother's?"

"It was nothing. Go on now."

He squinted at her. "You look terrible."

"And that's all I needed to finish off my fecking day. Thanks for that."

She started to shut the door in his face, but he put a shoulder to it. For a foolish minute, each pushed against the other. She tended to forget the man was stronger than he looked.

"Fine, fine, come in then. The day's been nothing but a loss in any case."

"Your head hurts, and you're tired and bitchy with it."

Before she could evade, he laid his hands on her temples, ran them over her head, down to the base of her skull.

And the throbbing ache vanished.

"I'd taken something for it already."

"That works faster." He added a light rub on her shoulders that dissolved all the knots. "Sit down, take your boots off. I'll get you a beer."

"I didn't invite you for a beer and a chat." The bad temper in her tone after he'd vanished all those aches and throbs shamed her. And the shame only added more bad temper.

He cocked his head, face full of patience and sympathy. She wanted to punch him for it.

She wanted to lay her head on his shoulder and just breathe.

"Haven't eaten, have you?"

"I've only just gotten home."

"Sit down."

He walked over to the kitchen—such as it was. The two-burner stove, the squat fridge, miserly sink, and counter tucked tidily enough in the corner of her living space, and suited her needs.

She grumbled rude words under her breath, but she sat and took off her boots while she watched him—eyes narrowed—poke around.

"What are you after in there?"

"The frozen pizza you never fail to stock will be quickest, and I could do with some myself for I haven't eaten either."

He peeled it out of the wrap, stuck it in the oven. And unlike her mother, remembered to set the timer. He took out a couple bottles of Harp, popped them open, then strolled back.

He handed her a beer, sat down beside her, propped his feet on her coffee table, a man at home.

"We'll start at the end of it. Your mother. A kitchen fire, was it?"

"Not even that. She burned a joint of lamb, and from her reaction, you'd think she'd started an inferno that leveled the village."

"Well then, your ma's never been much of a cook."

Meara snorted out a laugh, drank some beer. "She's a terrible cook. Why she got it into her head to have a little dinner party for Donal and his girl is beyond me. Because it's proper," she said immediately. "In her world, it's the proper thing, and she must be proper. She's bits of Belleek and Royal Tara and Waterford all around, fine Irish lace curtains at the windows. And I swear she dresses for gardening or marketing as if she's having lunch at a five-star. Never a hair out of place, her lipstick never smudged. And she can't boil a potato without disaster falling."

When she paused, drank, he patted her leg and said nothing.

"She's living in a rental barely bigger than the garden shed where she lived with my father, keeps it locked like a vault in defense against the bands of thieves and villains she imagines lie in wait—and can't think to open a bleeding window when she has a house full of smoke."

"She called for you then."

"For me, of course. She couldn't very well call for Donal, as he was at his work, and I'm just playing with the horses. At my leisure."

Then she sighed. "She doesn't mean it that way, I know it, but it *feels* that way. She never worked at a job. She married my father when she was but a girl, and he swept her up, gave her a fine house with staff to tend it, showered her with luxuries. All she had to do was be his pretty ornament and raise the children—entertain, of course, but that was being a pretty ornament as well, and there was Mrs. Hannigan to cook and maids to see to the rest."

Tired all over again, she looked down at her beer. "Then her world crashed down around her. It's not a wonder she's helpless about the most practical things."

"Your world crashed down as well."

"It's different. I was young enough to adjust to things, and didn't feel the shame she did. I had Branna and you and Boyle and Fin. She loved him. She loved Joseph Quinn."

"Didn't you, Meara?"

"Love can die." She drank again. "Hers hasn't. She keeps his picture in a silver frame in her room. It makes me want to scream bloody hell every time I see it. He's never coming back to her, and why would she have him if he did? But she would."

"It's not your heart, but hers."

"Hers holds on to an illusion, not to reality. But you're right. It's hers, not mine."

She leaned her head back, closed her eyes.

"You got her settled again?"

"Cleaned up the mess—she'd swamped the kitchen floor with water and potatoes—and I can be grateful she'd forgotten to turn the flame on under the potatoes so I didn't have that secondary disaster to deal with. She'll be having dinner at Ryan's Hotel with Donal and his girl now."

He rubbed a hand on her thigh, soothing. "On your tab."

"The money's the least of it. I rang Maureen, and had it out with her. It's her turn, fuck it all. Mary Clare lives too far. But from Maureen's, Ma could see Mary Clare and her children as well as come back here for visits. And my brother . . . His wife's grand, but it would be easier for Ma to live with her own daughter than her son's wife, I'm thinking. And Maureen has the room, and a sweet, easy-goer of a husband."

"What does your mother want?"

"She wants my father back, the life she knew back, but as that's not happening, she'd be happy with the children. She's good with children, loves them, has endless patience with them. In the end Maureen came around, for at least a trial of it. I believe—I swear this is the truth—I believe it'll be good for all. She'll be a great help to Maureen with the kids, and they love her. She'll be happy living there, in a bigger, finer house, and away from here where there are too many memories of what was."

"I think you're right on it, if it matters."

She sighed again, drank. "It does. She's not one who can live content and easy alone. Donal needs to start his life. I need to have mine. Maureen's the answer to this, and she'll only benefit from having her own mother mind the children when she wants to go out and about."

"It's a good plan, for all." He patted her hand, then rose at the buzz of the timer. "Now it's pizza for all, and you can tell me what's all this about Cabhan."

It wasn't the evening she'd imagined, but she found herself relaxing, despite all. Pizza, eaten on the living room sofa, filled the hole in her belly she hadn't realized was there until the first bite. And the second beer went down easy.

"As I told Branna, it was all soft and dreamy. I understand now what Iona meant when it happened to her last winter. It's a bit like floating, and not being fully inside yourself. The cold," she murmured. "I'd forgotten that."

"The cold?"

"Before, right before. It got cold, all of a sudden. I even took my gloves out of my pocket. And the wind came up strong. The light changed. It had been a bright morning, as they said it would, but it went gray and gloomy. Clouds rolling over the sun, I thought, but . . ."

She dug back now, mind clear, to try to see it as it had been.

"Shadows. There were shadows. How could there be shadows without the sun? I'd forgotten, didn't tell Branna. I was too wound up, I suppose."

"It's all right. You're telling me now."

"The shadows moved with me, and in them I felt warm—but I wasn't, Connor. I was freezing, but I *thought* I was warm. Is that sensible at all?"

"If you mean do I understand, I do. His magick's as cold as it is dark. The warmth was a trick for your mind, as the desire was."

"The rest is as I told you. Him calling my name, and me standing there, with my hand about to part the vines, wanting to go in, so much, wanting to answer the call of my name. And Roibeard and Kathel to my rescue."

"If you've a mind to walk from work to the cottage, or when you guide your customers, stay clear of that area, much as you can."

"I will, of course. It's habit takes me by there, and habits can be broken. Branna made me a charm in any case. As did Iona, and then Fin pushed yet another on me."

Connor dug into his pocket, pulled out a small pouch. "As I am."

"My pockets will be full of magick pouches at this rate."

"Do this. Keep one near your door here, and one in your lorry, one near your bed—sleep's vulnerable. Then one in your pocket." He put the pouch into her hand, closed her fingers over it. "Always, Meara."

"All right. That's a fine plan."

"And wear this." Out of his pocket he drew a long thin band of leather that held polished beads.

"It's pretty. Why am I wearing it?"

"I made it when I was no more than sixteen. It's blue chalcedony here, and some jasper, some jade. The chalcedony is good protection from magick of the dark sort, and the jade's helpful for protection from psychic attack—which you've just experienced. The jasper's good all around as a protective stone. So wear it, will you?"

"All right." She slipped it over her head. "You can have it back when we're done with this. It's cleverly done," she added, studying it. "But you've always been clever with your hands."

The instant the words were out, she winced inwardly at the phrase. "So, that's filled you in on the highs and lows of my day, and I'm grateful for the pizza—even if it came from my own freezer."

She started to get up, clear the dishes, but he just put a hand on her arm, nudged her back again.

"We haven't finished the circle yet, as we've been working backward. And that takes us to last night."

"I already told you nothing was meant by it."

"What you told me was bollocks."

The easy, almost cheerful tone of his voice made her want to rail at him, so she deliberately kept her tone level. "I've had enough upheaval for one day, Connor."

"Sure we might as well get it all over and done at once. We're friends, are we not, Meara?"

"We are, and that's exactly the point I'm making."

"It wasn't the kiss of a friend, even one upset and shaken, you gave me. Nor was it the kiss of a friend I gave you when I got beyond the first surprise of it."

She shrugged, to show how little it all meant—and wished her stomach would stop all the fluttering. You'd think she'd swallowed a swarm of butterflies instead of half a frozen pizza.

"If I'd known you'd be so wound up about a kiss, it wouldn't have happened."

"A man who wasn't wound up after a kiss like that would've been dead for six months. And I'm betting he'd still feel a stir."

"That only means I'm good at it."

He smiled. "I wouldn't argue with your skill. I'm saying it wasn't friend to friend, and distress. Not that alone."

"So there's a bit of lusty curiosity as well. That's not a surprise, is it? We're adults, we're human, and in the strangest of situations. We had a quick, hot tangle, and that's the end of it."

He nodded as if considering her point. "I wouldn't argue with that either, but for one thing."

"What one thing?"

He shifted so quickly from his easy slouch she didn't have an instant to prepare. He had her scooped up, shifted as well, and his mouth on hers.

Another hot tangle, fast and deep and deadly to the senses. Some part of her mind said to give him a punch and set things right, but the rest of her was too busy devouring what he gave her.

Then he tugged on her braid—an old, affectionate gesture, so their lips parted, their faces stayed close. So close the eyes she knew as well as her own took on deeper, darker hues of green with little shimmers of gold scattered through.

"That one thing."

"It's just . . ." She moved in this time, couldn't resist, and felt his heart race against hers. "Physicality."

"Is it?"

"It is." She made herself pull back, then stand—a bit safer, she thought, with some distance. "And more, Connor, we need to think, the both of us need to think. It's friends we are, and always have been. And now part of a circle that can't be risked."

"What's the risk?"

"We have sex—"

"A grand idea. I'm for it."

Though she shook her head, she had to laugh with it. "You'd be for it on an hourly basis. But it's you and me now, and with you and me what if there are complications, and the kind of tensions that can happen, that *do* happen, when sex comes through the door?"

"Done well, sex relieves the tensions."

"For a bit." Though just now the thought of it, with him, brought on plenty. "But we might cause more—for each other, for the others when we can least afford it. We need to keep ourselves focused on what's to be done, and keep the personal complications away from it as much as we can."

Easy as ever, he picked up his beer to finish it off. "That's your busy brain, always thinking what's next and not letting the rest of you have the moment."

"A moment passes into the next."

"Exactly. So if you don't enjoy it before it does, what's the point of it all?"

"The point is seeing clear, and being ready for the next—and the next after it. And we need to think about all of this, and carefully. We can't just jump into bed because we both have an itch. I care about you, and all the others too much for that."

"There's nothing you can do, not anything, that could shake my friendship. Not even saying no on this when I want you to say yes more than . . . well, more than I might want."

He stood as well. "So we'll both think on it, give it all a little time and see how we feel."

"That's the best, isn't it? It's just a matter of taking time to cool it down, think clear so we're not leaping into an impulse we could regret. We're both smart and steady enough to do that."

"Then that's what we'll do."

He offered a hand to seal the deal. Meara took it, shook.

Then they both simply stood, neither backing away, moving forward, or letting go.

"Ah hell. We're not going to think at all, are we?"

He only grinned. "Not tonight."

They leaped at each other.

10

GRAPPLING WASN'T HIS USUAL WAY, BUT THIS WAS something so . . . explosive he lost his rhythm and style. He grabbed whatever he could grab, took whatever he could take. And there was so much of her—his tall, curvy friend.

He all but ripped off her shirt to get to more.

No stopping now for either of them, for here ran needs and urges far beyond careful and rational thinking. Here was the moment, and the next and the next would have to wait.

This bright new hunger for her, just her, must be fed.

But not, he realized, standing in her living room or rolling about on the floor.

He scooped her up.

"Oh Jesus, don't try to carry me. You'll break your back."

"My back's strong enough." He turned his head to meet her mouth as he walked to her bedroom.

Crazy, she thought. They'd both gone completely mad. And she didn't give a single bleeding damn. He carried her, and though his purpose—and hers—was hurry, it was foolishly romantic.

If he stumbled, well, they'd finish things out where they landed.

But he didn't stumble. He dropped to the bed with her so the old springs squeaked in surprise, gave with a groan to nestle them both in a hollow of mattress and bedding.

And those hands, those magick hands were busy and beautiful.

She used her own to pull and yank off layers of clothes until, at last—God be praised—she found skin. Warm, smooth—with the good firm muscles of a man who used them.

She rolled with him, struggling as he did to strip off every barrier.

"Bloody layers," he muttered, and made her laugh as she fought with the buckle of his belt.

"We would, both of us, work outdoors."

"Good thing it's worth the unwrapping. Ah, there you are," he murmured and filled his hands with her bare breasts.

Firm and soft and generous. Beautiful, bountiful. He could write an ode to the glory of Meara Quinn's breasts. But at the moment, he wanted only to touch them, taste them. And feel the way her heartbeat kicked up from canter to gallop at the brush of his fingers, lips, tongue.

All that was missing was . . .

He brought light into the dark, a soft, pale gold like her skin. When her eyes met his, he smiled.

"I want to see you. Beautiful Meara. Eyes of a gypsy, body of a goddess."

He touched her as he spoke. No grappling now; he'd found his rhythm after all. Why rush through something so pleasurable when he could linger over it? He could feast on her breasts half a lifetime. Then there were her lips, soft and full—and as eager as his. And her shoulders, strong, capable. The surprisingly sweet stem of her neck. Sensitive there, just there under her jaw so she shivered when he kissed it.

He loved how she responded—a tremble, a catch of breath, a throaty moan—as he learned her body, inch by lovely inch.

Outside someone shouted out a half-drunken greeting, and followed it by a wild laugh.

But here, in the nest of the bed, there were only sighs, murmurs, and the quiet creak of the springs beneath them.

He'd taken the reins, she realized. She didn't know how it happened, as she'd never given them over to anyone else. But somewhere between the hurry and the patience, she'd surrendered them to him.

His hands glided over her as if he had centuries to pet and stroke and linger. They kindled fires along the way until her body seemed to shimmer in the heat, to glow under her skin like the light he'd conjured.

She loved the feel of him, the long back, the narrow hips, the hard, workingman's palms. He smelled of the woods, earthy and free, and the taste of him—lips, skin—was the same.

He tasted of home.

He touched where she ached to be touched, tasted where she longed for his lips. And found other secret places she hadn't known longed for attention. The inside of her elbow, the back of her knee, the inside of her wrist. He murmured to her, sweet words that reached into her heart. Another light to glow.

He seemed to know when the glow became a pulse, and the pulse a throb of need. So he answered that need, drawing the pleasure up and up before spilling her over into release.

Weak from it, dazed by the flood and the flow, she clung to him, tried to right herself.

"A moment. Give me a moment."

"It's now," he said. "It should be now."

And slid inside her. Took her mouth as he took her, deep and slow.

It should be now, he thought again. For she was open for him to fill. Warm and wet for him.

Her moan, a sound of welcome; her arms strong ropes to bind him close.

She rose to him, wrapped those long legs around him. Moved with him as if they'd come together like this, just like this, over a hundred lifetimes. In the glow he'd made, in the glow that gleamed now from what they made together, he watched her.

Dubheasa. Dark beauty.

Watched her until what they made overwhelmed him, and the pleasure deepened dark as her eyes. In the dark and the light, he surrendered to her as she had to him. And let her take him with her.

SHE LAY, BASKING. SHE'D EXPECTED—ONCE SHE'D ACCEPTED she was having sex with Connor—a rollicking rough and tumble. Instead she'd been . . . tended, pleasured, even seduced, and with a delicate touch.

And had no complaints whatsoever.

Now her body felt all loose and soft and weak in the loveliest of ways.

She'd known he'd be good at it—God knew he'd had the practice—but she hadn't known he'd be absolutely bloody brilliant.

So she could sigh now in utter satisfaction—with her hand resting on his very fine ass.

Just as she sighed, it occurred to her she couldn't possibly have measured up. She'd been taken by surprise, she thought, and surely hadn't done her best work—so to speak.

Was that why he was currently lying on her like a dead man?

She moved her hand, not quite sure now what to do or say.

He stirred.

"I suppose you're wanting me to get off you."

"Ah . . . Well."

He rolled, sprawled on his back. When he said nothing at all, she cleared her throat.

"And what now?"

"I'm thinking," he said. "That once we take a bit of a breather, we do it all over again."

"I can do better."

"Better than what?"

"Than I did. I was taken off-balance."

He trailed a finger lazily down her side. "If you'd done better, I might need weeks of a breather."

Unsure what that might mean, exactly, she pushed up enough to see his face. Since she knew what a satisfied male looked like, she relaxed again.

"So it went well for you then."

He opened his eyes, looked into hers. "I'm considering how to answer that, for if I tell the truth you might say: Since it went so well, that's all for you tonight. And I want you again before I've even caught my breath."

He slid an arm under her, drew her over, cuddled her in so they were nose to nose. "And did it go well for you?"

"I'm considering how to answer that," she said and made him grin.

"I've missed seeing you naked."

"You haven't seen me naked before tonight."

"Sure have you forgotten the night you and me and Branna and Boyle and Fin snuck out and away to swim in the river?"

"We never— Oh, that." Content, she tangled up her legs with his. "I was no more than nine, you git!"

"But naked all the same. I'll say you grew up and around very well indeed." He ran a hand down her back, over her ass, left it there. "Very well indeed."

"And you yourself, if memory serves me, were built like a puny stick. You've done well yourself. We had fun that night," she remembered. "Froze our arses, the lot of us, but it was grand. Innocent, all of us, and not a worry in the world. But he'd have been watching us, even then."

"No." Connor touched a finger to her lips. "Don't bring him here, not tonight."

"You're right." She brushed a hand through his hair. "How many, do you think, are where we are tonight who have all those years and memories between them?"

"Not many, I expect."

"We can't lose that, Connor. We can't lose what we are to each other, to Branna, to all. We have to swear an oath on it. We won't lose even a breath of the friends we've ever been, whatever happens."

"Then I'll swear it to you, and you to me." He took her hand, interlaced his fingers with hers. "A sacred oath, never to be broken. Friends we've ever been, and ever will be."

She saw the light glowing through their joined fingers, felt the warmth of it. "I swear it to you."

"And I to you." He kissed her fingers, then her cheek, then her lips. "I should tell you something else."

"What is it?"

"I've my breath back now."

And when she laughed, he rolled back on top of her.

SHE'D SHARED BREAKFAST WITH HIM BEFORE, COUNTLESS times. But never at the little table in her flat—and never after sharing the shower with him.

He could count himself lucky, she decided, that she'd picked up some nice croissants from the cafe when she'd gotten dessert for her mother.

Along with them she made her usual standby—oatmeal—while he dealt with the tea as she hadn't any coffee in the pantry.

"We're to meet tonight," he reminded her, and bit into a croissant. "These are brilliant."

"They are. I don't step foot into the cafe often as I'd buy a dozen of everything. I'll go by the cottage straight from the stables," she added. "And help Branna with the cooking if I can. It's good we're meeting regular now, though I don't know as any of us suddenly had a genius idea on what to do, exactly, and when to do it."

"Well, we're thinking, and together, so something will come."

He believed it, and the croissants only helped boost his optimism.

"Why don't I take you to the stables on my way, and just fetch you when we're both done? It'd save you the petrol, and seems foolish for us to each take our lorries."

"Then you'd have to bring me home after."

"That was the canny part of my plan." He hefted his tea as if toasting himself. "I'll bring you back, stay with you again if that's all right. Or you could just stay at the cottage."

She downed tea he'd made strong enough to break stone. "What will Branna think of this?"

"We'll be finding out soon enough. We wouldn't hide it from her, either of us, even if we could. Which we couldn't," he added with an easy shrug, "as she'll know."

"They'll all need to know." No point, Meara decided, being delicate about it all. "It's only right. Not just because we're friends and family, but because we're a circle. What we are to each other . . . that's the circle, isn't it?"

He scanned her face as she pushed oatmeal around in her bowl. "It shouldn't worry you, Meara. We've a right to be with each other this way as long as we both want it. None who care for us would think or feel otherwise."

"That's right. But then as far as my other family—my blood kin—I'd as soon not bring them into it."

"That's for you to say."

"It's not that I'm ashamed of it, Connor, you mustn't think that."

"I don't think that." His eyebrows lifted as he took a spoonful of her oatmeal, brought it up to her mouth himself. "I know you, don't I? Why would I think that, knowing you?"

"That's an advantage between us. It's that my mother would start fussing, and inviting you to dinner. I couldn't take another kitchen disaster on the heels of the last—and my finances can't take a bigger tab at Ryan's Hotel. In any case, she'll be off for her visit with Maureen soon—and unless that's a fresh disaster, it'll be a permanent move."

"You'll miss her."

"I'd like the chance to." She huffed out a breath, but ate some oatmeal before he took it into his head to feed her again. "And that sounds mean, but it's pure truth. I think I'd have a better time with her if there was some distance. And . . ."

"And?"

"I had a moment yesterday, while I was rushing over there, not sure what I'd find. I suddenly thought, what if Cabhan's been at her, as he'd been at me? It was foolish, as he's no reason to, and never has. But I thought as well of what you said about feeling better knowing your parents were away from this. I'll rest easier knowing that about my mother. This is for us to do."

"And so we will."

HE DROPPED HER OFF AT THE STABLES, THEN CIRCLED around to go home and change out of yesterday's work clothes.

He found Branna already up—not dressed for the day as yet, but having her coffee with Sorcha's spell book once again open in front of her.

"Well, good morning to you, Connor."

"And to you, Branna."

She studied him over the rim of her mug. "And how is our Meara this fine morning?"

"She's well. I've just dropped her at the stables, but wanted to change before I went to work. And wanted to see how you fared as well."

"I'm fit and fine, though I can say you look fitter and finer. You've had breakfast I take it?"

"I have, yes." But he liked the looks of the glossy green apples she'd put in a bowl, and took one. "Does this bother you, Branna? Meara and myself?"

"Why would it when I love you both, and have seen the pair of you careful to skirt round the edges of what my brilliant brain deduces occurred last night—for years."

"I never thought of her in that way before . . . Before."

"You did, but told yourself not to, which is different entirely. You'd never hurt her."

"Of course I wouldn't."

"And she'd never mean to hurt you." Which, Branna thought, was another thing different entirely. "Sex is powerful, and I think will only add to the strength and power of the circle."

"Obviously, we should've jumped into bed before this."

She only laughed. "The pair of you had to be willing and wanting. Sex only to take power? That's a selfish act, and damaging in the end."

"I can promise we were both willing and wanting." He bit into the apple, which tasted as tart and crisp as it looked. "And it's occurring to me I left you on your own last night."

"Don't insult me." Branna brushed that aside. "I can more than take care of myself and our home, as you well know."

"I do know it." He picked up the pot to top off her coffee. "And still I don't like leaving you on your own."

"I've learned to tolerate a houseful of people, even enjoy it. But as you know me you know I prize being on my own in a quiet house."

"As I'd switch the *prize* and *tolerate* around, it's a wonder we came from the same parents at times."

"It may be you were left on the doorstep and taken in out of pity. But you're handy enough to have around when a faucet's dripping or a door squeaks."

He pulled her hair, crunched his apple. "Still, you can't ask us to give you that quiet and alone too often till this is done."

"Sure I won't. I'm after making beef bourguignon for the horde of us tonight."

He raised his eyebrows. "Fancy."

"I'm in the mood for fancy, and you'll see someone brings some good red wine, and plenty of it."

"That I'll do." He tossed the apple core in the compost pail, walked over, kissed the top of her head. "I love you, Branna."

"I know it. Go on and change your clothes before you're late for work."

When he left, she sat looking away and out the window. She wanted him happy, more even than she wanted happiness for herself. And yet, knowing he was on his way to finding what he didn't yet know he wanted made her feel so painfully alone.

Sensing it, Kathel rose from beneath the table, laid his head in her lap. So she sat, stroking the dog, and returned to poring over the spell book.

IONA STEPPED INTO THE TACK ROOM WHERE MEARA organized the equipment needed for her first guided ride of the morning.

"It's coming time for another good going-over of everything in here," Meara said cheerfully. "I'm taking out a party of four, two brothers and their wives who've come to Ashford for a big family wedding on the weekend. Their niece it is, having the wedding at Ballintubber Abbey, where you and Boyle will marry next spring, then back to Ashford they'll all come for the reception."

"You and Connor had sex."

Meara looked up, and blinking dramatically began to pat herself front and back. "Am I wearing a sign then?"

"You've been smiling all morning, and singing."

"I've been known to smile and sing without having sex beforehand."

"You don't sing the whole time you're mucking stalls. And you look really, *really* relaxed, which you wouldn't, without sex, after a day like you had yesterday. Since you kissed Connor, you had sex with him."

"Some people are known to kiss without having sex. And don't you have a lesson in the ring on the schedule?"

"I have five minutes, and this is the first time I could catch you alone. Unless you want Boyle to know. It was wonderful, it was good or you wouldn't look so happy."

"It was wonderful and good, and it's not a secret. Connor and I both agree—as we're a circle, and something like this can change matters, though it won't—all should know we're together that way. Right now."

She gathered reins, bit, saddle, blanket. "So we are."

"You're good together— You're happy," Iona added, hauling up more tack herself and following Meara out. "So you're good together. Why do you say right now?"

"Because right now is right now, and who knows what tomorrow might be? You and Boyle can look forward—you're both built that way." She stepped into Maggie's stall, the mare she'd chosen for one of the women. "I'm a day-at-a-time sort on matters like this."

"And Connor?"

"I've never known him to be otherwise on any matter. That's for Caesar. Just leave it there and I'll tend to it. You have a lesson."

"At least tell me, was it romantic?"

"You've such a soft heart, Iona, but I can tell you it was. And that was unexpected, and really lovely." For a moment, just a moment, she leaned her cheek against Maggie's soft neck. "I thought, well, once it was clear we were going forward, we'd just tear in. But . . . he made the room glow. And me with it."

"That's beautiful." Iona stepped in, hugged Meara hard. "Just beautiful. Now I'm happy, too."

Iona led Alastar, her big, beautiful gray, already saddled and waiting, out of his stall, toward the ring. Smiled as she heard Meara singing again.

"She's in love," Iona murmured to her horse, and rubbed his strong neck. "She just doesn't know it yet." When Alastar nuzzled her, she laughed. "I know, she's still glowing some. I saw it, too."

Meara switched to humming as she led horses to the paddock, looped reins around the fence. She turned to go back for the last, spotted Boyle bringing Rufus along.

"Thanks for that. Since Iona's got a lesson going in the ring, I'll take the group around the paddock a bit, be sure they're as experienced as they say before we start off."

She looked up. "It's a fine day, isn't it? It's nice they've booked a full hour."

"And we've just had someone else ring up to book another four-group for noon. This wedding's bringing them along."

"I can take that as well." She had energy enough to ride and muck and groom all day and half the night. "I owe you for taking so much time away yesterday."

"We won't start owing around here," he said, "but it would help if you could as Iona's got two at half ten, Mick's doing a lesson at eleven, and with Patty at the dentist this morning, and Deborah booked for one o'clock, we're a bit squeezed. Still, I could do it myself."

"You hate doing the guideds, and I don't mind at all." She gave him a pat on the cheek, had him giving her a hard stare.

"You're a cheerful sort this morning."

"And why wouldn't I be?" she asked as four people strolled toward the stables. "It's a bright day at last, my mother's going for a long visit with a strong potential of a permanent move to Maureen's, and I had hot and brilliant sex with Connor last night."

"It's good your mother's having a visit with— What?"

Meara had to smother a snort at the way Boyle's mouth hung open. "I had sex with Connor last night, and this morning as well."

"You . . ." He trailed off, shoved his hands in his pockets, so absolutely *Boyle* she couldn't resist patting his cheek again.

"I suspect he's cheerful himself, but you can ask him yourself at the first opportunity. It's the McKinnons, is it?" Meara called out as she went, smiling all the way, to meet her morning group.

In short order, with the paperwork done, and her ignoring Boyle's questioning stares, she had her group outfitted and mounted.

"Well now, I can see you all know what you're about," she said when they'd walked and trotted around the paddock. She opened the gate for them, mounted Queen Bee.

"You've picked a fine morning, and there's no better way to see what you'll see than on the back of a horse. And how are you enjoying your stay at Ashford?" she began, sliding into easy small talk as she led them away from the stables.

She answered questions, let them chat among themselves, turned in the saddle now and again just to check—and to let them know they had her attention.

It was lovely, she thought, to ride through the woods with the sky blue overhead, with the earthy perfumes of autumn wafting on the soft and pretty breeze. The scents reminded her of Connor, had her smile brightening.

Then there he was, out and about with his own group on a hawk walk. He wore a work vest but no cap so his hair danced around his face, teased by that soft and pretty breeze. He shot her a grin as he baited his client's glove, and the wife readied her camera.

"Family of yours?" Meara asked as her group and Connor's called out to each other.

"Cousins—our husbands'." The woman—Deirdre—moved up to ride beside Meara for a moment. "We talked about trying the hawk walk ourselves."

"Sure and you should. It's a wonderful experience to take back with you."

"Do all the falconers look like that one?"

"Oh, that would be Connor who runs the school. And he's one of a kind." I had sex with him before breakfast, she thought, and shot a grin of her own back at him as she led her group on.

"Connor," she heard the woman say as she fell in behind Meara. "Jack, we should all book that hawk walk."

Under the circumstances, Meara couldn't blame her.

She led them along the river, enjoyed them, enjoyed the ride. She took them deep into the green where the shadows thickened, and out again where that blue sky shone over the trees.

When she began to circle them back, she saw the wolf.

Just a shadow in the shadows, with its paws sunk into mist. The stone around its neck gleamed like an eye even as the wolf itself seemed to waver like a vapor.

Her horse trembled under her. "Steady now," she murmured, keeping her gaze on the wolf as she stroked Queen Bee's neck. "You be steady now and the rest will follow your lead. You're the queen, remember."

The wolf paced them, coming no closer.

Birds no longer sang in the woods; squirrels no longer raced busily along the branches.

Meara took the necklace Connor had given her from under her sweater, held it out a little so the stones caught the light.

Behind her, her group chatted away, oblivious.

The wolf showed its fangs; Meara put a hand on the knife she wore on her belt. If it came, she would fight. Protect the people she guided, the horses, herself.

She would fight.

The hawk dived—from the blue, through the green.

Meara no more than blinked, and the shadow of the wolf was gone.

"Oh, there's one of the hawks!" Deidre pointed to the branch where the bird perched now, wings folded. "Did he get loose?"

"No, not at all." Meara steadied herself, put her smile back in place as she turned in the saddle. "That's Connor's own Roibeard, having a bit of fun before going back to the school."

She lifted her hand to the necklace again, and rode easily out of the woods.

11

THE MINUTE HE COULD GET AWAY, CONNOR DROVE around to the stables. Too many people about to talk, he decided immediately, but with Meara chatting with a group she'd just guided back, at least he knew just where she was and what she was doing.

He tracked Boyle down in the stalls, giving Caesar a rubdown.

"Busy days," Boyle said. "This wedding's brought in as much business as we can handle."

"And the same for us. We've our last two hawk walks of the day going now."

"We've two out ourselves, though Meara should be back anytime."

"She's just back." Absently, Connor stroked the big gelding as Boyle brushed him out. "Can you set her loose, or do you need her longer today?"

"We've the evening feedings yet, and Iona's at the big stables on a lesson."

"You'll keep her close then? I'll run back and settle my own business for the evening. Is Fin with Iona?"

"He's home if that's what you're meaning, and set to take her to your place when they're both done." Connor's tone had Boyle setting the currycomb aside. "There's a worry. What is it?"

"Cabhan. He was out today, stalking Meara on her guided. And myself a bit. Nothing came of it," Connor said when Boyle cursed. "And he wasn't quite there—not fully physically."

"Was he there or wasn't he?" Boyle demanded.

"He was, but more a shadow. It's a new thing, and something to discuss tonight when we're all together. But I'd feel easier if I knew you were with her until I'm done."

"I'll keep her with me." Boyle pulled out his phone. "And be sure Fin does the same with Iona. And Branna?"

"Roibeard's keeping a watch on all, and Merlin's with him. But I'll be happier altogether when the six of us are together at home."

IT TOOK NEAR AN HOUR TO SETTLE THE BIRDS FOR THE night, and clear up some paperwork Kyra left meaningfully on his desk. He took more time to add yet another layer of protection around the school. Cabhan had gotten into the stables once. He might try for the hawks.

By the time he'd done all that needed doing, locked up tight, the brightness had gone out of the day. Just shorter days, he thought as he stood a moment, opened himself. He felt no threat, no watchful presence. He let himself reach out to Roibeard, join with the hawk—and saw clearly the stables, the woods, the cottage, peaceful below, through his hawk's eyes.

There was Mick, squat as a spark plug, climbing into his lorry, giving a wave out the window to Patti as the girl swung onto her bike.

And there, spread below him, Fin's grand stone house, and the fields and paddocks. Iona soaring over a jump with Alastar.

A short glide, soaring on the wind and, below, Branna picking herbs in her kitchen garden. She straightened, looked up, looked, it seemed, right into his eyes.

And she smiled, lifted a hand before taking her herbs inside with her.

All's well, Connor told himself, and though there was always just a hint of regret, came fully back to earth. Satisfied, he climbed into the lorry.

He drove around to the stables—and felt a warm hum in his blood as he watched Meara come out with Boyle. She was a beauty for certain, he thought, an earthy one in a rough jacket and work pants, and boots that had likely seen hundreds of kilometers, on the ground and on horseback.

Later, he'd have the pleasure of removing those worn boots, those riding pants. And unwinding that thick braid so he could surround himself with waves of brown hair.

"Boyle, are you wanting a lift?" he called through the open window.

"Thanks, but no. I'll follow you over."

So he leaned left, shoved the door open for Meara.

She jumped in, smelling of horses and grain and saddle soap. "Christ Jesus, this was a day and a half shoved into one. The McKinnon party is leaving no stone unturned. We've got groups of them coming tomorrow up through two o'clock, with the wedding, I'm told, at five."

"The same for us."

Since she made no move, he put a hand on the back of her head, drew her over for a kiss. "Good evening to you."

"And to you." Her lips curved. "I wondered if you'd feel a little off center after thinking it over for a day."

"Not much time to think, but I'm balanced well and good."

He turned the lorry, headed away from the stables with Boyle falling in behind.

"Did you see the wolf?" he asked her.

"I did, yes. Boyle couldn't say much as we had the crew about nearly till you came, but he said you did as well. But as with me, it was more a shadow."

She shifted to face him, frowned. "Still, not only a shadow, as he bared his fangs, and I saw them clear, and the red stone. Did you send Roibeard?"

"I didn't have to; he went to you on his own. But I knew from him the wolf only kept pace with you for a minute or two."

"Enough for the horses to sense it. My biggest worry, to tell the truth, was that the horses would spook. Which they might have done, but I had a group of experienced riders. And they themselves? They saw and sensed nothing."

"I've been thinking on the whys and hows of that. I want to see what Branna and Fin and Iona have to say. And I want to ask you to stay tonight at the cottage."

"I don't have my things," she began.

"You have things at the cottage, enough to get you through. You can think of it as us taking turns. Stay tonight, Meara. Share my bed."

"Are you asking because you want me to share your bed, or because you're worried about me being on my own?"

"It would be both, but if you won't stay, I'll be sharing your bed."

"That's a fine answer," she decided. "It works well for me. I'll stay tonight."

He took her hand, leaned toward her when he stopped the lorry in front of the cottage. And could already feel the kiss moving through him before their mouths met.

The lorry shook as if from a quake, jolted as the wolf pounced.

It snarled, eyes and stone gleaming red, then with a howl echoing with triumph, leaped off. And was gone.

"Holy Jesus!" Meara managed an instant before Connor shoved out of the lorry. "Wait, wait. It might still be out there." She yanked at her own door, shoved, but it held firm against her.

"Goddamn it, Connor. Goddamn it, let me out."

He only flicked her a glance as Roibeard landed light as down on his shoulder.

In that moment, in that glance, it was like looking at a stranger, one sparking with power and rage. Light swirled around him, like a current that would surely shock to the touch.

She'd known him the whole of her life, she thought as her breath backed up in her lungs, but she'd never seen him truly, fully until that moment when the full force and fury of what ran in his blood revealed itself.

Then Branna rushed from the house, with Kathel thundering out with her. Her hair, raven black, flew behind her. She had a short sword in one hand, a ball of hot blue fire forming in the other.

Meara saw their eyes meet, hold. In that exchange she saw a bond she could never share, never really know. Not just of power and magick, but of blood and purpose and knowledge.

There she saw a kinship that ran deeper, wider even than love.

Before she'd caught her breath again, Fin's fancy car spun up. He and Iona bolted from either side. So the four of them stood, united, forming a circle, one where the light undulated and spread until it stung her eyes.

It died away, and it was only her friends, her lover, standing in front of the pretty cottage with its blaze of flowers.

Now when she pushed at the door, it sprang open—and she sprang out.

She marched straight to Connor, shoved him hard enough to knock him back a step. "Don't you ever lock me in or out again. I won't be closed off or tucked away like someone helpless."

"I'm sorry. I wasn't thinking clear. It was wrong of me, and I'm sorry for it."

"You've no right, no right to close me out of it."

"Or me," Boyle said, his face ripe with fury, when he strode up beside her. "Be grateful I don't break your head for it."

"It's grateful I am, and sorry as well."

Meara saw for the first time Alastar had come—he must have all but flown from the stables. So there was horse, hawk, and hound; the dark witches three; and the blood of Cabhan, with his own hawk standing now with Roibeard on the branch of a nearby tree.

And there was herself and Boyle.

"We're a circle or we're not."

"We are." Connor took her hands, gripped them only tighter when she started to yank them free. "We are. It was wrong of me. I jumped straight into the fury of it, and that was wrong as well. And foolish. I shut you out of it, both of you, and that showed you no respect. I'll say again, I'm sorry for it."

"All right then." Boyle shoved at his hair. "Bloody hell I could do with a beer."

"Go on in," Branna told him, glanced around at the others. "Help yourself to what you want. I need a moment with Meara. A moment with Meara," she repeated when Connor continued to grip Meara's hands. "Go, have a beer and open the wine Fin should've brought with him."

"And so I did."

Fin went to his car, fetched out three bottles. "Come on then, Connor. We could all do with a drink after this day."

"Yeah." With some reluctance Connor released Meara's hands, went inside with his friends.

"I've every right to be pissed," Meara began, and found her hands taken again.

"You do, yes, you do, but not only with Connor. I need to tell you that when I ran outside, I knew at once what he'd done, and I was relieved. I'm sorry for it, but I can't let him take full blame."

Stunned, and wounded to the core, Meara stared at Branna. "Do you think because Boyle and I don't have what you have, aren't what you are, we can't fight with you?"

"I think nothing of the kind, nor does Connor. Or Iona, and I imagine she'll be making this same confession to Boyle." When Branna let out a breath, the sound of it was regret.

"It was a moment, Meara, and the weakness was on our part, not yours. You fought with us on the solstice, and I don't want to think what might have happened without you, without Boyle. But for a moment, in the rush of it, I only thought, ah, they'll be safe. That was my weakness. It won't happen again."

"I'm still mad about it."

"I don't blame you a bit for that. But come inside, we'll have some wine and talk about all of it."

"There was nothing weak about the four of you," Meara said, but she started inside with Branna. "The power of you together was blinding. And Connor alone, before you came . . . I saw him on the solstice, but that was a blur of fear and action and violence all at once. I've never seen him as he was for that moment you speak of. Alone, with the hawk on his shoulder, and so full of what he is . . . *radiant* I suppose is the word, though it seems too soft and benign for it. I thought if I touched him now it would burn."

"He's slow to anger, our Connor, as you know. When he reaches it, it's fierce—but never brutal."

Before Branna shut the door she took a long last look at the woods, at the road, at the blaze of flowers along her cottage skirts. She went with Meara back to the kitchen where the wine was open, and the air smelled of the rich, silky sauce she'd spent a good chunk of her day preparing.

"It's near to ready," she announced and took the wine Fin poured her. "So the lot of you can make yourself useful getting the table set."

"It smells amazing," Iona commented.

"Because it is. We can talk about all of this while we feast. Connor, there's bread wrapped in the cloth there."

He got it, set it out, turned to Meara. "Am I to be forgiven?"

"I haven't gotten there yet. But I'm moving in that general direction."

"Then I'll be grateful for that."

Branna served the beef bourguignon on a long platter showcasing the herbed beef and vegetables in the dark sauce, surrounded by roasted new potatoes and garnished with sprigs of rosemary.

"It really is a feast," Iona marveled. "It must have taken hours."

"It did, so no one's allowed to bolt it down." Branna ladled it herself into her pretty shallow bowls before she sat. "And so, all of us have had a day or two." She spread her napkin across her lap before spooning up the first sample. "Meara, you should begin."

"Well, I suppose we all know where we were before this morning, but we've not been together to talk over today. I was guiding a group of four, and in fact, we rode by Connor, who had a group of his own. I took them around the longest route we use, even let them have a bit of a trot here and there, as they were all solid horsemen. It was when we'd circled back, and were coming through the woods, the narrow trail now. I saw the wolf in the trees, watching, keeping pace. But . . ."

She searched for the words. "He was like the shadows that play there, when the sun dapples through the leaves. More formed than that, but not formed. I felt I could almost see through him, though I couldn't. The horses saw or sensed, I couldn't say which, but the riders behind me, they didn't. They kept on talking together, even laughing. It was no more than a minute, and Roibeard flew in. The wolf, it didn't run away so much as fade away."

"A projection," Fin suggested.

"Not in the usual way." As he ate, Connor shook his head. "As I saw it as well. A shadow's close. My sense was of something not quite here, not quite there. Not as he was outside here, not a thing with weight and full form, but with power nonetheless."

"Something new then," Fin considered. "Balancing between two planes, or shifting between them, as he can shift time at Sorcha's cabin."

"It pulls from him though. If you watch the stone, his power source, it ebbs and flows." Meara glanced at Connor for confirmation.

"That's true enough, but as with any skill, the power of it grows as you hone it."

"The McKinnons, the people I guided," Meara continued, "they saw nothing."

"To them he was a shadow," Fin said. "Nothing more."

"A shadow spell." Branna considered it. "I've seen a thing or two in Sorcha's book that might be useful."

"And did you get the way of this from her book?" Fin asked as he ate. "For it's magick. I've had this dish at a tony restaurant in Paris, and it didn't match yours."

"It turned out well."

"It's brilliant," Boyle said.

"It is," Branna said with a laugh. "It takes forever as the sauce is fussy, and not something I'll do often. But today it gave me time to think in the back of my brain. He's pushing at Meara now as he did with Iona before. Testing the edge of things, we could say. And it's Meara, I think, because, in truth, it's Connor he wants to take a run at."

"He went for the boy first." Fin sipped wine as he considered. "A boy, an easy target he might think. But together, Connor and the boy hurt him, drove him away again. And that would be . . . disappointing."

"So he's after a bit of revenge," Boyle continued. "And got a good lick in when he took Connor on. But only a lick come to that. And next he takes aim at Meara."

"After she and Connor had their hot time in the lorry," Iona pointed out. "The power of a kiss."

"Oh, for pity's sake," Meara muttered.

"Sure it's true enough." Under the table, Connor danced his fingers up Meara's thigh and down again. "And when things progress as things do, he comes again. With a shadow spell."

"Could he do harm in that form that's not a form?" Meara wondered.

"I think yes. A delicate balance from what I know," Branna added. "And the conjurer of the spell would have to be able to shift—away, or into full form quickly—without losing that delicate balance."

"If he can do that, why didn't he come at me today? I had a knife, and I'm not helpless, but it would've been his advantage I'd think."

"He wants to unnerve you more than cause you harm," Fin told her. "Hurting you gives him some satisfaction, of course, as causing harm feeds him. But you'd be worth more to him in another area."

"He wants you," Connor said flatly, and with the bubble of that pure rage she'd seen rippling, "because I do. He thinks to seduce you—spellbind you or shake you enough so you don't fight, but run or plead—"

Her eyes fired, black suns. "Neither of those will ever happen."

"We won't underestimate him," Connor snapped back. "It's what he seeks so he can take you. And taking you the way he seeks would harm us all. He understands we're bound, but sees it as a binding for power—only that. Taking you breaks our circle. Be grateful he doesn't understand it's not just a binding for power, but one of love and loyalty. If he understood that, the power of that, he'd hunt you without ceasing."

"You've caught his eye," Fin added, "as he understands sex very well—though with none of its true pleasures or depth. It's another kind of power to him, and he has desire enough for the act of it."

"So the last day or two has been a kind of . . . mating dance?"

"That's not far from the mark," Branna said to Meara. "Sorcha writes of the weeks and weeks he tried to seduce her, bribe her, threaten her, wear down her mind and spirit. He wanted her power without question, but he wanted her body as well—and he wanted to make a child with her, I think."

"I'd slit my own throat before I'd let him rape me."

"Don't say that." The bubble of fury burst as Connor rounded on her. "Don't ever say such a thing again."

"Don't." Iona spoke quietly before Meara could fling words back. "Connor's right. Don't say that. We'll protect you. We're a circle, and we protect each other. You'll protect yourself, but you need to trust us to protect you."

"I'll say something here." Before he did, Boyle helped himself to another ladle of stew. "The four of you can't and don't fully understand what it is for Meara and me. We have our fists, our wits, a blade, instincts, strategies. But these are ordinary things. I'm not after poking at a spot still sore, but when a thought from you can lock us away, out of the mix, it comes home we've only those ordinary things."

"Boyle, you have to know—"

Fin stopped Iona, a light brush on her arm. "And I'll say something back to that—as an outsider. One step back," he insisted as Iona sent him a sorrowful look. "We're not the three, but with the three. Another delicate balance we could say. What we bring to the circle is as vital as the other end of that balance. The three might think it different from time to time, and some with the three might think different, but it is what it is, and that's for us all to remember and respect."

"You're eating at my table," Branna said quietly. "Food I made. I've given you respect."

"You have, and I'm grateful. But it's come time for you to open the door again, Branna, and let me work with you without me having to pry that door open. It's Meara we're speaking of, and the whole of it that hangs in that balance."

Branna's fingers tightened on the stem of her wineglass, then relaxed again. "You're right, and I'm sorry for it. And I see he's shaken us. That's a victory for him, and it ends now."

"We can't understand what it is not to be what we are. Iona would, I think," Connor continued, "as what she is, and has, was held back from her for so long. But I think you—and you as well, Fin—don't understand that for Branna and for me, knowing you're with us, when for Fin, going back to Paris and his fine restaurant would be an easier choice, for you, Meara, and for you, Boyle, not having power but being with us, is braver by far than going on with this, as Branna and I, and now Iona must do. We must, but you, all three of you choose. We don't forget that. Don't think, don't ever think, we do."

"We're not looking for gratitude," Boyle began.

"Well, you have it, want it or not. And admiration as well, even if there's been times, and will be again, we don't show it."

Rising, Branna got another bottle of wine, poured it all around. "For feck's sake, do you think I spend hours cooking a meal like this for myself? I do fine with a bacon sandwich. So we'll all of us stop feeling sorry for ourselves, or sorry to each other, and just be."

Very deliberately Meara scooped up more stew. "It's a gorgeous meal, Branna."

"Bloody right it is, and unless all of you want nothing but that bacon sandwich next time you come, we'll set all that business aside.

Now, why do we think Cabhan jumped on the bonnet of Connor's lorry?"

"I might be risking that bacon sandwich, though they're tasty enough," Fin said, "but answering that, for what I think myself, digs back into the other a bit."

"Answer." Branna waved a hand in the air. "I'll decide whether you eat at all next time."

"He wanted to see what would happen. He was fully formed."

"He was," Meara agreed. "Muscle, bone, and blood."

"But he was quick about it. A leap without warning—where Connor had no sense of it, nor did I, and we weren't far off. Then a leap back, wherever he's biding his time. But in that time, what did he learn?"

"I'm not following you," Boyle said.

"What did he see Connor do? Get out to face him alone—deliberately alone as he closed you and Meara inside. Protected you. And he saw Branna run out—armed, but again alone—to go to her brother."

"Then Iona and you," Meara added.

"He was gone by the time I joined, by the time we made the circle. Watching?" Fin shrugged. "I can't say for certain, but I had no sense of him."

"Nor did I," Connor said when Fin glanced at him.

"So it showed him Connor's first instinct is to protect. His woman— Oh, don't be so fragile about it," Fin said when Meara sputtered a protest. "His woman, his friend. Move the risk away and protect. Branna's is to go to Connor's side, as his would be to go to hers. But she protects as well, as she didn't move to release Meara or Boyle to increase the numbers."

"It was wrong of me as well, and I've apologized to Meara already. Now I apologize to you, Boyle."

"We've covered it all, and it's forgotten."

"He won't forget." Iona glanced around, understanding. "And he'll use what he knows, try to use it, work it in somehow."

"So we find a way to use what he knows, or thinks he knows, against him." Pleased with the idea, Meara grinned around the table. "How do we use me to trap him?"

"We won't be doing that." Connor put a firm cork in that idea bottle. "We tried it, didn't we, with Iona, and it didn't work—nearly lost her to him."

"If at first you don't succeed."

"Fuck it and try something else," Connor finished.

"I choose. Remember your own fine words. I'll ask you," she said to Fin. "Is there a way to use me to lure him?"

"I can't say—and not because I don't want to tangle with Connor, or Branna come to that. But because we'd all need time to think it through, and carefully. I'm no more willing than Connor to risk as close a call as we had with Iona on the solstice."

"I've no argument with that."

"We'll think on it, and all must agree in the end." He looked at Connor, got a nod. "And we'll work on it, use what we know, refine what we had, as it was close to the mark." He looked at Branna.

"It was, as Sorcha's poison was. But neither finished him. I can't find what we missed—and yes, we should work together. You've a good hand with potions and spells. We have until Samhain."

"Why Samhain?" Connor asked her.

"The beginning of winter, the eve of the beginning of the year itself for us—the Celts. I thought on this while making this meal. We thought the longest day—light over dark—but I think that was wrong. Maybe this is something we missed. Samhain, for we need some time, but as he's coming after one of us so blatantly, we can't take too much of it."

"On the night the Veil is thin," Connor considered. "And where it's said no password is needed to move from realm to realm. That could be it, one of the things we missed. He can pass easy as walking across the room. On that night, it may be we can do the same without struggling first to find where, or when."

"The night when the dead come to seek the warmth of the Samhain fire," Fin added, "and the comfort of their blood kin."

"The dead—ghosts now?" Meara demanded. "Witches aren't enough for us now."

"Sorcha," Branna said simply.

"Ah. You think she could come, add to the power. Sorcha, and the first three as well?"

"It's what we'll think on, work on. If we're all agreed to it."

"I like it." Boyle lifted his glass to Branna. "All Hallow's Eve it is."

"If we can hold him off that long, and learn enough," Branna qualified.

"We can. We will," Connor said decisively. "I've always been partial to Samhain—and not just for the treats. I had a fine conversation once with my great-granny on Samhain."

"Who was dead at the time, I suppose."

He winked at Meara. "Oh, gone years before I was born. When the Veil thins I'm able to see through it easier than other times. And since we're all thinking he's testing me, in particular, it might be I'm the lure we're after. And you thought of that," he said to Fin.

"It crossed my mind. We'll think a great deal more, talk it through, and work carefully. I can give you all the time you need, Branna. At any time."

"No ramblings coming up?" she asked carelessly.

"Nothing that can't be postponed or put off. I'm here till this is done."

"And then?"

He looked at her, said nothing for a long beat. "Then, we'll see what we see."

"He's only made us stronger." Iona took Boyle's hand. "Families fight, and they make mistakes. But they can come back stronger for it. We have."

"To squabbles and fuckups then."

Connor raised his glass, the rest lifted theirs, and with a musical clink, sealed the toast.

12

H E KNEW IT FOR A DREAM. IN HIS MIND'S EYE HE COULD
see himself, tucked warm and naked in bed with Meara, and
could—if he drifted back, feel her heart beat slow and steady
against his.

Safe and warm in bed, he thought.

But as he walked the woods, the chill hung in the night air, and
the clouds that flirted with the three-quarter moon deepened dark
shadows.

"What are we looking for?" Meara asked him.

"I don't know till I find it. You shouldn't be here." He stopped to
cup her face in his hands. "Stay in bed, sleep safe."

"You won't lock me in or away." Firmly, she gripped his wrists.
"You promised it. And it's my dream as much as yours."

He could send her back, into dreams where she wouldn't remember. But it would be the same as a lie.

"Keep close then. I don't know the way here."

"We're not home."

"We're not."

Meara lifted the sword she carried so the blade caught the filtered light of the moon. "Did you give me the sword or did I bring it in myself?"

"I don't know that either." Something shimmered over his skin, teased the edges of his senses. "There's something in the air."

"Smoke."

"Aye, and more." He lifted his hand, held a ball of light. He used it as a kind of torch, dispelling shadows to better see the way.

A deer stepped onto the rough path, its rack a crown of silver, its hide a glimmer of gold. It stood a moment, statue still, as if allowing them to bask in its beauty, then turned and walked regally through the swirl of mist.

"Do we follow the hart?" Meara wondered. "As in song and story?"

"We do." But he kept the light glowing. The trees thickened, and there was the scent of green and earth and smoke as the hart moved with unhurried grace.

"Does this happen often for you? This sort of dream?"

"Not often, but it's not the first—though the first I've had company from my side of things. There, do you see? Another light up ahead."

"Barely, but yes. It could be a trap. Can you feel him, Connor? Is he here with us?"

"The air's full of magicks." So full he wondered she couldn't feel it. "The black and the white, the dark and the light. They beat like pulses."

"And crawl on the skin."

So she could feel them. "You won't go back?"

"I won't, no." But she stayed close as they followed the hart toward the light.

Connor cast himself forward, let himself see. And made out the shape, then the face in the shadowed light.

"It's Eamon."

"The boy? Sorcha's son? We're back centuries."

"So it seems. He's older, still a boy yet, but older." So Connor cast out again, this time speaking mind to mind. *It's Connor of the O'Dwyers who comes. Your blood, your friend.*

He felt the boy relax—a bit. *Come then, and welcome. But you are not alone.*

I bring my friend, and she is yours as well.

The hart drifted off into the dark as the lights merged. Connor saw the little cottage, a small lean-to for horses, a garden of herbs and medicinal plants, well tended.

They'd made a life here, he thought, Sorcha's three. And a good one.

"You are welcome," Eamon repeated, and set his light aside to clasp Connor's hand. "And you," he said to Meara. "I thought not to see you again."

"Again?"

Now the boy looked closer, looked deep with eyes as blue as the hawk's-eye stone he wore around his neck. "You are not Aine?"

"A goddess?" Meara laughed. "No indeed."

"Not the goddess but the gypsy named for her. You are very like her, but not, I see, not her at all."

"This is Meara, my friend, and yours. She is one of our circle. Tell me, cousin, how long has it been for you since you saw me?"

"Three years. But I knew I would see you again. The gypsy told me, and I saw she had the gift. She came to trade one spring morning, and told me she'd followed the magicks and the omens to our door. So she said I had kin from another time, and we would meet again, in and out of dreams."

"In and out," Connor considered.

"She said we would go home again, and meet our destiny. You have her face, my lady, and her bearing. You come from her, she who called herself Aine. So I'll thank you as I did her for giving me hope when I needed it."

He looked at Connor. "It was after our first winter here, and the dark seemed never to lift. I pined for home, despaired of seeing it again."

He'd grown tall, Connor observed, and confident. "You've made a home here."

"We live, and we learn. It's good land here, and the wild of it calls. But we, the three, must see home again before we can make our own, and keep it."

"But it's not time yet, is it? I'll trust you'll know when it is. Your sisters are well?"

"They are, and thank you. I hope your sister is the same."

"She is. We're six. The three and three more, and we learn as well. He has something new. A shadow spell, a way to balance between worlds and forms. Your mother wrote something of shadows, and my Branna studies her book."

"As does my sister. I'll tell her of this. Or will you come in. I'll wake her and Teagan as they'd be happy to meet you both."

Eamon started to turn to the cottage door.

For Meara it all happened at once.

Connor whirled and Eamon with him as if they were one form. The big gray—and it gave her a jolt to see Alastar, the same as the stallion she knew—charged from the lean-to. Almost as one, Roibeard dived, Kathel leaped.

Before she could fully turn, Connor yanked her back and behind him just as the wolf sprang.

It came from nowhere, silent as a ghost, quick as a snake.

In a blur, it dodged Alastar's flashing hooves and charged. Straight at the boy, she realized, and without thought, shoved Eamon to the side, swung her sword.

She struck air, but even that sang up her arms to her shoulders.

Then the full force of the wolf struck her, sent her flying. Pain, the shock of it, the bitter, bitter cold of it ripped through her side. Instinct—survival—had her clamping her hands around its throat to hold back the snap of its jaws.

And again, it happened at once.

The hound attacked, and light burst so bright it burned the air to red. Shouts and snarls tore through that searing curtain while her muscles quivered at the strain of holding back those snapping jaws. She heard herself scream, felt no shame in it as the wolf screamed as well.

She saw rage in its eyes, murderous and crazed, before it wavered, faded, vanished as it had come. Out of nowhere.

Her name, Connor saying it over and over and over. She couldn't get her breath, simply couldn't draw in the air—air that stank like brimstone.

Warm hands on her side, warm lips on her lips. "Let me see now, let me see. Ah, God, God. Not to worry, *aghra*, I'll fix it. Lie quiet."

"I can help you."

She heard the voice, saw the face. Branna's face, but younger. She remembered that face, Meara thought through the pain, the liquid daze of it all. Remembered it from her own youth.

"You'll look like her in a few years. Our Branna's a rare beauty."

"Lie quiet, lady. Teagan, fetch—ah well, she already is. My sister's getting the rest I need. I'm skilled, cousin," she said to Connor. "You'll trust me to this?"

"I will." But he took Meara's hand. "Here now, darling, here, *mo chroi*, look at me. At me, into me."

So she went dreaming, dreaming into those green eyes, outside of pain, outside of all but him. And him murmuring sweet things to her as he did when they loved.

Then Iona—no Teagan, the youngest—Teagan, held a cup to her lips, and the taste on her tongue, down her throat, was lovely.

Now when she drew in breath, true and deep, it tasted the same—of the green and the earth, the peat fire, and the herbs thriving nearby.

"I'm all right."

"Another moment, just another moment. How could he come here?" Brannaugh asked Connor. "We're beyond him here."

"But I'm not. Somehow I brought him, gave him passage. A trap it was after all. Using me to get to you, Eamon, and your sisters. I led him here, led him to this."

"No, he used us both, our dreams."

"And drew us in as well," Brannaugh said. "There's none of his dark left in you, my lady. Can you sit now, easy and slow?"

"I'm fine. Better than I was before the wound. You have her skill, or she has yours."

"You stood for my brother. If you hadn't risked yourself, he would be hurt, or worse, for Cabhan wanted his blood, his death."

"Your sword." Teagan laid it over Meara's legs.

"There's blood on it. I thought the strike missed."

"You struck true."

"'Tis shadow magick," Brannaugh stated.

"It is," Connor agreed. "As long as I'm here, he can come again. I do you more harm than good by staying."

"Would you take this, if you please?" Teagan held out a flower topping its bulb. "And when you can, if you'd plant this near our mother's grave. She favored bluebells."

"I will, yes, soon as I'm able. I must go, must take Meara back."

"I'm fine," she said.

"I'm not. Have a care, all of you." He wrapped his arms tight around Meara, pressed his face into her hair.

She woke in bed, sitting up with Connor's arms around her, with him rocking her as he might a baby.

"I had a dream."

"Not a dream, or not only a dream. Shh now, give me a moment."

His lips pressed onto her hair, her temples, her cheeks, all slow and deliberate.

"Let me see your side."

"It's fine. I'm fine," she insisted as he shifted her, ran his hands over her. "In fact I feel someone dosed me with a magick elixir. And I suppose that's just what happened. How did it happen? Any of it, all of it?"

"Eamon dreamed of me and I of him. He drew me to him, and I drew you with me. And likely Cabhan set the stage for it all."

His hands fisted in her hair until he carefully relaxed them again.

"To use me, my dreaming, to attack Eamon."

"You pushed me behind you."

"And you did the same with Eamon. We do what we do." On a sigh, he laid his forehead on hers. "Your sword struck his flank, and his claws yours, but he was still part in shadow so the blade drew his blood, but didn't stop him. That's my theory on it."

"He came out of the air, Connor. How do we fight what comes out of the air?"

"As we did. The light drove him back—Eamon's and mine joined, then the girls."

"He screamed," Meara remembered. "It didn't sound like an animal, but a man."

"Balancing between worlds, and forms. It's catching him when he steps off on one or the other, I think. It's near dawn. It'll be an ugly business, but I'm waking Branna. I'll leave it to you to ring up the others. This is something to share with all and straightaway."

But first he cupped her face in his hands as he had in the dreaming time. "Don't be so fucking brave next time, for the next time might kill me where I stand."

"He was just a boy, Connor, and straight in its path. And he looks like you, or you look like him. The shape of the face," she added, "his mouth, his nose, even the way he stands."

"Is that so?"

"Harder to see it yourself, I'd think, but it's very so. I'll ring Iona, then she'll be in charge of waking Boyle, who can wake Fin."

"All right." He ran his hands through her hair, long and waving as he'd released it from its braid the night before. "Whoever gets downstairs first puts on the bleeding coffee."

"Agreed." Because she could see the worry in his eyes still, she leaned in to kiss him. "Go on, you've got the worst job between us in waking Branna when the sun's barely up."

"Have the first-aid kit ready." He rolled out of bed, yanked on his pants.

As he left, Meara reached over for her phone, and saw the bluebell. Thinking of Teagan, so like the girl Iona must have been, she rose, fetched a glass of water from the bathroom, set the bulb in it.

For Sorcha, she thought, then called Iona.

She made it down first, did her duty with the coffee. She considered making oatmeal, the only breakfast meal she had a decent enough hand with. And Connor nearly always scorched the eggs if he had charge of breakfast.

She was spared when Branna came in. Her friend wore blue and green striped flannel pants with a thin green top. She'd tied a little blue sweater over it, and that somehow matched the thick socks on her feet.

Her hair spilling free to her waist, Branna marched straight for the coffee. "Don't talk to me, not a word, until I've had my coffee. Put some potatoes on the boil, and when they're soft enough, chip them up for frying."

She drank the coffee black rather than adding the good dose of cream that was her usual.

"I swear an oath, there's a time coming soon when I'll not step near a stove for a month."

"You'll have earned it. I'm not talking to anyone in particular,"

Meara said quickly as she scrubbed potatoes in the sink. "Just making some general observations."

"Bloody Cabhan," Branna muttered, as she pulled things from the fridge. "I'll kill him with my own hands, I swear *another* oath, for forcing me to see so many sunrises. The eggs are going scrambled, and whoever doesn't like it doesn't have to eat them."

Wisely, Meara said nothing, but put the potatoes on the boil.

Muttering all the while, Branna put on sausage, started on the bacon, sliced bread from the loaf for toast.

Then downed more coffee.

"I want to see your side."

Meara stopped herself from saying she was fine, simply lifted up her shirt.

Branna laid her fingers on it—how did she know the exact spot—probed for a moment. Meara felt heat slide in, and out again.

Then Branna met her eyes, just moved in and wrapped around her tight.

"It's healed perfectly. Damn it, Meara. Damn it."

"Don't start now. I've had it from Connor already. You'd think I'd been gutted instead of getting a bit of a swipe."

"What do you think he was aiming for if not your guts?" But Branna stepped back, pressed the heels of her hands to her eyes. Breathed deep before she dropped them again.

"All right then. Let's get this bloody breakfast on. Connor Sean Michael O'Dwyer! Get your arse down here and do something with this breakfast besides eat it."

As he appeared seconds later, he'd obviously been waiting for her to settle. "Whatever you like. I can do the eggs."

"You'll not touch them. Set the table as it seems I'll be cooking for six the rest of my life. And when you're done with that, you can start on the toast."

The potatoes were frying when the others arrived.

"You're all right?" Iona went straight to Meara. "You're sure?"

"I am. More than all right as I'm bristling with energy from whatever potion they gave me."

"Let me see it." Fin nudged Iona aside.

"Am I going to have to lift my shirt for everyone?" But she did so, frowning a bit as Fin laid his hand on her. "Branna's already had a poke at me."

"He's my blood. If there's even a trace of him, I'll know. And there's none." Gently, Fin drew her shirt into place again. "I wouldn't have you hurt, *mo deirfiúr*."

"I know it. Sure there was a moment, and I wouldn't care to repeat it, but the rest? It was a fascination. You went with Iona once," she said to Boyle.

"I did, so I know the sensation. Like dreaming but more like walking, talking, doing while you dream. It makes you a bit light-headed."

"You should sit," Iona decided. "Just sit down. I'll help Branna finish breakfast."

"You'll not," Branna said definitely. "Boyle, you're the only one of the lot who doesn't have ham hands in the kitchen. Scramble up the eggs, will you, as I've nearly finished the rest."

He went over to the stove beside her, poured the beaten eggs from the bowl into a skillet where she'd melted butter.

"All right then?" he asked.

Branna leaned against him a moment. "I will be."

She turned the heat off under the potatoes, began to scoop them out with a slotted tool onto paper towels to drain. "Why didn't I feel any of it?" she wondered. "I slept straight through it all, never knowing a thing."

"Why didn't I, or Iona?" Fin countered from behind her. "It wasn't our dream; we didn't have a part in it."

"I was right in the same house, only just down the hall. I should've sensed something."

"I can see as you're the center of this world how you're deserving a piece of all of it."

When she rounded on him, eyes flashing, narrowed, Iona stepped up. "Stop it, just stop it, both of you. You're each blaming yourselves, and that's stupid. Neither of you is responsible. The only one who is, is Cabhan, so knock it off. My blood, my brother," she added before the pair of them could speak. "Blah, blah, blah. So what? We're all in this. Why don't we find out exactly what happened before we start dividing up the blame?"

"You're marrying a bossy woman, *mo dearthair*," Fin said to Boyle. "And a sensible one. Sit, Iona, and Meara as well. I'll get your coffee."

Iona sat, folded her hands neatly on the table. "That would be very nice."

"Don't bleed it out," Meara warned, and joined her.

At Branna's direction, Boyle piled eggs on the platter with the sausage, bacon, potatoes, fried tomatoes, and black pudding.

He carted it to the table while Fin served the coffee and Connor poured out juice.

"Take us through it," Fin told Connor.

"It started as they do—as if you're fully awake and aware and somewhere else all at once. In Clare we were, though I didn't know it at first. In Clare, and in Eamon's time."

He wound through the story as they all served themselves from the huge platter.

"A hart?" Branna interrupted. "Was it real, or did you bring it into it?"

"I wouldn't have thought of it. If I'd wanted a guide, I'd have pulled in Roibeard. It was a massive buck, and magnificent. Regal, and with a hide more gold than brown."

"Blue eyes," Meara added.

"You're right. They were. Bold and blue, like Eamon's, come to think of it."

"Or his father's," Branna pointed out. "In Sorcha's book she writes her son has his father's eyes, his coloring."

"You think it was Daithi," Connor considered, "or representing him. He might be given that form to be near his children, protect them as best he can."

"I hope it's true," Iona said quietly. "He was killed riding home to protect them."

"The hart that might have been Daithi's spirit guided us toward the light, and the light was Eamon. Three years in his time since we last met. He was taller, and his face fined down as it does when you're passing out of childhood. He's a handsome lad."

Now he grinned at Meara.

"He'd say that, as I told him they favor each other. Different coloring to be sure, but you'd know they're kin."

"He thought Meara was Aine—a gypsy," Connor explained. "One who'd passed through some time before, and told him they'd see home again."

"That's interesting. You have gypsy in your heritage," Iona pointed out.

"I do."

"And Fin named the filly he chose for Alastar Aine."

"I thought of that, and take it doesn't mean I resemble a horse."

"Of great beauty and spirit," Fin pointed out. "The name was hers—I never considered another. It was who she was the moment I saw her. Sure it's interesting, the connections, the overlaps."

"It's that I felt nothing while we talked, there outside the cottage. Nor did he," Connor considered. "We asked after family. I told him of the shadow spell. And it was when he asked if we'd come inside that it happened. One minute I felt nothing, then I felt him there. Just there an instant before the wolf leaped out of the air. And he felt it as well."

"You spun around together, like one person," Meara added. "It was all so fast. Connor pushed me back behind him, but it wasn't me, it was the boy, he wanted."

"And so she pushed Eamon aside, exposed herself, and swung the sword. Not even a second, no time to throw out a block of any kind. He rammed her full, clawed her. Her blood and his in the air. The hound charged. Eamon and I joined, and the girls rushed out. It was they who threw a block, stopping me from rushing forward, throwing what they had at him, so it was me who joined with them as there was nothing else to do in those few seconds. What we had was enough to give him pain, with Kathel, Roibeard, and Alastar going at him along with us. He screamed like a girl."

"Hey!"

He managed a grin at Iona. "No offense meant. Between us and Kathel, Alastar's hooves and Roibeard's talons, he went as he'd come. Gone, vanished, leaving only the stench of hell behind him. And Meara bleeding on the ground. And not two minutes, when I look back calm, not two minutes between."

"They've all been short, haven't they? Something to consider," Branna said. "It may be he only has enough power for those short bursts with this spell."

"For now," Fin added.

"For now is what we have. He hitched onto Connor's dream, slithered into it to try to get the boy—or one of the sisters if they'd greeted you, Connor. He can't get into the house, but into a dream, once you've moved out of its protection . . . I can see this. He can't get to them in that time, in that place, but could link to the dream to go there."

"Where the boy would've been vulnerable," Fin added, "in the half world of active dreaming. Then Cabhan waits on the edges of it, waits to attack—until you turn your back."

"Bloody coward," Boyle muttered.

"You said Meara spilled his blood. Where's your sword?" Branna demanded.

"At home. I never brought it here. 'Twas just in my hand in the dream."

"I'll go get it," Fin said. "Where do you have it?"

"It's on the shelf in the closet in my bedroom. I'll get you the key to the flat." When he only smiled, she sat back again. "Which you don't need at all, do you? Which is a thought that never occurred to me. Any of the four of you could walk right in as you please."

"I'll bring it. It won't take but a few moments."

"I appreciate the respect, as you know I don't approve of taking the easy way when a bit of effort and time does the job. But." Branna sighed. "We're beyond that, and it's foolish for you to drive into the village and back."

Fin merely nodded. He lifted his hand, and in a flash held Meara's sword.

Meara jolted, then laughed a little. "Well, that's brilliant, and it's so rare to see any of you do that sort of thing, I sometimes forget you can."

"Fin's a bit freer with it than Branna," Boyle pointed out.

"We all don't have the same boundaries." Fin turned the sword. "There's blood on it, and fresh enough."

"I won't have blood or swords at my table." Branna rose, took it from him. "It's enough to work with. I still have some from the solstice. But as you said, this is fresh—and it's from him when he was wounded during a shadow spell."

"I'll come back, work with you as soon as I can get away," Connor told her.

"So will I," Iona added. "We're really busy this morning, but I think my bosses might give me some flex time this afternoon."

Boyle ran a hand over Iona's cap of hair. "They might be persuaded.

I'll bring Meara back as well if you can use us. We can bring food if nothing else."

"It's quite a bit else." Branna continued to study the sword. "As there isn't enough of the fancy French stew to go full around a second time."

"We'll see to that then, Meara and myself, and come back around as soon as we can close things up at the stables. I'll send Iona off soon as I can."

"I'll come get her," Connor said. "I think we're back to no one wandering around on their own, at least for a bit. I can juggle the scheduling and be off by three if that suits."

"Well enough."

"I'll stay now." There was a beat of silence as Fin spoke. "If *that* suits."

"It does." Branna lowered the sword. "The lot of you can put my kitchen back to rights. I'll be in the workshop when you're done," she said to Fin, and walked out.

13

MEARA SPENT MOST OF HER NEXT FREE DAY AT HER mother's helping with the last of the packing up for what they were all calling The Long Visit. And as packing required making decisions—what should be taken, what should be left behind, what might be given away or simply tossed in the bin—Meara spent most of her free day with a throbbing headache.

Decisions, and Meara knew it well, put Colleen Quinn in a state of dithering anxiety. The simple choice of whether to take her trio of pampered African Violets nearly brought her to tears.

"Well, of course you'll take them." Meara struggled to find balance on a thin midway line between good cheer and firmness.

"If I leave them, you and Donal will have the bother of watering and feeding them, and if you forget . . ."

"I can promise not to forget." Because she'd take them straight to Branna, who'd know how to tend them. "But you should have them with you."

"Maureen might not want them in her house."

"Now why wouldn't Maureen want them?" Teetering on that thin line, Meara pasted a determined smile on her face as she lifted one of the fuzzy-leafed plants, pregnant with purple blooms. "They're lovely."

"Well, it's *her* house, isn't it?"

"And you're her mother, and they're your plants."

Decision made—by God—Meara set them carefully in boxes she'd begged off the market.

"Oh, but—"

"They'll ride safe in here." *Seven times seven is—bugger it—forty-nine.* "And haven't you said plants are living things, and how they respond to music and conversation and affection? They'd miss you and likely wilt, however careful I was with them."

Inspired, Meara sang "On the Road Again" as she tucked balled paper around the pots. At least that got a glimmer of a smile from Colleen.

"You've such a beautiful singing voice."

"I got it from my mother, didn't I?"

"Your father has a fine, strong voice as well."

"Hmm" was Meara's response to that as she multiplied in her head. "Well now, you'll want some of your photos, won't you, to put around your room."

"Oh." Colleen immediately linked her fingers together as she did when she didn't know whether to turn left or right. "I'm not sure, and how would I choose which. And—"

"I'll choose, then it'll be a nice surprise for you when you unpack. You know, I could do with some tea."

"Oh. I'll make some."

"That would be grand." And provide five minutes of peace.

With Colleen in the kitchen, Meara quickly snatched framed photos—captured moments of the past, of her childhood, of her siblings, and, though it didn't sit particularly well, of her parents together.

She studied one of her parents, smiling out with the lush gardens of the big house they'd once had surrounding them. A handsome face, she thought, studying her father. A fine, strapping man with all the charm in the world.

And no spine whatsoever.

She wrapped the photo to protect the glass of the frame, tucked it in the box. She might be of the opinion her mother would be better off without the constant reminder of what had been, but it wasn't her life to live.

And that life, right at the moment, fit into two suitcases, a shoulder tote, and three market boxes.

There would be more if the move became permanent—a word Colleen wasn't ready to hear. More packing to do, but much more than that, Meara was sure, more life to be lived.

Considering the job done—or nearly enough—she went back to the kitchen. And found her mother sitting at the tiny table, weeping quietly into her hands.

"Ah, Ma."

"I'm sorry, I'm sorry. I haven't made the tea. I feel at sea, Meara. I've lived in Cong and hereabouts all my life. And now . . ."

"It's not far. You'll not be far." Sitting, Meara took her hands. "Not even a full hour away."

Colleen looked up, tearfully. "But I won't see you or Donal as I do."

"It's just a visit, Ma."

"I may never come back here. It's what you're all thinking for me."

With little choice, Meara shouldered the guilt. "It's what we're all thinking you'll want once you're there a little while. If you stay in Galway with Maureen and Sean and the kids, we'll visit. Of course we will. And if you're not happy there, you'll come back here. Haven't I said I'll see the cottage is right here for you?"

"I hate this place. I hate everything about this place."

Stunned, Meara opened her mouth, then shut it again without an idea what to say.

"No, no, that's not right, that's not true." Rocking herself, Colleen pressed her hands to her face. "I love the gardens. I do. I love seeing them, front and back, and working in them. And I'm grateful for the cottage, for it's a sweet little place."

Taking a tissue from her pocket, Colleen dabbed away the tears. "I'm grateful to Finbar Burke for renting it to me for far less than a fair price—and to you for paying it. And to Donal for staying with me so long. To all of you for seeing someone rang me every day to see how I was doing. For taking me on little holidays. I know you've all conspired so I'll move off to Galway with Maureen for my own good. I'm not altogether stupid."

"You're not stupid at all."

"I'm fifty-five years old, and I can't roast a joint of lamb."

Because that brought on another spate of weeping, Meara tried another tact. "It's true enough you're a bloody terrible cook. When I'd come home from school and smell your pot roast cooking, I'd ask God what I'd done to deserve such punishment."

Colleen goggled for a long minute, tears shimmering on her cheeks. Then she laughed. The sound was a bit wild, but it was a laugh all the same.

"My mother's worse."

"Is that even possible?"

"Why do you think your grandda hired a cook? We'd have starved to death. And bless her, Maureen's not much better."

"That's why they invented take-away." Hoping to stem more weeping, Meara rose to put the kettle on. "I never knew you hated living here."

"I don't. That was wrong and ungrateful. I've a roof over my head, and a garden I'm proud of. I've good neighbors, and you and Donal close. I've hated it's all I have—another's property my daughter pays to keep around me."

"It's not all you have." How blind had she been, Meara wondered, not to see how it would score her mother's pride to live in a rental her child paid for?

"It's only a place, Ma. Just a place. You have your children, your grandchildren, who love you enough to conspire for your happiness. You have yourself, a terrible cook, but a brilliant gardener. You'll be a boon to those grandchildren."

"Will I?"

"Oh, you will. You'll be patient with them, and sincerely interested in their doings and their thoughts. It's different with a parent, isn't it? They have to consider constantly whether to say yes or no, now or later. They have to discipline and enforce as well as love and tend. You'll only have to love, and they'll soak all that up like sponges."

"I do miss having them closer, having the time to spoil them."

"So here's your chance."

"What if Maureen objects to the spoiling?"

"Then I'm off to Galway to kick her arse."

Colleen smiled again as Meara made the tea. "You've always been my warrior. So fierce and brave. I'm hoping I'll have grandchildren from you to spoil one day."

"Ah well."

"I've heard you and Connor O'Dwyer are seeing each other."

"I've been seeing Connor O'Dwyer all my life."

"Meara."

No avoiding it, Meara thought, and brought the tea to the little table. "We're seeing each other."

"I'm as fond of him as I can be. He's a fine man, and so handsome as well. A good heart and a kind nature. He comes to see me now and then, just to see how I'm faring, and to ask if there's any little thing he can do around the place."

"I didn't know, but it's like him."

"He has a way about him, and though I know the way of the world, I can't approve of . . . that is, the sex before marriage."

Holy Mary, Meara prayed, have mercy and spare me from the sex talk.

"Understood."

"I feel the same with Donal and Sharon, but . . . A man's a man, after all, and they'll want such things with or without Holy Matrimony."

"As do women, Ma, and I hate to break the news to you, but I'm a woman grown."

"Be that as it may," Colleen said primly, "you're still my daughter. And despite what the Church says on such matters, I'll hope you'll have a care."

"You can rest easy there."

"I'll rest easy when you're happy and married and starting a family in a home of your own. I'm as fond of Connor as I can be, as I said, but it's a fact he's an eye for the ladies. So have a care, Meara."

When she heard the front door open, Meara offered desperate thanks. "And here's Donal set to take you to Galway," she said brightly. "I'll get another cup for his tea."

SHE THOUGHT TO GO HOME, STARE AT THE WALLS UNTIL SHE felt less frazzled and guilty and generally out of sorts. And ended up driving straight to Branna's.

The minute she'd dashed into the workshop, she saw she'd made a mistake.

Branna and Fin stood together at the big work counter, their hands poised over a silver bowl. Whatever brew it contained glowed, a hard orange light that swirled up a thin column of smoke.

Branna held up a finger of her free hand, a signal to wait.

"Yours and yours and me and mine, life and death together twine. Blood and tears cast and shed mixed together thick and red. Fire and smoke will bubble true and seal your fate with this brew."

It bubbled up, frothed over, a virulent orange.

"Damn it!" Branna stepped back, fisted her hands on her hips. "It's still not right. It should go red, bloodred. Murderous red, and thick. We're still missing something."

"It's damn well not my blood," Fin said. "I've given you a liter already."

"A few drops is all, don't be such a baby." Obviously frustrated, Branna shoved at the hair she'd bundled on top of her head. "I've taken mine and Connor's and Iona's as well, haven't I?"

"And there's three of you to my one."

"Plus what we've used from the vial we have of his from the solstice, and what we're using from the sword."

"You can have mine if you need it," Meara offered. "Otherwise it seems I'm just in the way."

"You're not. It might be we can use another eye, another brain on this. But we're having a break so I can think on this," Branna decided. "We'll have some tea."

"You're upset," Fin said to Meara as Branna mopped up the counter. "You saw your mother off to Galway today."

"Just a bit ago, yes, and with much of the weeping and gnashing of teeth."

"I'm sorry." Immediately Branna came around the counter, rubbed Meara's arm. "I was blocked off in my own frustrations and didn't give a thought to yours. It was hard."

"In some ways more and in others less than I expected. But altogether exhausting."

"I've things I could do and leave the two of you to talk."

"No, don't go on my account. And this gives me the chance to talk to you about the rental."

"It's nothing you need worry over. As I told you, I can hold it until she's decided what she wants to do. It's been hers near to ten years now."

"It's good of you, Fin. I mean it."

Saying nothing, Branna walked over to make the tea.

"I think she won't be back—not to live," Meara said. "I think the change will boost her. The grandchildren, particularly the grandchildren, as she'll be living with some and closer to the rest. Added to it, Maureen's Sean will make a fuss over her, as he's always had a soft spot there. And the fact is, she's not happy on her own. She needs someone not just for conversation but direction, and Maureen will give her both."

"Then stop feeling guilty about it," Fin advised.

"I'm wading in it for a bit." Doing just that, Meara pressed her fingers to her eyes. "She cried so, and said things I didn't know were in her mind or her heart. She's grateful to you, Fin, for the cottage, for the ridiculously low rent you've charged all these years—and I never thought she had any idea about the money at all. But she did, she's grateful, and so am I."

"It's nothing, Meara."

"It is, to her, to me. I couldn't have managed my own rent and hers if hers hadn't been cheaper than dirt even with Donal kicking in, and then there'd have been murder for certain. So you kept her alive and me out of prison, so you'll take the gratitude that's given."

"You're welcome." Then he went to her, drew her in, as she'd started to cry. "Enough now, darling."

"It's just she started crying again when Donal and I loaded her things into the lorry, and she clung to me as if I were going off to war. Which I am, I suppose, but she doesn't know. I swear she's turned a blind eye to what three of my closest friends are about all these years, and now is only somewhat concerned that Connor and I are having sex outside Holy Matrimony."

Though he couldn't help the smile, Fin rubbed her back. "It sounds like a very full day for you."

"Ending with me booting my own mother out of her home."

"You did no such thing. You helped her break a chain that's kept her locked here when she'll be happier in a house filled with family. I'll wager she'll thank you for it before the year's out. Here now, *dubheasa*, dry your eyes."

He stepped back, patted his pockets, then pulled out a handkerchief swirling with color, and made her laugh.

"What's all this?"

"Always a rainbow after the storm." Then plucked an enormous and bright pink daisy from her hair. "And flowers from the rain."

"You'd make a fecking fortune at birthday parties."

"I'll keep that for backup."

"And I'm a complete git."

"Not at all." He gave her another hug. "Only a half a git at best."

He caught Branna's eye over Meara's head. And the smile she sent him stabbed straight into his heart.

SHE DRANK HER TEA, ATE THREE OF BRANNA'S LEMON biscuits, and though she knew next to nothing of writing spells and making potions, did her best to help.

She ground herbs using mortar and pestle—sage, fleabane, rosemary for banishing. She measured out the dust of a crushed black fluorite crystal, snipped lengths of copper twine, marking all amounts precisely in Branna's journal.

By the time Connor arrived, with Iona and Boyle with him, all the ingredients Branna and Fin had chosen were ready.

"We've failed twice with this today," Branna told them, "so we'll hope it's true third time's the charm. Plus we've had Meara's hand in it this time, and that's for luck."

"An apprentice witch are you?" Connor nipped her in for a kiss.

"Hardly, but I can grind and measure."

"Did you see your mother on her way?"

"I did, and mopped her up after she cried her buckets. Then came here where Fin mopped me up in turn."

"Be happy." This time Connor kissed her forehead. "For she will be."

"I'm closer to believing it as Donal texted me not an hour ago to say Maureen's family gave her a queen's welcome, with streamers and flowers, cake and even champagne. I can be a little shamed for not thinking Maureen had it in her to make the fuss, but I'll get past that the first time she pisses me off. Donal says she's giddy as a girl—Ma, not Maureen, so that's a cloud gone from over my head."

"We'll go up and take her out to dinner once we can get away easy."

A good heart, her mother had said. And a kind nature.

"You'd be taking a chance as you're having sex with her daughter outside Holy Matrimony."

"What?"

"I'll explain later. I think Branna wants your blood."

"From all," Branna countered. "As we took from all for the spell before the solstice."

"It didn't finish it." Boyle frowned at the bowl as Branna carefully added ingredients. "Why should this?"

"We have his blood—from the ground, from the blade," Fin said.

"That adds his power to it, it adds the dark, and the dark we'll use against him."

"Cloak the workshop, Connor." Branna measured salt into the bowl. "Iona, the candles if you will. This time we'll do it all together as we're all here, and within a circle.

"Within and without," she began, "without and within, and here the devil's end we'll spin." Taking up a length of copper, she twisted it into the shape of a man. "In shadows he hides, in shadows we'll bide and trap his true form inside. There to flame and burn to ash in the spell we cast."

She set the copper figure on the silver tray with vials, a long crystal sphere, and her oldest athame.

"We cast the circle."

Meara had seen the ritual dozens of times, but it always brought a tingle to her skin. The way a wave of the hand would set the wide ring of white candles to flame, and how the air seemed to hush and still within their ring.

Then stir.

The three and Fin stood at the four points of the compass, and each called on the elements, the god and goddesses, their guides.

And the fire Iona conjured burned white, a foot off the floor with the silver bowl suspended over it.

Herbs and crystals, blessed water poured from Branna's hand— stirred by the air Connor called. Black earth squeezed from Fin's fist dampened by tears shed by a witch.

And blood.

"From a heart brave and true." With her ritual knife Iona scored Boyle's palm. "To mix with mine as one from two."

And scored her own, pressed her hand to his.

"Life and light, burning bright," she said as she let the mixed blood slide into the bowl.

Connor took Meara's hand, kissed her palm. "From a heart loyal and strong." He scored her palm, his. "Join with mine to right the wrong. Life and light, burning bright."

Branna turned to Fin, started to take his hand, but he drew it back, and pulled down the shoulder of his shirt.

"Take it from the mark."

When she shook her head, he gripped her knife hand by the wrist. "From the mark."

"As you say."

She laid the blade on the pentagram, his curse and heritage.

"Blood that runs from this mark, mix with mine. White and dark." When she laid her cut hand on his shoulder, flesh to flesh, blood to blood, the candle flames shot high, and the air trembled.

"Dark and white, power and might, light and life burning bright."

The blood ran in a thin river down her hand, into the bowl. The potion boiled, churned, spewing smoke.

"In the name of Sorcha, all who came before, all who came after, we join our power to make this fight. We cast thee out of shadow and into light."

She tossed the copper figure into the bubbling potion, where it flashed—orange and gold and red flame, a roar like a whirlwind, a thousand voices calling through it.

Then a silence so profound it trembled.

Branna looked into the bowl, breathed out. "It's right. This is right. This can end him."

"Should I release the fire?" Iona asked her.

"We'll leave it to simmer, one hour, then off the flame overnight to cure. And on Samhain, we choke him with it."

"We're done for now then?" Meara asked.

"Done enough so I want to clear my head and drink a good glass of wine."

"Well then, we'll be back in a minute. I just need to . . ." She was already pulling Connor from the room. "Just need Connor for a moment."

"What is it?" He worried, as she had a death grip on his hand while she pulled him out the back of the workshop, through the kitchen. "Are you upset? I know the ritual was intense, but—"

"It was. It was. It was." She all but chanted it, dragging him on through the living area, up the stairs.

"Was it the blood? I know it can seem harsh, but I promise you it's needed to make the potion, to bespell it."

"No. Yes. Jesus. It was all of it!" Breathless, she shoved him into his bedroom, then back against the door to slam it.

Then she covered his mouth with hers, all but fusing their lips with the heat pouring from her.

"Oh," he managed, finally clueing in as she ripped his sweater up and away.

"Just give me." She peeled off the insulated shirt under the sweater, latched her teeth on his bare shoulder. "Just give me."

He'd have slowed things down—a bit—but she was already unhooking his belt, and what was a man to do?

He started tugging up her sweater—undressing a woman was one of the great pleasures of life—got tangled up with her very busy hands. He considered just ripping it away, then—

"Ah, to hell with all that."

The next thing Meara knew she was naked, and so was he.

"Yes, yes, yes." She gripped his hair, assaulted his mouth, moaned with pleasure when he took her breasts.

She'd never been so wild with lust, never known such quaking, roiling need. Perhaps something in the swirling air, the pulse of the fire, the stunning rise and merging of powers and magicks had punched into her.

All she knew was she'd had to have him or go mad.

He still tasted of it, that exotic flavor of magick—potent, seductive, edging toward the dark. She felt the ripples of it still working in him, not yet tamped down.

And wanted that, wanted him, wanted all.

His hands weren't patient now, but greedy and rough and quick. She wanted that as well, craved being touched and taken as if his life depended on it.

It felt as if hers did.

He whipped her around, forced her back to the door. She had an instant to look into his eyes—fierce and feral—before he drove into her.

She'd thought she'd go mad if he didn't take her, and now, being taken, went mad.

Her hips jackhammered, challenging him to match her ferocious pace. Her nails bit into him—back, shoulders—her teeth gnawed and scraped. Little pains, quick and hot, that fired into a crazed pleasure that enslaved him. His blood beat hammer strikes under the skin, so he thrust into her harder, faster, deeper in a brutal, breathless rhythm.

She cried out, a sound that joined shock and greed. And again, this time his name with a kind of wonder. When he gripped her hips, lifted her, she locked her legs around his waist.

He ravaged her throat, filled himself with the taste of her as he filled her with his lust until the last frayed tether snapped.

He broke, swore he felt the very air shatter like glass as she tightened around him, as her final cry died off into a shuddering sigh.

Limp, they slid down to the floor in a sweaty tangle of limbs.

"God. My sweet God." She drew in air like a drowning woman surfacing.

Struggling for breath, he managed a grunt, then flopped off her to lie on his back with his eyes closed and his chest heaving.

"Is the floor shaking?"

"I don't think so." He opened his eyes, stared at the ceiling. "Maybe. No," he decided. "I think we are—or more what you could call vibrating. There are bound to be aftershocks after an earthquake, I'm told."

He reached out blindly to pat her, and his hand landed on her breast. A fine place. "Are you all right then?"

"I'm not all right. I'm amazing and amazed. I feel like I've gone flying again. It was the way you looked—like you'd been lit up from the inside, and your hair flying around in the wind you'd made, and the power of it all beating like tribal drums. I couldn't help it. I'm sorry, but I couldn't control myself."

"You're forgiven. I'm a forgiving sort of man."

She sighed out a laugh, laid a hand over his. "And now here we are, naked and spent on your floor—and your room's a disaster of a mess as always."

He turned his head, glanced around. Not a disaster, exactly, he calculated. True enough there were shoes and boots and clothes and books scattered around. And he'd never seen the point—a severe and sharp bone of contention between him and his sister—on making a bed when you were only going to get back in it again.

To please her, he waved a hand, had the shoes and boots and clothes and books—and whatever else lay on the floor—pile up in a corner. He'd deal with it all—at some point.

But for now he waved his hand again, had rose petals raining down. She laughed, grabbed a handful from the air, then scattered them over his hair.

"You're a foolish romantic, Connor."

"There's not a thing foolish about romance." He drew her over, pillowed her head on his shoulder. "There, that's altogether better."

She couldn't argue, and yet. "We should go down. They'll be wondering what we're up to."

"Oh, I'll wager they know perfectly well what we're up to. So we'll take a little time."

A little, she decided. "I'll need my clothes again—from wherever you sent them."

"I'll get them back to you. But not quite yet."

She let herself be content with her head pillowed on his shoulder, and the air full of rose petals.

14

As September ticked on to October, Branna dragooned Connor and Iona into helping harvest the vegetables from her back garden. She set Iona on picking the fat pea pods, Connor to digging potatoes, while she pulled carrots and turnips.

"It smells so good." Iona straightened to sniff at the air. "In the spring when we planted, it all smelled fresh and new, and that was wonderful. And now it smells ripe and ready, and that's a different wonderful."

Connor sent Iona a baleful stare as he shoveled. "Say that when she has you scrubbing all this, and boiling or blanching or whatever the bloody hell it is."

"You don't complain when you eat the meals I make all winter with the vegetables I jar or freeze. In fact . . ."

She moved over, plucked a plump plum tomato from the vine, sniffed it. "I've a mind to make my blue cheese and tomato soup tonight."

Knowing his fondness for it, Branna smiled when Connor gave her the eye. "That's a canny way to keep me working."

"I'm a canny sort."

Harvesting put her in a fine mood. She might pluck and pick through the summer, but the basics of bounty she'd jar up for the coming winter gave her a lovely sense of accomplishment.

And the work, as far as Branna was concerned, only added to it.

"Iona, you could pick a good pair of cucumbers. I'll be making some beauty creams later, and I'll need them."

"I don't know how you manage to do so much. Keep the house, a garden, cook, make all the stock for your shop—run a business. Plot to destroy evil."

"Maybe it's magick." Enjoying the scent of them, the feel of them in her hand, Branna added more tomatoes to her bucket. "But it's the truth I love what it is I do, so most times it's not much like working."

"Tell that to the man with the shovel," Connor complained, and was ignored.

"You've plenty dished on your own plate," Branna said to Iona. "You don't seem to mind spending each day shoveling away horse dung, hauling bales of hay and straw, riding about the woods nattering to tourists who likely ask most of the same questions daily. Add all the studying and practice you've done on the craft since last winter when you could barely spark a candlewick."

"I love it all, too. I have a home and a place, a purpose. I have family and a man who loves me." Lifting her face to the sky, Iona breathed deep. "And I have magick. I only had hints of that, only had Nan as real family before I came here."

She shifted to the cucumbers, selected two. "And I'd love to be able to plant a little garden. If I learned how to can things, then I'd feel I'd done my part when Boyle ends up doing most of the cooking."

"There's room enough for one at Boyle's. Do you plan on staying there once you're married?"

"Oh, it's fine for now. More than fine for the two of us, and close to everything and everyone we want to be close to. But . . . we want to start a family, and sooner rather than later."

Branna adjusted the straw hat she wore more for the tradition of it than as a block from the sun that peeked in and out of puffy white clouds on a day that spoke more of summer than fall.

"Then you'll want a house, and not just rooms over Fin's garage."

"We're thinking about it, but neither of us wants to give up being close to all of you, or the stables, so we're just thinking about it." Bending back to her work, Iona picked a bright yellow squash. "There's the wedding to plan first, and I haven't even decided on my dress or the flowers."

"But you have what you want in mind for both."

"I have a sort of vision of the dress I want. I think— Connor, fair warning, as this will bore you brainless."

"The potatoes have already done that." He plucked them out of shoveled dirt for the bucket.

"Anyway, I want the long white dress, but I think more a vintage style than anything sleek and modern. No train or veil, more simple but still beautiful. Like something your grandmother might have worn—but a bit updated. Nan would give me hers, but it's ivory and I want white, and she's taller—and, well, it's not really it, as much as I'd love to wear a family dress."

She picked a cherry tomato, popped it warm into her mouth. "God, that's good. Anyway, I've been looking online, to get the idea, and after Samhain, I'm hoping you and I and Meara can go on a real hunt."

"I'd love it. And the flowers?"

"I've gone around and around on that, too, then I realized . . . I want your flowers."

"Mine?"

"I mean the look of your flowers, your gardens."

Straightening again, Iona waved a hand toward the happy mix of zinnias, foxglove, begonias, nasturtiums. "Not specific types or colors. All of them. All that color and joy, just the way you manage to plant them so they look unstudied and happy, and stunning all at once."

"Then you want Lola."

"Lola?"

"She's a florist, has a place just this side of Galway City. She's a customer of mine. I send her vats of hand cream as doing up flowers is murder on the hands. And she'll often order candles by the gross to go with her arrangements for a wedding. She's an artist with blooms, I promise you. I'll give you her number if you want it."

"I do. She sounds perfect."

Iona glanced toward Connor. He crouched on the ground studying a potato as if it had the answer to all the questions printed on its skin.

"I warned you I'd bore you brainless."

"No, it's not that. It got me thinking about family, about gardens and flowers. And the bluebell Teagan asked me to plant at her mother's grave. I haven't done it."

"It's too much of a risk to go to Sorcha's cabin now," Branna reminded him.

"I know it. And still, it's all she asked. She helped heal Meara, and all she asked was that I plant the flowers."

Setting down her bucket, Branna crossed over to him, crouched down so they were face-to-face. "And we will. We'll plant the bluebell—a hectare of them if that's what you want. We'll honor her mother, who's ours as well. But none of us are to go near Sorcha's grave until after Samhain. You'll promise me that."

"I wouldn't risk myself, and by doing that risk all. But it weighs on me, Branna. She was just a girl. And with the look of you, Iona. And I'm looking at you," he said to Branna, "just like I looked at Sorcha's Brannaugh, and I could see how she'd be in another ten years, and see how you were at her age. There was too much sorrow and duty in her eyes, as too often there's too much in yours."

"When we've done what we've sworn to do, the sorrow and duty will be done." She gave his grubby hand a squeeze. "They'll know it just as we do. I'm sure of that."

"Why can't we see, you and me together? And with Iona the three? Why can't we see how it ends?"

"You know the answer to that. As long as there's choice, the end is never set. What he has, and all that's gone before, it blurs the vision, Connor."

"We're the light." Iona stood with her bucket of pods, garden soil staining the knees of her jeans. And the ring Boyle had given her sparkling on her finger. "Whatever he comes with, however he comes, we'll fight. And we'll win. I believe that. And I believe it because you do," she told Connor. "Because with your whole life leading to this, knowing it did, you believe. He's a bully and a bastard hiding behind power he bartered for with some devil. What we are?" She laid a hand on her heart. "What we have is from the blood and from the light. We'll cut him down with that light, and send him to hell. I know it."

"Well said. And there." Branna gave Connor a poke. "That's our own Iona's St. Crispin's Day speech."

"It was well said. It's just a mood hanging over me. A promise not yet kept."

"One that will be," Branna said. "And it's not just that and digging potatoes that's put you in a mood—a sour one that's rare for you. Have you and Meara had a fight?"

"Not at all. It's all grand. I might worry here and there at the way Cabhan's taken too fine an interest in her. When it's one of us, we have weapon for weapon, magicks to magicks. She's only wit and spine, and a blade if she's carrying one."

"Which serves her well, and she wears your protective stones, carries the charms we made. It's all we can do."

"I had her blood on my hands." He looked down at them now, saw the wet red of Meara's blood rather than the good, dark soil. "I find I can't get around it, get past it, so I'm after texting her a half dozen times a day, making up some foolish reason, just to be sure she's safe."

"She'd knock you flat for that."

"I know it well."

"I worry about Boyle, too. And Cabhan hasn't paid any real attention there. It's natural," Iona added, "for us to have concerns about the two people we care about who don't have the same arsenal we do." She looked at Branna. "You worry, too."

"I do, yes. Even knowing there's nothing we can do we haven't done, I worry."

"If it helps, I promise I'm with her a lot during the workday. And when she takes out a group—ever since the wolf shadowed her—I braid a charm into her horse's mane."

Connor smiled. "Do you?"

"She indulges me, and so does Boyle. I've been adding them to all the horses as often as I can manage. It makes me feel better when we have to leave them at night."

"I gave her some lotion the other day, asked her to use it every day, to test it for me." Now Branna smiled. "I charmed it."

"The one that smells of apricots and honey? It's lovely." He kissed Branna's cheeks. "So that's thanks on a magickal and a romantic sort of level. I should've known the pair of you would add precautions. For me, she's never out of Roibeard's sight unless she's in mine."

"Well, give her over to Merlin for an hour or so—Fin would be willing. And go hawking." With a hand on his shoulder for a boost, Branna rose. "Put the potatoes in the little cellar and take your hawk out for a bit. I expect you could both use the time."

"What about the boiling and blanching and all the rest?"

"You're dismissed."

"And the soup?"

She laughed, gave him a light knock on the head with her fist. "Here's my thought. Tell Boyle I'll need Meara around here in . . ." Branna looked up at the beaming sun, calculated the time. "Three hours will work. Then the rest of you should be here by half-six. We'll have your soup, and a rocket salad as I'll have Iona cut it fresh, some brown bread, and cream cake."

"Cake? What occasion is this?"

"We'll have a *céili*. It's long past time we had a party here."

Brushing his hands on his pants, Connor pushed to his feet. "I can see I need to develop a sour mood more often."

"It won't work a second time. Go store those potatoes, go find your hawk, and be back here at half-six."

"I'll do all that. Thanks."

She went back, picked more tomatoes as now she'd be making the soup for six, and glanced over at Iona after Connor had gone.

"He doesn't know yet," Iona said. "He'd tell you if he did. You if no one else. So he doesn't know he's in love with her."

"He doesn't know yet, but he's coming around to it. Sure he's loved her all his life, so realizing it's another sort of love than he let himself believe takes some time."

Branna looked toward the cottage, thought of him, thought of Meara. "She's the only one he'll ever want a life with, or a lifetime. Others have and could touch his heart, but none but Meara could break it."

"She never would."

"She loves him, and always has. And he's the only one she'll ever want a life with, or a lifetime. But she hasn't his faith in love or its power. If she can trust herself and him, they'll make each other. If she can't, she'll break his heart and her own."

"I believe in love and its power. And I believe that when given the choice, Meara will reach for it, hold on to it, and treasure it."

"I hope more than I hope for almost anything else you're right."
Branna let out a breath. "Meanwhile, the two of them haven't yet
figured why no one else in the world has ever made them feel as they
do now. The heart, it's a fierce and mysterious thing. Let's get all this
inside, scrubbed off. I'll show you how to start the soup, then we'll
see how much we can jar before Meara comes."

SHE ARRIVED, TIMELY AND OUT OF SORTS.

Once she'd stalked through to the kitchen, she fisted her hands
on her hips, frowned at the shining jars of colorful vegetables cooling
on the counter, the soup simmering low on the stove.

"What's all this? If you've called me here to do kitchen work, you're
to be sorely disappointed. I've had enough work altogether today."

"We're nearly done," Branna said pleasantly.

"I'm having a beer." Meara completed her stalk to the fridge,
yanked out a bottle of Smithwick's.

"Is everything all right at the stables?"

Meara snarled at Iona. "All right? Oh, sure it's been more than all
right with us having a summer day in October and every blessed soul
within fifty kilometers deciding nothing would do but they ride a
horse today. If I wasn't taking out a group, I was doing rubdowns or
hauling saddles in, hauling them out."

She waved the beer in the air before opening it. "And didn't Caesar take it in his head to bite Rufus on the arse, and this after I told
the Spanish lady riding him to give the horses some space. So then I
had a near hysterical Spanish lady on my hands, and I can barely
understand her as she's hysterical *in* Spanish, and doing half the talking with her hands so the reins are flying about giving Caesar the
notion she wants a fine gallop."

"Oh God." Iona spoiled the attempt to sound concerned by chok-
ing off a laugh.

"Oh sure it's an amusement to you."

"Only a little, because I know it's all right, and you wouldn't have put her on Caesar if she couldn't ride."

"For all her hysterics, she rode like a bloody conquistador, and I have a suspicion she angled for the gallop all along. Fortunately, I was on your Alastar, and caught up with her easy. Grinning wide she was, though she tried to turn that around when I got hold of Caesar's bridle and pulled him up. And I swear to you—"

Now she pointed, face livid. "I swear to you the two horses had a hearty laugh over it all." She chugged down beer. "And after that one I had five teens. Five girl teens. And that I can't talk about at all or I might have Spanish hysterics myself. And you." She pointed again, an accusing jab at Iona. "You've a free day to play about in the gardens as you're sleeping with the boss."

"I'm such a slut."

"Well, there you are." Meara drank again. "And that's why I won't be doing any kitchen work or garden work, and if there's spells or enchantments to be done, I'll require another beer at the very least."

Branna glanced over toward the jars at a trio of tiny pops—a sign the lids had sealed. "That's a good sound. There's no work at all. We're having the day off."

This time Meara drank slowly. "Has she fallen under a spell herself?" she asked Iona. "Or has she been into the whiskey?"

"Neither, but there should be whiskey later. We're having a *céili*."

"A *céili*?"

"I've the first of my harvesting done, and the jarring as well. We've had a summer day in October." Branna dried off her hands, laid the cloth out. "So have your singing voice ready, Meara, and put on your dancing shoes. I'm in the mood for a party."

"Are you sure this isn't a spell?"

"We've worked and worried, planned and plotted. It's time we took a night. We'll hope he hears our music, and it burns his ears."

"I won't argue with that." More contemplatively now, Meara took another sip of beer. "I hate to risk spoiling this rare mood of yours, but I should tell you I saw him twice today—the shadow. First of the man, and next the wolf. Just watching, no more than that. But sure it's enough to play on the nerves."

"He does it for that, so we'll show him he can't stop us from living. And speaking of just that, I'll need you both upstairs."

"You're full of surprises and mystery," Meara decided. "Do the others know you're after having a party?" she asked as they started upstairs.

"Connor will let them know."

Branna led them into her bedroom, where, unlike Connor's, everything was perfectly in place.

She had the largest space—built to her specifications when she and Connor expanded the cottage. She'd painted the walls a deep forest green, and with the dark, tree-bark trim, she often thought it was like sleeping in the deep woods. She'd chosen the art carefully, following fancy with paintings of mermaids and faeries, dragons and elves.

She'd indulged herself with the bed, with a Celtic trinity knot carved into its high head- and footboard. A garden of pillows mounded on its thick white duvet. A chest, built and painted by her great-grandfather sat at its foot and held the most precious of the tools of her craft.

She fetched a long hook from her closet and, fitting it into the little slot in the ceiling, drew down the attic door and steps.

"I need to get something. I'll only be a minute."

"It always feels so peaceful in here." Iona walked to the windows that looked out over fields and woods to the roll of green hills beyond.

"They do good work between them, Branna and Connor. I envy her en suite bath with that big tub and the hectare of counter. Of course if I had that much counter in my bath, I'd clutter it up. And hers has . . ."

Meara went to the door, peeked in. "A pretty vase of calla lilies, fancy soaps in a dish, three fat white candles on gorgeous silver holders. I'd say it was witchcraft, but she's just brutal about tidiness."

"I wish some of it would rub off on me," Iona said as Branna came down the steps with a big white box. "Oh, let me help you."

"I've got it, 'tisn't heavy." She laid the white box on the white duvet. "So when we talked about weddings, and dresses and flowers and all of that, I had this thought."

After opening the box, she folded back layers and layers of tissue paper, then lifted out a long white dress.

Iona's gasp was exactly the reaction she'd hoped for.

"Oh, it's beautiful. Just gorgeous."

"It is, yes. My great-grandmother wore it on her wedding day, and I thought it might suit for yours."

Eyes wide, Iona took a quick step back. "I couldn't. I couldn't, Branna, it should be for you, for yours. It was your great-grandmother's."

"And she's your blood as well as mine. It wouldn't suit me, though it's lovely. The style's not for me. And she was petite, as you are."

Head cocked, Branna held the dress in front of Iona. "I'll ask you to try it on—indulge me in that. If it doesn't suit, if it isn't what pleases you, no harm done."

"Try it on then, Iona. You're frothing to."

"Okay, okay! Oh, this is fun." She began to strip, all but dancing as she did. "I never thought I'd be trying on a wedding dress today."

"You've the unders for a honeymoon." Meara raised her brows at Iona's lacy pale blue bra and matching panties.

"I've bought an entire new supply. It's proven to be an excellent investment." She laughed as Branna helped her step into the dress.

"Button up the back, will you, Meara?" Branna said as Iona carefully slid her arms in the thin lace sleeves.

"There are a million of them, and so tiny, and pretty like pearls."

"She was Siobhan O'Ryan, who married Colm O'Dwyer, and was

an aunt to your own grandmother, Iona, if I've got it all straight. The length's good as you'll be wearing heels, I imagine." Branna fluffed the tiers of lace-edged tulle.

"It might've been made for you the way it fits." Meara continued to fasten buttons.

"Oh, it's so beautiful." Smiling at herself in Branna's long mirror, Iona brushed fingertips over the lace bodice, down the tiered column of skirt.

"There! That's the lot,' Meara said as she did up the last buttons at the base of Iona's neck. "You look a picture, Iona."

"I do. I really do."

"The skirt's perfect, I think." Nodding, Branna walked around Iona as her cousin swayed this way and that to make the skirt sweep. "Soft, romantic, just enough fuss but not too much. But I'm thinking the bodice could use some altering. It's far too old-fashioned and far too modest. Vintage is one thing, covering you to the chin's another."

"Oh, but we can't change it. You've kept it all these years."

"What can be changed can be changed back again. Turn around here once." She turned Iona herself, putting her back to the mirror. "These should go." Branna swept her hands down the sleeves, vanishing them, glanced at Meara.

"Altogether better already. And the back here? Don't you think . . ."

Branna pursed her lips as Meara traced a low vee, then with a nod, traced it herself to open the back to just above the waist. "Yes, she's a lovely strong back and should show it off. Now the bodice."

Head angling this way, that way, Branna walked a circle around Iona. "Perhaps this . . ." She changed the bodice to a straight line just above the breasts with thin straps.

Meara folded her arms. "I like it!"

"Mmm, but it's not quite right." Thinking, imagining, Branna tried an off-the-shoulder style, with a hint of cap sleeves. Stepped back to study with Meara.

They both shook their heads.

"Can I just—"

"No!" And both of them snapped out the denial as Iona started to peek over her shoulder.

"The first you did was better by far."

"It was, but . . ." Branna closed her eyes a moment until the image formed. Then opening them, she waved her hands slowly over the bodice.

"That!" Meara laid a hand on Branna's shoulder. "Don't touch it. Let her look now."

"All right. If you don't like it, you've only to say. Turn around, have a look."

And the look said it all. Not just a contented smile now, but a stunned gasp followed by a luminous glow.

Bride-white lace formed a strapless bodice with the curve of a sweetheart neckline. From the nipped waist, the lace-edged tulle fell in soft, romantic tiers.

"She likes it," Meara said with a laugh.

"No, no, no. I love it more than I can say. Oh, Branna." Tears glimmered now as she met her cousin's eyes in the glass.

"The back was my notion," Meara reminded her, and had Iona angling to look. "Oh! Oh, Meara. It's fabulous. It's wonderful. It's the most beautiful dress in the world."

She spun around in it, laughed through the tears. "I'm a bride."

"Almost. Let's play a bit more."

"Oh please." As if to protect, Iona crossed her arms over the bodice. "Branna, I love it exactly as it is."

"Not with the dress, for it couldn't be more perfect for you. No veil you said, and I agree. What about something like this?"

She ran a finger over Iona's cap of sunny hair so Iona wore a rainbow of tiny rosebuds on a sparkling band. "That suits the dress, and you, I think—and something for your ears. Your Nan might have just the thing, but for now . . ." She added tiny diamond stars.

"That works well."

A dress, Branna thought, suited to the shower of sunlight and the glimmer of the moon. Suited for a day of love and promises, and a night of rejoicing.

"I don't have the words to thank you for this. It's not just the dress—how it looks, which is beyond anything I hoped for. But that it's from family."

"You're mine," Branna told her, "as is Boyle." She slid an arm around Meara's waist. "Ours."

"We're a circle as well, we three." Meara took Iona's hand. "It's important to know that, and value that. Beyond all the rest, we're a circle as well."

"And that's beyond anything I once hoped for. On the day I marry Boyle, my happiest day, you'll both stand with me. We'll stand, we three, the three and all six. Nothing can ever break that."

"Nothing can or will," Branna agreed.

"And now I see why you decided to celebrate. Spanish hysterics be damned," Meara announced. "I'm in the mood to sing and put my dancing shoes on."

15

THE KITCHEN SMELLED OF COOKING, AND THE PEAT FIRE
in the hearth. It glowed with light, shoving the bright, celebrational glow against the dark that pressed against the windows. The dog stretched by the fire, big head on big paws, watching his family with an amused eye.

There was music, full of pipes and strings, rollicking out of the little kitchen iPod while they put the finishing touches on the meal. Voices mixed and mingled, song and conversation as Connor swung Iona around in a quick dance.

"I'm still so clumsy!"

"You're not at all," he told her. "You're only needing more practice." He twirled her once, and twice on her laugh, then passed her smoothly to Boyle. "Give her a spin, man. I've primed her for you."

"And I'll break her toes when I trod on her feet."

"You're light enough on them when you've a mind to it."

Boyle only smiled and lifted his beer. "I haven't had enough pints for that."

"We'll tend to that as well." Connor grabbed Meara's hand, sent her a wink, then executed a quick complicated step, boots clacking, clicking on the glossy wood floor.

And Meara angled her head—a silent acceptance of the challenge. Mirrored it. Two beats later they clicked, stomped, kicked in perfect unison to the music, and, Iona thought, to some energetic choreography in their minds.

She watched them face each other, torsos straight and still while their legs and feet seemed to fly.

"It's like they were born dancing."

"I can't say about the Quinns," Fin commented, "but the O'Dwyers have always been musical. Hands, feet, voices. The best *céilies* hereabouts have forever been hosted by the O'Dwyers."

"Magickal," she said with a smile.

His gaze slid toward Branna, lingered a moment. "In all ways."

"And what about the Burkes? Do they dance?"

"We've been known to. Myself, I do better at it with my hands on a woman. And since Boyle's not making the move, I'm obliged to."

He surprised Iona by pulling her to him, circling her fast, then dropping into steps that took the dance into a half time. After a moment's fumbling, she caught on, matched him well enough, with his arms guiding her.

"I'd say the Burkes hold their own."

When he twirled her around, she levitated herself a few inches off the floor and made him laugh.

"As does the American cousin. I'm looking forward to dancing with you at your wedding. It may be I'll have to be standing in for the groom on that, while he stands on the sidelines."

"Now I see I've no choice in the matter, or find myself shown up by Finbar Burke."

Boyle snatched Iona away, solved the issue of his less talented feet by lifting her off hers and turning circles.

And Branna found herself facing Fin.

Connor saw the moment, squeezed Meara's hand in his.

"Will you?" Fin asked.

"I'm about to put dinner on the table."

He said, "Once," and took her hand.

They had a way, Connor thought, a smooth way of flowing along with the music, in time, in step, as if they'd been made to move together.

His soft heart ached for them, both of them, for it was love ashimmer in their steps. Around the kitchen, they turned, flowed, turned, eyes for each other only, easy and happy as they'd once been.

Beside him, Meara stopped as he had, and leaned her head against his shoulder.

For one lovely moment, all was right in the world. All was as it had been once, how it might be yet again.

Then Branna stopped, and though she smiled, the lovely moment shattered.

"Well now, I hope you've all worked up an appetite."

Fin murmured something to her, in Irish, but too soft and low for Connor to understand. Her smile fell toward sorrow as she turned away.

"We'll have more music after our meal, and there's wine aplenty." Movements brisk, Branna turned the music down. "Tonight's not for work or worries. We've food fresh from the garden tonight, and our own Iona made the soup."

That pronouncement brought on a long, hushed silence that hung until Iona rolled out a laugh. "Come on! I'm not that bad a cook."

"Of course you're not," Boyle said with the air of a man facing a hard, unhappy task. He went to the stove, spooned up a taste straight from the pot. Sampled, lifted his eyebrows, sampled again. "It's good. It's very good indeed."

"I don't know if a man in love's to be trusted," Connor considered. "But we'll eat."

They ate a bounty from the garden, kept the conversation light and away from all things dark. Wine flowed freely.

"And how's your mother faring in Galway?" Fin asked Meara.

"I'm not ready to say she's there to stay, but closer to it. I had a talk with my sister, who's that surprised it's a happy arrangement—for now in any case. My mother's working in the garden, and keeping it in trim. And she's struck up a bit of a friendship with a neighbor who's a keen gardener herself. If you could hold the cottage a bit longer—"

"As long as you need," Fin interrupted. "I've a mind to do a few updates there. When you've time enough, Connor, we could talk about a bit of work on the place."

"I've always time enough for that. I've missed the challenge and fun of building and fixing since we finished off the cottage. Did you truly do the soup, Iona, for it's more than good." So saying, he took another ladle from the tureen.

"Branna watched me like Roibeard, and took me through it step by step."

"I'm hoping you'll be remembering the steps, as I'll be asking you to make it at home."

Pleased, Iona grinned at Boyle. "We'll have to plant tomatoes. I'm pretty good with a garden. We could try some next year—in patio pots."

"Sure maybe we'll find something with a bit of land by then, and you can have a proper garden."

"It may be you'll be too busy with weddings and honeymoons next spring to plant tomatoes," Meara pointed out.

"And we've more than enough here to share," Branna added. "You haven't found a place that suits you more than where you are?"

"Not yet, and no hurry on it," Boyle said, glancing at Iona.

"None," she confirmed. "We like being close to all of you, and to the stables. In fact, we're both set on staying close, so until we find something that hits all the notes, we like just where we are."

"Building your own tends to hit those notes, as I've reason to know." Fin poured more wine, all around.

"You wrote a bloody opera when you built your house," Boyle commented.

"Sure what fun it was to have a hand in that," Connor remembered. "Though Fin was as fussy as your aunt Mary about everything from a run of tile to cabinet pulls.

"That's what makes it a satisfying endeavor, if you're in no particular hurry. There's land behind my own place," Fin continued, "where a house could be tucked nicely in the trees if someone liked the notion of that. And I'd be willing to sell a parcel to good neighbors."

"Are you serious?" Iona's spoon clattered against her bowl.

"About good neighbors, yes. I've no wish to be saddled with poor ones, even with plenty of space between."

"A cottage in the woods." Eyes shining, Iona turned to Boyle. "We could be excellent neighbors. We could be *amazing* neighbors."

"When you bought all that, you said it was to keep people from planting houses around you."

"People are one thing," Fin said to Boyle. "Friends and family—and partners—there's another thing entirely. We can take a look around some time or another if you've any interest."

"I guess now's too soon," Iona said with a laugh. "But then I don't have a single idea how to design or build a house."

"Sure you're lucky you have a couple of cousins who do," Connor pointed out. "And I know some good workmen here and about if you decide to go that way. Which would suit me down to the ground," he added, "if I've a vote in it. I can go hawking back there as I do, and have the benefit of stopping in for a bowl of soup."

"He thinks with his stomach," Meara commented. "But he's right enough. It would be a lovely spot for a cottage, and just where you want it to be. It's a fine notion, Fin."

"A fine notion, but he's yet to talk price."

Fin smiled at Boyle, lifted his glass. "We'll get to that—after your bride's had a look."

"A canny businessman he's always been," Branna said. "She'll fall in love and pay any price." But she said it with humor, not sting. "And it is a fine notion. More, it's saved me a quandary, for the field behind here is for Connor. But with Iona being family, I've been torn about it—even though . . . I've walked it countless times, and it never said Iona. I could never see you and Boyle making your home there, though you'd have been in sight of our own, and it's a pretty spot with a lovely view of things. I never could understand the way of that. Now I do. You'll have your cottage in the woods."

She lifted her glass in turn. "Blessed be."

BRANNA BROUGHT OUT HER VIOLIN AFTER THE MEAL, AND joined her voice with Meara's. Only happy tunes, and lively ones. Connor fetched the boden drum from his room, added a tribal beat. To Iona's surprise and delight, Boyle disappeared for a few moments and came back with a melodeon.

"You play?" Iona gaped at Boyle, at the little button accordion he held. "I didn't know you could play!"

"I can't, not a note. But Fin can."

"I haven't played, not a note, in years," Fin protested.

"And who's fault is that?" Boyle shoved the instrument at him.

"Play it, Fin," Meara encouraged. "Let's have a proper *seisiún*."

"Then no complaints when I make a muck of it." He glanced at Branna. After a moment she shrugged, tapped her foot, and began something light and jumpy. With a laugh, Connor danced fingers and stick over the colorful drum.

Fin caught the time and the tune, joined in.

Music rang out, paused only for more wine or a discussion of what should be next. Iona scrambled up for a notepad.

"I need the names of some of these! We'll want some of them at the wedding reception. They're so full of fun and happy." Imagining herself in her perfect wedding dress, dancing to all that lively joy with Boyle, surrounded by friends and family, she beamed at him. "The way our life together's going to be."

At Meara's long, exaggerated *awwww*, Boyle kissed Iona soundly.

So in the warm, bright kitchen there was laughter and song, a deliberate and defiant celebration of life, of futures, of the light.

Outside, the dark deepened, the shadows spread, and the fog slunk along the ground.

In its anger, and its envy, it did what it could to smother the house. But protections carefully laid repelled it so it could only skulk and plot and rage against the brilliance—searching, searching for any chink in the circle.

Meara switched to water to wet her throat, brought a glass over to Branna. She felt suddenly tired, and a little drunk. It was air she needed more than water, she thought. Air cool and damp and dark.

"After Samhain," Connor said, "we'll have a real *céilie*, invite the neighbors and those all around as Ma and Da did. Near Christmas, do you think, Branna?"

"With a tree in the window, and lights everywhere. With enough food to set the tables groaning. I've a fondness for Yule, so that would suit me."

It was rare for Connor to slide into her mind, but he did now.

He's close, circling close, pressing hard. Do you feel him?

Branna nodded, but kept smiling. *The music draws him like a wasp to the light. But we're not ready, not altogether ready to take him on.*

Here's a chance to try, and we shouldn't miss taking it.

Then tell the others, this way. We'll try the chance, and hope surprise is enough.

Connor saw, as Branna did, that Fin already felt that pressure, those dark fingers scrabbling against the bright. He saw Iona jolt, just a little, as he slid his thoughts into her head.

Her hand squeezed Boyle's.

He glanced toward Meara.

The instant he realized she wasn't there he felt her, *saw* her reach out to open the front door of the cottage.

The fear gripped his throat like claws, all but drawing blood. He shouted for her, in his mind, with his voice, and rushed out of the room.

Nearly half asleep, floating on the shadows soft and dim, she stepped outside. Here's what she needed, here's what she had to have. The dark, the thick and quiet dark.

Even as she started to draw in a deep breath, Connor caught her around the waist, all but threw her back into the cottage.

Everything shook—the floor, the ground, the air. To her stunned eyes, the dark mists outside the door bowed inward as if something large and terrible pushed its weight against them. Boyle slammed the door on it, and the dull roar—like an angry surf—that rolled with it.

"What happened? What is it?" Meara shoved against Connor, who'd thrown his body over hers.

"Cabhan. Stay back," Branna snapped, and flung the door open again.

A storm raged outside, the shadows twisting, knotting. Under them came a kind of high shriek and a rumble that was thousands of wings beating.

"Bats, is it?" Branna said in disgust. "Try as you might," she shouted, fists clenched at her sides. "Try your worst, then try again. But this is *my* home, and never will you cross the threshold."

"Jesus," Meara whispered as the mists thinned enough for her to see the bats. Like a living, undulating wall, red eyes gleaming, spiked wings beating.

"Stay here." Connor shouted against the din, then leaped up to join his sister. And with him, Iona and Fin moved to form a line.

"In our light you'll twist and turn," Connor began.

"In our flame you'll scorch and burn," Iona continued.

"Here merge the power of one and three," Fin added.

"As we will, so mote it be," Branna finished.

Meara, dragged back by Boyle, watched as the bats lit like torches. Hated herself for cringing as they screamed, as they burst, as smoking bodies twisted.

Ash fell like black rain, whipped in the terrible wind.

Then all went quiet.

"You're not welcome here," Branna murmured, then firmly shut the door.

"Are you hurt?" With the danger passed, Connor dropped to his knees beside Meara.

"No, no. God, did I let it in? Did I open us up to that?"

"Nothing got in." But Connor gathered her up, pressed his lips to her hair. "You opened nothing but the door."

"I had to. Felt I couldn't breathe, and wanted—craved—the dark and quiet." Shaken, she balled her hands, pressed them to her temple. "He used me again, tried to use me against all of us."

"And failed," Iona said crisply.

"He sees you as weak. Look at me now." Fin crouched down to her. "He sees you as weak as you're a woman, and no witch. But he's wrong, as there's nothing weak about or in you."

"And still he used me."

"He wanted you to go out, beyond the protections and charms." Connor brushed her hair away from her face. "He tried to lure you out, away from us. Not to use you, darling, but to harm you. For he's enraged by what we're doing here. The music, the light, the simple joy of it all. He'd have hurt you, if he could, for only that."

"You're sure of it? The music, the lights?" Meara looked from

Connor to Branna, and back. "Well then. We'll play louder, and if you'd do me a favor considering, use what you will to make the lights brighter."

Connor kissed her, helped her to her feet. "No, not a bit of weak in or about you."

LATE INTO THE NIGHT WHEN THEY'D PLAYED THEMSELVES out, Connor held her close against him in his bed. He couldn't seem to let her go. The image played in his mind—the dazed look on her face as she'd stepped from light to dark.

"It's mind tricks he's using, and he's enough of them, enough in him to slither through the shields." As he spoke, he traced a finger over the beads she wore. "We'll work on something stronger."

"He doesn't go after Boyle the same way. Is Fin right? It's because I'm not a man?"

"He preys on women more, doesn't he? He killed Sorcha's man to be sure, but he killed Daithi to torment her, to break her heart and spirit. And he tormented her again and again over that last winter. The history of it says he took girls from the castle and around."

"Yet it's the boy, Eamon, he's tried to get to."

"Take out the boy, and he'd see the girls as more vulnerable to him. He wants Brannaugh—both the one who was and our own. I feel it whenever I let him in."

She shifted. "Let him in?"

"Into my head—a bit. Or when I'm able to slip through, as he does, and get into his. It's cold, and it's dark, and so full of hunger and rage it's hard to understand any of it."

"But letting him in, even for a moment, is dangerous. He could see your thoughts as well, couldn't he—use them against us? Against you."

"I've ways around that. He doesn't have what I have, or only a whisper of it. What Eamon has as well, and he'd love to drain the boy of his power, take it for his own."

Idly, he stroked her hair, loose from its braid. Despite all, he found himself oddly content to just be with her, bodies warm and close, voices hushed in the dark.

"He bothered us so little before Iona came. With Fin he's been relentless since the day the mark burned into Fin's shoulder."

"He never speaks of it, our Fin, or rarely."

"To me he does," Connor told her, "and sometimes to Boyle. But no, even then it's rare. Things changed all around when Cabhan's mark came on him. And changed all around again when Iona came. He pushed at her those weeks, as she was not only a woman but so new and inexperienced, just learning all she had in her and how to use it. He thought her weak as well."

"She proved him wrong."

"As you have more than once already." He kissed her forehead, her temple. "But he won't stop trying. Harming you harms us all. That he can see well enough, even if he can't understand it, as he's never loved in the whole of his existence. How is it, do you think, to exist for so long, so many lifetimes, and never know love, giving it, being given it?"

"People live without it—or do for one lifetime—and don't torment and kill."

"I'm not meaning it as an excuse." Now he propped up on his elbow to look down at her. "He can bespell a woman and take her body, and her power if she has it. Lusting without love—without any love for anything or anyone—that's the dark. Those who go through their time with only that? I think they must be sad creatures, or evil ones. It's the heart that gets us through the hard times, and gives us joy."

"Branna says your power comes through your heart." Lightly, Meara traced a cross on it.

"That's her thinking, and it's true enough. I couldn't be if I couldn't feel. He feels. Lust and rage and greed, with nothing to lighten it. Taking what we are won't be enough. It will never be enough. He wants us to know the dark he knows, to suffer in it."

It made her want to shudder, so she stiffened herself against it. "You found that in his mind?"

"Some of it. Some I can just see. And for a moment tonight, I knew what he felt—and it was a kind of terrible joy that he would take you from me, from us. From yourself."

"You were inside me—in my head. He never called my name, not this time, but you did. I heard you call my name, and I stopped for just an instant. I felt like I stood on the edge of something, pulled in both directions. Then I was under you on the floor, so I don't know which way I'd have gone."

"I know, and not only because there's no weakness in you. Because of this." He lowered his head, met her lips lightly, lightly with his. "Because it's more than lust."

Nerves rose, a shiver of wings in her belly. "Connor—"

"It's more," he whispered, and took her mouth.

Soft, so soft and tender, his lips coaxing hers to give, seducing degree by aching degree. If his power came from the heart, he used it now, saturating her in pure feeling.

She would have said no—no, it wasn't the way for her, couldn't be the way. But he was already gliding her along on the sweet, onto the shimmer, into the shine.

His hands, light as air, skimmed over her, and even with such a delicate touch kindled heat.

Quiet, so quiet and stirring, his words asking her to believe what she never had. To trust what she both feared and denied.

In love, its simplicity, its potency. Its permanence.

Not for her. No, not for her—she thought it, but drifted on its silky clouds. What he gave, what he brought, what he promised, was irresistible.

For a moment, for a night, she gave herself to it. Gave herself to him.

So he took, but gently, and gave more in return.

He'd known, in the instant she'd stood between Cabhan's dark and his light, he'd known the full truth of love. He'd understood it came weighted with fear, and with risks. He'd known he might be lost in the maze of it, accepted he would work through its shadows, draw on its light and live his life riding its ups, its downs, its stretches of smooth, its sudden bumps.

With her.

A lifetime of friendship hadn't prepared him for this change, this tidal shift from easy love to what he felt for her.

The one. The only. And this he would cherish.

He didn't ask for the words back—they would come. But for now her yielding was enough. Those breathy sighs, the tremors, the thick, unsteady beat of her heart.

She rose up, swimming up and over a wave of pleasure so absolute it seemed to fill her body with pure white light.

Then it was him filling her, giving her more, and more and more until tears blurred her vision. As she peaked, as she clung for glorious moments to that bright and brilliant edge, she heard his voice, once again, in her mind.

This is more, he said to her. *This is love.*

"WHY DOES IT MAKE YOU SO UNEASY?"

"What?" Meara stared at him, then looked around. "Where are we? Is— Is that Sorcha's cabin? Are we dreaming?"

"More than a dream. And love is more than the lie you try to believe it is."

"It's Sorcha's cabin, but it stands under the vines that grow around it. And this isn't the time to talk about love and lies. Did he bring us here?"

She drew her sword, grateful the dream that wasn't a dream provided it.

"Love's the source of the light."

"The moon's the source of the light, and we can be glad it's full wherever and whenever we are." She turned a slow circle, searching shadows. "Is he near? Can you feel him?"

"If you can't yet believe you love me, you should believe I love you. I've never told you a lie, or not one that mattered, in your life."

"Connor." She sheathed her sword, but left her hand on the hilt. "Have you lost your senses?"

"I've gained them." He grinned at her. "It's your senses lost because you haven't the nerve to pick them up and hold them."

"I'm the one with the sword so mind what you say about my nerve."

He only kissed her before she shoved him away. "Not a weak thing in or about you. Your heart's stronger than you think, and it's going to be mine."

"I'm not going to stand here, of all places, and talk nonsense with you. I'm going back."

"That's not the way." Connor took her arm as she turned.

"I know the way well enough."

"That's not the way," he repeated. "And it's not yet time, as here he comes now."

Her fingers tightened on the hilt of her sword. "Cabhan."

Connor stilled her sword hand before she could draw, and took the white cobble out of his pocket. It glowed like a small moon in his palm.

"No. It's Eamon who comes."

She watched him ride into the little clearing, not a boy now, but a man. Very young, but tall and straight and so like Connor her heart jerked.

He wore his hair longer and braided back. He came quietly astride a tough-looking chestnut who, to her eye, could have galloped halfway across the county without losing its wind.

"Good evening to you, cousin," Connor called out.

"And to you and your lady." Eamon dismounted smoothly. Rather than tether the horse, he simply laid the reins over its back. The way the chestnut stood, like a carved statue in the moonlight, it was clear it wouldn't stray or bolt away from its master.

"It's been some time for you," Connor observed.

"Five years. My sisters and their men bide at Ashford. Brannaugh has two children, a son and a daughter, and another son comes any day. Teagan is with child. Her first."

He looked to the cabin, then over to his mother's gravestone. "And so we've come home."

"To fight him."

"'Tis my fondest wish. But he is in your time, and that is a truth that cannot be denied."

Tall and straight, with the hawk's eye around his neck, Eamon looked over at his mother's grave again.

"Teagan came here before me. She saw the one who will come from her. Saw her watching while Teagan faced Cabhan. We are the three, the first, but what we are, what we have, we will pass to you. This is all I can see."

"We are six," Connor said. "The three and three more. My lady, my cousin's man, and a friend, a powerful friend." And since the boy was now a man, Connor thought, the time had come to speak of it. "Our friend Finbar Burke. He is of Cabhan's blood."

"He is marked?" Like Meara, Eamon laid a hand on the hilt of his sword.

"Through no act of his own, no wish of his own."

"The blood of Cabhan—"

"I would trust him with my life, and have. I would trust him with the life of my lady, and I love her beyond reason—though she doesn't believe it. We are six," Connor repeated, "and he is one of us. We will fight Cabhan. We will end him. I swear it."

Connor drew Meara's sword and, taking it, stepped over to the gravestone. He scored his palm, let the red drip onto the ground. "I swear by my blood we will end him."

He reached in his pocket, unsurprised to find the bluebell. He used the sword to dig a small hole, and planted it. "A promise given and kept."

He stirred the air with a finger, pulled the moisture out of it, and let blood and water pour on the ground.

Stepping back, he watched with the others as the flower grew, and the blooms doubled.

"I rode away from her." Eamon stared at the grave. "There was no choice, and it was her will and her wish. Now I come home a man. Whatever I can do, whatever power is given me, I will do, I will use. A promise kept." He held out a hand to Connor. "I cannot trust this spawn of Cabhan's, but I trust you and yours."

"He is mine."

Eamon looked at the grave, at the flowers, at the cabin. "Then you are six." He touched his amulet, the twin of Connor's, then the stone on the leather binding Connor had given him. "All we are is with you. I hope we'll see each other again, when this is done."

"When it's done," Connor agreed.

Eamon mounted his horse, then smiled at Meara. "You should believe my cousin, my lady, as what he speaks, he speaks from his heart. Farewell."

He turned his horse, rode off as quietly as he'd come.

Meara started to speak—and woke with a jolt in Connor's bed.

He sat beside her, a half smile on his face as he studied his bloodied palm.

"Jesus Christ. You never know where you'll end up when you lie down beside the likes of you. Mind yourself! You'll get blood on the sheets."

"I'll fix it." He rubbed palm to palm, stanched the blood, closed the shallow wound.

"What was that about?" she demanded.

"A bit of a visit with family. Some questions, some answers."

"What answers?"

"I'm after figuring that out. But the flower's planted, as Teagan asked of me, so that's enough for now. He looked fine and fit, didn't he, our Eamon?"

"You'd say so as you've a resemblance. Cabhan would know they'd come back."

"They don't end him, but neither does he end them. Like the flowers, that's enough to know for now. It's for us to end, I know that as well."

"And how do you know?"

"I feel it." He touched a finger to his heart. "I trust what I feel. Unlike you for instance."

After an impatient glance she shoved out of bed. "I have to go to work."

"You've time for a bite to eat. You needn't worry as there's not enough time for me to poke at you properly about my feelings and yours. But there'll be time for that soon enough. I love you to distraction, Meara, and while it comes as a surprise to me, I'm happy being surprised."

She grabbed up her clothes. "You're romanticizing the whole business, and cobbling it all together with magicks and risks and blood and sex. I expect you'll come to your senses before long, and for now, I'm using the loo, and getting myself ready for work."

She marched off.

He grinned after her, amused he had such a fine view of her back-side as she stalked through the door of the bath he shared with Iona.

He'd come to his senses, he thought—though it had taken most of his life to get there. He could wait for her to come to hers.

Meanwhile . . . He studied his healed palm. He had some thinking to do.

16

WOMEN WERE A CONSTANT PUZZLE TO CONNOR'S mind, but their mysteries and secret ways accounted for some of their unending appeal to him.

He considered the woman he loved. Courageous and straightforward as they came on all matters—except those of the heart. And there she turned as fearful as a trapped bird, and just as likely to fly off and away given the smallest opening.

And yet that heart held strong and loyal and true.

A puzzle.

He'd spooked her, no question of that, with his declaration of feelings. He loved her, and for him true love came once and lasted forever.

Still, as he'd rather see her fly free—for now—than batter herself against the cage, he roused Boyle.

Having Boyle go into the stables with Meara—earlier than either needed to be—accomplished two things. She'd have his friend with her, and the three would have some time to talk alone.

Rain blew across the trees and hills, shivered against the windows. He let the dog out, walked out himself, circling the cottage—as they'd done the night before—checking to be certain no remnants of Cabhan's spell remained.

His sister's flowers bloomed, bold, defiant colors against the gloom with the grass beyond them a thick green blanket. And all he felt in the air was the rain, was the wind, was the strong, clear magicks he'd helped light himself in a ring around what was theirs.

When he paused at Roibeard's lean-to, the hawk greeted him with a light rub of his head to Connor's cheek. That was love, simple and easy.

"You'll keep an eye out, won't you?" Connor skimmed the back of his knuckle down the hawk's breast. "Sure you will. Take some time for yourself now, and have a hunt with Merlin, for we're all safe for the moment."

In answer, the hawk spread his wings, lifted. He circled once, then soared to the woods, and into them.

Connor walked around again, went in through the kitchen door— holding it open as Kathel came up behind him.

"Done your patrol, have you then? And so have I." He gave the dog a long stroke, a rub along the ears. "I don't suppose you'd go up and give our Branna a nudge to get me out of making breakfast?"

Kathel simply gave him a look as dry as any hound could manage.

"I didn't think so, but I had to try it."

Accepting his fate, Connor fed the dog, freshened the water in the bowl. He lit the fires, in the kitchen, in the living room, even in the workshop, then had to calculate he could stall no more, and got down to it.

He set bacon sizzling, sliced up some bread, beat up eggs.

He was just pouring the eggs into the pan when Iona and Branna came in together—Iona dressed for work, Branna still in her sleep clothes with that before-my-coffee scowl in her eyes.

"Everyone's up so early." Knowing the rules, Iona let Branna get to the coffee first. "And Boyle and Meara already gone."

"She wanted to change, and promised Boyle she'd fix him some breakfast for taking her around."

"Mind those eggs, Connor, you'll scorch them," Branna said, as she did whenever he made breakfast.

"I won't."

"Why is it you have to turn up the flame to hellfire to cook every bloody thing?"

"It's faster is why."

And damn it, he nearly did scorch them because she'd distracted him.

He dumped them on a plate with the bacon, tossed on some toast, then plopped it all in the middle of the table. "If you'd stirred yourself sooner, you could've made them to your liking. Now you'll eat them from mine, and you're welcome."

"It looks great," Iona said brightly, and finger combing her cap of bright hair, sat.

"Ah, don't pander to him just because he's made a meal, and for the first time in weeks." Branna sat with her, gave Kathel's ears a scratch.

"It's not pandering if you're hungry." Iona filled her plate. "We're going to get cancellations today." She nodded toward the steady, soaking rain. "Not only rain, but a cold one, too. Normally I'd be sorry about that, but today I think we could all use the extra time."

She sampled some eggs. They were very . . . firm, she decided.

"If it's as slow as I think it may be," she continued, "I can probably get off early. I can come work with you, Branna, if you want."

"I've some stock to finish up as I didn't work on it yesterday. I'll need to get it done and run it into the shop. But I'll be here by noon,

I'd think. Fin and I've finished the changes to the potion we used on the solstice. It's stronger than it was, but the spell needs work, as does the timing, and the whole bloody plan."

"We've got time."

"The days click by. And he's growing bolder and bolder. What he tried last night—"

"Didn't work, did it now?" Connor countered. "What are his devil bats now but ash blown by the wind, washed by the rain? And it gave me a notion or two, the whole business of it."

"You've a notion, have you?" Branna lifted her coffee.

"I have, and a story to tell as well. I looked for Eamon in dreams, and he for me. So we found each other."

"You saw him again."

He nodded at Iona. "I did, and pulled Meara into it with me. He was a man, about eighteen, as he said it had been five years since he'd last seen me. His Brannaugh has two children with a third to come, and Teagan is carrying her first."

"She was pregnant—Teagan," Iona added, "when I saw her, in my own dream."

"I remember, so this would have been for me the same time in their world as it was for you. It was, for me as for you, at Sorcha's cabin."

"You know better than to go there," Branna snapped, "in dreams or no."

"I can't tell you in truth if it was my doing or his, for I promise you I don't know even now. But I knew we were safe there, for that time, or I would have pulled it back. I wouldn't have risked Meara again."

"All right. All right then."

"They'd come home," he continued, and lathered toast with jam, "and that was bittersweet. They know they'll fight Cabhan, and they know they won't win, won't end him, as he's here in our time, our place. I told him we were six, and that one of our six had Cabhan's blood."

"And did that float well?" Branna wondered.

"He knows me." Connor tapped a hand on his heart. "And he trusts me. So in turn, he trusts mine, and Fin is mine. He had the pendant I gave him as well as the amulet we share. I had the little stone he gave me, and when I took it out, it glowed in my palm. You had the right of that, Branna. It has power."

"Well, I wouldn't put it in a sling and play David to Cabhan's Goliath, but it's good to keep it with you."

"So I do. And more, I had the bluebell."

"Teagan's flower," Iona added.

"I planted it, fed it with my blood, with water I drew from the air. And the flowers bloomed there on Sorcha's grave."

"You kept your word." Iona brushed a hand over his arm. "And you gave them something that mattered."

"I told him we'd end it, as I believe we will. And I think I know something that we missed on the solstice. Music," he said, "and the joy of it."

"Music," Iona repeated even as Branna sat back, speculation in her eyes.

"What drew him here last night, so enraged, so bold? Our light, yes, and we'll have that. Ourselves, of course. But we made music, and that's a light of its own."

"A joyful noise," Iona said.

"It is that. It blinds him—with that rage against the joy. Why couldn't it bind him as well?"

"Music. We made music that night last spring, do you remember, Iona? Just you and I and Meara here. I brought out my fiddle, and we played and sang, and he lurked outside, all shadows and fog. Drawn to it," Branna said, "drawn to the music even as he hated it—hated that we had it in us to make it."

"I remember."

"Oh, I can work with this." Branna's eyes narrowed, her lips curved. "Aye, this will be something to stir into the pot. It's a good thought, Connor."

"It's brilliant," Iona said.

"I tend to agree with that." Grinning, Connor shoveled in the last of his eggs.

"I'm sure Meara said the same."

"She may, when I tell her. I only came around to it this morning," he added, "and she was in a fired hurry to get on her way."

"Why was that? I've still got nearly a half an hour before I have to get to work." And because she did, Iona rose for a second cup of coffee. "If she'd waited, Boyle and I could've . . . Oh." Her eyes rounded. "Did you have a fight?"

"A fight, no. She went into a fast retreat, as I expected she would, when I told her I loved her. Being Meara, it'll take her a bit of time to settle into it all."

"You figured it out." Dancing back, Iona wrapped her arms around him from behind his chair. "That's wonderful."

"It wasn't a matter of figuring . . . Maybe it was that," he reconsidered. "And she's some slower on coming to the conclusion. She'll be happier when she does, and so will I. But for now, there's a certain enjoyment in watching her try to squirm around it."

"Have a care, Connor," Branna said quietly. "It's not a stubborn nature or a hard head that holds her back. It's scars."

"She can't live her life denying her own heart because her shite of a father had none."

"Have a care," Branna repeated. "Whatever she says, whatever she thinks she believes, she loved him. She loves him still, and that's why the hurt's never gone all the way quiet."

Irritation walked up his spine. "I'm not her father, and she should know me better."

"Oh no, darling, it's that she's afraid she is—she's like her father."

"Bollocks to that."

"Of course." Branna rose, began to clear. "But that's the weight she carries. As much as I love her, and she loves me, I've never been able to lift it away, not altogether. That's for you to do."

"And you will." Iona pushed away from the table again to help. "Because love, if you just don't let go, beats anything."

"I won't be letting go."

Iona paused to kiss the top of his head. "I know it. The eggs were good."

"I wouldn't go as far as that," Branna said, "but we'll do the washing up since you cooked . . . after a fashion."

"That's fine then, as I need to call Roibeard in and get on to work."

He got his jacket from the peg, and a cap while dishes clattered. "I do love her," he said as the words felt so fine, "I love her absolutely."

"Ah, Connor, you great git, so you always have."

He went out into the rain thinking his sister was right. So he always had.

A FOUL MOOD, AN EDGY MANNER, AND A TENDENCY TO snipe equaled an assignment to the manure compost pile.

A filthy day for a filthy job, Meara thought as she changed into her oldest muck boots, switched her jacket for one of the thicker barn coats. But then again she was feeling fairly filthy. And since she couldn't deny she'd picked a fight with Boyle—after snapping at Mick, snarling at Iona, and brooding her way through the rest of the morning—she couldn't blame Boyle for banishing her to shit duty.

But she did in any case.

He'd given her guided to Iona—hardy souls from the midlands who weren't put off by the sodding rain. Mick had a ring lesson, so the sodding rain didn't matter for that, not a bit. Nor did it matter to

Patty, who was cleaning tack, or to Boyle, who'd closed himself off
in his office.

So it was left to her to tromp around in the sodding rain, and to
the majestic turning of the shit pile.

She wrapped a scarf around her neck, pulled a cap low on her head,
and clomped her way out—carting a shovel and a long metal stick—
well behind the stables to what was not-so-lovingly referred to as Shite
Mountain.

A stable of horses produced plenty for the mountain, and this by-
product—if she wanted to use a fancy term—had to be dealt with.
And wiser, eco-minded souls did more than deal. They used.

It was a process she approved of, on normal days. On days she
wasn't pissed off at the world in general. On days when it wasn't raining fecking buckets.

Manure, properly treated, became compost. And compost
enriched soil. So Fin and Boyle had built an area—far enough the
odors didn't carry back—to do just that.

When she reached Shite Mountain, she cursed, realizing she left
her iPod and earbuds back at the stable. She wouldn't even have music
to distract her.

All she could do was mutter as she pulled the old, empty feed bags
off the big pile, and began to use the shovel to turn the manure.

Proper compost required heat to kill the seeds, the parasites, to
turn manure into a rich additive. It was a job she'd done countless
times, so she continued automatically, adding fertilizer to help break
down the manure, turning the outer layers into the heart and the
heat, making a second pile, adding ventilation by shoving the stick
down deep.

At least she didn't have to drag out the hose as the sodding rain
added all the water required to the mucky mix.

Mucky mix, she thought, putting her back into it. That's just what
Connor had tossed them into.

Why did he have to bring love into it? Love and promises and notions of futures and family and forever? Hadn't it all been going well? Hadn't they been doing fine and well with sex and fun and friendship?

Now he'd said all those words—and said many of them in Irish. A deliberate ploy, she thought as she shoveled and turned and spread. A ploy to twist up her heart. A ploy to make her sigh and surrender.

He'd made her weak—he had, he had—and she didn't know what to do with weakness. Weakness was an enemy, and he'd set that enemy on her. And more, he'd made her afraid.

And she'd started it all, hadn't she? Oh, she only had herself to blame for the situation, for the trouble it was bound to cause all around.

She'd kissed him first, she couldn't deny it. She'd taken him into her bed, changing what they were to each other.

Connor was a romantic—she'd known that as well. But the way the man flitted from woman to woman, she couldn't be blamed entirely for never expecting proclamations of love.

They had enough to deal with, didn't they? The time to All Hallow's Eve grew shorter every day, and if they had a true and solid plan for that, she'd yet to hear it.

Connor's optimism, Branna's determination, Fin's inner rage, Iona's faith. They had all that, and Boyle's loyalty as well as her own.

But those didn't amount to strategy and tactics against dark magicks.

And instead of keeping his brain focused on finding those strategies and tactics, Connor O'Dwyer was busy telling her things like she was the beat of his heart, the love of all his lifetimes.

In Irish. In Irish while he did impossible things to her body.

And hadn't he looked her straight in the eye in the morning, after they woke from that strange dreamworld, and said straight out he loved her?

Grinned at her, she thought now, steaming up. As if turning her world upside down was a fine and funny joke.

She should've knocked him out of bed onto his arse. That's what she should've done.

She'd set things right with him, by God she would. Because she wouldn't be weak, not for him or anyone. She wouldn't be weak and afraid. Wouldn't have her heart twisted up so she made promises she'd only break.

She wouldn't let herself become soft and foolish like her mother. Helpless to care for herself. Shamed and mourning the betrayal dealt like an axe blow by a man.

More—worse—she wouldn't let herself become careless and selfish like her father. A man who would make promises, even keep them as long as his life stayed smooth. Who would heartlessly break them, and the hearts of those who loved him, when the road roughened.

No, she'd be no man's wife, no man's burden, no man's heartbeat. Especially not Connor O'Dwyer's.

Because, God help her, she loved him far too much.

She felt a sob rising up, brutally choked it back.

A temporary thing, she promised herself as she spread the bags over the compost piles again. This kind of burning in the heart couldn't last.

No one could survive it.

She'd be herself again soon, and so would Connor. And all this would be like one of those strange dreams that weren't dreams.

She told herself she was steadier now, that the physical labor had done her good. She'd go back, smooth things over with Mick, especially, and the others as well.

"You've done your penance," she said out loud, stepped back, turned.

And her father smiled at her.

"So here you are, my princess."

"What?"

A bird sang in the mulberry tree, and the roses bloomed like a fairyland. She loved the gardens here, the colors, the scents, the sounds of the birds, the song of the fountain as the water poured into the circling pool from a jug held by a graceful woman.

And loved all the odd corners and shaded bowers where she could hide away from her siblings if she wanted to be alone.

"Lost in dreams again, and didn't hear me calling." He laughed, the big roll of it making her lips curve even as tears stung her eyes.

"You can't be here."

"A man's entitled to take a pretty day off to be with his princess." Smiling still, he tapped the side of his nose with his index finger. "It won't be long before all the lads in the county will start coming around, then you won't have time for your old da."

"I always would."

"That's my darling girl." He took her hand, drew her arm through the crook of his. "My pretty gypsy princess."

"Your hand's so cold."

"You'll warm it up." He began to walk with her, around the stone paths, through the roses and the creamy cups of calla lilies, the aching blue of lobelia with the sun showering down like the inside of a broken pearl.

"I came just to see you," he began, using that confidential voice, adding the sly wink as he did when he had secrets to tell her. "Everyone's in the house."

She glanced toward it, the three fine stories of brick, painted white as her mother had wished. More gardens surrounded the large terrace, then led to a smooth green lawn where her mother liked to have tea parties in good summer weather.

All tiny sandwiches and frosted cakes.

And her room there, Meara thought, looking up. Yes, her room right there, with its French doors and little balcony. A Juliet balcony, he called it.

So she was his princess.

"Why is everyone in the house? It's such a bright day. We should have a picnic! Mrs. Hannigan could make up some bridies, and we can have cheese and bread, and jam tarts."

She started to turn, wanted to run to the house, call everyone out, but he steered her away. "It's not the day for a picnic."

For a moment she thought she heard rain drumming on the ground, and when she looked up, it seemed a shadow passed over the sun.

"What is that? What is it, Da?"

"It's nothing at all. Here you are." He broke a rose from the bush, handed it to her. She sniffed at it, smiled as the soft white petals brushed her cheek.

"If not a picnic, can't we have some tea and cake, like a party, since you're home?"

He shook his head slowly, sadly. "I'm afraid there can be no party."

"Why?"

"None of the others want to see you, Meara. They all know it's your fault."

"My fault? What is? What have I done?"

"You consort and conspire with witches."

He turned, gripping her shoulders hard. Now the shadow moved over his face, had her heart leaping in fear.

"Conspire? Consort?"

"You plot and plan, having truck with devil's spawn. You've lain with one, like a whore."

"But . . ." Her head felt light, dizzy and confused. "No, no, you don't understand."

"More than you. They are damned, Meara, and you with them."

"No." Pleading, she laid her hands on his chest. Cold, cold like his hands. "You can't say that. You can't mean that."

"I can say it. I do mean it. Why do you think I left? It was you, Meara. I left you. A selfish, evil trollop who lusts for power she can never have."

"I'm not!" Shock, like a blow to the belly, staggered her back a step. "I don't!"

"You shamed me so I couldn't look upon your face."

The sobs came now, then a gasp as the white rose in her hand began to bleed.

"That's your own evil," he said when she threw it to the ground. "Destroying all who love you. All who love you will bleed and wither. Or escape, as I did. I left you, shamed and sickened.

"Do you hear your mother weep?" he demanded. "She weeps and weeps to be saddled with a daughter who would choose the devil's children over her own blood. You're to blame."

Tears ran down her cheeks—of shame, of guilt and grief. When she lowered her head, she saw the rose, sinking in a puddle of its own blood.

And rain, she realized, falling fast and hard.

Rain.

She swayed a little, heard the bird singing in the mulberry, and the fountain cheerfully splashing.

"Da . . ."

And the cry of a hawk tore through the air.

Connor, she thought. Connor.

"No. I'm not to blame."

Drenched by the rain, freed by the cry of the hawk, she swung out with the shovel. Though she took him by surprise, he leaped back so it whooshed by his face.

A face no longer her father's.

"Go to hell." She swung again but the ground seemed to heave under her feet. As it did she swore something pierced her heart.

On her sharp cry of pain, Cabhan bared his teeth in a vicious smile. And he spilled into fog.

She managed a shaky step forward, then another. The ground continued to heave, the sky turned and turned over her head.

From a distance, through the rain and the fog, she heard someone calling her name.

One step, she told herself, then another.

She heard the hawk, saw the horse, a gray blur speeding through the mists, and the hound streaking behind him.

She saw Boyle running toward her as if devil dogs snapped at his heels.

And as the world spun and spun, she saw with some amazement Connor leap off Alastar's bare back.

He shouted something, but the roaring in her head muffled the sound.

Shadows, she thought. A world of shadows.

They closed in and swallowed her.

She swam through them, choked on them, drowned in them. She heard her father laugh, but cruelly, so cruelly.

You're to blame, selfish, heartless girl. You have nothing. You are nothing. You feel nothing.

I'll give you power, Cabhan promised, his voice a caress. *It's what you truly want, what you covet and crave. Bring me his blood, and I'll give you power. Take his life, and I'll give you immortality.*

She struggled, tried to claw her way through the shadows, back to the light, but couldn't move. She felt bound, weighed down while the shadows grew thicker, thicker so she drew them in with every breath.

Every breath was colder. Every breath was darker.

Do what he asks, her father urged her. *The witch is nothing to you; you're nothing to him. Just bodies groping in the dark. Kill the witch. Save yourself. I'll come back to you, princess.*

Then Connor reached for her hand. He glowed through the shadows, his eyes green as emeralds.

Come with me now. Come back with me. I need you, aghra. *Come back to me. Take my hand. You've only to take my hand.*

But she couldn't—didn't he see—she couldn't. Something snarled and snapped behind her, but Connor only smiled at her.

Sure you can. My hand, darling. Don't look back now. Just take my hand. Come back with me now.

It hurt, it hurt, to lift that heavy arm, to strain against binding she couldn't see. But there was light in him, and warmth, and she needed both so desperately.

Weeping, she lifted her arm, reached out for his hand. It was like being pulled by her fingertips out of thick mud. Being dragged a centimeter at a time, and painfully, while some opposing force pulled her back.

I've got you, Connor said, his eyes never leaving hers. *I won't let you go.*

Then she felt as if she exploded, a cork out of a bottle, into the clear.

Her chest burned, burned as if her heart had turned into a hot coal. When she tried to draw in air, it seared up into her throat.

"Easy now, easy. Slow breaths. Slow. You're back now. You're safe. You're here. Shh now, shh."

Someone sobbed, wrenching, heartrending. It took her minutes to realize the sounds came from her.

"I've got you. We've got you."

She turned her face into Connor's shoulder—God, God, the scent of him was like cool water after a fire. He lifted her.

"I'm taking her home now."

"My house is closer," she heard Fin say.

"She'll be staying at the cottage until this is finished, but thanks. I'm taking her home now. But will you come? When you can, will you come?"

"You know I will. We all will."

"I'm with you now, Meara." She heard Branna's voice, felt Branna's hand stroke her hair, her cheek. "I'm right here with you."

She wanted to speak, but nothing came out but those terrible, tearing sobs.

"Go with them," Boyle said. "Go with them, Iona. It should be the three with her. I'll see to Alastar. Take the lorry and go with them."

"Come soon."

Meara turned her head enough to see Iona running for Boyle's lorry, climbing behind the wheel. Running through the rain, through the mists while the world rocked back and forth, back and forth like the deck of a ship in a storm.

And the pain in her chest, in her throat, in every part of her burned like the fires of hell.

She wondered if she'd died. If she'd died damned as the father who wasn't her father had said.

"Shh now," Connor said again. "You're alive and you're safe, and you're with us. Rest now, darling. Just rest now."

On his words, she slipped into warm sleep.

17

SHE HEARD VOICES, MURMURING—SOFT, SOOTHING. SHE
felt hands, stroking—light, gentle. It seemed she floated on a
warm pallet of air with the scents of lavender and candle wax all
around. Bathed in light, she knew peace.

Murmuring became words, garbled and indistinct, as if spoken
through water.

"It's rest she needs now. Rest and quiet. Let the healing do its
work." Branna's voice, so weary.

"She's some color back, doesn't she?" And Connor's, anxious,
shaky.

"She does, and her pulse is steady again."

"She's strong, Connor." Now Iona, a bit hoarse as if from sleep or
tears. "And so are we."

Then she drifted again, floating, floating into comforting silence.

Waking was like a dream.

She saw Connor sitting beside her, eyes closed, his face illuminated by the glow of the candles all around the room. It was as if he'd been painted in pale, luminous gold.

Her first conscious thought was it was ridiculous for a man to be that handsome.

She started to say his name, but before she could speak it, his eyes opened, looked directly into hers. And she knew by the color, the intensity of the green, more than the candlelight illuminated him.

"There you are." When he smiled the intensity faded, and it was only Connor and candlelight. "Lie still and quiet, just for a moment."

He held his hands over her face, closed his eyes again, as he skimmed them down, over her heart, back again. "That's good. That's fine now."

He removed something from her forehead, her collarbone, leaving the faintest tingle behind.

"What is that?" Was that her voice? That frog croak?

"Healing stones."

"Was I sick?"

"You were, but you're doing well now."

He lifted her a little, removed stones from under her back, under her hands, put them in a pouch and closed it tightly.

"How long was I asleep?"

"Oh, near to six hours now—not long in the grand scheme."

"Six hours? But I was . . . I was . . ."

"Don't look for it yet." His tone, brisk, cheerful, had her frowning. "You'll be a bit foggy yet, and feel weak and shaky. But it'll pass, I promise you. And here, you'll drink this now. Branna left it for you to drink—and all of it—as soon as you woke."

"What is it?"

"What's good for you."

He propped her up on pillows before taking the stopper from a slim bottle filled with red liquid.

"All of that?"

"All." He put the bottle in her hands, cupped his own around them to guide it to her lips. "Slow now, but every drop of it."

She prepared for medicine, and instead sipped the cool and lovely. "It's like liquid apples, blossoms and all."

"That's some of it. All now, darling. You need every drop."

Yes, more color in her cheeks now, Connor thought. And her eyes were heavy, but clear. Not blind and staring as they'd been when she'd succumbed to Cabhan's spell, when she'd lain lifeless on the wet grass.

The image flashed back into his mind, made his hands shake. So he pushed it aside, looked at her now.

"You'll have some food next." It took every ounce of will to keep his voice steady and carve a little cheer into it. "Branna's made up some broth, and we'll see how you do with that and some tea first."

"I think I'm starving, but I can't really tell. I feel I'm only half here. But better. The drink was good."

She handed him back the bottle; he set it aside as carefully as a man placing a bomb.

"Food next." He managed a smile before he laid his lips on her forehead. Then simply couldn't move.

She felt him tremble, reached for his hand. He gripped hers so hard she had to bite back a gasp. "It was bad?"

"It's fine now. All's well now. Oh God."

He pulled her to him, so tight. He'd have pulled her inside him if he could. "It's all right now, it's all fine now," he said over and over, to comfort himself as much as her.

"I don't know how he got past the protection. It wasn't strong enough. I didn't make it strong enough. He took the necklace from you, and I never believed he could. He took it away, and stole your breath. I should've done more. I will do more."

"Cabhan." She couldn't quite remember. "I was . . . turning the manure. The compost. And then . . . I wasn't. I can't see it clear."

"Don't fret." He brushed at her hair, at her cheeks. "It'll come back when you're stronger. I'll make you another necklace, a stronger one. I'll have the others help me, as what I did with the other wasn't enough."

"The necklace." She reached up where it should have hung around her neck. Remembered. "It's in my jacket. I took it off, didn't I?"

As she struggled to remember, Connor slowly eased away.

"You took it off?"

"I was that mad. I took it off, stuffed it in my jacket pocket. I snapped at poor Mick—and everyone else as well, so Boyle . . . Yes, Boyle sent me out to the compost pile. I put on one of the barn coats, left my own jacket behind."

"You weren't wearing it at all? And the pocket charms I made you?"

"In my pocket—in the jacket I left in the stables. I didn't give it a thought because . . . Connor."

He stood abruptly, and in his face she saw only cold rage.

"You took it off, left it behind because I gave it to you."

"No. Yes." It was all such a muddle. "I wasn't thinking properly, don't you see? I was so angry."

"Because I love you, you were angry enough to go out, without protection."

"I wasn't thinking of it that way. I wasn't thinking at all. I was stupid. I was beyond stupid. Connor—"

"Well then, it's done, and you're safe enough now. I'll send Branna up with the broth."

"Connor, don't go. Please, let me—"

"You need the quiet now to finish the healing. I'm not able to be quiet now, so I can't be with you."

He went out, closed the door between them.

She tried to get up, but her legs simply wouldn't hold her. Now she, a woman who'd prided herself on her strength, her health, had to crawl back into bed like an invalid.

She lay back, breath unsteady, skin clammy, and her heart and mind spinning with the consequences of one careless act done in temper.

When Branna came in with a tray she could have wept with frustration.

"Where's he gone?"

"Connor? He needed some air. He's been sitting with you for hours."

Branna arranged the tray—an invalid's tray with feet so it would sit over the lap of the sick and the weak. Meara stared at it with absolute loathing.

"You'll feel stronger after the tea and broth. It's natural to be shaky and weak just now."

"I feel I've been sick half my life." Then she looked up, cleared her own frustrations enough to see the fatigue and worry in Branna's eyes. "I'm poor at it, aren't I? Never been sick more than a few hours. You've seen to that. You always have. I'm so sorry, Branna. I'm so sorry for this."

"Don't be foolish." Eyes weary, hair bundled up messily, Branna sat on the side of the bed. "Here now, have some of the broth. It's the next step."

"In what?"

"Getting back to yourself."

Since she wanted that—she couldn't mend things with Connor when she could barely lift a spoon—she began to eat. The first taste was like ambrosia.

"I thought I was starved, but I couldn't really feel much of anything. It's wonderful to feel hungry, and this is brilliant. I can't piece it all together. I remember it, most of it, clear enough until I started back to the stables, then it goes dim."

"Once you feel yourself again, you'll remember. It's a kind of protection."

"Oh God." Meara squeezed her eyes shut.

"Is there pain? Darling——"

"No, no——not that kind. Branna, I did something so stupid. I was upset, in a black temper so I just couldn't think sensible. Connor—— well, he said he loved me. The kind of love that leads to marriage and babies and cottages on the hill, and it just threw me into upheaval altogether. I'm not fit for that sort of thing——everyone knows it."

"No one knows anything of the sort, but I won't argue you think it. You should stay calm, Meara." Branna stroked a hand along Meara's leg. "Rest easy now to help yourself be well again."

"I can't be calm and rest easy when Connor's gone off as mad at me as he's ever been. And worse, even worse."

"Why would he be mad at you?"

"I took it off, Branna." Her fingers rubbed at her throat, where the necklace should be. "I wasn't thinking, I swear. I was just caught up in the temper. So I took off the necklace he gave me and pushed it into my pocket."

The hand stroking to soothe stilled. "The blue chalcedony with the jade and jasper beads?" Branna said carefully.

"Yes, yes. I just shoved it into my pocket, along with the charms. And I was picking fights with everyone within arm's reach until Boyle had enough of me. He sent me out to the compost, and as it's filthy work, and it was raining buckets, I switched my jacket for a barn coat. I didn't think——didn't even remember I'd taken the necklace off, you see. I wouldn't have gone out without it. I swear, even in a mad, I wouldn't have done that purposely."

"You took off what he gave you out of love, what he gave you to protect you, what he loves, from harm. You cut through his heart, Meara."

"Oh, Branna, please." She sobbed in air as Branna rose, walked to the window to stare out at the dark. "Please don't turn me away."

Branna spun back, her own temper bright in her eyes. "That's a cold and cruel thing to say."

All the color dropped out of Meara's cheeks again. "No. No. I——"

"Cold and cruel and selfish. You've been my friend, my sister in all but blood since my first memory. But you could think I'd turn you away?"

"No. I don't know. I'm so confused, so twisted up inside."

"The tears are good for you." Voice brisk now, Branna nodded. "You don't shed them often, and they're good for you now. A kind of purging. There are five people in this house—no, that's not true as Iona and Boyle have gone off now that you're awake to pack up your things for you."

"Pack up my——"

"Quiet. I've not finished. Those five people love you, and not one of us deserves you're thinking we would stop because you've done something hurtful."

"I'm sorry. I'm sorry."

"I know you are. But I'm here, Meara, standing between you and Connor, loving you both. He blamed himself, you see, for not giving you stronger protection."

"I know." Her voice hitched and shook on every word. "He said. I remembered. I told him. He left me."

"He left the *room*, Meara, you idjit. He's Connor O'Dwyer, as good and loyal and true a man as there ever was. He's not your bleeding father or a man anything like him."

"I don't mean . . ." It flooded back, the force and clarity of it leaving her gasping for air.

"Calm. Be calm." Branna rushed to her, gripped her hands, pushed her will against the panic. "You will be calm, and breathe easy. In my eyes, look in my eyes. There's calm, and there's air."

"I remember."

"Calm first. No harm comes here, and no dark. We scried the candles, laid the herbs and stones. Here is sanctuary. Here is calm."

"I remember," she said again, and calmly. "He was there."

"You'll let yourself settle a bit, and as much as I want to know it all, we'll wait until we're all together. You'll only have to tell it once."

And Connor, Branna thought, deserved to hear it all.

"What did he do to me? Can you tell me that? How bad was it?"

"Drink the broth first."

Impatient, and stronger already, Meara just lifted the bowl, drank it down straight. And made Branna laugh a little.

"Now you've done it."

"Tell me— Oh!"

It was like a jolt of electricity, or a good, quick orgasm, or a direct hit by a lightning bolt. Energy shot straight into her, rocking her back.

"What *is* that?"

"Something you're meant to drink slowly, but leave it to you."

"I feel I could sprint all the way to Dublin. Thank you."

"You're welcome. We'll just leave this for later." Cautious now, Branna moved the tea out of reach.

"I could eat a cow and still have room for pudding." But she reached for Branna's hand. "I'm sorry. Truly."

"I know it. Truly."

"Tell me, will you, what he did to me? Was it poison, like Connor?"

"It wasn't, no. You were open and defenseless, and he would know it. He used his shadows, and I think it blocked it all for a time. But they cleared enough, for he can't keep that box, as Connor called it, shut tight for long. The lot of us were coming. He'd have known that as well, so he acted quickly and with cruelty. The spell he cast, you could call it a kind of Sleeping Beauty, but it's not so pretty as a fairy tale. It's a kind of death."

"I . . . He killed me."

"No, it's not so clean. He took your breath; he stopped your heart. It's a kind of paralysis that anyone who didn't know would take for death. Without intervention, it could last for days or weeks. Even years. Then you would wake."

"Like, what, a zombie?"

"You would wake, Meara, and you would be mad. You would claw or dig your way out if you could, or die raving. Or . . . he would come for you, at a time of his own choosing, and make you his creature."

"Then I would be dead," Meara declared. "All that I am would be gone. He couldn't have done this to me if I'd worn the protection Connor gave me."

"No. He could hurt you, he could try to draw you to him, but he couldn't cast such a spell on you when you're protected." She paused a moment. "It was Connor who breathed life back into you. He reached you first. He brought you back—your breath, your heart. Then the rest of us came together as he pulled you out of the sleep. Even in those few minutes, Meara, you'd been drawn deep. You could only sob and sob, and shake. He had to slide you into sleep again, healing sleep, so you could be calm while we worked."

"The candles, the stones, the herbs. The words. I heard you—you and Connor and Iona."

"Fin as well for a bit."

Five people who loved her, Meara thought, all sick and afraid because she'd been foolish.

"He could've broken us, because I was childish."

"That's true enough."

"I'm shamed and sorry, Branna, and so I'll say to all. But if I could speak with Connor first."

"Of course you should."

"Could you help me clean up a bit?" She managed a wobbly smile. "I've been a bit dead, and probably look it."

BECAUSE IT CONTINUED TO RAIN, CONNOR SAT IN BRANNA'S workshop, drinking his second beer and brooding at the fire.

When Fin walked in, he scowled. "You'd be wise to feck off. I'm not fit company."

"That's a pity." Fin dropped into a chair with a beer of his own. "You said she'd waked and was better—but little else. Branna's yet to come back down, and as Iona and Boyle just came in with cases of her things, I'd like to know just what the bloody hell better might be."

"Awake, aware. She drank the potion, and her color was good when I left her."

"All right then." Fin took a sip of beer, waiting for the rest. When it didn't come, he prepared to pry the lid off, then Boyle came in.

And better yet.

"I hauled clothes and boots and Christ knows, enough for a month or more that Iona swears is all essential. Then I was dismissed, which is just fine with me."

He dropped down, as Fin had, with a beer.

"Branna said she'd rallied well, and was having a shower. A hell of a thing, a scare like that. A hell of a thing." He drank deep from the beer. "I sent her out there. She was snappish and snarly, and I'd had enough of it, and sent her off to Shite Mountain. I should've kept her inside, working on tack. I shouldn't have—"

"It's not your fault." Connor shoved up, paced around. "Don't take any kind of blame on this, for it's not yours. She took it off. I told her I loved her. And to think I was entertained at the way she stormed about after, claiming she had to get to the stables straightaway."

"So, that's why I lost a full hour's sleep this morning. And," Boyle added, "that's what crawled up her arse like a scorpion."

"She took what off?" Fin asked, circling back.

"The necklace, the blue chalcedony with jasper and jade I gave her for protection. She took it off, went out without it, because I told her I loved her."

"Ah, God." Fin rolled his eyes heavenward. "Women. Women drive men to madness, and is there any doubt as to why? Why, the question should be, do we want them about when they devil us at every turn?"

"Speak for your own women," Boyle suggested. "I'm more than fine with my own."

"Give it time," Fin said darkly.

"Ah, feck off. She was in a temper," Boyle added, watching Connor. "It was foolish and reckless, but, well, as someone who's a temper of his own, it's the easiest thing in the world to do the foolish and reckless when caught up in one."

"We could have lost her."

"That will never happen," Fin vowed.

"She was gone, for moments—that might as well have been years for me." It shook Connor, belly deep, to think it. To know it. "You saw it yourself, Boyle, as you reached her seconds after I did."

"And in those seconds it felt as if the blood drained out of my body. I wanted to start CPR, and you tossed me back with a flick of your hand."

"I'm sorry for that."

"No need. You knew what needed to be done, and I was in the way. You breathed light into her. I've never seen the like."

Seeing it again, Boyle took a breath of his own.

"You're straddling our girl on the ground, calling out for gods and goddesses, and your eyes, I swear to you, went near to black. And the wind's whirling, the others come running, and you lifted your arms up, like a man grabbing on to a lifeline. And you pulled light out of the rain, pulled it out of the rain, into yourself so you burned like a torch. Then you breathed it into her. Three times you did that, burning hotter every time so I near expected you to go to flame."

"Three times is needed," Fin said. "With fire and light."

"And I saw her draw in air. Her hand moved, just a bit in mine." Boyle took another long drink. "Christ."

"I owe you all," Meara said from the doorway. She stood with her hands clasped, her hair loose, and her eyes filled with emotion. "I have to ask if I could have a moment alone to speak to Connor. Just a few moments, if you wouldn't mind."

"Of course not." Boyle got up quickly, moved to her, hugged her hard. "You look fine." Drawing back, he gave her back a hearty pat, then walked straight out.

Fin got up more slowly, studying the tears swirling in her eyes. He said nothing at all, but kissed her lightly on the cheek before going out.

Connor stood where he was. "Did Branna give you leave to be up and about?"

"She did. Connor—"

"It's best if you tell what happened to all, at one time."

"I will. Connor, please, forgive me. You have to forgive me. I couldn't bear it if you didn't, couldn't bear knowing I ruined it all. I was wrong, in every way wrong, and I'll do anything, anything you need or want or ask to mend this with you."

Her shame, her sorrow poured out, all but pooled at his feet. And still he couldn't bring himself to move toward her.

"Then answer me one question with truth."

"I won't lie to you, whatever the truth costs. I never have lied to you."

"Did you take off what I gave you because you thought I might have used it to hold you, to keep you with me, to make you feel for me?"

Shock ripped through the sorrow, pushed her one stumbling step back. "Oh no, God no. You would never do such a thing. I would never think any such thing, never of you. Never, Connor, on my life."

"All right." That, at least that, stanched the worst of a bleeding heart. "Be calm again."

"It was temper," she said, "temper and . . . fear. Honest, be honest," she ordered herself. "Fear more than anything, and that sparked the temper, and together the roar of it made me blind and deaf to any sort of sense. I swear to you, I *swear* I never meant to go out without it. I forgot. I was so turned around and wound up, that when Boyle booted me out, I changed jackets without a thought I'd left all the protection in the other."

She had to stop, press her fingers to her eyes. "Read me. Go in here—" She moved her fingers to her temple. "Read my thoughts, for you'd find the truth."

"I believe you. I know when I hear the truth."

"But will you forgive me?"

Was it as hard for her to ask, he wondered, as for him to accept? He thought perhaps it was. And still they needed to clear it all before the answers.

"I gave you something that mattered to me because you mattered."

"And I was careless with it, and with you. Careless enough to cost us all." She took a step toward him. "Forgive me."

"I give you love, Meara, of the kind I've never given to another. But you don't want it."

"I don't know what to do with it, and that's a different thing. And I'm afraid." She pressed both hands to her heart. "I'm afraid because I can't stop what's happening in me. If you don't forgive me, if you can't forgive me, I think something inside me would die of grief."

"I forgive you, of course."

"You're more than I deserve."

"Ah, Meara." He sighed it. "Love isn't a prize given on merit, or something to be taken back when there's a mistake. It's a gift, as much for the giver as the one who's given it. The day you'll take it, hold it, you won't be afraid."

He shook his head before she could speak. "It's enough. You're more weary than you know, and you've still a tale to tell. You should sit, and we'll see what Branna's cooked up as, Jesus, it's been a long time since breakfast."

When he crossed to her, she reached for his hand. "Thank you.

For the light, for the breath, for my life. And thank you, Connor, for the gift."

"Well now, that's a start," he told her, and led her back to the kitchen.

SHE TOLD THE STORY HALTINGLY WHILE SHE DUG INTO THE spaghetti and meatballs—a particular favorite. It seemed she couldn't get enough to eat or drink—though she found even a few sips of wine made her unsteady.

"You'll do better with water tonight," Branna told her.

"I think part of me knew it wasn't real, but it looked and felt and smelled and sounded so real. The gardens, the fountain, the paths, just as I remember them. The house, the suit my father wore, the way he tapped his finger to the side of his nose."

"Because he built the spell on your thoughts and images." Fin poured her more water.

"The way he called me princess." Meara nodded. "And how it could make me feel like one when he paid special attention to me. He was . . ."

It pained her to speak of it. "He was the fun in our home, you see. His big laugh, and how he'd slip us extra pocket money or a bit of chocolate like it was a secret shared. I worshiped him, and that all came back, those feelings, as we walked around the garden with a bird singing in the mulberry tree."

She had to stop a moment, gather herself. "I worshiped him," she repeated, "and he left us—left me—with never a backward glance. Sneaking off like a thief, and indeed it turned out he was just that, as he took everything of value he could with him. But there, in the gardens, it was all as it had been before. The sun shining, and the flowers, and feeling so happy.

"Then he turned on me, so quickly. He'd left because of me, he said, because I was friends with you. I'd shamed him by consorting, conspiring—he used those words—with witches. I was damned for it."

"A trick, using some of your thoughts again," Branna explained, "then twisting them."

"My thoughts? But I never thought he left because we were friends."

"But you've thought, more than once, his leaving was your fault. I don't have to slip into your mind to know it," Connor added.

"I know it's not true. I'm meaning I know he didn't leave because of me."

"And still it can make you doubt yourself." Iona sent her a look of understanding. "Make you wonder, when you're feeling low, what it is about yourself they can't love. I know how it is, and how hard it is to accept someone who should love you absolutely, doesn't. Or not enough. But it wasn't me, and it wasn't you. It was them, the lack in them."

"I know it, but you're right. Sometimes . . . The rose he gave me began to bleed, and he said I was a whore for lying with a witch. But I certainly never had before my father left us. And God, come to it, the man was too much of a coward ever to say such things to anyone's face."

She paused, stared down at her plate. "He was so weak, my father. It's hard admitting you loved something—someone so weak."

"We can't choose our parents," Boyle said, "any more than they can choose us. We all just have to muddle through best we can."

"And loving . . ." Connor paused until she lifted her eyes to his. "It's never something to be ashamed of."

"What I loved was an illusion, as much as what I saw today. But I believed in both, for a while. And with this, today, I felt things change when he said those things to me, those hard things he, for all his flaws, would never have said. I heard the rain again, and I heard Roibeard, and I knew him for a lie. I had the shovel. I hadn't when I walked with him, but now I did again. I swung it at him, swung it at his head, but he was quick. I swung it again, but the world started to turn and rock. And you, Connor, riding up like a demon on Alastar, and Boyle running from the stables, and Kathel and . . . He smiled at me—Cabhan now and nothing like my father."

She saw it clearly now, that cruelly handsome face smiling. "And it felt like something stabbed my heart—so sharp and cold—as he smiled and swirled away in the fog."

"Black lightning," Boyle stated. "That's what it looked like to me, just a flash of it from the stone he wears."

"I didn't see it." Meara lifted her water glass, drained it again. "I tried to walk, but it was like swimming through the mud. I felt sick and dizzy, and I couldn't feel the rain now as the shadows closed so thick.

"I couldn't get out of them, couldn't seem to move, couldn't call out. And there were voices in the shadows. My father's, Cabhan's. Threats, promises. I . . . He said, he would give me power. If I took Connor's life, he'd give me immortality."

She groped for Connor's hand, comforted when he took it. "I couldn't get out, and it all got darker and darker. I couldn't speak or move, as if bound up, and it was so bitter cold. Then you were there, Connor, talking to me, and there was light. You were the light. You told me to take your hand. I didn't know how, but you said to take your hand."

"And you did."

"I didn't think I could, it hurt so. But you kept saying I could. Kept telling me to take your hand and go with you."

She linked fingers with him now, a strong grip.

"When I did, it was like being pulled out of a pit while something fought to drag me back, pulled out and out, and the light, it was blinding. Then I felt the rain again. It hurt, everything, all at once. My body, my heart, my head. The shadows were horrible, but I wanted to go back where I didn't feel the pain."

"Part of it was shock," Branna said. "And what he'd used to take you. Then the abrupt yank back. It's why Connor put you to sleep."

"I owe you all."

"We're a circle," Boyle began. "Nothing's owed."

"No, I do. Owe you for coming for me—and yes, any of us would for the other. And I owe you my apology for being so foolish as to give him the chance to take me. And doing that put us all at risk."

"It's done." Boyle reached over, poked her shoulder.

"It is," Branna agreed. "Now you'll have some tea and quiet up in bed."

"I've slept enough."

"Not nearly enough, but you can take your tea out by the fire until you're ready to go up."

"I'll tuck you up."

Meara frowned at Fin. "I can move my arse from here to there."

"Now then, you're not after an argument after such a fine apology, are you?" He settled it by going around the table, plucking her right out of her chair. "You're a sturdy girl, Meara Quinn."

"Oh, am I now?"

He shot Connor a grin over his shoulder, carted her into the sofa. He gave the fire a little boost with a finger flick, then set her down, pulled the pretty throw over her while she eyed him balefully.

"I hate being tended."

"So do I, like poison. That's why I'm doing it. You deserve a bit of a pinch."

"Go on then, make me feel guiltier than I already do."

"No need for that." He sat down, just above her hip, gave her a brief study. And pulled the blue chalcedony out of his pocket. "I thought you might want this."

"Oh. How did you—"

"It was a quick trip to the stables to fetch your jacket, and this out of the pocket." He dangled it by the band. "Do you want it or no?"

"I do, very much."

He laid it around her neck himself. "Have more of a care with it, and with him."

"I will." She looked up, into his eyes. "I swear it. Thank you. Thank you, Fin."

"You're welcome, and maybe we'll see if there's any cakes to go with that tea."

He started out, glanced back. She held the stones in her palm, stroked them gently with a finger.

Love, he thought. It could make you a fool or a hero. Or both at once.

18

M EARA WOKE IN CONNOR'S BED. ALONE. THREE WHITE candles glowed in clear glass domes on his dresser. Some magickal health thing, she supposed—as the scent of lavender—sprigs of it under the pillow along with more crystals—was likely meant for health and restful sleep.

The last she remembered, as she scanned back, she'd stretched out on the sofa downstairs, tucked in by Fin, waiting for the others to come in for their tea.

She wondered if they had.

It annoyed her she'd dropped off again like a sick child. And annoyed her more to find herself alone in bed.

When she eased out of bed, she found her legs a little wobbly, which added a third annoyance. She'd felt so strong after drinking the broth, found it lowering to realize she wasn't fully recovered.

Someone had changed her into her nightwear, and that was lowering as well.

She walked, a bit drunkenly, into the bath, peered at herself in the mirror over the sink. Well, it was God's holy truth she'd looked better, but she'd looked worse.

She frowned as she saw her toothbrush, the creams she used, other toiletries tucked neatly into a basket on the narrow counter.

They'd moved her in, hadn't they, while she slept. Just packed her up, settled her in without so much as a by-your-leave.

Then she remembered why, and sighed.

She deserved it, and had no ground to stand on. She'd put herself and everyone else at risk, given them hours of worry. No, she wouldn't question the decision; she wouldn't complain.

But she would damn well find Connor.

She cracked open the door leading to Iona's room. If Boyle and Iona had gone to Boyle's, as they did most nights now, Connor would be using this room. Though he should be using his own, with her.

Rain pattered, and without even a hint of moonlight she waited for her eyes to adjust to the dark before she tiptoed into the room. She heard breathing, moved closer. She had a mind to just crawl right in with Connor, and they'd see what he had to say about it.

Then as she leaned over the bed for a closer look, she clearly saw Iona, tucked up with Boyle, her head on his shoulder.

A sweet picture, she thought—and a private one. But before she could back away, Iona whispered, "Are you feeling sick?"

"Oh, no, no, I'm sorry." Meara hissed it out. "So sorry. I woke, and I came in looking for Connor. I didn't mean to wake you."

"It's all right. He's on the sofa downstairs. Do you need anything? I can make you some tea to help you sleep again."

"I feel like I've slept a week."

"And some of us haven't slept through one bloody night," Boyle muttered. "Go away, Meara."

"I'm going. I'm sorry."

She went out through the hall door, heard the rumble of Boyle's voice, the murmur of Iona's laugh before she shut it behind her.

Fine for them, she thought, all curled up warm together, and here she was sneaking around in the middle of the night trying to find her man.

She was halfway down the steps before it struck her.

Her man? When had she started thinking of Connor as "her man"? She was fuddled up, that was all, just fuddled up from magicks dark and light. She wasn't thinking any way at all, not clearly, and should probably go straight back up to bed.

Sleep it all off.

But she wanted him, that was the hell of it. She wanted her head resting on his shoulder as Iona's was on Boyle's.

She made her way down.

He'd wrapped himself up in the throw on the sofa that was too short for him so his feet ended up propped on the arm of it, and his face half smashed into the pillow angled on the other arm.

The only way a man could be near to comfortable under the circumstances would be by drinking himself unconscious first. She shook her head, set her hands on her hips, and wondered how he managed to look so fecking adorable, considering.

They'd banked the fire so it burned low with simmering coals red as a beating heart. The light flickered over him, adding a bit of the devil to the adorable.

Regardless, she had some words to say to him, and he was about to hear them.

She started forward, eyes on his face, and tripped over the boots he'd tossed aside.

She landed on him, hard and full, getting an elbow in the belly for her trouble. So the first word she said to him was *oof*.

And his response was a muttered, "What the fuck!" as he levered up, grabbed her shoulders as if prepared to give her a good toss. Then he said, "Meara?" and pushed the hair out of her face.

"I tripped over your gigantic boots and into your bony elbow."

"You may have collapsed one of my lungs. Here." He shifted her, managed to sit with her half sprawled over his lap.

It was far from the way she'd intended things to go.

"Are you feeling sick then?"

Even as he lifted a hand to her brow as if to check for fever, she batted it aside. "Why is everyone thinking I'm sick? I'm not sick. I woke, that's all there is to it. I woke as I've slept most of a day and half a night away."

"You needed to," he said, altogether reasonable. "Do you want some tea?"

"I can see to my own tea if I'm in the mood for bloody tea."

"Sure you're in some mood or the other."

Tears wanted to fight their way through the annoyance, and she wouldn't have it. "You said you'd forgiven me."

"I did. I have. Here now, you're cold."

She batted again as he started to wrap the throw around her. "Leave off, will you leave off fussing over me." Those insistent tears kept pushing up, shocking, shaming, stupefying her. "Just leave off."

She tried to push away, roll up and off, but he wrapped his arms around her, held her in, held her tight. "Just calm yourself down, Meara Quinn. Be still a moment. Be quiet a moment."

The effort of trying to pull away exhausted her, left her out of breath and ever closer to tears. "All right, I'm calm."

"Not yet, but in a moment. Take a breath or two." He rocked her gently, looked toward the fire, boosted the flames.

"Don't tend to me, Connor. It makes me want to blubber."

"Blubber away then. It's all reaction, Meara, all natural from what was done to you, and what needed to be done to counter it."

"When will it stop?"

"It's less than it was, isn't it now? And will be even less in the morning with more calm, more rest. Have a bit of patience."

"I hate patience."

He laughed, brushed his lips over her hair. "That I know, but you have it. I've seen it myself."

But she had to dig and dig deep for it, Meara thought. Connor simply owned it, like the color of his eyes, the timbre of his voice.

"I don't hate your patience," she murmured.

"That's good to know as it would be a hard thing to rid myself of it to please you. Tell me now, did something wake you, or did you wake natural?"

"I just waked, and you weren't there." She heard it, the petulance in her voice. She could only hope that was part of the reaction as well, or else she'd learn to hate herself before much longer.

"If you forgive me, why are you sleeping down here with your feet hanging over the end of the sofa?"

"You needed quiet and rest, that's all." Because he trusted her calm now, he managed to shift them both so they wedged together in the corner of the sofa, looking toward the fire. "You were asleep before we brought out the tea, and never stirred when I carried you up, and Branna got you in your nightclothes. It's healing, darling, the sleep's a healing thing, and your mind and body, even your spirit took what it needed."

"I thought you didn't want to be with me, and I hunted you down to fight about it."

"Then I'm glad you tripped over my boots as this is nicer than a fight."

"I'm sorry."

"There's no need to keep being sorry." He traced a finger over the stones around her neck.

"Fin went to the stables and got it for me."

"I know."

"I won't take it off again."

"I know."

Trust, patience, forgiveness. No, she didn't deserve him, she thought, and pressed her face to his throat. "I hurt you."

"You did, yes."

"How do you love so easy, Connor? So free and easy. I don't mean how it always was with us, or how it is for you with Branna."

"Well, I'm new with it myself, so I don't know for certain. I can say it was like holding something you've had so long and is just another part of you. Then tilting that something a little. You know how you hold a piece of glass, then change the angle just a bit, and it catches the sun, makes that beam? You can kindle a fire that way, just tilting the glass. Something like that, and what was already there tipped and caught all the light."

"It could tip another way, and lose it again."

"Why would it when the light's so lovely? Do you see the fire there?"

"I do, of course."

"All it takes is a bit of tending, a stir, more fuel, and it'll burn day and night and night and day, give you light and warmth."

"You could forget to stir it, or run out of fuel."

Laughing, he nuzzled at her neck. "Then you'd be careless, and shame on you for it. Love needs tending, is what I'm saying. It's some work to keep the light and the warmth, but why would you want to be cold in the dark?"

"No one would want to, but it's easy to forget to tend things."

"I expect sometimes both tend, and other times one may tend more as the other forgets for a bit, then it might shift over again."

It was all a matter of balance, he thought, with some care and effort tossed in.

"What's easy isn't always what's right, and it may take a reminder here and there. Over it all, Meara, I've never known you to just settle on the easy. You've never been afraid of the work."

"What I can lift or carry or clean or put my back into, no. But emotional work is another matter."

"I haven't seen you shirk on that area either. You don't credit yourself near enough. Friendships take tending as well, don't they? How have you managed to remain such good, strong friends, not only with me, but Branna, Boyle, Fin, now Iona? Then there's family," he said before she could comment. "And families take considerable tending. You've done more than many would for yours."

"Yes, but—"

"And grumbling about it doesn't matter," he said, anticipating her. "It's the doing that counts at the end of the day."

He kissed her between the eyes. "Trust yourself."

"That's the hard part."

"Well then, practice. You didn't learn how to ride a horse by standing back and wondering if you might fall off."

"I've never in my life fallen off a horse."

"There, you see my point in it all."

It was her turn to smile. "Aren't you the clever one?"

"That makes you the lucky one, to have such a clever man in love with you. With patience enough to let you practice until you catch up."

"It makes my heart shake when you say it," she admitted. "It makes me so afraid when you say it to me my heart shakes."

"Then you'll tell me when it stops shaking and grows warm instead. Now try to sleep again."

"Here?"

"Here's where we are, and we're cozy, aren't we? And the fire's nice. Do you see the stories in the fire?"

"I see the fire."

"There're stories in the embers, in the flames. I'll tell you one."

He spoke of a castle on a hill, and a brave knight on a white stallion. Of a warrior queen skilled with bow and sword who rode the sky on a golden dragon.

All so fanciful, she thought, and so pretty she nearly saw what he drew with his words.

And she drifted off to sleep again with a smile on her face, and her head pillowed on his shoulder.

IT TOOK THREE DAYS BEFORE SHE WAS ABLE TO BE UP AND awake more than down and asleep. She spent the whole of the first day in bed, on the sofa, or doing what small chores Branna would assign her. But by the second, she felt able to return to the stables for part of the day, help with grooming, feeding.

And made her apologies to her coworkers.

By the third, she'd found Meara again.

It felt so good she sang as she shoveled shit.

"Look at you, giving Adele a run for her money."

"The woman's got a brilliant throat." Meara paused, smiled back at Iona who leaned on the open stall door. "Sure I never really understood that saying about how at least you have your health. Never really sick a day in my life. A strong constitution and a best friend who's a witch with exceptional healing powers saw to that. Now that I've been down, I'm learning to give thanks for being up again."

"You look great."

"And feel even better."

Meara wheeled the barrow out of the stall, and Iona stepped in to sweep it out. With their changed positions, Meara glanced right, left, to be certain they were alone.

"Since I'm better, will you tell me how bad it all was?"

"You don't remember? You had all the details before, once you came out of it."

"No, I remember. What I'm meaning is how bad was it, Iona? How close did he come to destroying me? I didn't feel right asking Branna or Connor before," she added when Iona hesitated. "But I'm on my feet now, and I'm asking you. Knowing the whole of it's the last of the healing I think I'll need."

"It was very bad. I've never dealt with anything like that before. Well, I don't think the others had either, but they knew more about it. The first moments, from what Branna told me, were critical. The deeper you went under, the harder it would be to bring you back, and the more likely . . . there could have been a kind of brain damage."

"A madness."

"Of a kind, I think. And memory loss, a psychosis. Branna said Connor reaching you so quickly made all the difference."

"So he saved my life, and my sanity as well."

"Yes. After that, the next hour or two were critical points. Branna knew just what to do, or she bluffed really well while barking out orders to Connor and me. I didn't realize how scared I was until we were finished; it was all just do, and do now. Then Fin came and having him added to it. And Boyle. He sat, held your hand right through the ritual. It took over an hour, and you were so white and pale and still. Then your color started to come back, not much, but a little."

"I'm making you cry. I don't mean to make you cry."

"No, it's okay." Iona dashed the tears away, and together they cut the binding on the fresh bale. "Your color came back, and Boyle said he felt your fingers move in his. And that's when I realized how scared I'd been—when the worst, according to Branna, was over."

"He put me down hard," Meara said as she loosened the straw with a pitchfork. "That's a tick in his column."

"Maybe, but we brought you back, and here you are spreading fresh straw for Spud's stall. That's a bigger tick in ours."

The silver lining, Meara mused. Iona could always find one. And maybe it was time she started searching them out herself.

"I'm after keeping it that way. I'll be putting in some time with my sword. I need the practice."

Needed practice, she thought as they moved to the next stall, on many things.

CONNOR DID SOME CLEANING OF HIS OWN, BUT WHAT HE considered end-of-the-day work. Birds must be fed, and as with horses, their area cleaned regularly of droppings. According to his personal calendar it was time for the hawks' bath to be cleaned and sanitized.

He wanted the labor. He'd needed the sheer physicality and mindless rote of it the last day or so while Meara recovered. It took effort to maintain his own calm, for her sake, to add some cheer to keep her spirits up when she'd been weakened and tired, and so unlike herself.

With some women you brought flowers or chocolate. With Meara—not that some blossoms and candy were out of place—she did better with bits and pieces of village gossip, or tales of work, of the people who'd come by the schools or stables.

He'd done his best to supply her, to prop his boots up, lift a pint and regale her with stories—some of which he embellished, others he made up of whole cloth.

And what he'd wanted to do was hunt Cabhan down, to dare the bastard to show himself. He wanted to whip a wind so fierce it would rend his bones and freeze his blood.

The thirst for vengeance ran so strong he was constantly parched.

And knew better, Jesus, knew better, he thought as he scrubbed the tub while the birds perched and watched him. But knowing and feeling weren't the same thing at all. He could hope that the labor burned the thirst out of him.

Then he saw her, walking across the wide gravel yard. He left everything, went out and through to meet her.

"What are you doing walking about alone?" he demanded.

"I could ask the same of you, but as I know what you'll say to that I won't and avoid it all. Iona and Boyle dropped me off before they went to Cong for a pint and a meal, so I haven't been alone at all, as I'm not now."

She glanced around. "You're late at this, aren't you, Connor? Where's everyone else?"

"We finished up the last hawk walk, and I sent the lot of them on. Brian had some studying for this online class he's taking, and Kyra had herself a hot date. And for the rest, I thought they could use an extra hour free."

"And you wanted some time alone with your friends," she added with a nod toward the hawks.

"There was that as well. I have to finish up here, since I've started it all."

"I'll come back with you, if that's all right. Then you'll give me a lift back to the cottage."

He walked her back. The birds ruffled a bit at the visitor, gave her a long stare.

"I haven't had time to visit much in the last months," she commented. "The young ones don't know me, or not well."

"They'll come to." He got back down to finish the cleaning. "How'd the day all go for you then?"

"Just as it should. I took out two guideds." She angled her head at his sharp look, pulled out the stones she wore from under her scarf. "And Iona insisted I take Alastar—*and* she braided fresh charms in his mane. I saw nothing but the woods and the trail. I won't be reckless, Connor. For my own sake, yes, but also because I never want to put you or the others through what I put you through once already."

She paused a moment. "I need the work and the horses as you need the work and the hawks."

"You're right. I hope he felt you. I hope he felt how strong and able you are, despite him."

He began to fill the tub, listened to the water pour.

"You think I don't know you're angry," she said quietly. "But I do know it. I'm angry as well. I've wanted to end him, always, because it's needed, because of you and Branna and Fin. But now I don't only want to end him—I want to give him pain and misery first, to *know* he suffers. I don't tell Branna as she'd never approve. For her it's only about right and wrong, light and dark—birthright and blood. And I know that's how it should be, but I want his pain."

From his crouch, he looked up at her. "I would give it to you, and more. I would give you his agony."

"But we can't." Hunkering down beside him, she touched his arm lightly. "Because Branna's got the right of it, and because it would change you. To seek revenge only? To seek to cause pain and suffering to pay him back for what he did to me? It would change you, Connor. I think it wouldn't change me, but that's the lack in me."

"It's not a lack at all."

"It's how I'm built, so we'll all have to live with it. But you're the light, and there's reason for that. End him, it must be done. But it must be done as it should be done. And if there's pain, it's because it had to be, not because you willed it."

"You've done some thinking on this."

He measured out the additives, then as he always did, stirred the water with his hands over the surface, adding that light she spoke of, for the health and well-being of his birds.

"God, yes, and far too much on it. And in thinking far too much on it, I came to understand you needed to know I felt as you do, but it isn't what I want from you, or for myself. I want what we are, the six of us. I want us to be right. And when we end him, and it's done, for us to know we were right. I want no shadows over us, no shadows over you. That's revenge enough for me."

"I love you, Meara. I love that you'd understand this, come clear to it, and tell me. I've been torn, in a way I've never been."

"Don't be. Know I'm telling you what's in my heart. I want us to be right."

"Then we will be."

Satisfied, relieved, she nodded. "And it's time to talk of it all again. I know you've all let it go the last few days."

"You weren't up to it."

"I'm more than up to it now." She pushed up, flexed her biceps to make him smile. "So we'll talk again, the six of us."

"Tonight?"

"Tonight, tomorrow night if need be. We'll see what the others say."

"I'll finish up then." He looked at her, smiled.

For some women it was flowers, he thought, or chocolate.

For Meara?

"Hold your arms out."

"What? Why would I?"

"Because I ask you. Hold your arms out."

She rolled her eyes, but did as he asked. He stretched his hands toward the birds, the young ones, sent his thoughts to them.

With the flow of his hands, they lifted, a soft whoosh of wings— the young hawks—and rose up to circle her, to make her laugh.

"Hold still, and don't worry about your jacket or your skin, I've taken that in the measure."

"What— Oh!"

They landed light and graceful along her outstretched arms.

"We've trained them well, though this isn't in their lessons. Still they don't seem to mind it. And they'll know you, Meara, now they will."

"They're beautiful. They're so beautiful. When you look in their eyes you think they know more than we do. So much more."

She laughed, and at the sound of it, the terrible thirst that had dogged him for days finally eased.

19

They had tea, with whiskey for those who wanted it, in the living room of the cottage. Branna set out a plate of gingerbread biscuits and considered her domestic duties done.

"Where do we begin?" she wondered. "Do we still agree on Samhain?"

"It gives us a fortnight," Boyle pointed out. "And from what I can see we could use the time. But . . ."

"But." Fin opted for whiskey and poured himself two fingers, neat. "He's come at us hard. We weren't ready for him, and that's clear enough."

"It was my fault."

"Fault isn't the point of it, Meara," Fin interrupted. "He lurks and slithers about at his will, and could come at any one of us in a moment of vulnerability. He's been at Iona, and now at you. From the pattern of it, if we don't end this, he'll go at Branna next."

"Let him come." Branna calmly took a sip of tea.

"You're far too cocksure of yourself," Fin snapped back. "Arrogance isn't power or a weapon."

"You've never had trouble wrapping yourself in it good and tight."

"Stop." Connor stretched his legs out, shook his head. "The pair of you. Save the pokes and barbs for when we've time for them. He may well go at Meara again, but she won't be foolish a second time."

"My oath on that."

"And it's just as likely he could take a pass at Boyle, or Fin or myself if he saw an opportunity."

Risking having an accusation of arrogance tossed at him, Connor shrugged. "And though I think Fin's right, if he tires of going for Meara, he'll turn his attentions on Branna, knowing that doesn't speak to what we do, when we do it, and how we send him on to hell for all and done."

"He's right. Protecting ourselves, that's defense—and it's essential," Iona added. "But it's our offense that needs to be perfected."

"She's been watching matches with me." Boyle gave her a quick grin. "We were close the last we went for him, sent him off bleeding and howling. But it wasn't enough. What will be?"

"The potion's stronger than it was, and that makes it a risk. One we'll have to take." Fin flicked a glance at Branna, got her nod.

"We thought to take him by surprise on the solstice," Connor pointed out, "and he took us. Even then, as Boyle said, we got close to it. If we make our stand at Sorcha's cabin, he'll have the advantage of shifting the time, and we couldn't know when he'd take us, or if he could, as he did, manage to separate us so we'd end up scattered, using power to reform again."

"If not there," Meara asked, "where?"

"It's a place of power, for us as well as him. I think it must be there. But you're right, Connor," Branna added. "We can't be separated. I'm thinking the three as a unit, and Fin, Boyle, and Meara as another—and those joined in a way that can't be broken. This we can do—and this we *will* do this time."

"Can we block him from the time shift?" Iona wondered.

"We could, I think, if we knew how he does it. But to counter such a spell, we'd need the elements of it. It's working blind there," Branna said in frustration.

"We shift first." Connor leaned forward, took a biscuit. "You're not the only one who can study and ponder and plot." He gestured toward Branna with the biscuit, then bit in. "But you're the only one who can make such brilliant gingerbread. We take the offensive, and shift from the start."

"And how, scholar, should we find the way to do that—which will take considerable doing—would we lure him to when we are?"

"We know the way to do it already," he reminded his sister. "Iona did it herself when she'd no more than gotten her toe dipped in her own magickal waters."

"I did?" After a blink, Iona pumped her fist in the air. "Go, me."

"I've done it myself," he added, "alone and with Meara, and met our long-ago cousins."

"Dream travel?" Branna put down her teacup. "Oh, Connor, that's a reckless thing."

"It's reckless times, and we'd have to be smart about it."

"It's bloody brilliant," Fin said, and earned Connor's grin, Branna's scowl.

"He's talking of casting a dream net over the six of us at once."

"I know it. That's what's bloody brilliant. He'd have to be on the same level, wouldn't he, to come at us? And it would be in the time and place of our choosing."

"He couldn't turn it on us," Connor pointed out, "as he wouldn't know the elements of the spell we cast, any more than we know the elements of his. It's him who'd have to come to us, and he'd lose the power to shift our ground."

"Give me a moment." Boyle lifted a hand, then used it to scratch his head. "Are you saying we'd go against Cabhan in our sleep?"

"A dream spell's different from natural sleep. It's not like you're lying there snoring them off. You've done a bit of it yourself," Connor recalled. "Pulled in with Iona into her dream—and didn't you give the bastard a good punch in the face while you were at it?"

"I did, and woke with his blood on my knuckles. But a dream battle? I've accepted all the lot of you can do as I've lived with it most of my life, but this strains the tether."

"He'd never expect it," Meara speculated. "Can it really be done?"

"All six at once, and with no one left behind at the wheel you could say." Struggling to look at the pros, the cons, the balance of them, Branna shoved both hands through her hair. "Sure it's nothing I've ever done. I'd be easy trying it with the three, facing him off that way, and the three of you back here—Fin at that wheel for certain to steer us back should we lose balance or direction."

"It's the six of us," Meara said decisively, "or not at all."

"Meara, I'm not talking this through in the way of insulting you. Any of you. But dream casting six together, and two of them without powers."

"Not so cocksure now?" Fin asked, with just a little bite.

"Oh, feck off," Branna snapped.

"And back at you, darling, for suggesting that I or Boyle or Meara would stay back like obedient pups while you waged the war."

"That's not my meaning."

"It's how it feels." Meara turned to Connor. "And you?"

"The six of us," he said without hesitation, "or none at all."

"All or none," Boyle agreed.

"Yes." Nodding, Iona took his hand. "If anyone can work out how it can be done, Branna, it's you."

"Ah, Jesus, bloody hell, let me think." She shoved the teacup aside, poured whiskey—more generously than Fin had.

She tossed it back like water.

"I've always admired your head for whiskey," Fin said as she shoved to her feet to pace.

"Be quiet. Just be quiet. Six at once," she repeated as she paced, "in the name of Morrigan, it's madness. And two of them armed with nothing but wit and fist and sword for all that. And one of them bearing Cabhan's mark. Just shut up about it," she snapped at Fin, who'd said nothing at all, "it's fact."

"They're armed with more than wit and fist and sword, and have more than a mark unearned." Connor spoke quietly. "They have heart."

"Do you think I don't know it? Do you think I don't value it, above all?" She stopped, closed her eyes a moment. Sighed. "You've turned this upside down on me, Connor. I need to work my way through it. It's not like one of us going into a magickal dream and taking along the one lying with us, the one we've been intimate with. And that has its own risks, as both Boyle and Iona know well."

"It's not, no. This would be a deliberate and conscious thing, a planned thing, a casting of our own." Connor lifted his hands, spread them, palms up. "With as many protections as we can build into the spell. But there'll be risks, yes, but risks however we go about it. And on Samhain, when the Veil thins, is the perfect time for this."

He rose, went to her, took her hands. "You'd leave them behind if you could—and I would as well. That's for love and friendship—and because this is a burden and duty that came to us. To you, to me, to Iona. Not to them."

He kissed her hands lightly. "But that would be wrong for so many reasons. We're a circle, three by three. It was always meant to be the six of us, Branna. I believe that."

"I know it. It's clear to me as well."

"You fear you'll fail them. You won't. You won't, and the burden of it isn't yours alone."

"We've never done it before."

"I'd never floated so much as a feather before I came here," Iona reminded her. "And now?"

She lifted her hands, palms up. The sofa where she sat beside Boyle rose smoothly, soundlessly, did a slow circle, then lowered back to the ground.

"Fair play to you," Fin said, amused.

"You taught me, you and Connor. You opened me to what I have and what I am. We'll figure out how to do it, and do it."

"All right. All right. I can't stand one against five. And it is a bloody brilliant idea. Reckless and frightening and brilliant. I know a potion I could tinker with that should work, and we'll write the spell—and I'll need every hour of that fortnight."

"And you have us to help you tinker," Connor pointed out.

"I'll need you all as well. Still, I'd be easier if we have what would be a kind of control outside the dream net."

"Would they have to be right here—with us, I mean?" Meara asked.

"Physically you're meaning?" Connor glanced over at her, considered. "I don't see why."

"Then you have your father, the two of you. And there's Iona's grandmother. That's blood and purpose shared, isn't it? And love as well."

"And more bloody brilliance!" On a laugh, Connor turned to Meara, plucked her straight out of her chair to spin her around. "That would do, and do very well. Branna?"

"It could—no, it would. And if I'd cleared the buzzing out of my head, I'd have seen it. Iona's Nan, our da, and . . ."

She turned to Fin. "Your cousin Selena. Would she be willing? Three's a better number than two, and gives it all power and blood from each of us. Three would balance, I'd think, should we need to be righted again."

"She would be more than willing. She's in Spain, but I'll contact her. I'll speak with her about it."

"Then that part's settled. I'll study on it."

"I have been," Connor told her. "The potion, to open the vision, shared by all inside the ritual circle. Best done outside, in the air. We take our guides as well, the horse, the hound, the hawk."

Branna started to speak, reconsidered. "You have studied on it."

"I have. Fin, your horse, your hawk—and I don't suppose you can come up with a hound in the next fortnight? Three for three."

"I have one. I have Bugs."

"Little Bugs?" Iona began, thinking of the barn dog at the big stables.

"Little as you are, game as you are. Three for three," Fin repeated with a nod. "Horse for Boyle, hawk for Meara, hound, such as he is, for me. It's well thought, Connor."

"It's you who must link them to the others, as they come from you."

"So I will."

"And so inside the circle, our circle and our guides," Connor said. "Our circle, the six, hands joined as the spell is spoken, as the spell is cast. And minds linked as well, which I will do. Minds, hearts, hands linked, and we go together, on the dream, to the night of All Hallow's Eve, to Samhain, in the year Sorcha's Brannaugh, Eamon, and Teagan returned to Mayo."

"Their presence adds power." Branna sat again, reached for a cookie herself. "The night the Veil thins. We may draw their power, and Sorcha's with ours. No, he could never expect this. There's time enough to perfect the potion and the spell. And then, to draw him there. That's for Meara."

"It's for me?"

Branna huffed at her brother. "You haven't spoken to her of it."

"Between one thing and the other, no. It's you he wants to use this go," Connor told her, "so it's you who'll use him. You'll sing him there."

"Sing?"

"Music, light, joy—emotions. Flames to his moth," Connor explained. "When he comes, it must be as quick as we can make it, giving him no time to slip away again."

"We go much as we did on the solstice," Branna began.

"No." Now Fin pushed to his feet. "We failed there, didn't we?"

"We have a new strategy, a stronger weapon."

"And if he once again manages to draw the three apart again, even if only for a moment? If the spell, the ritual, the end, must come from you, then he must be held off while you cast him out. We engage him. Boyle, Meara, and I. We cost him blood and pain before. We'll do worse this round. We'll do worse while you do what's best."

"Do you want his end, Fin, or do you want his blood?"

"I want both, and so do you, Branna. You can't shed it for gain or for joy."

"Nor should you."

"And I won't. We won't. But we'll shed it and worse in defense of the three. In defense of the light. If there's joy in it as well? A witch is still human for all that."

"I'm with Fin on it," Boyle said. "Iona's mine. And all of you my family. I'll stand for her, for you. I won't stand back."

"They've said what I'd say." Meara shrugged. "So that's done." She set her hands on her knees. "So, as I have it, in a fortnight's time, we'll all—including horses, hounds, hawks, go dreaming ourselves back a few centuries. I'll sing, and like the Pied Piper's tune to rats, that will lure Cabhan. Three of us fight, three of us cast the spell to destroy him. When the job's done we take our bows, then wake up back here where we should take another bow for certain, as we've vanquished evil. Then I suppose we should all go to the pub for a pint."

"That puts it all in a nutshell," Connor decided.

"All right then. I think there should be whiskey all around as we're all raving lunatics." She let out a breath, picked up a biscuit and bit in. "But at least one of us does indeed make brilliant gingerbread."

Amused, Connor poured whiskey all around, lifted his glass, tapped it to Meara's. "Whether we're victorious or buggered, there's no five others I'd rather stand with. So fuck it all. *Sláinte*."

And they drank.

THEY HAD WORK TO DO AND PLENTY OF IT. BRANNA BARELY left her workshop. If her nose wasn't in a spell book—Sorcha's, her great-grandmother's, her own—she was at her work countertesting potions or writing spells.

When the life around them allowed, Connor joined her, or Iona or Fin. Meara found herself in the position of fetching, carrying, cooking—or splitting that chore with Boyle.

As often as she could she pulled one of them out for sword practice.

And all watched the woods, the fields, the roads for any sign.

"It's been too quiet." Meara easily parried Connor's advance on one of the rare occasions she managed to drag him away from work or witchcraft.

"He's watching, and waiting."

"That's just it, isn't it? He's waiting. I've barely seen a shadow of him for days now. He's keeping his distance. He's waiting for us to make the move as he knows we've one to make."

She thrust, feinted, then swung up, nearly disarming him.

"You're not paying attention in the least," she complained. "If these blades weren't charmed I could've sliced your ear off."

"Then I'd only half hear your voice, and that would be a pity."

"We should go at him, Connor."

"We've a plan, Meara. Patience."

"It's not about patience, but strategy."

"Strategy, is it?" He twirled his free hand, stirred a little cyclone of air. When she glanced toward it, he moved in, and had his sword to her throat. "How's that?"

"Well, if you're after cheating—"

"And Cabhan will play nicely, of course."

"Point taken." She stepped back. "What I'm saying is we should feint." She jabbed, shifted, jabbed again. "Make him think we've gone at him, let him score a point or two. He'll think we've made our move, so he won't expect it when we do."

"Hmm. That's . . . interesting. Have you anything in mind?"

"You're the witch, aren't you, so you and your like would have to come up with the ritual of it."

Lowering her sword, she worked through what she'd only half baked in her head.

"But what if we did it near here—near the cottage where we could retreat, as retreat would be part of it. Let him think he's routed us."

"That's a hard swallow, but I see where you're going. Come on then." He grabbed her hand, pulled her into the workshop where Branna funneled a pale blue liquid into a slim bottle. Iona crushed herbs with mortar and pestle.

"Meara's an idea."

Eyebrows drawn together, Branna focused on the liquid sliding gracefully into the bottle. "I'm still working on the last idea that's come around."

"It's perfect, Branna." Iona stopped as Branna slid a crystal stopper into the bottle.

"And how many dream spells for six, and their guides, have you cast?"

"This will be my first." But Iona smiled. "And it's perfect. You should have seen the stars," she told Connor and Meara. "Tiny blue stars rising up, circling around the cauldron as she finished it."

"I think it's right." Branna rubbed the small of her back. "I added the amethyst as you suggested, Connor, and I think it's right. It needs to cure out of the light for at least three days."

She lifted it, carried it over to a cupboard.

"Let me make you some tea," Iona began, but Branna shook her head.

"Thanks, but no. I've had enough tea these last days to do me for six months. I'm after some wine."

"Then we'll have some wine while you hear Meara's idea. Better, don't you feel like cooking something?" Connor tried out a winning smile. "Aren't you feeling a longing for your own kitchen, darling? This is the sort of idea that goes well with a good bowl of soup, and the full circle of us."

Meara gave him a shove. "I think it's a good idea, and it should be heard by everyone. But I can make the soup while you sit and have your wine."

"I'll make it, because despite the fact that my brother's thinking with his belly, I do miss my kitchen. We've vegetables in the garden still." She pointed at Connor. "Go fetch some."

"What's your pleasure?"

"Any and all. I'll make it up as I go. And since you've had some fine idea, Meara, you can tell me of it while I have the wine. I don't see why I should wait for the others. Leave that, Iona. We'll get back to it. Let's have a little kitchen time."

Meara thought she was doing some making it up as she went as well. And by the time everyone arrived, she'd refined things a bit.

"So," she finished, "by doing something now without any real stake in winning, we'd have him thinking we'd made our attack, bungled it, or at least failed at it. We're forced to retreat to the cottage—where we're protected. Confused-like, you know? And bitter. If we've had our arse handed to us, he wouldn't think we'd launch another attack in a matter of days."

"If we go halfway, he could do real damage," Boyle pointed out. "Why not go full-out?"

"We still need the time left for the plan we settled on. I've been working the spell around the night we chose," Branna explained. "I wouldn't want to try it on another. It must be Samhain."

"Her point is by losing we have a better chance of winning." Connor gave Boyle a bump on the shoulder. "And I know losing, even by design, goes down hard."

"We'd have to make it flashy. He won't be fooled by something that looks weak and tossed together." But Fin smiled. "And we could give plenty of flash. Fire and storm, quake and flood. We throw the elements at him. It wouldn't be right—not on its own in any case, but it would be loud and strong and it would feel bloody fierce."

"A call to the elements." Now Branna began to smile. "Oh, we could make it fierce indeed. Even rock him on his heels a bit. We'd need to shield, for we've neighbors here. The field—the rise behind the gardens."

"That's farther than I'd thought," Meara began. "If we're going to be routed, that's a long road to retreat and safety."

"We don't retreat," Connor said. "At least not at a run. We fly."

"Fly?" Meara let out a long breath. "I think I'll have some more wine on that notion."

"That makes a statement, too." Iona did the honors with the wine. "We're defeated, and have to fly to safety. When would we try it?"

"We're on a waning moon." Connor glanced toward the window. "That could be useful. I'd like a go at it tonight, but I think closer to the real attack. Two nights more? If we get any singes from it, we'd have time to mend them."

"Two nights more." Branna walked over to stir her soup.

EVEN A FEINT REQUIRED PLANNING.

The three added more protection around the house. If Cabhan

believed them weakened, he might try to come in for the coup de grace. They couldn't afford a single chink.

Meara thought of it as a kind of play. Though some would be scripted, and she'd gone over her part of it a dozen times and more, some would have to be written and delivered on the spot.

"I'm nervous," she confessed to Connor. "More nervous than I was on the solstice."

"You'll be fine. We all will. Remember defense is the first goal here. Offense is just a happy bonus."

"It's nearly time." As if to warm them, she rubbed her hands together. "He may not even come."

"I think he will. He'll believe you're weak, and that we're fractured. He'll see a chance, want to take it. It's family he doesn't understand, and the bonds of friendship. But he'll understand what we lure him with."

He took her hand, walked with her into the workshop where the others had already gathered.

Even for this, Meara thought, the ritual must be kept.

So they lighted the ritual candles, watched while the smoke from the cauldron rose in a pale blue.

Branna took the ritual cup she placed in the circle, and spoke words familiar now.

"This we drink, one cup for six, from hand to hand and mouth to mouth to fix with wine our unity. Six hearts, six minds as one tonight as we prepare to wage this fight. Sip one, sip all, and show each one here answers the call."

Three times they passed the cup, hand to hand, mouth to mouth.

"A circle are we, two rings forming one three by three. Tonight we ask for strength and power to see us through the dark hour. Four elements we will call to bring about Cabhan's fall. Fire, earth, water, air we'll stir into a raging sea. As we will, so mote it be."

The three closed the circle.

"We're ready. The circle's been cast, the spell begun. If we have time to cast a circle on the rise, so much the better." Branna looked at Meara. "You'll know when to start."

She hoped so.

They walked to the rise, carrying candles, cauldron, weapons, and wands, shielded from sight—but for Cabhan's. Connor told her they'd left a window for him.

As they topped the rise, he reached for her hand. She pulled sharply away.

And the play began.

20

"I TOLD YOU TO STAY CLEAR OF ME."

"Ah now, Meara, it was just a pint in the pub."

"Talk runs like a river, Connor, so I know just how you spent your time in the pub." She sent him a look of absolute disgust. "And while I was barely able to stand after what was done to me. On your account done to me."

"Jesus, Meara, it was just a bit of a flirt. Some conversation, a bit of fun."

"Have all the fun and *conversation* you want, but don't think you'll come cozying up to me after." Deliberately she quickened her pace. "I know your ways. Who better?"

"What do you want?" He hunched his shoulders as they climbed the gentle rise. "I needed a bit of a breather, is all, after being cooped up day after day in the cottage or slammed with work at the school. You could do little but sleep for hours at a go."

"And why was that?" She stopped, rounded on him. "It's you and your magicks put me flat, isn't it?"

He planted his feet, glared back at her. "It's me and my magicks saved your bleeding life!"

"And while I was clinging to that life, you're off *conversing* with Alice Keenan at the pub."

"Enough, enough, enough!" Branna blasted at both of them. "There's no time for this. Didn't I tell you my star chart has tonight as our best chance to finish this? We can't do what needs doing with the two of you sniping at each other."

"I'm here, aren't I?" Meara jerked up her chin. "I'm here putting my life on the line yet again because I said I would. I keep my word. Unlike some."

"A man buys a girl a pint, and suddenly he's a liar?"

"Lay the candles, Connor." Branna shoved them at him. "And focus on what's at hand. By the gods, couldn't you have waited till we'd done this before sniffing around Alice Keenan?"

On an outraged hiss, Meara dumped her pack on the ground. "Oh, so it's fine and well for him to run around behind me after I've been useful?"

"That's not what I meant," Branna said, her tone sharp, dismissive. "Stop acting the gom."

"Now I'm the gom? You would take his part, even knowing he was off with that sleveen."

"Stop, will you all stop?" Iona put her hands over her ears.

"Best stay out of it," Boyle advised.

"I can't stay out of it. They're my family, and I can't take any more of this sniping and bickering. Give me those." She snatched the candles from Connor, began to secure them in a circle on the rise. "How can we work together, do what we've all sworn to do, if we're fighting?"

"Easy for you to say." Meara slammed a hand on the hilt of her sword. "When you've Boyle acting the lap dog for you at every turn."

"I'm no one's dog, Meara, and mind yourself."

"Didn't I tell you tonight wasn't the time?" Fin drew his athame out of its sheath, examined it in the light of the waning moon.

"If I said up, you'd say down," Branna shot back. "For the spite of it."

"And wasn't it you who said it must be the solstice? And here we are, months later, at your bidding again."

"And I wonder still how much you held back that night. If my bidding was done, you would never be here, you would never be with us."

"Branna, that's too much." Connor laid a hand on her shoulder. *He's coming,* he told her, told the others. *Fast.*

"Too much or not enough hardly matters now. We're here."

Branna swept her hand out, lighted the candles. She set the bowl at the northmost point.

Behind her, Connor touched his fingers lightly to Meara's.

She drew in a breath, and braced for it.

Fog dropped, a thick curtain, and with it came a bitter, bone-deep cold. A roaring ripped through it, shivered over the high grass.

Even as she drew her sword, Connor whipped her aside.

She felt something streak by her, grazing her arm, leaving a frigid burn of pain behind. She didn't have to feign the fear and confusion. Both rose up in her like a flood.

Then Connor's voice sounded in her head. *I'm with you. I love you.*

She spun, moving back-to-back with Boyle, readied to attack or defend.

The ground trembled under her feet as Fin called to earth.

"Danu, goddess and mother, by your power will this earth quake and shudder."

Even protected by the ritual, Meara nearly pitched forward when the ground heaved.

"On Acionna, on Manannan mac Lir I call," Branna shouted. "On Cabhan's head your wrath will fall."

Rain poured out of the sky, as if some deity had turned the course of a raging river.

Through the fog, the deluge, she saw glowing streaks of black winging like arrows. And to her shock, the fog hissed. It curled around her leg like a snake. Instinctively she sliced out at it, rent it. Black blood splattered from the mists.

Balls of fire catapulted out, burning the black arrows to cinder on Iona's call. "Power of fire in Brighid's name to scorch the dark with light and flame."

She felt Boyle lurch, whirled to defend, and saw him hack at a thorny tendril of fog striking toward Fin.

She dove under, sliced and struck, then had to cling to the ground as it heaved up under her.

"Sidhe, heed your servant, your son, and with your breath bring his damnation."

She watched Connor, a flame within the flames lift his arms high. As she struggled to her feet she saw the boiling sky above open. And whirl.

Came the lightning, spearing out of the dark to strike the quaking earth. Even the rain sparked with fire. She saw Iona fall, saw Boyle spring over to lift her. Flames shot from her hands at the wolf, at the man, at the twisting, snaking branches of fog.

She fought her way through, back toward the circle where the candles still glowed like beacons. Back toward Connor, who'd gripped Branna's hand, then Iona's, so the three of them lit, candles themselves.

It howled, the wolf.

It laughed, the man.

The candles, wax and witch, sputtered and began to dim.

"Pull it back!" Branna shouted. "We've lost it. We've lost the night. It's drained from us. Flee, while we can."

Connor gripped Meara around the waist—strong hands, face

fierce, sheened with sweat, with blood. "I'll steer clear of you after I save your life a second time."

Spinning through the air, showers of stars, sparks of fire. Light so brilliant she had to squeeze her eyes tight, turn her head.

Falling, too fast, too fast, so the speed sucked the air from her lungs.

The next she knew she was sprawled over Connor on the kitchen floor with his heart galloping under her like a runaway horse.

A terrible roar swept over, around, rattling the windows. Great fists pounded at the doors, the walls, so the cottage shook. For a moment Meara braced for it to collapse on their heads.

Then there was silence.

The others lay, like survivors of some terrible smashup. Kathel leaped over her to Branna, licked at her face, whined.

"I'm all right, there now. We're all right."

"That should convince him we'd gone to war tonight, as it bloody well convinced me." Connor stroked Meara's hair as he shifted her. "Are you hurt?"

"I don't know. I don't think so. You're bleeding."

He swiped his fingers over a gash on his temple. "Didn't dodge fast enough."

"Here, let me see to it." Branna scooted over. "Iona—"

"I know what you need." As she ran toward the workshop, Meara tugged up her trouser leg, saw the livid bruise circling just above her ankle.

"Here, let me see to that." Even as Branna tended him, Connor reached out, laid his hands on the bruising.

"The fog—it turned to snakes. And thorns. It grew thorns."

"Not thorns, teeth." Fin, his face shiny with sweat, sat on the kitchen floor with his back braced against a cupboard.

"You're hurt. A bit of that for Connor's head," Branna snapped to Iona as she pushed up to go to Fin. "See that it's clear and clean. Were you bitten?" she demanded of Fin.

"I'm just winded."

She pressed her hand to his chest. "It's more. Let me see."

"I'll tend to myself when I've my breath back."

"Oh, bollocks." With a flash of her hand, she stripped him to the waist.

"If you're after getting my clothes off, we could do with some privacy."

"Shut it." She looked over her shoulder, spoke urgently. "Iona, the balm!"

"I'll see to myself," Fin began.

"I'll put you under if you don't be still, be quiet. You know I can and will. Connor, I need you."

"How bad is it?"

He saw for himself when he pushed across the kitchen floor.

Raw and black puncture wounds ran down both sides of Fin's torso, as if a monstrous jaw had closed over him.

"They're not deep." Branna's voice stayed low and steady. "Thank the gods for that. And the poison . . ." She looked up sharply. "What did you do to stop the spread of it?"

"I'm his blood." Breathing labored, Fin spoke slowly, almost too precisely. "What he makes from his weakens in mine."

"There's pain," Connor said.

"There's always pain." But he hissed out a breath as Branna worked deeper. "Christ Jesus, woman, your healing's worse than the wound."

"I have to draw it out, weakened or not."

"Look at me, Fin," Connor ordered.

"I'll take my own pain, thanks."

Connor merely gripped Fin's jaw in his hand, turned his head.

He's taking the pain, Meara realized. Taking Fin's pain so the healing goes quickly. And so, she knew, Branna couldn't take it herself.

Boyle got out the whiskey, so she stood to fetch glasses. Then sitting on the floor again, passed them out when Branna sat back, nodded.

"That will do."

"A bit more of a dust-up than we reckoned on." Mirroring Fin, Connor leaned back against the cupboards. His own face shone now, from the sweat of the effort, of the pain. "But we singed his ass more than a bit, and we're safe and whole."

"He'll think we're cowed," Branna said. "He'll think we're bickering among ourselves, licking our wounds, questioning if we should ever try such a thing again."

"And when we go at him in two days' time, we'll burn him to ashes before he knows we've duped him. A fine show, one and all." He lifted his glass. "A notion of brilliance, Meara my darling, and one that may have turned the tide good and hard. It's hardly a wonder I love you."

He drank, as did the others, but Meara held her glass and studied him.

"No taste for your whiskey?" he asked her.

"I'm waiting for my heart to shake. It may be I'm in a bit of shock. Why don't you tell me again? We'll see if it gets through."

He set his glass aside, walked over on his knees to where she sat on the floor. "I love you, Meara, and ever will."

She downed the whiskey, set the glass down, rose up on her knees to face him. "No, it's not shaking. But really, what sort of weak and foolish heart shakes in fear of love. Will yours?" She laid her hand on his chest. "Let's see if it does. I love you, Connor, and ever will."

"It may have stopped for a second." He closed his hand over hers, held it to him. "But there's no fear, there's no doubt. Do you feel that? It's dancing, with joy."

She laughed. "Connor O'Dwyer of the dancing heart. I'll take you." She threw her arms around him, met his mouth with hers.

"Would you like us to move along then?" Boyle replied. "Give the two of you your privacy there on the kitchen floor?"

"I'll let you know," Connor murmured, then went back to kissing his love.

He stood, plucked her up, swept her up, gave her a toss to make her laugh again. "On second thought, we'll get out of your way."

He carried her from the room on more laughter.

"It's what you've always wanted," Fin said to Branna.

"What I knew could be, felt should be, and yes, what I wanted." She let out a sigh. "I'll put on the kettle."

LATER, WRAPPED UP WITH MEARA IN BED, THE HOUSE QUIET around them, and moonlight coming through the window, Connor asked her.

"Was it the battle that did it? The knowing of life and death that steadied your heart?"

"You took his pain."

"What? Who?"

"Down in the kitchen. Though he didn't want it of you, you wouldn't let him hurt, so you took Fin's pain. I thought, That's who he is, down into it. A man who'd take on the pain of a friend—or anyone else for that matter. A man of power, of kindness. Of fun and music and loyalty. And he loves me."

She laid a hand on his cheek. "I've loved you as long as I can remember, but I wouldn't let myself have it, have that gift you spoke of, or give it. That was fear.

"And I thought, when I watched you tonight, in the horrible heat of battle, in the bright lights of the kitchen, how can I let myself be too afraid to have what I love? Why do I keep convincing myself I might be like my father, or let what he did define the whole of my life? I owe Cabhan a debt."

"Cabhan?"

"He thought to hurt and shame and shake me by bringing the image of my father to me. And he did, right enough, but that was from me. And seeing plain what I held in me, I could start seeing the truth. He didn't leave me, or my mother, or the rest of us. He left his own shame and his mistakes and failures because he couldn't stand and look at them in the mirror."

"You always stand, you always look."

"I try, but I didn't look from the right angle. I didn't let myself tip the glass. It's my mother who stayed, with the shame he left her with, who lived—in her own dithering way—with mistakes and failures that were his. And she stood, and stayed, for me and my family, even after we were grown. She's happy now, free of that whether she knows it fully or not. I'm free of it as well. So I owe Cabhan a debt. But it won't stop me from doing all I can to send him to hell."

"Then I owe him a debt alongside you. And we'll send him to hell together."

IT WAS HARD OVER THE NEXT TWO DAYS OUTSIDE OF THE cocoon of the cottage to stop himself from radiating joy. He had to go about his work, and avoid contact with Meara until they were inside that sanctuary.

He felt Cabhan probing once or twice, but lightly, cautiously. And there were bruises there, oh yes, they'd given the bastard a few bruises for his trouble.

He'd come into it weaker than he'd been—and thinking their circle damaged when it was stronger and more vital than it had ever been.

And yet.

"You have doubts," he said to Branna. Only hours remained, so he'd come home to help however he could.

"It's a good scheme."

"And still?"

She took out the dream potion, padded it carefully in a silver box that had come down through their family, placing it alongside the bloodred brew she hoped would end Cabhan.

"A feeling, and I don't know if it's a true one. I wonder if I was so confident on the solstice that now I doubt when it's time to try again. Or if there's truly something I'm not seeing, not doing that needs seeing, needs doing."

"It's not only on your shoulders, Branna."

"I know it. Whatever Fin thinks, I know that very well." She gathered the tools she'd cleansed and charmed to wrap in a roll of white velvet.

She opened a drawer, took out a smaller silver box. "I have something for you, whatever tonight brings."

Curious, he opened it, saw the ring, the deep glow of the ruby in hammered gold. "This came to you, down from our great-grandmother."

"Now it's yours if you want it for Meara. She's my sister, and that bind only tightens when you give her the ring. Another circle, and it should be hers. But only if it's what you want."

He came around the work counter, drew her in. "After the night's done. Thank you."

"I want it ended, now more than ever. I want to see you and Meara make your lives together."

"We'll end it. We're meant to."

"Your heart's talking."

"It is, and if your head wasn't talking so bloody loud, you'd hear your own." He drew her back. "If you won't trust your heart, trust your blood. And mine."

"I am."

He gathered his own tools and readied himself for the night to come.

They met at the big stables, and at Fin's request, Connor saddled Aine, the white filly Fin bought to breed with Alastar.

"I thought Fin was taking Baru, his stallion."

Connor glanced back at Meara. She wore sturdy boots, rough pants, a thick belt with her sword and sheath carried on it. He knew Iona had braided charms in her hair.

And she wore his necklace over a flannel shirt.

"So he is. We're to take Aine, and Iona and Boyle take Alastar. The third horse makes the getting there easier."

"So we're riding to Sorcha's cabin."

"In a way. You're prepared for what's to come?"

"As well as I can be."

He reached across the saddle for her hand. "We'll come through it."

"I believe that."

Together, they led the horse out to join the others in the pale light of a crescent moon. "Once we're there it must go quickly, without a missed step. My father, Iona's grandmother, Fin's cousin, they'll have ahold of things, and they'll bring us back should things go wrong."

"You'll bring me back," she said.

Once he'd mounted, she swung up behind him. He glanced at Boyle and Iona already on a restless Alastar.

Wants to be going, he does, to be doing.

He saw Fin gather up the little mutt, mount the black stallion, then hold his hand down to Branna.

"It's hard for her," Connor murmured. "To go with him this way."

"Hard for him as well."

But Branna mounted, then signaled to Kathel. The hound raced off. Overhead Roibeard called, and Fin's Merlin answered.

"Hold on to me," Connor advised, and the three horses leaped forward in a gallop.

Then they flew.

"Sweet Jesus!" Meara's big laugh followed the exclamation. "This is brilliant! Why haven't we done this before?"

The wind streamed by, cool and damp, while clouds winked over the moon and away again. The air filled with the scent of spice and earth, of things going bold before they settled down to rest.

They flew, riding the air above that earth, into the deep, and straight through the vines to Sorcha's cabin.

"Quickly now," Connor told her.

He had to leave her to move to Branna and Iona, to cast the circle, a hundred candles, the bowls, the cauldron.

Branna opened the silver box, removed the dream potion.

"Spirits ride upon this night. We come to join them with our light. In this place and in this hour, we call upon bright things of power. We are the three, and are three more. Together we walk through the door and into the dreaming there to find the meaning of our destiny. So we drink one by three and one by three."

She poured the potion into a silver cup, lifted it up. Lowered it, sipped.

"Body, blood, mind, and heart, into the dreaming we depart."

She passed the cup to Fin. He sipped, repeated the words, and then to Iona, and around the circle.

It tasted of stars, Connor thought as he took his turn, one by three.

He joined hands, his sister's, Meara's, and with her circle said the words.

"With right, with might, with light we seek the night. A dream-walk back in time, Cabhan's evil to unwind. To the time of the return of Sorcha's three. As we will, so mote it be."

There wasn't a floating as he'd experienced before, but a kind of swimming through mists and colors with voices murmuring behind, before, and images just on the edges of his vision.

When the mists cleared, he stood as he had been, with his circle, and his hand clasped with Meara's, his other with Branna's.

"Did we go back?"

"Look there," Connor said to Meara.

Vines covered the cabin, but it stood. And bluebells bloomed on the ground beneath the gravestone.

The horses stood with the hawks on branches above them. Kathel sat calm as a king beside Branna, while Bugs quivered a little between Fin's boots.

"We're all here, as we should be. You'll call him now, Meara."

"Now?"

"Start," Branna confirmed, and took out the vial filled with red. "Draw him in."

Inside the vial brilliance pulsed and swirled. Liquid light, magick fire.

"In the center of the circle." Connor took her by the shoulders, kissed her. "And sing, whatever happens."

She had to steady herself, calm her heart, then open it.

She'd chosen a ballad, sang in Irish though he doubted she knew the meaning of all the words. Heartbreaking they were, and as beautiful as the voice that lifted over the clearing, into the night, and across all the dreaming time.

He'd ask her to sing it for him, he decided, when they were done with dark things, when they were alone. She would sing it again, for him.

"He hears," Fin whispered.

"It's a night that calls to black and white, to dark and light. He'll come."

Branna stepped out of the circle, then Connor, then Iona.

"Whatever happens," Connor said again. "Sing. He's coming."

"Aye." Fin stepped out of the circle, leaving Boyle to guard Meara. He drew a sword, and set it to burning.

It came on the fog, a shadow that became a wolf. It stalked toward the line of four witches, then whirled and leaped at the circle.

Boyle blocked Meara's body with his, but the wolf leaped back from the fireball Iona threw.

It paced the clearing, eyed the horses until Alastar pawed the ground, then it rose up to a man.

"Do you think to try for me again? Do you think to destroy me with song and your weak white magick?" He waved a hand and the flame on Fin's sword died.

Fin simply lifted it, caught the fire again.

"Try me," Fin suggested, and stepped forward in front of the three.

"My son, blood of my blood, you are not my enemy."

"I am your death." Fin leaped forward, swinging out, but cleaved only fog.

The rats came, a boiling flood of them, red eyes feral. Those that streamed to the circle screamed as they flashed into flame. But Meara saw one of the candles gutter out.

Now she drew her sword and sang.

Aine reared, hooves flashing. Her eyes rolled in fear. Fin grabbed her reins, used the sword to set a ring of fire around her. While the two stallions crushed the rats, the hawks dived for them.

The bats spilled out of the sky.

Connor saw another candle wink out.

"He's attacking the circle to get to her. It must be now, Branna."

"We have to pull him closer."

Connor threw his head back, called the wind. The torrent of it tore through those thin wings until the air filled with smoke and screaming.

Meara's voice wavered as a single twisted body fell at the circle's edge, and a third candle went out.

"Steady, girl," Boyle murmured.

"I'm steady." Drawing in air, she lifted her voice over the screams.

"I'll slice open your throat and rip your heart out through it."

Cabhan, his eyes nearly as red as his stone, threw black lightning at the circle.

Boyle took an opening, jabbed through with his knife, drew first blood. The explosion of air knocked him back. The blood on the tip of his knife hit the ground and sizzled black as pitch.

"It has to be now," Connor shouted, and began the chant.

The power rose up, clear heat. Again he heard voices, not only Meara's and Iona's, but others. Distant, murmuring, murmuring through the thinning Veil. Over them Meara's song rang, filled his heart with more.

Fin swept his sword so the candles reignited, so the flames ran straight.

The rats turned away, flowing toward the three. Cabhan dropped to all fours. The wolf charged Kathel.

Connor felt Branna's fear, turned with her as did Iona to shoot power toward the wolf. But the ground heaved under it—Fin's work. Kathel's jaws snapped over the wolf's shoulder, and Roibeard dived.

It screamed, fought its way clear to run toward the trees beyond the clearing.

"Cut it off," Connor shouted. "Drive it back." But his heart stopped when both Boyle and Meara ran clear of the circle to join Fin.

It darted right, turned and, desperate, began to charge. Meara's sword flamed. The tip of it scorched fur before the wolf checked, turned again.

Out of the corner of his eye, Connor caught movement. He glanced over, saw three figures by the cabin. A wavering vision, as their voices struggled to reach through the Veil.

Then he knew only his sister, Iona, only the three and the hot rush of power.

She suspended the vial in front of them, and with hands linked, minds linked, powers linked, they hurtled it toward the wolf.

The light exploded, a thousand suns. It charged into him, through him.

"By the power of three you are ended. With our light your dark is rended. With our light this web is spun, with our blood you are undone. No life, no spirit, no magicks left for thee. As we will so mote it be."

The light flashed again, brighter still. It bloomed in his eyes, simmered in his blood. And through it, again, he saw three figures. One held out a hand to him, reaching. Reaching.

Then they were gone, and so was the light. The dark fell, lifted only by moonglow and the circle of candles. Breaking his link with the three, Connor rushed to Meara.

"Are you hurt? Anywhere?"

"No, not a bit."

"You weren't to stop singing, you weren't to step out of the circle."

"My throat got dry." She smiled, her face smeared with soot, and threw her arms around him. "Did we end it? Did we end him?"

"Give me a moment." Ash and blood littered the ground, tiny splotches of black still burned. "By the gods what's left of him should be here. Give me a moment."

"He's not. I can feel him." Fin swiped blood from his face. "I can feel him, I can smell him. I can find him. I can finish him."

"You can't leave the clearing." Branna grabbed his arm. "You can't or you may not get back."

Face fierce, Fin wrenched his arm free. "What difference does it make if I end him, end this?"

"This isn't your place."

"And it isn't your choice."

"Nor can it be yours," she said, and flung him back into the circle. "Connor."

"Bloody hell."

With considerable regret, he rushed Fin, pinned him, and got a fist in his face for the trouble before Boyle joined in.

"Quickly." Branna laid a hand on Connor's shoulder, took Meara's hand, nodded to Iona as the men grappled on the ground.

She closed her eyes, broke the spell.

Through the dark and light again, through the colors and mists to the clearing with the ruins of a cabin and the call of an owl.

"It wasn't for you to stop me."

"Not only her," Connor said, rubbing his jaw as he eyed Fin. "It was for all of us. We can't do without you."

"Can you be sure?" Meara demanded. "Can you be sure we didn't finish him?"

Saying nothing, Fin stripped off his coat, yanked the sweater under it over his head. The mark on his shoulder showed raw and red, beating like a heart.

"What is this?" Branna demanded. "You feel his pain?"

"Your blood saw to that. He's wounded, but who can say if it's mortal. I could have finished him."

"If you'd left the clearing, you'd have been lost," Connor said. "You're with us, Fin. Your place, your time is here. We didn't finish him. I felt him as well before Branna broke the spell. But not here, not now. And this time, we've some bumps and bruises and nothing more—if we're not counting your fist in my face—and he's battered and bleeding and torn, half blind as well—I got that much. He may not survive the night."

"I can ease the pain."

Fin only stared at Branna. "I'll keep it all the same."

"Fin." Iona stepped forward, rose to her toes to cup his face in her hands. "*Mo dearthair*. We need you with us."

After a moment's struggle, Fin lowered his forehead to hers, sighed. "Ah well."

"We should go back." Meara handed Bugs to Fin, where the dog wiggled in his arms and lapped at his face. "We may not have finished it, but we did good work tonight. And for myself, I sang my throat dry as the moon."

"It's not finished." Branna crossed over to Sorcha's gravestone, traced a finger over the words carved there. "Not yet finished, but it will be. I swear it will be."

They mounted, filthy, weary. Connor hung back, just a bit, looking over his shoulder at the clearing before they went through the vines. "I saw them—I need to tell the others."

"Saw who?"

"The three. Sorcha's three—the shadows of them. Eamon with a sword, Brannaugh with a bow, Teagan with a wand. Some part of them was there, came through and into the dreaming. They tried to get through to us."

"We could have used them—more than their shadows."

"That's the truth all around." He turned Aine toward home. "I thought, for a moment and more, I thought we'd done it."

"So did I. You wanted to go with Fin. Wanted to go with him and finish it, whatever the cost."

"I did, but I couldn't."

"Because it wasn't meant."

"More than that. I couldn't leave you." He stopped Aine so he could turn to her, touch her face. "I couldn't and wouldn't leave you, Meara, not even for that.

"I've something for you."

He dug in his pocket, pulled out the silver box, opened it so the ruby pulled at the moonlight.

"Oh, but, Connor—"

"It's a fine ring, and I'll see that it fits—as you fit me, and I fit you. It's come down through the family. Branna passed it to me so I could give it to you."

"You're proposing to me on horseback when we both smell of brimstone?"

"It strikes me as romantic and memorable. Look here." He slid it onto her finger, gave it a little tap. "See, it fits, as I said. You'll have to marry me now."

She looked at the ring, back at him. "I suppose I will then."

He caught her in a kiss as sweet as it was awkward.

"Hold on now," he told her.

And they flew.

SEEKING ITS LAIR, IT CRAWLED OVER THE GROUND, MORE shadow than wolf, more wolf than man. Its black blood scorched the earth behind it.

It knew only pain and hate and a terrible thirst.

And the terrible thirst was vengeance.

Keep reading for an excerpt from
the two-hundredth novel
by Nora Roberts

THE COLLECTOR

Now available from Piatkus

S HE THOUGHT THEY'D NEVER LEAVE. CLIENTS, ESPECIALLY
new ones, tended to fuss and delay, revolving on the same loop
of instructions, contacts, comments before finally heading out the
door. She sympathized because when they walked out the door they
left their home, their belongings, and in this case their cat, in someone else's hands.

As their house sitter, Lila Emerson did everything she could to send
them off relaxed, and confident those hands were competent ones.

For the next three weeks, while Jason and Macey Kilderbrand
enjoyed the south of France with friends and family, Lila would live
in their most excellent apartment in Chelsea, water their plants, feed,
water and play with their cat, collect their mail—and forward anything of import.

She'd tend Macey's pretty terrace garden, pamper the cat, take
messages and act as a burglary deterrent simply by her presence.

While she did, she'd enjoy living in New York's tony London Terrace just as she'd enjoyed living in the charming flat in Rome—where
for an additional fee she'd painted the kitchen—and the sprawling
house in Brooklyn—with its frisky golden retriever, sweet and aging
Boston terrier and aquarium of colorful tropical fish.

She'd seen a lot of New York in her six years as a professional house
sitter, and in the last four had expanded to see quite a bit of the world
as well.

Nice work if you can get it, she thought—and she could get it.

"Come on, Thomas." She gave the cat's long, sleek body one head-
to-tail stroke. "Let's go unpack."

She liked the settling in, and since the spacious apartment boasted a second bedroom, unpacked the first of her two suitcases, tucking her clothes in the mirrored bureau or hanging them in the tidy walk-in closet. She'd been warned Thomas would likely insist on sharing the bed with her, and she'd deal with that. And she appreciated that the clients—likely Macey—had arranged a pretty bouquet of freesia on the nightstand.

Lila was big on little personal touches, the giving and the getting.

She'd already decided to make use of the master bath with its roomy steam shower and deep jet tub.

"Never waste or abuse the amenities," she told Thomas as she put her toiletries away.

As the two suitcases held nearly everything she owned, she took some care in distributing them where it suited her best.

After some consideration she set up her office in the dining area, arranging her laptop so she could look up and out at the view of New York. In a smaller space she'd have happily worked where she slept, but since she had room, she'd make use of it.

She'd been given instructions on all the kitchen appliances, the remotes, the security system—the place boasted an array of gadgets that appealed to her nerdy soul.

In the kitchen she found a bottle of wine, a pretty bowl of fresh fruit, an array of fancy cheeses with a note handwritten on Macey's monogrammed stationery.

Enjoy our home!

—Jason, Macey and Thomas

Sweet, Lila thought, and she absolutely would enjoy it.

She opened the wine, poured a glass, sipped and approved.

Grabbing her binoculars, she carried the glass out on the terrace to admire the view.

The clients made good use of the space, she thought, with a couple of cushy chairs, a rough stone bench, a glass table—and the pots of thriving flowers, the pretty drops of cherry tomatoes, the fragrant herbs, all of which she'd been encouraged to harvest and use.

She sat, with Thomas in her lap, sipping wine, stroking his silky fur.

"I bet they sit out here a lot, having a drink, or coffee. They look happy together. And their place has a good feel to it. You can tell." She tickled Thomas under the chin and had his bright green eyes going dreamy. "She's going to call and e-mail a lot in the first couple days, so we're going to take some pictures of you, baby, and send them to her so she can see you're just fine."

Setting the wine aside, she lifted the binoculars, scanned the buildings. The apartment complex hugged an entire city block, and that offered little glimpses into other lives.

Other lives just fascinated her.

A woman about her age wore a little black dress that fit her tall, model-thin body like a second skin. She paced as she talked on her cell phone. She didn't look happy, Lila thought. Broken date. He has to work late— he says, Lila added, winding the plot in her head. She's fed up with that.

A couple floors above, two couples sat in a living room—art-covered walls, sleek, contemporary furnishings—and laughed over what looked like martinis.

Obviously they didn't like the summer heat as much as she and Thomas or they'd have sat outside on their little terrace.

Old friends, she decided, who get together often, sometimes take vacations together.

Another window opened the world to a little boy rolling around on the floor with a white puppy. The absolute joy of both zinged right through the air and had Lila laughing.

"He's wanted a puppy forever—forever being probably a few months at that age—and today his parents surprised him. He'll remember today his whole life, and one day he'll surprise his little boy or girl the same way."

Pleased to end on that note, Lila lowered the glasses. "Okay, Thomas, we're going to get a couple hours of work in. I know, I know," she continued, setting him down, picking up the half glass of wine. "Most people are done with work for the day. They're going out to dinner, meeting friends—or in the case of the killer blonde in the black dress, bitching about not going out. But the thing is . . ." She waited until he strolled into the apartment ahead of her. "I set my own hours. It's one of the perks."

She chose a ball—motion-activated—from the basket of cat toys in the kitchen closet, gave it a roll across the floor.

Thomas immediately pounced, wrestled, batted, chased.

"If I were a cat," she speculated, "I'd go crazy for that, too."

With Thomas happily occupied, she picked up the remote, ordered music. She made a note of which station played so she could be sure she returned it to their house music before the Kilderbrands came home. She moved away from the jazz to contemporary pop.

House-sitting provided lodging, interest, even adventure. But writing paid the freight. Freelance writing—and waiting tables—had kept her head just above water her first two years in New York. After she'd fallen into house-sitting, initially doing favors for friends, and friends of friends, she'd had the real time and opportunity to work on her novel.

Then the luck or serendipity of house-sitting for an editor who'd taken an interest. Her first, *Moon Rise*, had sold decently. No bust-out bestseller, but steady, and with a nice little following in the fourteen-to-eighteen set she'd aimed for. The second would hit the stores in October, so her fingers were crossed.

But more to the moment, she needed to focus on book three of the series.

She bundled up her long brown hair with a quick twist, scoop and the clamp of a chunky tortoiseshell hinge clip. While Thomas gleefully chased the ball, she settled in with her half glass of wine, a tall glass of iced water and the music she imagined her central character, Kaylee, listened to.

As a junior in high school, Kaylee dealt with all the ups and downs—the romance, the homework, the mean girls, the bullies, the politics, the heartbreaks and triumphs that crowded into the short, intense high school years.

A sticky road, especially for the new girl—as she'd been in the first book. And more, of course, as Kaylee's family were lycans.

It wasn't easy to finish a school assignment or go to the prom with a full moon rising when a girl was a werewolf.

Now, in book three, Kaylee and her family were at war with a rival pack, a pack that preyed on humans. Maybe a little bloodthirsty for some of the younger readers, she thought, but this was where the path of the story led. Where it had to go.

She picked it up where Kaylee dealt with the betrayal of the boy she thought she loved, an overdue assignment on the Napoleonic Wars and the fact that her beautiful blond nemesis had locked her in the science lab.

The moon would rise in twenty minutes—just about the same time the Science Club would arrive for their meeting.

She had to find a way out before the change.

Lila dived in, happily sliding into Kaylee, into the fear of exposure, the pain of a broken heart, the fury with the cheerleading, homecoming queening, man-eating (literally) Sasha.

By the time she'd gotten Kaylee out, and in the nick, courtesy of a smoke bomb that brought the vice principal—another thorn in

Kaylee's side—dealt with the lecture, the detention, the streaking home as the change came on her heroine, Lila had put in three solid hours.

Pleased with herself, she surfaced from the story, glanced around.

Thomas, exhausted from play, lay curled on the chair beside her, and the lights of the city glittered and gleamed out the window.

She fixed Thomas's dinner precisely as instructed. While he ate she got her Leatherman, used the screwdriver of the multi-tool to tighten some screws in the pantry.

Loose screws, to her thinking, were a gateway to disaster. In people and in things.

She noticed a couple of wire baskets on runners, still in their boxes. Probably for potatoes or onions. Crouching, she read the description, the assurance of easy install. She made a mental note to e-mail Macey, ask if she wanted them put in.

It would be a quick, satisfying little project.

She poured a second glass of wine and made a late dinner out of the fruit, cheese and crackers. Sitting cross-legged in the dining room, Thomas in her lap, she ate while she checked e-mail, sent e-mail, scanned her blog—made a note for a new entry.

"Getting on to bedtime, Thomas."

He just yawned when she picked up the remote to shut off the music, then lifted him up and away so she could deal with her dishes and bask in the quiet of her first night in a new space.

After changing into cotton pants and a tank, she checked the security, then revisited her neighbors through the binoculars.

It looked like Blondie had gone out after all, leaving the living room light on low. The pair of couples had gone out as well. Maybe to dinner, or a show, Lila thought.

The little boy would be fast asleep, hopefully with the puppy curled up with him. She could see the shimmer of a television, imagined Mom and Dad relaxing together.

Another window showed a party going on. A crowd of people—well-dressed, cocktail attire—mixed and mingled, drinks or small plates in hand.

She watched for a while, imagined conversations, including a whispered one between the brunette in the short red dress and the bronzed god in the pearl gray suit who, in Lila's imagination, were having a hot affair under the noses of his long-suffering wife and her clueless husband.

She scanned over, stopped, lowered the glasses a moment, then looked again.

No, the really built guy on the . . . twelfth floor wasn't completely naked. He wore a thong as he did an impressive bump and grind, a spin, drop.

He was working up a nice sweat, she noted, as he repeated moves or added to them.

Obviously an actor/dancer moonlighting as a stripper until he caught his big Broadway break.

She enjoyed him. A lot.

The window show kept her entertained for a half hour before she made herself a nest in the bed—and was indeed joined by Thomas. She switched on the TV for company, settled on an *NCIS* rerun where she could literally recite the dialogue before the characters. Comforted by that, she picked up her iPad, found the thriller she'd started on the plane from Rome, and snuggled in.

OVER THE NEXT WEEK, SHE DEVELOPED A ROUTINE. THOMAS would wake her more accurately than any alarm clock at seven precisely when he begged, vocally, for his breakfast.

She'd feed the cat, make coffee, water the plants indoors and out, have a little breakfast while she visited the neighbors.

Blondie and her live-in lover—they didn't have the married

vibe—argued a lot. Blondie tended to throw breakables. Mr. Slick, and he was great to look at, had good reflexes, and a whole basket of charm. Fights, pretty much daily, ended in seduction or wild bursts of passion.

They suited each other, in her estimation. For the moment. Neither of them struck Lila as long-haul people with her throwing dishes or articles of clothing, him ducking, smiling and seducing.

Game players, she thought. Hot, sexy game players, and if he didn't have something going on, on the side, she'd be very surprised.

The little boy and the puppy continued their love affair, with Mom, Dad or nanny patiently cleaning up little accidents. Mom and Dad left together most mornings, garbed in a way that said high-powered careers to Lila.

The Martinis, as she thought of them, rarely used their little terrace. She was definitely one of the ladies-who-lunch, leaving the apartment every day, late morning, returning late afternoon usually with a shopping bag.

The Partiers rarely spent an evening at home, seemed to revel in a frantic sort of lifestyle.

And the Body practiced his bump and grind regularly—to her unabashed pleasure.

She treated herself to the show, and the stories she created every morning. She'd work into the afternoon, break to amuse the cat before she dressed and went out to buy what she thought she might like for dinner, to see the neighborhood.

She sent pictures of a happy Thomas to her clients, picked tomatoes, sorted mail, composed a vicious lycan battle, updated her blog. And installed the two baskets in the pantry.

On the first day of week two, she bought a good bottle of Barolo, filled in the fancy cheese selections, added some mini cupcakes from an amazing neighborhood bakery.

Just after seven in the evening, she opened the door to the party pack that was her closest friend.

"There you are." Julie, wine bottle in one hand, a fragrant bouquet of star lilies in the other, still managed to enfold her.

Six feet of curves and tumbled red hair, Julie Bryant struck the opposite end of Lila's average height, slim build, straight brown hair.

"You brought a tan back from Rome. God, I'd be wearing 500 SPF and still end up going lobster in the Italian sun. You look just great."

"Who wouldn't after two weeks in Rome? The pasta alone. I told you I'd get the wine," Lila added when Julie shoved the bottle into her hand.

"Now we have two. And welcome home."

"Thanks." Lila took the flowers.

"Wow, some place. It's huge, and the view's a killer. What do these people do?"

"Start with family money."

"Oh, don't I wish I had."

"Let's detour to the kitchen so I can fix the flowers, then I'll give you a tour. He works in finance, and I don't understand any of it. He loves his work and prefers tennis to golf. She does some interior design, and you can see she's good at it from the way the apartment looks. She's thinking about going pro, but they're talking about starting a family, so she's not sure it's the right time to start her own business."

"They're new clients, right? And they still tell you that kind of personal detail?"

"What can I say? I have a face that says tell me all about it. Say hello to Thomas."

Julie crouched to greet the cat. "What a handsome face he has."

"He's a sweetheart." Lila's deep brown eyes went soft as Julie and Thomas made friends. "Pets aren't always a plus on the jobs, but Thomas is."

She selected a motorized mouse out of Thomas's toy basket, enjoyed Julie's easy laugh as the cat pounced.

"Oh, he's a killer." Straightening, Julie leaned back on the stone-gray counter while Lila fussed the lilies into a clear glass vase.

"Rome was fabulous?"

"It really was."

"And did you find a gorgeous Italian to have mad sex with?"

"Sadly no, but I think the proprietor of the local market fell for me. He was about eighty, give or take. He called me *una bella donna* and gave me the most beautiful peaches."

"Not as good as sex, but something. I can't believe I missed you when you got back."

"I appreciate the overnight at your place between jobs."

"Anytime, you know that. I only wish I'd been there."

"How was the wedding?"

"I definitely need wine before I get started on Cousin Melly's Hamptons Wedding Week From Hell, and why I've officially retired as a bridesmaid."

"Your texts were fun for me. I especially liked the one . . . 'Crazy Bride Bitch says rose petals wrong shade of pink. Hysteria ensues. Must destroy CBB for the good of womankind.'"

"It almost came to that. Oh no! Sobs, tremors, despair. 'The petals are pink-pink! They have to be rose-pink. Julie! Fix it, Julie!' I came close to fixing her."

"Did she really have a half-ton truckload of petals?"

"Just about."

"You should have buried her in them. Bride smothered by rose petals. Everyone would think it was an ironic, if tragic, mishap."

"If only I'd thought of it. I really missed you. I like it better when you're working in New York, and I can come see your digs and hang out with you."

Lila studied her friend as she opened the wine. "You should come with me sometime—when it's someplace fabulous."

"I know, you keep saying." Julie wandered as she spoke. "I'm just not sure I wouldn't feel weird, actually staying in— Oh my God, look at this china. It has to be antique, and just amazing."

"Her great-grandmother's. And you don't feel weird coming over and spending an evening with me wherever, you wouldn't feel weird staying. You stay in hotels."

"People don't live there."

"Some people do. Eloise and Nanny did."

Julie gave Lila's long tail of hair a tug. "Eloise and Nanny are fictional."

"Fictional people are people, too, otherwise why would we care what happens to them? Here, let's have this on the little terrace. Wait until you see Macey's container garden. Her family started in France— vineyards."

Lila scooped up the tray with the ease of the waitress she'd once been. "They met five years ago when she was over there visiting her grandparents—like they are now—and he was on vacation and came to their winery. Love at first sight, they both claim."

"It's the best. First sight."

"I'd say fictional, but I just made a case for fictional." She led the way to the terrace. "Turned out they both lived in New York. He called her, they went out. And were exchanging 'I dos' about eighteen months later."

"Like a fairy tale."

"Which I'd also say fictional, except I love fairy tales. And they look really happy together. And as you'll see, she's got a seriously green thumb."

Julie tapped the binoculars as they started out. "Still spying?"

Lila's wide, top-heavy mouth moved into a pout. "It's not spying. It's observing. If people don't want you looking in, they should close the curtains, pull down the shades."

"Uh-huh. Wow." Julie set her hands on her hips as she scanned the terrace. "You're right about the green thumb."

Everything lush and colorful and thriving in simple terra-cotta pots made the urban space a creative oasis. "She's growing tomatoes?"

"They're wonderful, and the herbs? She started them from seeds."

"Can you do that?"

"Macey can. I—as they told me I could and should—harvested some. I had a big, beautiful salad for dinner last night. Ate it out here, with a glass of wine, and watched the window show."

"You have the oddest life. Tell me about the window people."

Lila poured wine, then reached inside for the binoculars—just in case.

"We have the family on the tenth floor—they just got the little boy a puppy. The kid and the pup are both incredibly pretty and adorable. It's true love, and fun to watch. There's a sexy blonde on fourteen who lives with a very hot guy—both could be models. He comes and goes, and they have very intense conversations, bitter arguments with flying crockery, followed by major sex."

"You watch them have sex? Lila, give me those binoculars."

"No!" Laughing, Lila shook her head. "I don't watch them have sex. But I can tell that's what's going on. They talk, fight, pace around with lots of arm waving from her, then grab each other and start pulling off clothes. In the bedroom, in the living room. They don't have a terrace like this, but that little balcony deal off the bedroom. They barely made it back in once before they were both naked.

"And speaking of naked, there's a guy on twelve. Wait, maybe he's around."

Now she did get the glasses, checked. "Oh yeah, baby. Check this out. Twelfth floor, three windows from the left."

Curious enough, Julie took the binoculars, finally found the window. "Oh my. Mmmm, mmmm. He does have some moves. We should call him, invite him over."

"I don't think we're his type."

"Between us we're every man's type."

"Gay, Julie."

"You can't tell from here." Julie lowered the glasses, frowned, then lifted them again for another look. "Your gaydar can't leap over buildings in a single bound like Superman."

"He's wearing a thong. Enough said."

"It's for ease of movement."

"Thong," Lila repeated.

"Does he dance nightly?"

"Pretty much. I figure he's a struggling actor, working part-time in a strip club until he gets his break."

"He's got a great body. David had a great body."

"Had?"

Julie set down the glasses, mimed breaking a twig in half.

"When?"

"Right after the Hamptons Wedding Week From Hell. It had to be done, but I didn't want to do it at the wedding, which was bad enough."

"Sorry, honey."

"Thanks, but you didn't like David anyway."

"I didn't not like him."

"Amounts to the same. And though he was so nice to look at, he'd just gotten too clingy. Where are you going, how long will you be, blah blah. Always texting me, or leaving messages on my machine. If I had work stuff, or made plans with you and other friends, he'd get upset or sulky. God, it was like having a wife—in the worst way. No dis meant to wives, as I used to be one. I'd only been seeing him for a couple months, and he was pushing to move in. I don't want a live-in."

"You don't want the wrong live-in," Lila corrected.

"I'm not ready for the right live-in yet. It's too soon after Maxim."

"It's been five years."

Julie shook her head, patted Lila's hand. "Too soon. Cheating bastard still pisses me off. I have to get that down to mild amusement,

I think. I hate breakups," she added. "They either make you feel sad—you've been dumped; or mean—you've done the dumping."

"I don't think I've ever dumped anyone, but I'll take your word."

"That's because you make them think it's their idea—plus you really don't let it get serious enough to earn the term 'dump.'"

Lila just smiled. "It's too soon after Maxim," she said, and made Julie laugh. "We can order in. There's a Greek place the clients recommended. I haven't tried it yet."

"As long as there's baklava for after."

"I have cupcakes."

"Even better. I now have it all. Swank apartment, good wine, Greek food coming, my best pal. And a sexy . . . oh, and sweaty," she added as she lifted the glasses again. "Sexy, sweating dancing man—sexual orientation not confirmed."

"Gay," Lila repeated, and rose to get the takeout menu.

THEY POLISHED OFF MOST OF THE WINE WITH LAMB KABOBS—then dug into the cupcakes around midnight. Maybe not the best combination, Lila decided, considering her mildly queasy stomach, but just the right thing for a friend who was more upset about a breakup than she admitted.

Not the guy, Lila thought as she did the rounds to check security, but the act itself, and all the questions that dogged the mind and heart after it was done.

Is it me? Why couldn't I make it work? Who will I have dinner with?

When you lived in a culture of couples, it could make you feel less when you were flying solo.

"I don't," Lila assured the cat, who'd curled up in his own little bed sometime between the last kabob and the first cupcake. "I'm okay being single. It means I can go where I want, when I want, take any job that works for me. I'm seeing the world, Thomas, and okay, talking to cats, but I'm okay with that, too."

Still, she wished she'd been able to talk Julie into staying over. Not just for the company, but to help deal with the hangover her friend was bound to have come morning.

Mini cupcakes were Satan, she decided as she readied for bed. So cute and tiny, oh, they're like eating nothing, that's what you tell yourself, until you've eaten half a dozen.

Now she was wired up on alcohol and sugar, and she'd never get to sleep.

She picked up the binoculars. Still some lights on, she noted. She wasn't the only one still up at . . . Jesus, one forty in the morning.

Sweaty Naked Guy was still up, and in the company of an equally hot-looking guy. Smug, Lila made a mental note to tell Julie her gaydar was like Superman.

Party couple hadn't made it to bed yet; in fact it looked as though they'd just gotten in. Another swank deal from their attire. Lila admired the woman's shimmery orange dress, and wished she could see the shoes. Then was rewarded when the woman reached down, balancing a hand on the man's shoulder, and removed one strappy, sky-high gold sandal with a red sole.

Mmm, Louboutins.

Lila scanned down.

Blondie hadn't turned in yet either. She wore black again—snug and short—with her hair tumbling out of an updo. Been out on the town, Lila speculated, and it didn't go very well.

She's crying, Lila realized, catching the way the woman swiped at her face as she spoke. Talking fast. Urgently. Big fight with the boyfriend.

And where is he?

But even changing angles she couldn't bring him into view.

Dump him, Lila advised. Nobody should be allowed to make you so unhappy. You're gorgeous, and I bet you're smart, and certainly worth more than—

Lila jerked as the woman's head snapped back from a blow.

"Oh my God. He hit her. You bastard. Don't—"

She cried out herself as the woman tried to cover her face, cringed back as she was struck again.

And the woman wept, begged.

Lila made one leap to the bedside table and her phone, grabbed it, leaped back.

She couldn't see him, just couldn't see him in the dim light, but now the woman was plastered back against the window.

"That's enough, that's enough," Lila murmured, preparing to call 911.

Then everything froze.

The glass shattered. The woman exploded out. Arms spread wide, legs kicking, hair flying like golden wings, she dropped fourteen stories to the brutal sidewalk.

"Oh God, God, God." Shaking, Lila fumbled with the phone.

"Nine-one-one, what is your emergency?"

"He pushed her. He pushed her, and she fell out the window."

"Ma'am—"

"Wait. Wait." She closed her eyes a moment, forced herself to breathe in and out three times. Be clear, she ordered herself, give the details.

"This is Lila Emerson. I just witnessed a murder. A woman was pushed out a fourteenth-story window. I'm staying at . . ." It took her a moment to remember before she came to the Kilderbrands' address. "It's the building across from me. Ah, to the, to the west of me. I think. I'm sorry, I can't think. She's dead. She has to be dead."

"I'm dispatching a unit now. Will you hold the line?"

"Yes. Yes. I'll stay here."

Shuddering, she looked out again, but now the room beyond the broken window was dark.